I0610770

Parlatheas Press Titles:

The Cayn Trilogy:

Son of Cayn
City of Cayn
Blood of Cayn

Chronicles of Damage Inc.:

Phantoms of Ruthaer
Mask of the Vampire*

* Forthcoming

Son of Cayn

The Cayn Trilogy
Book One

Jason McDonald
Alan Isom
Stormy McDonald

Parlatheas Press, LLC
Hollywood, SC

DEDICATIONS

To my stepdad, for opening my eyes to a world of opportunity.
– Jason

To my father, for doing things right and introducing me to J.R.R. Tolkien and his fabulous works.
– Alan

To my dad: a teller of tales, a bringer of laughs, and the greatest teacher a daughter could have.
– Stormy

CHAPTER 1
FIRE

August 3, 4235 K.E.

11:43pm

Feral eyes appeared in the flickering shadows, their depths reflecting the tendrils of fire playing along the study's bead-board ceiling. Time slowed as paint on the underside of the tongue-and-groove planks bubbled and peeled.

"I can save you," whispered a hollow voice from the darkest shadow.

Baroness Aleksandra Madasgorski-Krakova stared into those yellow eyes, her rage and frustration making her reckless, and yelled, "Did you do this!? Did you set fire to my house!?"

"I only do what my master requires," the voice replied smoothly.

Fists clenched at her sides, Aleksandra stood in the center of the room, dressed in an elegant, wine-colored gown made from the finest silk. A gown intended for only the most extravagant occasions, such as tonight, before it had all come crashing down around her.

A portion of the ceiling collapsed, and flames erupted in the corner of the study, blasting waves of heat into the room. The fire found new fuel in the rosewood bookshelves as it trailed down the wall. Burning light streamed in from the gaping hole above, revealing the conflagration that was the second floor.

Aleksandra felt detached from the world. Even though the fire roared all about her, it seemed muted compared to the agonized screams echoing outside the study. Many of them trailed out the front door, while others simply choked off. Perhaps the flames had taken them, or maybe they had succumbed to the smoke. She wondered if one of those screams belonged to her husband, Gavriil.

It had all happened so fast. Their guests, all the social elite of Upper Pazard'zhik — the Capital City of Trakya — had arrived earlier that evening. There had been wine, food, and gossip aplenty. She recalled meeting her husband as he ascended from the basement. He had just come from checking on the wretched souls collected for tonight's ceremony — the ones to be sacrificed — and making certain all the preparations were in order. His eyes had gleamed with a rare excitement. "Skoro, lyubimi." *Soon, my beloved.*

Three Sha'iry — D'yakon Krovos and his two Anshu underlings — mingled amongst their guests. It was perfect. Using the party as an excuse to gather, none would have suspected the dark magics performed beneath their feet.

The night's workings would have sealed the fate of the Trakyans and paved the way for her husband to assume the throne. Somehow, she seethed, the Kral discovered their plans and sent in his agents. That damnable Marcus Marchenkov, second-in-command of the Ochi i Ushi na Kral — *the Eyes and Ears of the King* — marched through her doorway with the militsiya as if orchestrating a raid in a common bordello and directed his men to search everywhere, upstairs and down.

"Nikoĭ da ne izbyaga," she had heard him command. *Let no one escape.*

Shortly thereafter, the basement door had burst open. Men, women, and children, all filthy and ragged, rushed forth through her beautiful home. With military efficiency, the Kral's men ushered them out the front door. The rank stench of their unwashed bodies still filled her nostrils.

Her full lips trembled with emotion as she gazed around her. The air shimmered as if she were the victim of some strange mirage. Her books, her desk, her paintings — everything she had collected over the years — were ablaze.

She glared into the heart of the shadows. Had it started the fire as a distraction to save her, or was the destruction a perverse form of punishment? Some considered fire to be a holy rite, one that purged evil. This fire was born of evil, and she swore only evil would come of it.

With a sharp gasp, Aleksandra swayed to one side and pressed a hand to her chest. Sutekh, her dark god, was nearby. She felt him snatch away her husband's soul. A searing pain coursed through her body, as though the dark god had ripped out her heart as well. All that remained to her was an empty void.

The shadow's eyes watched her intently, but she avoided looking directly into them a second time. She'd had plenty of practice over the years. Each time she looked into its eyes, the demon enjoyed reminding her of her coming-of-age gift. She shuddered despite the heat.

Out in the street, the militsiya shouted orders, and someone called her name. Hopefully, Marcus would think she was dead like her husband. Regaining her composure, she shouted, "I will have my revenge, demon!"

A terrible, twisted form stepped from the shadows, its very existence a mockery of creation, and it came for Aleksandra with open arms. "All is not lost. Come with me, and we will have our revenge together. Let us finish what your husband started."

She hesitated, weighing her limited options. With one last look around her ruined study, Aleksandra embraced the demon. The two vanished just as the ceiling collapsed. Flames geysered into the night sky as the house tumbled in upon itself, debris burying the basement as though it still had something to hide.

CHAPTER 2
AND VENGEANCE
August 22, 4235 K.E.

7:38am

Somewhere on the White River, an old fisherman stood at the bow of his small flat-bottomed boat. Holding the net between his teeth and with both his gnarled hands, he twisted and released it in one swift motion. The net unfurled in a perfect circle and hit the water with a soft splash.

After waiting a few moments for the net to sink to the bottom of the river, he hauled it back up using the thin line tied to his wrist. Small panfish wiggled within its confines, throwing sparkles of water this way and that. The old fisherman grabbed the net and emptied the few fish onto the deck, where they flopped wildly.

Glancing at them, he counted four big enough to eat; the others were too small, so he stooped down and threw them back into the river. The fisherman carefully checked his net for tangles and snags before standing up. Once satisfied, he clenched the edge of the net between his teeth and made to cast again.

From the corner of his eye, he spotted a dark shape gliding through the early morning fog. Curious, he lowered his net as the single-masted cog floated past. Buzzards with bald, scaly, blood-colored heads perched on the yards. A gentle breeze swept past him, heavy with the scent of death.

Something akin to fear crept up the fisherman's spine. He had lived on the banks of the river his entire life and never seen a sight like this one. Putting down his net, the old fisherman hauled up his anchor. Taking a seat on the bench, he reached for his oar and aimed toward the small cargo vessel.

"Na palube!" the old man called out. No response.

As he approached, he studied the cog carefully. The fisherman noted with interest that it rode low in the water, a signal it was still laden with cargo. Suspicious, he looked around to see if anyone was watching. He tossed the anchor and let it catch the rail of the riverboat like a grapnel. With a strength that belied his age, he hauled himself up the anchor line the short distance onto the deck.

Once aboard, he found himself surrounded by clusters of buzzards. The large, black birds splayed their wings to hide their meal. The old man kicked at one and sent it scurrying. What lay beneath caused him to quickly turn his head and avert his eyes, but the image of the ghastly corpse stayed with him. Retching over the side, the old man lost his breakfast.

With an ungainly, hopping lope, a buzzard dashed across the deck toward another rotten morsel, exposing two more bloated corpses. Collecting himself, the fisherman cautiously approached the bodies and knelt beside the one wearing what looked like the remnants of a captain's uniform.

The vultures had pecked away most of the flesh, but for some reason had avoided the arm. Searching closer, he saw the captain held something clenched in his fist. He reached down and pried open the stiff fingers, expecting to find a glint of gold or silver. Instead, he found something wrapped inside a wad of wax paper. The old fisherman stared in confusion when he unwrapped a partially dissolved bar of pearlescent grey soap that smelled faintly of lavender.

At its center, a tiny speck of black oil appeared. It slid free of the soap and quivered as though alive. The fisherman backed away but not before the black oil leapt toward his extended finger and seeped into his skin.

CHAPTER 3
THE INTERVIEW

October 11, 4235 K.E.

1:08pm

Extending from the base of the Escarpment to the northern shores of the Cherno More, the warehouse district of Lower Pazard'zhik consisted of expansive timber buildings and earthen yards stockpiled with bulk materials or crated goods ready for delivery. Outside their stone border walls and arched gateways, men's shouts and the whinny of horses intermingled as pedestrians and horse-drawn wagons fought for the right of passage.

A line of warriors stretched out a wide-open gate, into the muddy street, and around the corner. Some wore plain leathers, while others wore hodgepodge pieces of armor mounted to boiled leather or rusted chain backing. They all carried weapons, most scuffed and scarred from frequent use.

"Excuse me." All eyes turned toward the voice.

Whistling, the rotund newcomer, dressed in a light grey tunic, dark brown breeches, and mud-stained boots, used his bulk to forge his way through the line of men. The man had a youthful, clean-shaven face framed by shoulder-length brown hair that appeared to be slightly damp. From the way he wore his clothes, it was hard to tell if he was obese or just big boned. Two belts wrapped around his tunic: one of wide leather, the other a thin belt that held a brown leather sporran decorated with Gaelic scrollwork. Based on the size, it wouldn't hold much more than three or four small books. Rings decorated each finger of both his hands. Most were plain bands of silver; however, one was an onyx and hematite signet ring bearing a dagger-pierced globe, and another bore arcane symbols and three kite-shaped emeralds.

Once past the line of warriors, he stopped and studied the stone wall surrounding the compound and yard inside. It was exactly as Marcus had described to him. He raised an eyebrow. It didn't look like a den of evil. It looked like a typical, albeit well to do, teamsters' compound. However, Marcus had been certain there was a connection between

Dragahn's team of wagons and the Krakov Estate, and he was here to find it. Studiously avoiding making eye contact with the giant half-orc at the end of the line, he proceeded toward the arched gate.

Ignoring the grumbles and hostile stares, he greeted the gatekeeper, who pointed him toward the nearby postern door where a primitive sign, written in Trakyan, read "откриване на работа: готвач." *Job Opening: Cook.* Underneath, a crude arrow pointed inside. Thanking him, the man cast a quick glance back toward the line of warriors before disappearing inside.

He passed through a spacious common room with a long central table and massive two-sided fireplace that also served the cookery. Following the acrid smell of burnt beans and smoke to the open door of a small office, he found a slim, olive-complected teenager with a shock of black hair standing beside a half-empty bucket of water. Next to him, a barrel-chested, balding man with a leathery face hunched over a plain desk, studying a long supply list. Precise checks appeared beside most of the items.

"Jasper Thredd from Tydway," the man from outside announced as he strode in.

"What do you want?" the older man replied tiredly, never looking up.

"I'm here for the cook position."

"Already filled," he said dismissively, still not looking up from his task. It was obvious his opinion of cooks, and maybe people in general, had dwindled with each applicant.

Jasper glanced back toward the common room and made a show of sniffing the air. Taking his pipe from a pocket in his tunic, he filled the bowl with tobacco and lit it with a match. The sweet smell cut through the burnt stench and cleansed the air, leaving behind a faint aroma of wintergreen.

"Are you sure?" Jasper asked, clenching the pipe between his teeth. "I have some experience with jerky and beans and other road grub. Coney stew is one of my specialties."

The youth stepped forward with an open smile. "I sure hope you can cook better than that last person."

Setting aside the list with a groan, the older man studied this new applicant. His eyes lingering on the odd rings, he held out his hand, and Jasper presented his letter of introduction. After reading over it briefly, he said, "Tydway — you're a long way from home."

"Yes, sir. I am," Jasper replied.

"Name's Dragahn," the caravan chief said, returning the letter. Nodding toward the teenager, he added, "And that's Lucky. What can you cook?"

"How much time do I have?" Jasper asked. He closed his eyes and answered his own question. "If I were you, I'd want someone who could whip up a hearty meal within fifteen to twenty minutes — thirty tops. I'm not sure how long it takes you to get everything stowed away after a long ride, but no one wants to wait on a meal. Am I right?" Jasper said with a chuckle, patting his stomach.

"Sure, whatever," Dragahn replied. "Lucky, take him to the larder and let him cook the brisket."

"The brisket? You sure?" Lucky asked.

"It'll be alright, kid," Jasper said. "Trust me."

Donning a fur kalpak with the brim turned up, the youth led Jasper outside to the earthen courtyard, where the smell of horse sweat immediately assailed them. Squatting in the far corner, an impressive, A-framed timber barn was abuzz with activity. Workers moved about, walking heavy draft horses, carrying bales of hay, and getting everything ready for the long ride ahead.

To their left, the line of men at the main gate wound around and disappeared into a much smaller office building on the opposite side of the yard.

Lucky turned right, and they passed in front of a wide, single-story warehouse sharing a common wall with the main hall housing Dragahn's office. Just outside the warehouse door, workers lined the bottom of several long wooden crates with straw. Beside them, bars of soap, individually wrapped in wax paper, sat on pallets. As the workers filled a crate with soap, they stuffed straw in the gaps and put a final layer on top before nailing it shut. The crate was then carried inside the warehouse and loaded onto a wagon.

Jasper followed Lucky across the yard, half-listening as the boy leapt from subject to subject. "I'm Yosif; most people just call me Lucky. Only been with the company for six months. Came down from the mountains hoping to see some action. I like to gamble sometimes, guess that's why I like this job. That last trip was a mess. We lost our cook.

Everyone expected me to learn, and then the chief came down with food poisoning. Man, was that gross! Then everyone got sick. Everyone says I'm lucky 'cause I didn't get sacked. Name stuck, and now that's what everyone calls me."

Lucky stopped talking when they reached the larder, a standalone shed along the back wall of the compound tucked between the stable yard and the warehouse. Pulling the key from his belt-pouch, the teen unlocked the door and opened it.

Slabs of smoked brisket and bacon hung from the rafters beside strips of jerky and strings of dried fruits and vegetables. Cyrillic marks on the barrels and bags clearly identified what was inside — items like potatoes, beans, flour, and corn meal. Everything was ready for travel at a moment's notice. Beside the barrel of flour, Jasper found several crates of fresh chicken eggs. With some sliced bacon, a few eggs, and a potato, he headed toward the door.

"That's not what the chief asked you to cook."

"Can't properly cook brisket in fifteen to twenty minutes, and Dragahn knows it. It would take at least three to four hours to do it up right," he explained simply. "And hey, if I don't burn the water, I'll at least do a better job than your last cook."

Lucky shrugged and said, "Sure, but you're not going to get points for following directions."

4:16pm

The line of warriors at the gate moved slowly. By the time the last of them made it inside the compound and to the small office, the sun perched atop the highest peak of the snow-capped mountains that surrounded Pazard'zhik on three sides.

Everyone in the courtyard watched the seven-foot tall, charcoal-skinned half-orc as he stepped up to the open office door. Long, oily black dreadlocks partially concealed the plain leather mask hiding his face. Before entering, he reached around and cinched one of the wide straps around his waist. A leather loop and bone toggle supported a massive, double-headed battle-axe with curved blades similar to a labrys. The long steel haft, wrapped in worn strips of brown leather, hung down almost to the ground.

The door shut behind the masked half-orc with an ominous click. A single candle lit the room, feeding the shadows more than giving off light. Behind an ornately carved mahogany desk sat a small, pale man with an effeminate face and cropped, brown hair. A thin, gold chain hung loose about his neck.

The giant stepped forward.

"What's your name?" the slight man asked in a soft voice. His large, dark eyes studied the half-orc intently.

"Grendel."

"Time to get out of town?"

Grendel shrugged.

"Remove your tunic and weapon."

Grendel hesitated but did as told, revealing a heavily muscled torso of flat, greyish black.

The man walked around his desk, saying, "My name is Sachin. I'm looking for someone to be my bodyguard. Do you have any training for this type of work?"

"A little," Grendel replied, his eyes following the small man's path.

"The teamsters get half a silver lev for every mile they travel; I'm willing to pay twice that. But understand, you would work for me — not Dragahn. Agreed?"

Grendel nodded.

Sachin walked behind Grendel, tracing a finger along his waist, and came around the other side. It took every ounce of discipline for Grendel not to flinch.

"I have some experience with mixed breeds like you," Sachin said. "It's been a while, and not all those experiences have been good."

Grendel felt like a piece of meat under Sachin's scrutiny. The man took note of his every feature, every scar, and how Grendel's eyes shimmered with a glint of purple in the low light.

"Your eyes are an odd color for a half-orc. They put me in mind of shadow-shrouded leaves in the dark heart of the forest. And I've never seen eyeshine like yours before." Sachin pursed his lips in thought and said, "I would guess your father was an orcné... maybe something more, but your mother was definitely human. Perhaps you have her eyes. Tell me, half-orc, do you see the world through your father's eyes or your mother's?"

Grendel tensed at the casual mention of his mother without answering, not knowing how.

"Based upon your height and obvious strength, I suspect you have some eoten blood in you. Take off your mask and kneel," Sachin commanded.

Again, Grendel hesitated. Slower this time, he complied.

Sachin stepped in front of Grendel and stared intently at his face. Grendel stared back. He knew what the small man saw and felt ashamed. He hated his heavy browed, bestial features. He hated his broad, flat nose, broken in his youth and never set. They gave him an abhorrent appearance that, along with the pair of ape-like canines protruding up past his lower lip, evoked fear in everyone he met. It was why he wore the mask.

However, he saw no fear in Sachin, only a spark of curiosity. "You have the markings of both eotenas and orcnéas," Sachin said quietly, continuing his observations.

"You know more about me than I do," Grendel commented.

"Like I said, I have some experience with mixed breeds. Makes for a nasty combination, doesn't it? Have you ever feasted on human flesh?"

"No," Grendel rumbled.

"Ever wanted to?"

"No," Grendel replied, a little less confident this time.

Sachin gave him a pensive look as he stepped back. "You're obviously not afraid of fighting; some of your scars run deep. It appears you've been tended by a skilled healer, and you tell me you've never tasted human flesh. What kind of half-orc are you?"

"What do you mean?"

"Hwæt syndon gé?" Sachin asked.

Uncomprehending, Grendel waited.

"You are not from any of the local tribes. Where are you from? And don't lie to me."

Grendel didn't say anything. He simply stared at the carvings on the desk.

"Tell me," Sachin urged.

"I am from J'Bel."

"Is that a family name or the name of your tribe?"

"I have no tribe; no family," Grendel said with finality. He stood and replaced his mask — one way or the other the interview was over.

"Well, son of Cayn, can you handle yourself in a fight?"

4:41pm

Outside, all the workers and stable hands had stopped what they were doing and formed a ring around five armed men in the center of the courtyard. Grendel noticed the sudden flurry of wagers being laid when Sachin escorted him out of the office. Standing back from the crowd, Jasper and two other men watched from a distance. He wished his friend, Chert, was here.

After taking his axe, Sachin motioned for Grendel to step inside the circle.

"Gentlemen, this is the final part of the interview," Sachin announced, addressing the warriors. "This is simply a test of skill and fitness — not a fight to the death. Each of you must face the others without weapons, dressed as you are. The last man standing will be chosen for the job. If you wish to remove yourself from the competition, now is your chance."

An olive-complected teamster with a thick, black beard entered the ring to collect the weapons. He wore black pants stuffed in the tops of tall brown boots and a dusty white tunic under a brown fur vest. A wide studded belt wrapped his waist, and on his head, he wore a traditional fur kalpak.

The men in the circle had had time to size each other up, calculating odds, but when the masked half-orc stepped into their midst, they instinctively huddled together. As the teamster passed, one warrior threw up his hands and said to Grendel, "Half-orc, you can have it."

After the first candidate left, three more followed. Grendel felt the hostile stares from the crowd. Without doing anything, he had turned them against him. From behind his leather mask, he glanced about, waiting for a challenger, someone with enough courage to face him.

Finally, two grizzled-looking veterans stepped forward. One wore a brown and green leather tunic riveted with steel studs and heavy leather breeches. The other wore a hodgepodge of ornate bronze plate armor, steel chain, and black leather, and on his head, he wore an open-faced steel helmet. Covering his hands were a pair of black leather gloves with small bronze plates sewn onto the backs and around the knuckles.

Both men kept their gazes fixed on Grendel as he crossed his forearms in front of his heart and dipped his head. He lifted his eyes and grumbled, "Alea iacta est." *The die is cast.*

Sachin gave a quick nod, and the two veterans spread out, trying to flank the taller half-orc. Grendel stood his ground in the middle of the circle, reading his opponents. They were both experienced fighters, but they hadn't fought together before. While their numbers gave them a slight advantage, he hoped they would not work well as a team.

Yelling, the warrior in brown and green leather rushed forward. Grendel meant to stop him with a single punch, but the man bent his knees and slipped inside it. He drifted forward, striking Grendel with a flurry of punches to the body.

Grendel surged like an onrushing wave, and the warrior leapt back in a vain attempt to get outside the half-orc's reach. Lashing out with a kick, Grendel caught his opponent a glancing blow to the hip. It was just a touch, but the force behind it was enough to send him spinning.

With Grendel distracted, the one in bronze armor attacked from behind and landed a heavy punch to the kidney. Grendel bellowed as he swung around, catching the man with the back of his hand, causing the helmet to ring like a bell. The man stumbled, dazed.

Grendel advanced on the man in bronze armor.

With a mighty leap, the warrior in studded leather pushed hard against Grendel's back, shoving him forward. Using the other's momentum, the man in bronze plowed a swift punch into the giant's forehead. Reinforced by the bronze-plates of his gauntlet, it snapped the half-orc's head backward with a loud, meaty thud and sliced through the thin mask.

Grendel saw stars. He lurched to one side and brought up his forearms to shield his face from his attackers.

Using the giant's body to hide his actions from the crowd, the warrior in studded leather grabbed Grendel with one hand and pulled a dirk with the other.

Grendel felt more than saw it. He jerked, deftly catching the leather clad warrior with his elbow. Blood spattered the crowd as the man flew back and landed in the dirt. The knife skittered across the yard with a metallic scrape. Rough hands hauled the injured man out of the ring, leaving the remaining two combatants alone with one another.

Grendel quickly rounded on the man in bronze plate. They circled each other, watching. Waiting.

The man held his ground and shouts of encouragement rang out from the crowd. More money exchanged hands, and someone yelled, "Kill the half-orc!"

Moving forward with his arms loose at his sides, Grendel slowly closed the gap between him and his opponent. The bronze-clad warrior, taking advantage of the opening, let out a shout and launched a right cross at Grendel's head.

With a sudden burst of speed, Grendel flowed with the punch and spun sideways, bringing up both his hands as if to block. With a quick flick of the wrist, Grendel's massive right hand caught his opponent's forearm and circled it around, turning the palm so that it faced up. Opening his left hand, he cupped the warrior's fist and wrist, trapping them.

Continuing with a rolling, twisting motion, Grendel locked his opponent's wrist and pushed the man's fingers down toward his own forearm. Steadily increasing the pressure, the bones in the man's arm jammed, forcing him to the ground.

When Grendel finished, the warrior was on his knees, pain contorting his features.

"Yield, or I will break it," Grendel growled, still holding the arm. A hush came over the crowd. The man in bronze slumped and finally nodded.

Silence reigned for a heartbeat. Murmurs and disgruntled boos broke out in the ring of spectators and from everywhere came the sound of money changing hands.

Narrow-eyed, Grendel stared at the crowd, adrenaline rushing through his body. This wasn't like the arena where he grew up, where people appreciated the art of the fight. This was a cock fight, and he felt like he had killed the ringmaster's prized gamecock. A part of him wanted to kill them all. Swallowing, he tamped down the violence inside him and put it back inside its cage.

"Someone, go find Pyotr!" a voice shouted.

Sachin appeared out of the crowd and stared at Grendel, an odd look on his face. "You bleed red, orcné, not black."

Grendel, who didn't even know he was bleeding, raised his hand to his forehead. His fingers came back wet.

Returning the axe, Sachin said, "See to that cut and report back to me. You have the job."

A haggard man carrying a satchel rushed out of the stables. "Give me room!" he yelled as he shoved people aside.

Everyone stepped back as Pyotr grabbed the man in studded leather by the head with both hands. The man was awake but still groggy. Bloody drool trailed down one side of his slack chin. Pyotr inspected the mouth; teeth were missing. Using his thumbs, he expertly set the jawbone back into place. Next, he took bandages from his satchel and wrapped them around the man's head.

"Does anybody know this person?" he asked loudly.

"I do," one of the warriors who had opted out of the fight replied.

"Get him out of here," he said, dismissing them.

Finding the half-orc, Pyotr gestured toward the gash over Grendel's eye and said, "Let me take a look at that."

"Are you a doctor?" Grendel asked thickly, his eyes shining in the evening light.

"No. Now, shut up while I look at you."

Lucky, who had just walked up with Jasper, started laughing. "He's our animal doctor. I wouldn't trust him with serious injuries, like if you lost your arm or something, but he's good in a pinch."

Pyotr looked sternly at Lucky but didn't say anything. Grendel took off his mask and knelt so the doctor could minister to his cut. "This will need stitches to stop the bleeding... or I can cauterize it. Lucky, go get me some water."

Lucky thought a moment and then disappeared back into the main hall.

"Pyotr, you should let that half-orc bleed," said the teamster who had collected the weapons.

"Viktor, shut up and get those voĭni out of here."

"What can I do?" Jasper asked.

"When Lucky gets back, you two hold him down. I need him to keep still."

Jasper looked incredulously at the doctor and then at Grendel, but before he could respond, Lucky returned, carrying a bucket. In his hand, he also carried several semi-clean rags, which he gave to Pyotr. The doctor pulled a glass vial of clear liquid out of his satchel. He fished out a long needle and threaded it with some stiff horsehair. He placed them both into the vial, closed it, and shook it, making sure the hair was thoroughly saturated.

"What's your name, half-orc?" he asked, using a water-soaked rag to clean the wound.

"Grendel."

"Mine's Pyotr. I don't know how much this is going to hurt. If you were one of us, I'd recommend some of the chief's hooch." Lucky handed Pyotr a metal flask.

"Where did you get that?" Pyotr asked. "If the chief knew you had it, he'd have you flayed." He turned to Grendel, offering the flask. "Do you want this?"

"No."

"Fine, then I'll have some." With that, he opened it and took a quick swig.

"You two," Pyotr said, pointing to Jasper and Lucky, "hold him down." The two exchanged nervous looks as they gingerly gripped Grendel's arms. "No, not like that... Tight! Hold him tight!"

Pyotr removed the needle and thread from the vial and, starting just beyond the wound, shoved the needle through the dark skin to the other side, pulled it as tightly as possible, tied the knot, and cut the thread. Pyotr repeated this six times, and through it all, Grendel never moved, not even a twitch.

Next, the horse-doctor took the half-orc's plain, leather mask and rinsed off the blood in the water bucket. It looked like cowhide to Pyotr, lacking the coarser grain of bull skin. The leather was soft and well worn, making it easy to repair.

Just as Pyotr tied the last knot, Dragahn walked over. He nodded to the horse doctor and said, "You done with the half-orc?"

"Da," Pyotr said, handing Grendel back his mask.

While Grendel donned it, Dragahn said to Jasper, "We'll be using the next few days to do our final preparations. I won't need you tomorrow, but it would be good for you to meet the men."

"What do you have in mind?"

"Cook that brisket like I asked you to," Dragahn said with a smile.

CHAPTER 4
ENCOUNTERS

October 11, 4235 K.E.

5:28pm

The long shadow of Upper Pazard'zhik blanketed Lower Pazard'zhik when Jasper stepped inside the nearby krŭchma. Historic tapestries depicting different scenes of both daily life and glorious battles covered the walls. Like most kruchmi, the menu was extensive, providing choices for all tastes and fancies, from the simplest of stews to exotic chicken hearts with blue saffron. In the corner, a duo played soft music. Varicolored sheets of sailcloth, pinned at the ceiling's center and radiating out to the crown molding, rippled and billowed each time the door opened.

Jasper found a place at the bar and ordered a small meal and a drink. He had just started chewing when he heard, "Hey!" behind him. He turned and saw Lucky approaching through the crowd.

"Have a seat," Jasper said after swallowing. "You want me to order you something?"

"No, can't stay long... running errands," he answered.

"For Dragahn?"

"Naw, Sachin... gives me the creeps... from Upper Pazard'zhik," Lucky said quietly, looking around to see who might be listening. He continued in a rush, "I'm glad I found you. Chief told me to tell everyone we're leaving day after tomorrow. Got our permits, need to get everything ready for the haul. Wants you to come in early tomorrow morning to load the chuck wagon. Figures since you have to cook it, you can stock it."

"I'll be there."

Patting Jasper on the back, Lucky said, "Dovizhdane," and disappeared outside.

Jasper quickly finished his meal, guzzled his drink, and laid some coins on the bar.

Just outside the warehouse district, he walked down the street, back toward Dragahn's compound. The business traffic from earlier was gone, replaced by small groups of men who went from one noisy krŭchma to another.

Jasper pulled his cloak tighter to ward off the evening chill. A mist was falling, transforming the candles set in the windows of the open businesses into diffused blotches of light.

A voice spoke from a nearby shadow. "How did it go? I heard about the fight." The words, though quiet, were distinct and held the soft lilt inherent with the language of the elves.

Jasper paused, ostensibly to fill and light his pipe, and replied in elven, "You know, Xandor, it's kind of spooky when you do that." Then he said, "It went fine. Grendel survived, and I got the job. I take it Marcus released the permits."

"He did," replied Xandor. "Can you work with a half-orc?"

"Sure. How are you faring with a dwarf?"

"It's too soon to tell," Xandor replied. The unease in his voice was obvious.

Jasper said, "Don't worry. I trust Marcus, and if he trusts them, then so do I."

"What about this Dragahn?"

"Not sure yet. I'll get to know him better once we're on the road."

"When are you leaving?"

"Day after tomorrow."

"We'll be ready. You have a room in the inn across the street. Meet you in the morning."

Rather than reply, Jasper crossed the street, surreptitiously dropping a small scrap of paper behind him.

CHAPTER 5
XANDOR AND CHERT

October 12, 4235 K.E.

2:00am

A distant clock bell echoed across the sleeping city of Lower Pazard'zhik. The mist was gone, but slow-moving clouds obscured all traces of moonlight. Outside the reach of the occasional oil lamp, two figures made their way down the street toward Dragahn's compound.

The first was a tall, lean man with blonde hair, square jaw, and narrow face that marked him as a clansman from the Alashalian Mountains far to the southeast. He walked with a purposeful stride that could quickly eat up the miles. Peeking above his shoulders through custom slits in his mottled cloak were the well-used, leather-bound hilts of twin longswords strapped across his back.

The other was a stocky dwarf who almost came up to the man's elbow. His thick, reddish-brown beard and mustache spilled from his hooded cloak, hiding most of his face. Wild, bushy eyebrows stuck out in all directions and competed with his bulbous nose for prominence. A silver hammer dangled from a belt loop at his side.

Across from the teamster's compound, Xandor side-stepped into an alley. The dark greys and greens of his cloak blended with the shadows. So long as he remained still, no one — not even the dwarf — would be able to pick him out of the darkness.

Hand resting on his hammer, Chert continued down the street to the next intersection, where he turned left into a narrow street behind the compound. The echo of his footfalls died.

Xandor waited silently, getting a feel for the airflows and watching for a seemingly nonexistent militsiya patrol. Picking his moment, he crossed the street and melted into another pool of shadow. There, he leapt and grabbed the wall's top, hoping there wouldn't be any broken glass or other nasty surprises. Heaving a mental sigh of relief when his fingers curled over smooth stone, he pulled himself up and perched briefly at the top, listening to the rhythms of the night to determine if anyone had observed him.

Below, a narrow lane separated the back of the stone wall from the rear of the warehouse. In one direction, the lane led to the rear entrance of the main hall where a glowing oil lamp provided some illumination. In the other, darkness swallowed the passage before it reached the warehouse's corner.

Positioning himself at the edge of the light, he lowered himself to the ground. After listening to make sure all was quiet, he took out the piece of paper Jasper had dropped and studied it while he waited.

It wasn't long before he heard the soft slither of sand and pebbles crumbling to the ground beside him. He turned and saw a slight crack form in the perimeter wall as the stone blocks and their mortared joints shifted. The crack grew wider as more and more joints compressed, but the sound remained as soft as that of sand in an hourglass. Pudgy fingers emerged from the wall, followed quickly by the dwarf's stocky form. The stone and mortar slid back to their original position, showing no traces of his passage.

Chert looked in both directions, and then at Xandor, who motioned toward the far end of the warehouse. With the dwarf leading the way, the two immersed themselves in total darkness. Practically blind, Xandor followed, keeping one hand on Chert's shoulder.

They rounded the corner, and a long shadow stretched across the narrow alley mouth. Silhouetted by a lamp from the courtyard, a bullmastiff approached cautiously, sniffing the air. Xandor's grip on the dwarf's shoulder tightened, stopping him.

The dog's low growl grew louder as it edged closer, but when Xandor stepped in front of Chert, the dog and his growls inexplicably stopped.

Crouching as he moved forward, Xandor murmured to the dog in smooth tones. He offered it a jerky treat from his pouch with one hand and warned Chert back with the other. The dog approached with his head low to the ground and gingerly took the dry meat. Behind the first, two more mastiffs appeared. Xandor continued his murmuring and produced two more jerky treats.

All three dogs stood by the tall man and looked up expectantly, their tails wagging. One leaned into him, nearly knocking him to the ground. Chert smothered a laugh when Xandor turned to him with a helpless expression and shrugged.

With the bullmastiffs following, Xandor walked casually toward the nearest oil lamp, supported by a corner bracket on the warehouse wall, and snuffed it out. Continuing on, Chert, Xandor, and their entourage of dogs turned toward the main entrance to the warehouse. As they went, Xandor murmured again; however, this time, the tone and words changed. The dogs backed away and laid down.

At the warehouse entrance, Chert scanned the courtyard one more time before giving Xandor a quick nod. In front of them stood a pair of thick, wooden doors, barred by a long oak timber. At one end, the timber had been set snugly into a metal socket bolted to the wall just beyond the door, while the other end was held in place by a hinged bracket closed with a padlock.

After Chert finished examining the locking mechanism, he whispered, "Xandor, I can't open this without permanently damaging it. Any ideas?"

Xandor reached into his pouch, pulled out a slender graphite rod, and slid it into the lock. The black bar slowly expanded until it filled the hole, pushing the tumblers above the lock's shear line. With a twist and soft click, the padlock opened. He put away the rod as Chert worked the bracket and moved the timber out of the way. Looking around to make sure no one had heard, the two pushed the door open just enough to get a glimpse inside.

The dwarf's eyes shone with a gold tint as they scanned the dark room. It was one vast, open space with two intermediate rows of solid oak columns supporting rough-hewn timber roof trusses. Between the columns sat three broad-wheeled wagons — two filled with crates, while the last and shortest one was empty except for a tall box at the rear.

While Chert closed the door behind them, Xandor pulled out a slender bone stylus and shook it. A reddish glow spread out from his hand, providing just enough light for them to see a few feet ahead.

Xandor cautiously approached the wagons, listening for any sounds of danger. Not hearing any, he pulled out a thin journal and began taking notes.

Walking around the loaded wagons, he roughly sketched their shape and listed the equipment. Water barrels hung on either side, along with toolboxes for any potential repairs. The wheels were iron-rimmed, with the front pair a little smaller than those in the rear, causing the wagon's front end to dip slightly. He noted that the bed and driver's seat were constructed using thin hardwood planks that were more conducive to speed than comfort or safety. He continued around the front and stepped over the long tongue-and-neck yoke that lay on the ground, waiting for the horses. Eight crates sealed with shiny silver nails filled the bed of each cargo wagon.

At the chuck wagon, Xandor flipped to a fresh page. He drew a diagram of the tall wooden box with its hinged face, made to fit in the back of the wagon. He reached up and lowered the odd-looking panel. As he did, spindle legs rotated out and the inside surface of the lid became a worktable. Inside, cast-iron pots and pans filled the box, along with a small, three-legged stand used for cooking over a campfire.

Looking underneath the wagon, Xandor noted a heavy piece of canvas stretched, hammock-style, across the underbelly.

While Xandor checked the wagons, Chert searched among the nearby stacks of empty pallets, various tools, bits of wax paper, and the scattering of straw. When finished, he joined Xandor, who stood in the back of one of the larger wagons, leaning over a crate.

Chert climbed up and focused his attention on the nails along the edge of the lid. He closed his eyes and whispered the dwarven word, "áhátian." The nails glowed with an inner light, and the wood panels around them slightly blackened. Then the dwarf said, "ácwencan." Immediately, the nails hissed and steamed as if doused in freezing water. When the dwarf tugged on the lid, the brittle nail heads snapped. Putting the lid aside, he took out a pair of pliers filched from the toolbox and tugged out one of the nail shanks.

Xandor scowled at the dwarf and whispered, "Chert, we'll have to replace those."

"Aye, lad, I know. There's a hammer and more nails in the box where I found these pliers," he replied quietly. While Chert continued to pull nails, Xandor searched the crate thoroughly. There was only straw and bundles of wax paper.

Satisfied, Xandor reached in, pulled a bundle out, and unwrapped it, revealing a plain bar of soap. Using his knife, he shaved a sliver off one end. Chert handed him a scrap of wax paper in which to wrap his shaving. After tucking away the sliver of soap in his pouch, he rewrapped the bar and placed it back in the crate exactly where he found it. He moved to the next bundle and unwrapped it — another plain bar of soap. Rewrapping it, he moved to the next one and the next one.

By the time Xandor finished, Chert had returned with the hammer and enough nails to repair the damage he had done to the crate. Between the two of them, they replaced the lid, pushing and tapping the nails back into the original holes.

They had just hopped down from the wagon when they heard someone outside the door yelling at the dogs, the words slurred.

"Enough, Pyotr, you drunken kopele!" someone shouted in the distance. In response, two men laughed.

"Tseluni me otzad!" Pyotr yelled back, but the laughter outside only increased. "These lazy dogs are just sitting here."

"Did you give them something from your flask?"

The man outside grumbled something incoherent. Chert and Xandor waited just inside the doors, peeking through a slim crack. Hunched over the three dogs, Pyotr kicked one in the ribs, too drunk to cause any real damage, and yelled, "Get up!"

With a firm grasp on Xandor's arm, Chert held the tall man back. The dog seemed completely unfazed by the assault. Someone from the main hall joined them. "Do you think they were drugged?"

"Viktor, you think everyone is drugged. No! They are not drugged — just look at them. They're... They're happy!" Pyotr threw his hands up in exasperation.

Holding a small hand lantern, Viktor laughed at the horse doctor. "Come on. I'll help you inside before you fall in any konski tor." The two were just about to walk away when Viktor noticed the door to the warehouse.

"Didn't we lock that door earlier?"

Pyotr was a bit unsteady as he gazed bleary-eyed at the warehouse. "How would I know? I was in the barn."

They walked up to the doors and opened them all the way. The light from the oil lamp in Viktor's hand illuminated the three wagons, but deep shadows filled the corners of the building.

"Branimir! Daniil!" Viktor yelled. "Come over here and bring more lights. I want to make sure everything's in order."

Two men, both dark haired and heavily bearded, rushed over to Viktor. Daniil, the younger of the two, was wiry thin and seemed to have a nervous twitch. He held up his light in a shaky hand and peered into the warehouse. Beside him, Branimir added his light to Daniil's and lit up the yard.

The door to the small office opened. "What's going on out here?" Sachin asked as he crossed the courtyard, Grendel right behind him.

Viktor turned as Sachin approached and replied, "Pyotr noticed something strange about how the dogs were acting, so I came over to see for myself. That's when I saw the warehouse wasn't locked."

Sachin pursed his lips and frowned in concentration as he picked up the padlock. He took the oil lamp from Daniil and was about to step inside when he seemed to think better of the idea. Instead, he asked, "Grendel, do you see anything? I know your vision is much better than ours in the dark."

"No, sir, but let me look around. Just keep that light back so I can see," Grendel replied calmly as he walked inside.

Hand on the hilt of his knife, Xandor watched the half-orc take his time. He searched all the corners, looking behind all the columns and up into the roof framing. Meanwhile, the other men checked the crates on the wagons and made sure nothing had disturbed them. When Grendel finished, he returned to Sachin and shook his head. "Nothing."

"Everything seems in order," Daniil said. "All the crates are here, and it doesn't look like anyone messed with them."

"Make sure it gets locked this time," Sachin ordered as he handed the padlock to Viktor. "I'll talk to Dragahn about replacing those dogs in the morning. Meanwhile, have someone guard the door."

"Yes, sir," Viktor replied.

While Sachin and Grendel returned to the office, Viktor closed the warehouse doors and slid the beam back into place. "Branimir, after I lock this, I want you to walk the grounds. Daniil, stand guard at the door until morning. I'll wake the chief and let him know it was unlocked. He may want to search the warehouse himself. I know how important this trip is to him."

Several minutes after the doors closed, Xandor slipped quietly out from the bottom of the wagon hammock and Chert appeared from behind a column. Xandor remained where he was, blind in the darkness until the dwarf walked over and took him by the arm. The two abandoned the idea of going out the front door. Instead, they worked their way to the middle of the common wall between the warehouse and the main hall. This wall, unlike the other three warehouse walls, was made of stone.

Chert closed his eyes, focusing his concentration, and stuck his fingers, palms facing outward, into a mortar joint. At first, a small crack appeared as he moved his hands apart, then gradually grew as Chert applied more pressure. The wythes of stone split open, revealing a cramped room beyond.

At the far end, light from under the door provided enough illumination for Xandor to tell they had found a storage closet. Pulling a bronze Korsun cross on a thin leather thong from under his tunic collar, he touched it to his lips and gave the Eternal Father a quick prayer of thanks.

Perspiration dotted the dwarf's forehead as he widened the fissure enough for them to crawl through, and then held it for Xandor, who quickly slid in, leaving room for Chert to enter behind him. As soon as they were clear of the crack, Chert released the stone, and the wall snapped back into place with a low rumble.

Xandor cringed at the noise. The two kept still, listening for any sign that someone had heard. After a few long minutes, they crept across the room. Seeing no movement under the door, Chert quietly turned the knob.

Outside was a long corridor that led toward a lit hall — probably the common room marked on Jasper's map. Echoes of two men discussing the dogs' odd behavior traveled to them. Xandor and Chert quickly tried the first door on the left. Finding it unlocked, they ducked inside.

Several workbenches and tables, laden with mounted lathes, stone sanders, and other tools crowded the room. Sawdust lay piled along the edges and in the corners. Not hesitating, they made their way toward the rear exit.

Xandor jumped up and grabbed the top of the wall as Chert prepared to open his way down below. Luckily, the streets were vacant when the two suddenly appeared on the opposite side. They crossed the street and then separated, both traveling circuitous routes to be sure no one followed them.

5:38am

It was an hour before dawn when Jasper was startled out of his favorite dream. He blinked owlishly at Xandor and the lit candle beside his bed.

Once his eyes were able to focus, he scrutinized the tall man and the short dwarf. "What have you been up to?"

"We went by the warehouse and picked up a piece of that soap for you. Can you take a quick look at it?"

Jasper stood up in his nightgown and cap and rolled his shoulders, then moved his head side to side. "Just trying to get the blood to flow," he said as the two watched him curiously. "Next time, I get to wake you up." The two studiously looked at the other items in the room, eliciting a soft chuckle from Jasper. "I'm ready. Let me see it."

Xandor reached into his pouch, pulled out the scrap of wax paper, and handed it to Jasper.

Whispering to himself, Jasper stared at the small bit of pearly grey soap nestled inside its wrapping for a long minute. Tilting the soap in his hand, tiny blue-green flecks reflected the candlelight.

"Seems normal enough," he said as he broke it unevenly.

Putting both pieces to one side, Jasper retrieved a half-empty jug of water. With a quick chant, a partially formed, semi-transparent sphere of energy appeared, floating just above the dressing table. He poured a tiny amount of water into the magical container, causing it to have a semispherical shape as it conformed to the lower portion of the ball. Holding the candle and the smaller piece of soap over the water, he touched it to the flame. As he did, a few milky drops fell. When the melted soap passed the upper surface of the sphere, Jasper muttered a single word and made a gesture with his hand reminiscent of putting a lid on a pot.

With a barely audible pop, the sphere sealed. The liquid soap slid slowly down the surface of the arcane vessel into the water. Suddenly, the water came alive as it hissed and splattered the inside surface.

Chert and Xandor leapt back. "Is it supposed to do that?" Chert asked cautiously.

"Yep, that's just the lye. Fellas, this is normal soap. Did you find anything else?"

The two glanced at each other, disappointed in the night's haul. Chert dug into his pouch, pulled out several nail shanks and popped nail heads, and laid them on the edge of the dresser.

"What's that?" Jasper asked.

"Those are the nails they used to fasten the crate lids. I grabbed them just before we left," Chert said sheepishly.

Jasper picked up a nail head and examined it. "That's funny," he said. It bore the remains of some type of sigil, something he couldn't quite discern. He inspected the cut portion. "This nail is silver with a copper core."

The three stared at each other, uncertain what this new information might mean, but convinced it would lead them to the connection Marcus wanted them to find.

After Xandor and Chert left, Jasper sat on the edge of his bed and studied the sphere of energy. The water had stopped boiling. Droplets coated the sphere's sides and upper curve, and a shallow puddle covered a layer of white residue in the bottom. The lye, he told himself. An uneasy feeling settled in his gut. Dismissing it, he slid his chamber pot under the sphere and made a quick gesture with his fingers. The sphere disappeared, and its contents dropped toward the bucket. As it did, the tiniest speck of black oil fell with it. Instead of falling straight down, the black speck shot toward Jasper's hand and seeped into his skin.

Knocking over the chamber pot, Jasper leapt back. He stared at his hand, turning it this way and that, but there was no sign of the black speck. He let out a deep sigh and told himself the black speck was nothing more than a figment of his imagination.

CHAPTER 6
MEET THE TEAMSTERS

October 12, 4235 K.E.

7:22am

Jasper arrived at the warehouse that morning to find Dragahn reviewing the previous night's events with his men. One of the workers had just handed him a small piece of metal from the ground near a wagon. Nearby, several men busily sealed the joints between the tightly fitted wood planks with tar while others stretched tough, white canvases across each bed, covering the crates.

Dragahn stuck the metal in his belt pouch and motioned Jasper over. "We need to discuss a few things before we leave tomorrow morning. I'll be here for a little longer so go on to the main hall and I'll meet you there."

When Dragahn entered the common room, Jasper was pouring himself a second cup of Turkestani kahve from a black kettle by the fireplace. "Want some?"

"That sounds great." After he had taken a few sips, Dragahn said, "I've been a caravan chief for almost ten years now. Started in the stables, younger than Lucky, and worked my way up the ranks." After a pause, he continued, "I'm forty-three years old and finally have a real chance here to turn the kind of profit that will let me live comfortably when I'm old and grey. The last thing I want is for you to mess things up and this trip go sour. A bad cook means a bad trip. I should know."

"Sure thing, Chief. The last thing I want is to poison everyone." There was a hint of laughter in the cook's voice, and a jovial glint in his eye.

Dragahn searched Jasper's face, obviously not finding the comment funny, then held up three fingers. "There are three things you need to know. First and foremost is that we have no room for sluggards on this trip. You pull your own weight, or you get left behind. Second, we are not part of the Teamster's Guild. They normally leave us alone, but I want you to be aware so you can keep your eyes open. Third, our hand signals. We have prearranged signals used by the drivers and the riders to communicate during the trip. I don't expect you to know them all, but you need to know the important ones. Daniil will instruct you this evening. Make yourself available."

Jasper nodded.

"Now, let's talk about some basics before we meet the others. Our team consists of three wagons, along with four guards on horseback. I'll be in the lead, driving the chuck wagon, Sachin the second, and Pyotr will be driving the third. I want to cover forty miles in a ten-hour day, including time for one break. Jasper, that will be your time. That break must be efficient; if we are delayed, it will disrupt our whole schedule.

"So you know, there will be towns along the way where we'll change horses. These stops will also give us a chance to adjust our supplies, as necessary. That way, we won't have to slow down." Dragahn looked at Jasper and asked, "Any questions?"

"A couple," Jasper replied. "Can you tell me where we're going, and how long we'll be out there? Or is that privileged information?"

Dragahn frowned and answered, "It's no secret. We're going east of the White River to the Rhodinan country of Michurinsk. I expect it will take us a month or so to get there and back if the weather holds. Don't worry, these trips usually go fast, but that's why your job is so important. You'll not only be our cook but, at one point or another, be someone these men can gripe to — including me."

"Yes, sir."

"When we're done meeting everyone, I want you to oversee the loading of the chuck wagon. It's the last wagon to get ready."

Jasper nodded and said, "Don't you worry, sir. I'll take care of it."

"Be sure to coordinate with Pyotr, because we also need to find room for the sweet feed and hay bales. Fortunately, we'll only have a short ride for the first leg of the trip, but I want you to be thinking about how we can store additional bales when the time comes."

Dragahn drained his cup and asked, "You ready to meet the rest of the team?"

"Yes, sir."

As they crossed the courtyard and between the various workers who came up asking questions, Dragahn continued, "You've already met Lucky, Sachin, and Pyotr. I want to introduce you to our four horsemen — Viktor, Bogdan, Branimir, and Daniil."

Jasper spotted Grendel and Sachin in the warehouse. They stood over the shoulder of one of the workers as he used a bar to pry the lid off a crate. A worried expression crept across his face. Had they discovered the crate Xandor and Chert broke into?

At the barn, the horses nickered and kicked the walls. Nearby, Pyotr shouted at the stable hands, demanding they move faster. He turned when he heard the two approach and said, "We're expecting Viktor's riding horses to arrive before lunch."

"Good. Pyotr, you met our new recruit?"

Pyotr looked at Jasper briefly and nodded. "We met."

"Where are Viktor and the others?"

"Daniil and Branimir had a late night, so they're sleeping it off. Viktor's over there with Bogdan, inspecting the horses. Again."

With a nod, Dragahn motioned Jasper to follow him into the drive bay of the barn. Only somewhat familiar with horse breeds, Jasper could still tell the horses in these stalls were remarkable. The massive, dappled-grey workhorses with muscular bodies and large feet were Percherons, a breed of draft horse that originated in northern Francesca. Considered second only to the famous Lundellan Chargers, Dragahn and his teamsters would be using ten of them to haul the three wagons. However, the difference between these beasts and most other draft horses was their impatience. Bred to work — and work hard — the horses were excited and eager for the run.

Two olive-complected men with thick, black beards stood observing the horses. Jasper recognized Viktor from the previous day's fight. The other had broader shoulders and a boyish face. Both wore the traditional kalpak, fur vest, and wide studded belt common to the labor class of Lower Pazard'zhik.

"Viktor and Bogdan, I want to introduce our newest member," Dragahn said. "This is Jasper."

The two stopped their conversation and stared at the cook, quickly sizing him up. Viktor stepped away from the stall door with his hand held out. "Good to meet you. It will be great having you as part of our team."

Jasper clasped the horseman's calloused hand and matched his firm grip.

"What do you think of the horses?" Dragahn asked.

"Chief, they'll work great," Viktor said. "Pyotr's been complaining about them all morning."

"I heard that, you bastard," Pyotr yelled as he stomped off.

Dragahn looked back over his shoulder and said, "What's wrong with him?"

Viktor and Bogdan replied, "Hangover," as they turned and resumed their morning duties.

"We should get our last four mounts this afternoon," Dragahn said.

Jasper looked around and asked, "How many people do you have working here?"

Dragahn stared at Jasper; the question obviously caught him off guard. He thought a moment before answering and said, "Twenty-five, if you include yourself and that half-orc Sachin hired."

"I'll want to spend a little time preparing dinner today, if that's alright, especially if I need to feed that many people," Jasper said. "And I'll need Yosif's help."

"Go ahead. Do what you need to, but don't forget the chuck wagon has to be ready today."

"Yes, sir, I haven't forgotten."

Inside the larder, Jasper pulled together some coarse salt, black peppercorns, paprika, cayenne pepper, some dried oregano leaves, cumin seeds, and garlic. He took his stash to the cookery, where he found Lucky waiting for him.

The cramped kitchen, while attached, lay on the other side of the two-sided fireplace, and had the musty feel of a stone bunker. The soot-stained hearth took up most of one wall and held grilles, tongs, and three different sized cauldrons. On the opposite wall was a deep counter with a granite top. Above it dangled an array of utensils. Below were shelves filled with a hodgepodge of metal pans and bowls. In the corner, a wooden bucket and rope lay next to the short stone wall surrounding the well.

"What's that?" Lucky asked.

"Seasoning," Jasper replied. "Can you go get the meat?"

"Sure," Lucky said before running out the door. When he returned, the two men cut three strips of flat-cut brisket from the slab and placed them in shallow pans. Lucky watched Jasper strike each piece of meat with a tenderizing hammer.

"Don't just stand there gawking. Get more wood for the fire and set up the grille."

Like a shot, Lucky bolted out of the room.

Turning the meat over, Jasper scored the layer of fat several times, brushed the surface with olive oil, and then smothered it thoroughly with his spice mix. The cook bowed his head, closed his eyes, concentrated, and whispered a few words. Once finished, he straightened, startled to find Lucky staring at him from the doorway, his arms filled with wood.

"Did you cast a spell?" Lucky asked.

"Just a prayer — of sorts."

12:16pm

Grendel stood outside the small office, giving Sachin some privacy. The half-orc had watched him trace their route past the Stena, the wall marking the eastern border of Trakya, to some place called Chernigov. He hadn't realized he had done anything wrong until Sachin flipped over the map and ordered him out.

He felt frustrated. Frustrated that his ward had him standing guard while everyone else worked through lunch. Frustrated that the only real threat here was boredom.

Two sweating teamsters carrying bales of hay walked past the office. One stopped and said, "Half-orc, you get kicked out? If you're looking for something to do, you can carry this bale."

The other laughed and said, "He didn't get kicked out. He probably ate Sachin and now he's looking for dessert. The man dug into his pouch and pulled out a jerky stick. Holding it up in front of Grendel, he said, "Do you want this?"

"Bogdan, stop that," the first teamster said.

"Why? I'm just having a little fun. Besides, we all know he shouldn't even be here."

Grendel eyed them as they continued toward the barn. He swallowed his anger and tried not to let their words get to him, but he couldn't help overhearing one mention that his mother had probably been raped.

Gritting his teeth, Grendel crossed his arms and focused on the people walking the street beyond the gate. Being a half-orc in a human city, his skin had grown thick against their taunts. He wondered if it would have been different being a half-human in an orc city. If what little he'd heard of his father's people were true, he imagined his lot might have been worse.

Letting out the breath he was holding, he spotted Dragahn staring at him. The teamster chief turned away, but the look in his eyes had been clear: half-orcs didn't belong.

1:02pm

Jasper returned to flip the meat and refill the water; three more hours, and the brisket would be ready. Some of the more curious workers kept finding their way into the common room to stare at him through the fireplace.

Dragahn stepped inside, and the men scattered. "Jasper, you're distracting my men."

"Not on purpose, sir."

"Do something about it," Dragahn said as he walked back out.

Jasper thought for a moment before he yelled, "Yosif!"

The youth ran up. "Yes, sir?"

"Stand guard and keep everyone out while I'm gone."

"Yes, sir."

Jasper was half-way across the room when he thought better of it. He turned back to Lucky, his face serious. "Don't touch that meat. If you do, I'll know."

Before Lucky could say anything, Jasper drew close and whispered, "It's just as easy to serve long pork, and no one here would ever know the difference."

"L-long pork?" Lucky stammered.

Jasper prodded the youth's chest.

Lucky's eyes grew wide, and his mouth formed an O. Rooted in place, he watched Jasper leave. At the door,

Jasper turned and touched the side of his nose with his forefinger.

By mid-afternoon, the last four horses arrived, saddled and ready for riding. Daniil, Bogdan, Branimir, and Viktor each picked a horse, led them into the corral, and in short order, were riding around the compound.

It was easy for Jasper to see the importance breeding made with the two types of horses. Standing about fifteen hands, the rounceys were sleek and lean while the Percherons were hefty and all muscle.

While he walked back and forth between the warehouse and larder, Jasper kept an ever-watchful eye on the door to the small office and Grendel standing guard beside it. Marcus mentioned they'd be working with a half-orc, but Jasper had his doubts. Grendel seemed more a typical bruiser than one capable of subterfuge.

There had been no sign of Sachin. The door remained closed most of the day, with only the occasional arrival of a courier to suggest someone was inside.

Surprisingly, very little was mentioned about the previous evening. The teamsters proved to be a tight group and, try as he might, Jasper had trouble getting them to loosen up around him.

An hour before the meat would be done, Jasper excused himself again. The chuck wagon was packed, with space left over for the sweet feed and a few bales of hay.

3:46pm

Dragahn was stunned by the smells coming from the main hall. Most of the smoke went up and out the chimney, but occasionally, the wind shifted, and the smell filled the courtyard. It was worse when the door opened, which for some reason, people kept forgetting to shut.

As mealtime approached, everyone became curious. Pedestrians milled outside the gate — some even venturing inside the compound.

"Get them out of here!" Dragahn yelled at Viktor. "And close that gate!"

The horseman quickly gathered his men and herded the small crowd back outside.

Pyotr emerged from the barn. "What's going on?"

"Jasper's cooking," Dragahn replied.

4:02pm

Jasper walked into the cookery to wash up. When he finished, he sent a relieved Lucky to collect cups and utensils while he prepared the side dishes. Several volunteers arrived to help, and within a few minutes, the common room had transformed into a banquet hall fit for the Kral.

Viktor, Daniil, Bogdan, and Branimir burst through the door and claimed seats next to one another. Similar in appearance with their combed dark hair, thick beards, and clothing styles, they could have been brothers. However, to Jasper, it appeared Viktor, being the oldest, set the tone for the other three. He suspected the four horsemen probably competed with one another over a lot of things.

Next through the door was Pyotr. The horse doctor had cleaned up and seemed sober enough. Dragahn, who led the rest of the stable hands and workers into the main hall, followed him closely.

Once everyone was seated, Lucky and Jasper busied themselves with setting the food on the table. There were sliced sweet potatoes, grilled and coated in a thick brown sugar and cinnamon glaze, pinto beans, and even a salad of carrots and cabbage, which Lucky had helped put together. With a flourish of true showmanship, Jasper and Lucky set three plates topped with sliced brisket upon the table. Everyone immediately dug in.

Lucky glanced at Jasper, who gave him a surreptitious nod. The youth quickly found a seat and joined the other teamsters.

As Jasper passed from person to person to make sure everything was to their liking, Grendel appeared at the doorway. The cook gave the person he was talking with a pat on the back and walked over to the half-orc.

"Sachin would like for you to prepare him a dish," Grendel said.

"Sure. Give me some help, and I'll fix you one as well."

"Do not bother. I am not hungry."

Jasper gave the bodyguard a skeptical look before slipping into the cookery to collect a tray with dinnerware for both Sachin and the half-orc. Conversations around the banquet table fell to whispers as he filled the plates with a portion of each dish and presented the tray to Grendel. Stunned silence settled over the room when Jasper said, "No one leaves my kitchen hungry."

CHAPTER 7
THE WATCHERS

October 12, 4235 K.E.

10:26pm

A waning gibbous moon cast pale light on Lower Pazard'zhik and set the snowy mountain peaks surrounding the city aglow.

High up in a belfry, Xandor took another swallow of water from his canteen and peered over the compound wall. The last light inside the main hall had gone out. Behind him, a church bell hung ominously close. Fortunately for him, this church didn't ring the bell every hour. Down in the sanctuary, Chert rested in a pew, hopefully keeping half an eye on the bell rope.

Xandor and Chert had spent the entire day taking turns watching the teamsters' compound. It had taken some fast talking and an exchange of messages with Marcus to convince the priest to allow Xandor and Chert access to the bell tower. The Ochi i Ushi's second-in-command had enough authority that, come nightfall, the priest and his acolytes had retired to their dormitory, letting Xandor and Chert have the church to themselves.

Studying the dark outlines of the sleeping warehouse, Xandor went through the events of the day. If this was a smuggling operation, they were doing an excellent job hiding it. There had been nothing in those crates. He kept coming back to the soap, but the soap was ordinary — wasn't it? And what about the nails? Jasper had said they were silver. He wanted to kick himself for missing that oddity.

They had watched Sachin, but the man had done what Xandor would have done — find out if any of the crates had been opened and count the bars to see if any were missing. Xandor could almost hear the grumbling when Sachin ordered the workers to take all the crates off the wagons and check each one. Dragahn tried to intervene, but whatever was said between the two didn't reach his ears.

One thing did stand out — Sachin replaced the nails, but he did not use the spares from the toolboxes. He used nails from a pouch he carried.

11:55pm

It was close to midnight when Xandor decided it was time to wake Chert. He had not seen anything suspicious, just the sporadic rounds made by the city guard. It was no wonder they had been able to break into the teamster compound so easily.

Mindful of his silhouette, Xandor peered from the belfry window one last time. Closing the trapdoor behind him, he climbed down the ladder and entered the chapel proper. Flickering light from votive candles on a small side altar lit his way as he approached a pew that snored softly.

"Chert, wake up."

The dwarf's hand jerked toward his hammer.

"It's just me," Xandor murmured.

"Holy ground, and I still don't feel safe," Chert muttered. He scrubbed the sleep from his eyes before standing to return the hammer to his belt.

As he walked toward the door, Xandor replied quietly, "It's not the church; it's the people we meet. They bring out the best in us."

"Where are we going?" Chert asked with a massive yawn.

"Upper Pazard'zhik. Marcus sent a message asking us to visit Advocate Hristova's office."

The two headed toward the Majna i Vira, a massive stone edifice carved into the three-hundred-foot escarpment separating Upper Pazard'zhik from Lower Pazard'zhik. As they drew closer, the runic symbols of strength and durability etched into the building face seemed to glow with an inner power. Inside, two cylindrical shafts spanned the height of the cliff and contained massive lifts used to transport both goods and people. To either side of the Majna i Vira, a pair of tall, rectangular towers with hip roofs supported switchback stairs, partially cut into the cliff face.

Torches set into wall sconces flanked each of the entrances. Xandor and Chert approached the guards standing in front of the left-hand stairwell. Wearing blue and black checkered tabards over plate armor, they eyed the newcomers curiously but didn't say anything.

Xandor pulled out a folded piece of thick parchment. Handing it to one of the guards, he said, "My partner and I need to go upstairs."

After reading the document, the guard snapped to attention and replied, "Of course, Sir." The other guard glanced at the paper and straightened like he was about to be inspected by the Kral himself.

The first guard produced a key and unlocked the door. "Gentlemen, please allow me to escort you to the top."

1:34am

Chert and Xandor bent over a desk inside an upstairs corner office, rifling through the drawers. The drapes over the windows were pulled tight, and the door was closed. Soft light from Xandor's stylus illuminated a small portion of the room. The placard on the other side of the door read, "Адвокат Христова."

After a moment, the dwarf sighed heavily and asked, "Do we even know what we are looking for?"

Xandor shook his head as he scanned a document with an official seal at the top. "Anything out of the ordinary."

"Like a silver nail?"

"Something like that."

Marcus' message earlier in the evening said one of Advocate Hristova's servants had visited Sachin that morning. It was a long shot, but Xandor figured this would be their only opportunity to check it out.

The law office seemed aboveboard, but it was hard to tell. The few papers they found were mostly plats, and the rest were estate documents. They had already searched for a safe, but if there was one here, they couldn't find it.

A door shutting downstairs made them stop.

Xandor doused his light and gently pulled back the drapes. When he did, a sudden movement caught his eye — not a flash of color or even the flickering of a light. It was pure motion which didn't blend with the rhythms of the night.

Fading back into the shadows, Xandor searched the street.

There it was again. Someone, or something, was crossing the street away from their building. Had they been followed? Slowly, Xandor let the drape settle back in place. He pointed to his eyes and then pointed outside.

His eyes shining in the darkness, Chert opened the door and peered down the hallway. All was clear.

Xandor peeked out the window again. No one.

The two crept down the hall, toward the stairs. A pungent aroma wafted up from below. The smell grew stronger as they descended and made the two men light-headed. Chert said a quick prayer and the air cleared a little, but they still needed to find a window. Following the peculiar odor to the rear of the building, the pair found a door with a flickering light glowing underneath it.

Xandor unsheathed his longswords while Chert cautiously cracked open the door. The odor ploughed out of the room like a solid object, and they both raised their hands to cover their coughing. Inside, fire behind the iron grate of a wood burning stove cast odd shadows on the tongue-and-groove wall paneling. At the opposite corner sat a wooden scrivener desk, its chair tipped over. Beside it, a man lay sprawled on the floor, surrounded by accounting ledgers.

Rushing to the man's side, Xandor felt for a pulse. "He's dead, but the body's still warm."

Chert followed the odor to the wood stove. He wasn't familiar enough with herbs to identify the poison, but there was no doubt that whatever it was, had been thrown into the fire on purpose. He followed the vent pipe to a bend in the metal joint where smoke poured out a small gap. Climbing a stool, the dwarf gripped both sections of the hot pipe with his bare hands and pushed them together, closing the hole. Woozy, he nearly fell, but Xandor caught him and helped him to the floor.

The main door to the building burst open, and torch flame lit the corridor. "This is the militsiya!" someone shouted. "We have the place surrounded!"

Chert looked to Xandor for some plan, but the man just shrugged, his motions slow and clumsy. For his part, Chert felt as if someone had stuffed a wad of cotton into his head. Using his hammer as support, he tried to stand but all he managed was a kneeling position.

Xandor gave the dwarf a meaningful look that said, 'I hope this works.' Leaning against the door, he pulled out his folded parchment and yelled, "Back here! A man's been poisoned!"

Footsteps quickly followed the sound of Xandor's voice. Armored men with crossbows filled the corridor. Their sergeant stepped into the room and studied the two trespassers. Their calm demeanor seemed to surprise him.

"Be careful," Xandor warned. "There's some kind of poison in the stove."

The militsiya sergeant glanced around at the ledgers on the floor, the residual pungent odor making his eyes water. Kneeling, he rolled the prone man over and felt for life. When he discovered the man was dead, he stood and gave Xandor a hard stare. "Who are you?"

Xandor handed the sergeant the parchment. As the guard read it, his eyes grew wide.

"What's one of the Kral's rangers doing here?"

"We're working with the Ochi i Ushi."

"We'll see about that." He held out his hand and ordered, "Your weapons."

Chert and Xandor glanced at each other as they slowly handed the guard their weapons, hilt first.

"I'm taking these men with me," he said aloud and motioned for three of his men to follow him. "The rest of you continue the search and let me know if you find anything."

"Where are we going?" Chert asked thickly, still groggy from the smoke.

"Zatvor." *Jail.*

"What?" Xandor exclaimed. He made to grab the sergeant and said, "You can't!"

The soldiers in the hallway gripped their weapons tighter, preparing for a fight. Stepping easily away from Xandor's hand, the sergeant said hotly, "I don't care who you are. A man is dead. You will do exactly what I say."

Xandor glanced from the sergeant to Chert and back to the sergeant. "Fine. We'll do it your way, but you're letting the killer escape."

The militsiya escorted their prisoners outside, where the fresh air cleared Chert's head. As they moved down the street, the dwarf caught a glimpse of someone standing in an alley. His wild and unruly hair glinted red in the torchlight. By the looks of him, he was one of the clansmen who hailed from the mountainous region along the northern border of Trakya. Why was he here?

The two made eye contact, and Chert read the satisfaction in the other man's eyes. He tapped Xandor on the elbow, but when he turned back, the man had disappeared.

True to his word, the sergeant led them to a single-story, stone zatvor with a crenellated parapet and barred windows.

Maybe the two could have made a run for it, or maybe they could have fought their way free. Still under the effects of the poisonous fumes, Xandor decided to take time and think — there was more going on here than they had been told.

A quick knock broke Xandor from his reverie. A heavy wooden door opened, and the sergeant ushered the two men into a guard room flanked by several closed doors. An arched opening led to a hallway lined with six by eight cells.

4:00am

A hacking cough woke Xandor. Limned by torchlight, a nobleman wearing a waist-length black doublet approached them. He carried a leather satchel with silver double-headed eagles emblazoned on each side. Symbols of the Ochi i Ushi na Kral — *the Eyes and Ears of the King* — they represented the organization tasked with protecting Trakya from both internal and external threats. His politician's eyes scanned the various occupants in the cells before settling on the ranger and the dwarf.

"Chert," Xandor said, pushing him awake. The dwarf and ranger rose when the nobleman stopped at their cell.

"Dobŭr vecher, Marcus," Xandor said. "We didn't expect to see you today."

"Dobŭr vecher, Xandor," Marcus replied, then shook his head. "I didn't expect to have to get you out of jail today."

Marcus opened the cell door and led them down the hall. They followed him into the sergeant's office, where he took the seat behind the desk. Their jailors were nowhere to be found.

"I expected better," Marcus said flatly. Suddenly overcome with another coughing fit, he turned his head, grabbed a handkerchief, and held it to his mouth. When he finally caught his breath, he said, "I know the two of you haven't worked together before, but I need you at your best. You getting arrested creates complications, especially if we're to keep this investigation under the table."

"Marcus, it won't happen again," Xandor replied.

Beside him, Chert nodded and said, "Yes, Sir."

"Were you able to find anything at the Advocate's office?" asked Marcus.

"No, what about you?"

"The dead man was a scrivener," Marcus answered. "If I had to guess, some of their ledgers are missing. Maybe just one. We found burnt pages in the stove."

"Who tipped off the militsiya?" Xandor asked.

"One of the patrolmen said he saw someone go inside. Must have been you."

Xandor thought back. He was certain they had not been spotted. "What's going on here, Marcus?"

"I was about to ask you the same question."

"We searched the warehouse and wagons and didn't find anything except for soap and some weird silver nails they used to fasten the crate lids."

"Did you talk with Jasper?"

"A little. He said the soap was normal. You still think there's a connection between the Krakov Estate we raided and this caravan?"

Marcus pushed back from the desk and ran his hand through his hair. "Yes. No. I don't know. All I do know is we never found the Baroness' body and D'yakon Krovos escaped. They're out there somewhere, and I don't believe their scheme is finished."

At the mention of the dark priest's name, Xandor turned grim and there was an air of restrained violence about him.

Chert laid a calming hand on Xandor's forearm and said, "Pull us out now if you think this caravan is digging for pyrite."

"No," Marcus said, shaking his head. "There are too many strange rumors coming from beyond the Stena, many centered on the White River. People talking about ships of death sailing south and humanoids seen massing near Chernigov. Dragahn's been out there twice this year already, and I need to know why — something other than what's written on his itinerary."

"What about Advocate Hristova?" Xandor asked. "What's her part in all this?"

"She's funding the caravan, and she was a guest at the Krakov Estate," Marcus replied. He turned his eyes toward his satchel and a worried expression crossed his face. "A member of the merchant's guild at a social event like that is suspicious. Nobility and the mercantile class typically don't mix."

"Why not?"

"For the same reason a business owner doesn't socialize with his employees. It undermines their authority. Hristova's money runs deep, but not deep enough for Krakov and his peers to ignore her peasant lineage. One thing is certain. It would not look good for the Ministry of Revenue if word got out the Advocate was connected to something illegal.

"The message we received, plus the information you provided me regarding Krakov's connection to the Sha'iry activity in Pazard'zhik, was instrumental in gaining the Kral's approval for the raid. That's one of the reasons I asked your Highlord and the Iron Tower if I could use you. I couldn't openly investigate Advocate Hristova's business without hard evidence. I needed your help. And now with your arrest all that may be compromised."

"What about the soap?"

"What about it?" Marcus asked. "You just said Jasper deemed it normal. It's very popular with the upper-class and has been for some time. I even have a bar of the stuff at home. Gentlemen, we have nothing."

"What do you want us to do?" asked Xandor.

After pondering Chert and Xandor a moment, Marcus stood. "Follow the caravan and discover what you can. I'll find a roundabout way to check on Advocate Hristova here in town and see if anything turns up."

Xandor gave a curt nod and held out his hand. "I hope you beat that cough."

"Me too." As he shook Xandor's hand, Marcus said, "Be careful. Yana worries about you."

Xandor smiled at the mention of her name. "Tell your sister not to. There's more chance of her falling out of the sky with those contraptions she rides than something happening to us."

4:30am

The redhaired Northman watched Marcus leave the zatvor. He left alone, with no signs of the Kral's ranger. Behind the Northman, another man with wild red hair stepped close enough so as to not be overheard. "Mladen, we need to go. Mag'osnik Asenov awaits us at the mage's guild."

"You bring the D'yakon's book?" Mladen asked.

"It's right here," Ognian replied, patting the over-sized courier pouch at his side. "I still don't understand why the guild can't magic the soap to Chernigov instead of having it travel by caravan."

"I overheard Gregori tell the D'yakon that the soap is triggered by two things: water or powerful magic. So, they're stuck transporting it by wagons."

"What about Dragahn? He has to be suspicious by now."

"Don't worry about him. I've got it all taken care of. He won't make it through tomorrow."

"Mladen, I hope you're right. Otherwise, it will be our asses."

CHAPTER 8
LEAVING PAZARD'ZHIK

October 13, 4235 K.E.

6:36am

The sun had not yet risen, and the vague outlines of the buildings were just becoming visible when Dragahn exited the main hall. Dressed in his thick wools and fur kalpak, holding a steaming tin cup of kahve, he stopped a few yards from the door and took a sip. Inhaling the crisp morning air, he breathed in the excitement of the moment. In front of him, workers had already hauled the wagons out of the warehouse and into the frost-covered courtyard. Others led the Percherons out of the barn, their harnesses fastened, and grey blankets draped across their backs.

Holding his own cup of kahve, Pyotr shuffled from the hall and joined Dragahn. The two remained silent, watching Viktor and his men hitch the draft horses to the vehicle tongues. Once the horses were in place, they fidgeted and stamped the ground.

Following right behind Viktor and his men, Sachin double checked the wagons and horses, giving them a final inspection. When Dragahn had first met the cargo owner's representative, he'd had his doubts Sachin could handle the draft horses, but now, seeing him interact with the animals, he again realized this slight man was an expert horseman and had a way with the beasts. Watching the half-orc out the corner of his eye, Dragahn wondered if Sachin had the same effect on Grendel. Why had the man chosen a half-orc? Everyone knew the creatures were notoriously untrustworthy, and the few he'd met lacked any real courage.

Preceded by the sound of his footsteps, Jasper passed Pyotr and Dragahn, opened the chuck box, and rearranged some of the items to make room for a small box containing several clay jars with hinged lids.

Stable boys led the new rounceys from the barn and held them steady for Viktor and his horsemen to mount before handing over the reins.

The sky continued to brighten. Dragahn finished the last dregs of his kahve and yelled, "All right, ladies, load up!"

In the front, Dragahn and Jasper took their places on the chuck wagon; next came Sachin and Grendel, followed last by Lucky and Pyotr. Viktor and Branimir trotted to the front of the line while Daniil and Bogdan remained to guard the rear.

With a flick of the wrist, the caravan chief snapped the reins, and the Percherons moved forward at an easy walk. The two horsemen in front, along with the stable hands, helped direct the morning traffic away from the gates as they opened. Once clear, the team turned and headed toward the east bridge. People and animals dodged out of their way as the team travelled quickly through the muddy streets.

7:00am

Speeding through Lower Pazard'zhik, they passed row after row of warehouses and other broad, wood framed buildings. Most bore Cyrillic symbols indicating guilds such as smiths, weavers, or carpenters. Jasper thought back to yesterday's speech and hoped they wouldn't have any trouble.

At first, the jumble of buildings prevented Jasper from visually gauging their proximity to the eastern gate. A dim rumble, felt more than heard, grew as they progressed, and Jasper caught fleeting glimpses of the River Maritsa plunging over the escarpment. Gradually, the larger buildings gave way to smaller shops and inns, catering to travelers, and allowed for a grander view of the river's sparkling waters.

The rumble became a dull roar. Ahead stood an ancient archway fashioned from black basalt covered with dwarven runes, most of which had become illegible with the passage of time. Beyond lay a fifty-foot-wide stone bridge. Underneath, two rows of regularly spaced columns founded on the bottom of the Maritsa supported its massive double-barrel vaults, which spanned both side-to-side and front-to-back. Along each side of the deck, short stone parapets prevented wagons from falling into the river.

Being so early in the morning, their three wagons were the first to arrive. When the team was within eyesight of the archway, a dozen soldiers dressed in fur-lined sable and azure tunics moved from their positions and barred further progress.

Dragahn called for a halt, and he and Viktor dismounted as one of the guards approached. A braided, gold cord decorated his right shoulder. The chief pulled out his itinerary and manifest, all the while giving the guard a friendly nod.

"Good morning, Sergeant Deyan."

"Morning, Dragahn," the sergeant replied sourly. "Where are you headed this early?"

Dragahn handed him his papers with his left while shaking the sergeant's hand with his right. As he did, Jasper caught the glint of silver passing between the two men.

The sergeant unfolded the papers and checked for all the appropriate approvals. Seeing everything in order, he motioned for two of his men to come forward.

"Let's take a look," Sergeant Deyan said, passing by the chuck wagon with Dragahn following him.

Viktor yelled for Bogdan and Daniil to open the canvas. They quickly dismounted and handed the reins off to a waiting Lucky. The two horsemen pulled back the canvas enough to reveal the eight crates.

The sergeant pointed to one, and together, Bogdan and Daniil slid out the crate while the two guards watched. Bogdan produced a pry bar and gently opened the lid.

One of the guards reached inside, picked out a wrapped bar of soap, opened it, and put it back. "It's soap, Sergeant," he reported.

Sergeant Deyan looked over his shoulder with a bored expression and said, "Yep, it's soap. Make a note of it in our log."

The two horsemen closed and refastened the lid with nails pulled from a bulging doeskin pouch, then raced to the rear wagon and peeled back the canvas. Sergeant Deyan picked another crate at random, the two men opened it, he looked inside, and they closed it back up. As soon as the three guards moved away from the rear wagon, Bogdan and Daniil quickly straightened both canvases and remounted. Curiosity piqued, Jasper watched as they drew beside Sachin and returned his pouch of nails.

Dragahn walked with the sergeant and one of his guards, making inquiries about the weather and road conditions. As they talked, Sergeant Deyan studied each driver and passenger. He stopped when he came to Grendel.

"What's your name?" he demanded.

"Grendel," the half-orc replied.

"We don't see your kind here often. Where are you from?"

"J'Bel."

If Sergeant Deyan had heard of the place, Jasper couldn't tell. The sergeant gave Grendel a lingering look before turning to Sachin. "Better keep it on a tight leash."

Waving his arm, Sergeant Deyan signaled for the guards at the archway to move aside. He produced a pair of crimping pliers and stamped their itinerary. When he was done, he handed it back to Dragahn and said loudly, "You're cleared. Have a safe journey."

Before Dragahn walked away, the sergeant added quietly, "Keep your eyes open, Dragahn; the guild knows you're making another run."

"I will. Thank you, Deyan."

The sergeant patted one of the Percherons on the flank and headed back to his men as Dragahn and Viktor resumed their positions.

Just before the team moved out, Dragahn reached down, pulled a scarf out from his belt pouch, and wrapped it around his head. He looked at Jasper and pulled out another one. "Wear this. It'll protect you from the dust and dirt."

CHAPTER 9
AMBUSH

October 13, 4235 K.E.

7:41am

"Hyah," Dragahn yelled, flicked his wrist, and the team started across the bridge.

To their left, the River Maritsa cascaded over the escarpment into the waterway below, where it wound its way into the Cherno More. The morning sun broke the horizon and caught the rising mist, decorating the waterfall with shimmering rainbows. For one precious moment, the beauty of the scene quieted every thought racing through Jasper's mind. With a deep sigh, he turned back to the road ahead.

Another stone arch guarded the end of the bridge. Once part of a larger structure, the ruins of an old wall extended several feet to either side and marked the edge of the city. The guards on this side of the bridge were only stopping traffic going west, so the team moved past them at a brisk pace. Just beyond the arch, the road forked. Dragahn steered the horses away from the southern shipyard and docks and continued east. The road climbed gradually as it wound into the mountains.

For the first two hours, the team rode with the sun in their eyes. The temperature rose, and it didn't take long for Jasper and Dragahn to toss their jackets into the wagon-bed behind them.

Viktor rode alongside their wagon, chatting with Dragahn while keeping an eye out for trouble. The Percherons made good progress on the well-maintained roads, walking at an easy pace. Everyone had an opportunity to enjoy the beautiful countryside as it gently rose and fell, but in the near distance, high, snow-capped mountains towered over both sides of the road like fanged crenellations.

Jasper watched in silence as cottars harvested their late season crops or winterized their homes. Irregularly spaced walls of stacked stone crisscrossed the countryside. Some delineated property boundaries while others separated the different fields used for crop rotation. Jasper guessed a good many were built just to store the vast number of rocks they found while plowing.

The homes they passed varied significantly, based on family wealth. Most were small, single-room buildings while others were two-room cottages. Then there were the estates of the wealthier landowners — dark stone buildings with roofs of clay tile or slate. They sprawled across the land like small villages.

Outside one particular estate, emaciated horses grazed on the sparse grass. Dragahn grumbled, "People don't care for their horses."

"Pardon?" the cook replied.

Dragahn gestured toward a small horse ahead. As it stood munching grass, Jasper could count the animal's ribs. "This time of year, everyone is getting ready for the first snow, so they end up practically starving their animals. Horses need more than grass."

Jasper shrugged. "What else can they do? They have to save the good stuff for later."

Dragahn stared at the nearby stone residence; smoke rose from the chimney. "They've got enough money to build those fancy houses, seems like they'd use some of it for the horses this time of year." He nodded at a cottage as they passed, directing Jasper's gaze toward the smoke seeping through a simple hole in the thatched roof. "It's a lot easier to tell the wealthy from the poor out here."

With this new insight, Jasper understood the chief a little better. He glanced sideways at Dragahn and wondered how someone who had worked his way up through the ranks could get caught up in smuggling. Was it the quick money or something else?

Shortly after their conversation, the small cottages and estates gave way to heavily wooded country, teaming with wildlife. After a stretch, the forest ended and small farms with cleared plots dominated the landscape again.

The road traffic varied as the day progressed, and to Jasper's untrained eye, Viktor's team did an excellent job clearing a path when it became congested.

Dragahn didn't say much after they passed into the more rural countryside, so Jasper pulled out his pipe and enjoyed a bowl of tobacco. As he understood it, their first destination, the town of Stamboliyski, was a good day's ride from the river.

Earlier, Dragahn had told the cook he preferred to ride six hours first thing, break, and then push for another four hours. That would make their scheduled stop an hour or so after noon. It was with some anticipation that Jasper watched the sun, gauging when it would be lunchtime.

As the hour approached, they entered a roadside village. Dark stone cottages with small gardens lined both sides of the road. Behind them were barren fields. They passed a weathered wooden sign welcoming travelers.

Suddenly two men ran out in front of the caravan pushing a wheelbarrow filled with burning straw. They stopped in the middle of the road, threw their arms up in the air, and shouted at the horses.

Thick black smoke blanketed the street, filling everyone's nostrils and stinging their eyes. The two Percherons in front of Jasper reared and screamed, threatening to overturn the chuck wagon.

Gripping the seat tightly, Jasper whipped his head around to see two more men run out behind Yosif and Pyotr's wagon, also pushing a flaming wheelbarrow. Smoke quickly obscured the road behind. Jasper looked left and right, hoping someone would see and send help. None came.

Dragahn stood in the seat to get more leverage and yelled while cracking the air with his whip, making the horses run through the thick curtain of smoke. Wrapping his leg around one of the seat supports, Jasper grabbed Dragahn's belt to steady him.

Several men with bows, using the houses for partial cover, started shooting.

Daniil went down first with a shot to the chest, followed by Bogdan's horse. Bogdan collapsed with his mount, his cry echoing off the walls of the cottages.

Galloping beside Jasper and Dragahn, Viktor pulled out his short bow. "Sons of bitches shot Daniil!" he yelled. Viktor stood in his stirrups and shot the closest bandit in the shoulder as he flew past.

"Keep everyone moving!" Dragahn ordered.

From both sides of the street, more bandits appeared and aimed their bows at the chief. Calming his mind, Jasper concentrated and whispered a quick word. One by one, the arrows streaking toward Dragahn snapped and fell short of their mark, striking some unseen barrier.

Through sheer force of will, Dragahn steered his galloping horses at a group of archers. The wagon careened wildly as he cracked the whip repeatedly, gaining speed. At first, the men raised their bows but then dove aside when they realized the wagon wasn't stopping.

Once out of the smoke, Dragahn sat down and threw a quick glance back. Behind him, Sachin and Pyotr's teams followed, led mostly by herd mentality. Viktor and Branimir raced along in their wake, with tendrils of smoke trailing after them, as if the dark cloud was unwilling to give them up so easily.

Wild parting shots followed them out of the smoke. Most landed harmlessly in the dirt, but a few lodged themselves in the side of Pyotr's wagon.

11:54am

Well over the stiffness from his night in jail, Chert jogged beside the mounted ranger. His plate and chain armor made a soft, shushing jingle with each step.

Xerxes, Xandor's horse, was a strongly built, glossy black Andalusian with a long, thick mane and tail. Standing approximately fifteen hands, the animal's eyes shone with intelligence, and it unnerved the dwarf how ranger and horse could communicate without words. Then again, Chert was suspicious of any animal taller than he, which explained why Xandor rode, and he jogged.

They intentionally set a slow, easy pace, not wanting to catch up to the caravan. Maybe it was the slow pace that lulled him into a sense of peacefulness. In any case, when Xerxes perked his ears, Xandor straightened in his saddle.

"What is it?" the dwarf asked.

"Don't know, but that looks like trouble up ahead. Let's investigate."

With that, Xandor reached down and hauled the dwarf up behind him. Chert barely got a grip on Xandor's leather jerkin before Xerxes leapt forward into a full gallop, pounding down the road toward the smoky village.

1:06pm

Tears streaking his dusty face, Bogdan watched his fellow horsemen disappear into the veil of smoke, the thunder from their hooves still ringing in his ears. He looked around and spotted where Daniil had fallen. With some digging and scraping, he crawled out from under his horse and over to Daniil to see if he was alive.

His hand still hovering over Daniil's mouth and nose, Bogdan cried out when a sharp pain lanced through his leg. He peered through the smoke and saw a man dressed in chain armor holding a longbow — this time the arrow was aimed straight at his heart.

"Kheil!" someone shouted and both men looked around. Smoke swirled, but nothing was there.

The bandit dropped his longbow and drew his sword. He waved the point around trying to clear the smoke. In the distance, the staccato pounding of horse hooves diminished, leaving an eerie silence interrupted by the occasional crackle of flames.

"Antonoff, hurry up!" one of the bandits yelled. Their leader turned, still holding his longsword. Footsteps scraped on the road as the other bandits moved out of the alleyways.

A gentle breeze blew down the street, and the thick smoke took on odd shapes. The smoke cleared a little more to reveal Xandor standing in the middle of the street with both his longswords drawn.

"This is none of your business, stranger," Antonoff said to Xandor. The leader's eyes flicked to one of his men. Responding to the look, the bandit raised his bow and aimed it at the ranger's back.

With a blur of motion, Chert drew his hammer and hurled it. The hammer struck the archer's forehead with a loud, meaty thud. It rebounded and flew back to Chert's waiting hand before the bandit hit the ground.

Antonoff leapt at Xandor, making an overhead sword slash as he charged. It was a strong attack but poorly executed.

Recognizing a thug instead of a professional, Xandor met the oncoming attack high and swept it outside with his left-hand sword. Panic crept into the bandit's eyes as Xandor punched him, pulping his nose and cracking teeth. To finish him off, Xandor smashed his right-hand sword pommel down on the bandit's forearm, breaking bones and disarming him.

Antonoff staggered back, and Xandor kicked his feet out from under him. The bandit fell heavily, screaming when he tried to break his fall with a shattered wrist.

Blood streamed from Antonoff's nose and mouth as he stared at the ranger in shock, but before the bandit could recover his wits, Xandor placed the tip of his sword against the man's neck.

"Call them off," Xandor growled. "Now."

"No need, Xandor," Chert replied. "They're all running away. Doubt they would hear you."

Voices filled the street as cottage doors opened. Men and women streamed out, wanting to lend a helping hand or curious to see what had happened. Xandor nodded toward Chert and inclined his head toward Antonoff.

"Who's in charge here? Why didn't you stop this?" Xandor asked, his eyes searching amongst the crowd. They all cowered back. All except for one man, who stood staring down his nose at Xandor and had the look of someone who perpetually smelled something foul.

"Who, sir, are you?" the man asked.

Xandor sheathed his weapons and handed him the folded parchment. The man paled and quickly handed back the paper as if it might bite. Behind him, "one of the Kral's rangers" was repeated a number of times.

The man visibly shook as he looked around at the dead bodies. "It wasn't supposed to happen this way."

Xandor grabbed the man by the collar with both hands and asked, "Who are you?"

"I'm the village proprietor."

1:58pm

The thunder of the Percherons' four-beat gait cut through the peaceful countryside. Dragahn held the reins loosely, letting the draft horses have their way. When they tried to veer off the road, he gently nudged them back on course, but otherwise, he was content to let them run. Viktor and Branimir galloped alongside the wagon teams and helped steer when nudging didn't work.

Once the village was far behind them, Dragahn's gentle nudging turned into a tug-of-war as he hauled back on the reins, urging the Percherons to a walk so they could cool down. The horses sweated profusely, and bloody patches marred their fur where the harnesses had rubbed raw spots. When Dragahn felt the Percherons had relaxed enough after their panic, he called a halt.

As soon as the wagons stopped, Viktor looked back down the road to see if anyone followed. Beyond the tree line, they could still see a faint trace of smoke.

"Dammit to hell!" Viktor yelled as he took his sword and hacked the nearest tree to splinters. Dragahn caught up with him and ushered him out of earshot.

Dipping into his bag, Pyotr examined each of the horses and applied a topical ointment when he came across a sore or other abrasion. Then he checked the men.

Lucky and Branimir each had water barrels, letting the horses slake their thirst. Sachin walked around each of the wagons, checking for damage and making sure everything was tied down. Like a tall shadow, Grendel followed him step for step.

While everyone worked, Jasper prepared lunch. When it was ready, he offered plates to those who were hungry. It was a somber crowd who sat around and stared at their food.

Nobody said anything when Dragahn and Viktor returned. Both lost in thought, they declined their meals, and it soon became obvious lunch was over before it began.

Dragahn looked around at his team and said, "Let's go. We still have a job to do."

CHAPTER 10
STAMBOLIYSKI

October 13, 4235 K.E.

5:46pm

Dusk had fallen by the time Dragahn and his team arrived in Stamboliyski. Behind them, the snowy mountaintops glowed blood red. The teamsters passed gambrel-roofed shops lining both sides of the road. Split geodes and polished crystals of calcite, quartz, and citrine decorated the windows of those specializing in semiprecious minerals. In front of the shops, people on boardwalks stopped and stared, gawking at the arrow shafts still lodged in the wagon sides, and the Percherons trudging along with their heads down.

Up ahead, Dragahn spied their destination — a small warehouse tucked behind a two-story hostel and stables. He led the Percherons through a narrow alleyway that opened into a flagstone courtyard. With an audible sigh, he stopped his wagon and waited until the others pulled up alongside.

Viktor and Branimir dismounted and greeted the superintendent, who stood waiting outside the warehouse. Meanwhile, Dragahn handed his reins to Jasper. He climbed down and headed inside the hostel to claim their rooms.

Standing beside his wagon, Pyotr stretched his aching muscles. "I'm getting too old for this laĭna. Lucky, make yourself useful and go help the stable hands. I want these teams fed, rubbed down, and into their stalls before nightfall."

Lucky laughed as he hopped lightly to the ground. "You sound like my grandmother! Maybe you should go in and warm your old bones by the fire." The youth easily dodged a halfhearted kick and dashed away to the stables.

Grendel left Sachin with the wagons. Searching the area, he tried to get a good look at what passed for the hostel's security. Logistically, he could see a number of problems — too many windows, too many exits, a single-story porch, and no obvious watchmen. He shook his head, trying to figure out how he could protect his charge.

Finding Viktor, Grendel asked, "Does that happen often?"

Viktor looked up at the giant, worry lines creasing his forehead. "Does what happen often?"

"The ambush."

"No."

"What about when we get beyond the Stena?"

A haunted expression crept onto Viktor's face, quickly replaced by a harsh glare. "Don't worry about that, half-orc. Worry about your job."

"That is why I am asking."

Viktor answered, "Then ask Sachin. He's the one who knows the most about where we are going."

Grendel turned when Lucky reappeared with several teens. They unhitched the Percherons and guided them into the stables. Once the horses were out of the way, the teens pushed the wagons into the warehouse under Sachin's direction. By the time everything was stowed, stars dotted the night sky.

Dragahn exited the hostel, and Sachin and the teamsters gathered around him. Grendel remained off to the side, searching the street for signs of trouble.

"Everything's set. Here are your keys," Dragahn said as he passed them around. "The inn was overbooked, so I let them convince me to take only four rooms, but we all get a free meal at the tavern across the street." He pointed at Lucky and Branimir, the youngest members of their team. "Wake up is at six, so don't get carried away."

7:02pm

Standing at the door to the local krŭchma, Grendel and the teamsters let the noise and smells wash over them. The place was hopping with business, and they had to wait until the barmaid found two tables she could push together. A half-hour passed before she motioned to Dragahn, letting him know their table was ready.

When Grendel stepped inside, everyone in the tavern stopped talking and stared at the masked giant. His footsteps echoed on the hardwood floors and chairs scraped as he walked past.

As soon as everyone was seated, the team ordered a round of drinks and food. Dragahn and Pyotr sat next to one another and discussed the road ahead but kept coming back to the ambush and to a place called Tsarevets. It seemed the upcoming town held memories as bad as the village behind them.

The other patrons slowly resumed their conversations and went back to their meals.

"To Daniil and Bogdan," Viktor said, holding his tankard high and then taking a swallow. "To Daniil and Bogdan," everyone repeated as they drank.

Grendel stared at his full cup, remembering their last encounter.

"Do you think they made it?" Branimir asked. "There was so much smoke, I didn't get a good look."

"Neither did I," Lucky said.

Conversation died and turned into an awkward silence while the teamsters tried to piece together what had happened. A sense of foreboding crept across the table.

Grendel finished his drink in one long swallow. Staring around at the different faces, he began to wonder if any of them would survive this trip.

Jasper took out his pipe, lit it, and nodded discretely toward one of the younger, more attractive serving girls. "Yosif, here she comes."

The one he pointed out came flitting out of the kitchen, balancing multiple platters on one arm. She practically danced her way across the room as she evaded men and dodged furniture. The girl set the platters down in front of each of the waiting teamsters.

"Did you see that? She managed our whole order from memory!"

"It wasn't her memory I was admiring, Jasper," the teen replied with a wry smile.

Jasper laughed, "I kinda figured."

Viktor and Branimir joined the discussion, and before long, everyone at the table seemed to be returning to themselves. Everyone, that is, except Sachin, who seemed genuinely uncomfortable with something, but Grendel couldn't tell if it was the crowd or the bawdy turn of the conversation.

9:46pm

When everyone had left but Pyotr and Jasper, the horse doctor began to fidget as if he was wrestling with himself. He took a few more swallows of his drink and slurred, "I saw what you did for Dragahn."

Jasper stared intently at the horse doctor and puffed his pipe. White smoke billowed about his face, briefly obscuring it.

"You saved his life," Pyotr continued.

"I grabbed his belt. It was the only thing I could think of," Jasper replied.

"No, I mean that other thing you did. Deflecting those arrows."

"I'm not sure what you're talking about."

Pyotr glanced around nervously before leaning forward and lowering his voice. "You're a wizard, aren't you?"

Jasper visibly relaxed and gave him a friendly slap on the shoulder. "I'm a cook."

"Whatever. I know what I saw."

"I was there too, Pyotr. Arrows were flying, smoke was everywhere, and the horses were about to flip our wagon. If anything, it was Dragahn who pulled off some serious magic. We were dead if he hadn't gotten those horses moving in the right direction."

"You're right," Pyotr said, his words coming out slurred. "It's just that I could've sworn I saw..."

Jasper interrupted his thought by raising his cup. "Let's drink to tomorrow being a much better day, shall we?"

With a nod, Pyotr raised his cup and downed his drink. Pushing his chair back, he stood up and swayed precariously on his feet. Jasper tipped the barmaid generously and helped the doctor back across the street.

On the way out, he saw Xandor and Chert walking toward the tavern. They both nodded, and a sigh of relief escaped Jasper as he continued to the inn.

CHAPTER 11
MLADEN AND OGNIAN

October 13, 4235 K.E.

11:36pm

Advocate Lena Hristova lay in bed with her husband, Petreski. Except for the news the caravan had left the city, the day had been horrible. Someone poisoned her scrivener, and the militsiya had commandeered her office. On top of it all, her two sons, Bruno and Erich, had not returned home yet, but that was not completely unexpected, considering they had just received nice bonuses. They would probably be out all night. The revenue and profit stream from selling and distributing soap had exceeded her expectations, especially after Sachin had opened up the trade route to Michurinsk.

Her husband thought going beyond the Stena and selling soap east of the White River was crazy, but Sachin had convinced her to try it. They had ended up selling the soap at three times its normal price, which more than paid for Dragahn's team. Of course, she had not fully disclosed their total profit and had adjusted some of the numbers in their accounting ledger to help with taxes. The Kral would never suspect.

Now Sachin was gone, and they could lay low for the winter. She had moved their money around into some of her other ventures, so all she had to do now was to wait for the mud season to pass and the trade routes to reopen. With that thought, she snuggled next to her husband and fell asleep.

Sometime during the night, a rank, unpleasant odor woke her. Looking around through sleep-filled eyes, Lena saw two ghostly shapes near her bed. She wanted to scream, but a strange lethargy filled her, making it impossible to move or speak. The dark forms floated toward her. In the back of her mind, she recognized the fragrance in the air: hemlock and opium. Her husband was next to her, still asleep. She tried to reach for him, but her limbs wouldn't respond. The forms stood next to the bed, and her eyes drifted from one to the other.

With a drug-laden detachment, she observed the figures were not really ghosts; they were men. Tattooed whorls covered the skin on their bare chests, necks, and arms — tattoos that slid across their torsos, making it difficult for Lena to focus on them. She struggled against the lethargy, but with the struggle came the realization the drugs were too entrenched in her system.

One of the men pulled Lena roughly out of bed and threw her over his shoulder. He carried her outside, dumped her in the back of a wagon, and covered her with a rough canvas.

The horse-drawn wagon slowly exited the estate through the service entrance. It moved down the hill, but instead of going to the Majna i Vira, which was closed for the evening, the two men steered it toward a street that paralleled the escarpment for several blocks. They stopped in front of a three-story hostel built along the top. A sign hung from the front porch ceiling read, "Дългата капка." *The Long Drop.*

Mladen jumped down from the wagon and knocked loudly. A lamp by the door lit his pale skin and bushy red hair. The tattoo swirls along his arms and neck had stopped moving, and a leather tunic hid his chest.

"Who is it?" a voice asked from the other side of the door.

"D'yakon Krovos sent us," Mladen said in a thick accent.

He heard scrambling as the lock was pulled back, and the door opened to reveal a scrawny man wearing a dirty apron. Acne scars marred his cheeks and temples. The man looked up and down the street to see if anyone else was around. Beckoning, he said hurriedly, "Come inside."

At the edge of the porch light, Ognian, a mirror of the first man, jumped down and pulled back the canvas. The Northman hoisted Lena over one shoulder and carried her inside. The proprietor guided them through the main hall into the kitchen and opened what, at first, appeared to be a closet door.

"We use this shaft to get rid of trash... among other things. It goes all the way to Lower Pazard'zhik; at this time of night, there shouldn't be anyone at the bottom."

"There better not be," Mladen said.

"There won't," the proprietor assured them as he released a catch in the shaft and opened a hidden panel beside the door. Thick rope stretched from a winch through the ceiling. Flipping a pair of levers, he turned the winch crank to lower a dumbwaiter into view.

"Once you get to the bottom, ring the bell and I'll pull it back up."

The tight compartment had just enough space for a single person to enter if they weren't claustrophobic. Mladen climbed into the cab and squatted with his knees under his armpits. The proprietor looked at the other Northman and said, "We do this, and my debt is clear. Right?"

After a brief nod from Ognian, the man in the apron lowered the dumbwaiter. The winch gears clicked with each turn of the hand-crank. It took about fifteen minutes for the cab to reach the escarpment bottom, and the rope to go slack.

A few moments went by before they heard the tiny bell, and the proprietor hauled the empty cab back up. As soon as it was ready, Ognian shoved Lena into the cab, and it went down again. Again, the tiny bell rang.

Before Ognian entered the waiting cab, he handed the proprietor a small bag of gold leva.

The man eyed the bag greedily and removed one of the coins. He rubbed it between his fingers, then bit it. Grunting with satisfaction, he dropped it back in the bag. "What's this for?" he asked.

"Your silence," answered Ognian.

At the bottom, the two Northmen found themselves standing inside one of a series of interconnected buildings amidst piles of trash. The rats had all hidden, but they still heard skittering and scratching amongst the refuse.

"Everything taken care of?" Mladen asked.

Ognian nodded. "Bit a coin right in front of me. Probably got both hands in it now. He'll be dead before sunrise."

While Mladen carried Lena to the building's front, Ognian went outside and found the stable where the trashman's mule and wagon were kept. After making sure the streets were clear, he drove it to the main door and knocked three times.

The door slid open, and Mladen stepped out with Lena. They loaded her into the back of the wagon and covered her body with a greasy tarp. The two Northmen then backed the wagon into an alley and waited.

A nearby church bell tolled one time, and Mladen flicked the reins. They wound their way through Lower Pazard'zhik to Dragahn's warehouse. In a dark, narrow street hugging the back of the perimeter wall, he pulled up with barely a finger's width between the wagon wheel and the stone barrier, allowing Ognian easy access to the top.

Reaching into his pouch, Ognian fished out a few scraps of meat and threw them over the wall. Three hounds immediately raced out of the shadows to investigate. They swallowed the chunks whole and then snuffled around, hoping to find more. It took a couple of minutes before the poison took effect, but when it did, the dogs fell over without a sound.

Ognian jumped over the wall while Mladen drove the wagon around to the compound gate. Crossing the courtyard, he quickly found the latch and swung it open just wide enough for the wagon to enter.

Light flared outside the main hall, and a man holding a lantern asked, "Who's there?"

The warehouse courtyard was dark and silent, so the man took a step away from the doorway. Nothing seemed out of the ordinary until he heard the mule stomp the ground, and he spotted the wagon behind it. At the edge of his light, the body of one of the dogs lay as if asleep.

A person stepped over the dog's body. His torso, covered with tattoos, seemed to shift and swirl with the shadows. There was a glint of steel, and a knife flew through the air, striking the man at the door in the throat. Oil and blood mixed on the dusty ground when he fell and his lantern broke.

Without a sound, Ognian retrieved his weapon and the broken lantern. Going inside, the Northman searched the hall and found two other men sleeping in their bunks. He slit their throats where they lay and dragged their bodies into the courtyard.

Mladen had the warehouse door open and the wagon with Lena inside. He filled the bed with straw and soaked it with lamp oil.

Together, the two Northmen dragged the other bodies inside the warehouse and placed them near the wagon. Closing the door, they waited outside, listening.

Inside the warehouse, Lena tried to see where she was, but her mind played tricks on her. She kept having visions of tattooed men standing over her, silent and staring. If she could have screamed, she would have, but it was all she could do just to gasp one more breath.

An orange glow lit the interior of the warehouse, and Lena realized where she was. Moving only her eyes, she glanced to the left and to the right. The crackling sound of fire reached her ears first, followed by the smell of smoke.

With a roar, flames leapt up into the roof timbers and spread across the floor. Driven by an insatiable hunger, they reached the wagon and found the oil-soaked straw.

Blood pounding in her temples, Lena struggled harder, and her mind began to clear. She felt movement in her toes and fingers, but with it came the searing heat. Gasping, her lungs filled with smoke and scorched air, and she convulsed with a coughing fit.

Fire consumed the wagon, and she felt the lick of the flames against her bare skin. It burned away the drug-induced grip on her lungs, and Advocate Lena Hristova screamed.

CHAPTER 12
THE CHURCH OF TSAREVETS

October 14, 4235 K.E.

6:00am

As promised, Dragahn was up early, banging on doors in the corridor. "Get your laǐna and meet me at the krŭchma."

Food was on the table by the time Viktor entered the tavern with two young men in tow, who he introduced as Andrei and Teodor. "Chief, we need more horsemen after what happened yesterday and these men come highly recommended by the stablemaster," Viktor said. "They also come with their own horses."

Dragahn sipped his kahve and stared up at the pair. They were in their late teens and looked like they would follow orders. He turned back to Viktor and gave him an approving nod. Viktor grinned, slapped the men on their backs, and led them to empty seats.

The caravan chief waited for people to push away their plates. Once the last man finished his breakfast, Dragahn stood and tapped his spoon against the side of his tin cup. "I want everyone's attention."

Conversations around the table stopped, and the men turned to face Dragahn.

"We lost two good men yesterday," he said as he met each man's gaze. "I've been wracking my brain trying to figure if I could have done something different, if I could have seen it coming." He paused to reflect a moment before continuing, "Word reached me late last night that the men who attacked us were run off, and their leader was captured by the Kral's men. I don't know if Daniil or Bogdan made it. I want everyone here to know this trip is voluntary. We're only one day out of Pazard'zhik. From here, the danger only increases. If anyone wants to turn back, now's your chance."

Dragahn waited while the men considered his words. Viktor stood and said, "Chief, I'm in this 'til the end." One by one, each man stood, nodding his affirmation. Sachin and

Grendel were the last to rise. When they did, Viktor added, "Just make sure we get paid."

After everyone sat back down, Dragahn continued, "If all goes well in Tsarevets, we'll arrive in Veliko Tarnovo this afternoon. Then, we'll have three nights on the road." He looked over at Jasper. "I'm sure our cook will have something special prepared."

Jasper smiled mysteriously and said, "Nothing too special. Just a little of this and a little of that."

"We almost had to sell tickets for your last *nothing too special*," Lucky laughed. Everyone nodded, remembering how they had to bar the gates to keep people from coming in off the street.

"Well, if everyone's ready."

The land was dark as they passed the last building of Stamboliyski. The sun had not yet risen, but the eastern sky was beautifully painted with pastel hues. Following the road as it turned southeast, Dragahn gave the signal to speed up, and the Percherons responded instantly.

Viktor stayed close to the front, ever watchful for another ambush. He rode with one hand on the reins and the other on his short bow.

They traveled over rolling terrain flanked by more picturesque, snow-capped mountains. The sun rose higher and higher, and bright shades of blue replaced the pastel colors of the morning as the day warmed. Herds of animals dotted the fields bordering the road. Some darted away at the sound of the cantering horses, but most barely looked up from their grazing.

Everyone breathed a collective sigh of relief when the two massive towers of Tsarevets appeared in the distance, marking the edge of the second escarpment. At first, the towers were mere smudges on the horizon, but as the team approached, they came into focus. Above each tower, the flag of Trakya — a rampant sable lion on an azure field — fluttered in the wind.

The road twisted back and forth as it wound its way through the rocky terrain and over a wooden drawbridge spanning a dry moat. Flanking each side of the bridge stood two squat corner turrets that hosted evenly spaced arrow slits. At the top, siege weapons peeked out from behind thick embrasures. Men with harsh faces glared down at them, making it perfectly clear what would happen if something went wrong.

Not intimidated by the massive fortress, Jasper practically bounced with excitement. He had heard the Church of Tsarevets boasted vividly painted frescoes. He nudged the caravan chief as they waited for the heavy portcullis to rise and mentioned the church for the third time. Dragahn gave him a sidelong glance but otherwise seemed preoccupied.

Jasper squinted and tried to catch a glimpse of the church but was interrupted when a wiry man dressed in the blue and black striped robes of the Gatekeeper emerged from a concealed sallyport. Different than the others, his fur kalpak was tall with a sharp taper, resembling a mountain. Behind him came a procession of armored guards.

"Afternoon, Officer Kostadin," Dragahn called out as he and Viktor dismounted.

"What's your destination, and what are you carrying?" the customs officer demanded.

Pulling out his itinerary and manifest, Dragahn handed them to the officer. The officious man stared at the sheets and took his time reading, checking each page for the proper seals. After he finished, he said, "Bring them inside."

When the last of the wagons cleared the entrance, the portcullis dropped behind them and clanged ominously into the flagstone pavement. Dragahn halted the Percherons, and the teamsters dismounted and congregated near the chuck wagon.

As Grendel moved to join them, the gate guards followed his path with their crossbows. A pair of guards atop each of the towers and several others along the walls trained weapons on the half-orc as well.

The custom's officer approached Dragahn, followed by a dozen young men dressed in fur-lined leathers, carrying small crowbars and sporting tool belts. He made a few gestures, and the men split into three groups, one for each wagon.

"I want all these crates open!" he yelled.

"What!?" Dragahn said. "That'll take all day."

Officer Kostadin eyed Grendel before turning to the caravan chief. "I want to see everyone's papers. Now."

With a frown, Dragahn signaled his team, and they fell in line, their papers in hand.

"Sir, this is our third time through," Dragahn complained. "Can't you cut us some slack? We're carrying the same soap to the same destination."

The customs officer took each of their papers, read them, and handed them back. When he reached Grendel, he stopped and gave the half-orc a hard look. Handing back the paper, he said to Sachin, "This is a military post. Khumanoidi must have an escort. If he is found without one, he will be shot. Is that clear?"

Sachin nodded and said, "Yes, sir."

Stepping past Grendel, he finished checking their papers and recited loudly for all to hear, "You are allowed to select one representative to remain behind, observe, and confirm we do not damage your cargo. When we are done, I will send someone for you. It will take us a while to go through the rest of your wagons. During that time, we will feed and water your horses. You and your men may visit the Church and the public house located in the inner courtyard while you wait." He paused to let his words sink in. "You are not allowed to leave Tsarevets while we perform our inspection. You are not allowed access to your wagons during this time. If you try, my men have orders to kill you. Is that clear?"

"Yes, sir," Dragahn griped. "Pyotr, stay here and keep an eye on things." Not giving Pyotr a chance to argue, he pointed to the dour-faced horse doctor and said, "Sir, this man is my representative."

Officer Kostadin nodded and walked back to the wagons with a grumbling Pyotr trailing behind him.

As they passed him, Sachin tossed Pyotr the doeskin pouch of nails and ordered, "Make sure those crates are sealed tight when they're done."

Motioning for his men to huddle up, Dragahn said quietly, "Let's get through this without any trouble."

Jasper frowned and asked, "Is this a slow day for them?"

"No, Officer Kostadin takes his job very seriously." Under his breath, Dragahn added, "I should've known having a half-orc on our team would cause trouble here."

"Why didn't you go around?"

"Can't. It's the only way down the second escarpment."

1:14pm

Against the keep wall, a long clapboard building served as a makeshift cafeteria and public house. Jasper walked inside with the team and stopped, letting his eyes adjust to the dimness. The proprietor, a whitehaired man with skin like cracked leather, worked behind the counter, wiping a few tin cups.

Military regalia covered the walls, representing different campaigns in which the owner had been involved. Off-duty soldiers filled most of the seats. Dragahn led them across the room to a pair of empty tables. Conversations stopped mid-sentence as patrons turned to follow the masked half-orc's progress. More than a few hands crept toward weapons.

"Hey!" The owner's gruff shout drew all eyes to him. "We don't serve their kind here."

Everywhere, Jasper saw soldiers staring at the half-orc.

Grendel's eyes narrowed as he scanned the crowd. He took up a defensive posture in front of his charge and waited.

With a loud sigh, Dragahn gave Sachin a quick gesture. Sachin faced the soldiers. His jaw jutted forward, and Jasper wondered if the small man planned to have the half-orc stay. Instead, Sachin leaned toward Grendel and said, "Go stand by the door. I'll be there to escort you outside shortly."

Grendel glared at Sachin but then relented with a slight nod.

Jasper, who had just taken his seat, stood back up and announced, "I'll stay with Grendel, too."

Dragahn grabbed Jasper by the arm as he passed and said, "Let Sachin do it. These soldiers have spent the bulk of their careers protecting our borders from all kinds of enemies, including khumanoidi like Grendel." Glancing at the half-orc, the chief continued, "He might be good at his job, maybe even halfway civilized, but I understand why they don't welcome him."

Jasper looked at Dragahn and then at each of the team members. "Grendel is one of us, not some bloodthirsty invader. If he can't eat here, then neither will I."

Turning to leave, Jasper saw Lucky staring at him. From the boy's expression, it was obvious he wanted to follow Jasper, but couldn't quite bring himself to do it.

Nearby, the soldiers resumed their meals, but their conversations had turned to comments about the half-orc and others like him. Several patrons continued to cast suspicious glares in the team's direction.

With a final nod toward Lucky, Jasper strode across the dining area. Before he reached the door where Grendel waited, a grizzled soldier blocked his path. "You keep a short leash on that kopele khumanoid," the scarred veteran warned.

"Yes, sir," Jasper said. He led Grendel out and across the courtyard, toward the Church of Tsarevets. Outside its ornate arched entry, he stopped to admire the bas relief friezes and the lifelike statues of saints standing atop carved columns between the stained-glass windows. The scuff of boots on flagstones snapped Jasper out of his reverie. Behind him, the shadow of the church pinnacle and wheel-cross fell across several soldiers watching Grendel with undisguised hate.

Jasper and Grendel entered the main doors of the vaulted church and stopped. Lit by massive chandeliers of black iron, the central aisle separated two columns of dark, maple pews and led to a raised altar surrounded by brightly colored frescoes that carried onto the ceiling. Set in the corner, an ornate pulpit, trimmed in silver and gold, towered over the rows of seating.

Along either side, more frescoes adorned the plaster walls, each depicting a different parable. Between each scene, a stained-glass window glowed brightly in the sunlight.

"If you don't mind, I'd like to look around. Will you be alright here?" Jasper asked.

"Yes," Grendel replied.

Grendel sat in the back and watched Jasper move from fresco to fresco like a kid in a candy store. For the first time, he regretted accepting Marcus' offer. Why had Chert talked him into this assignment?

"He's a strange one, isn't he?"

Grendel nearly jumped out of the pew. Sachin sat next to him, holding two small plates of food. "I forget just how evil men can be."

"Not evil, just unaccustomed to things that are different," the half-orc replied.

"Son of Cayn, make no mistake, they are evil. If you had been by yourself, you and I both know there would have been a fight. Even if it took the whole garrison, those soldiers would have killed you."

Taking his time to think and absorb Sachin's words, Grendel watched Jasper cross in front of the altar and examine the frescoes on the other side. Finally, he replied, "At least I would have died fighting."

A young acolyte entered the church. He dipped his fingers into a small bowl of holy water and touched his forehead before entering the nave. He walked up to the altar and knelt, bowing his head in a short prayer. Whispering, "Soþlice," the young acolyte stood and prepared to greet the church's visitors. His eyes grew wide at the sight of the huge half-orc and small man seated together at the rear of the sanctuary. With a slight shiver, he turned to find a pudgy man making an intent study of the murals. "Sir," he said, "you might be interested in this."

Jasper swung around and saw the young cleric pointing to a circular stained-glass window with a saw-toothed edge overlooking the north transept. The glass was a deep mauve and represented a meditation wheel. In the center was a translucent crystal flower in the shape of the dog rose.

"We just installed it a month ago."

"It's very beautiful; where did it come from?" Jasper asked, his voice hushed with awe.

"It's from the old monastery near Chernigov, along the White River."

"Did they get tired of it?"

The acolyte laughed. "No, the orcs took over that area when they took the city. A noble Rhodinan family recently donated this one to us. I don't recall their name, but they've rescued several pieces of art from that old monastery. This one had so much smoke damage it had to be sent to Pazard'zhik to be restored."

"Did they have to cut the wall for the window to fit?"

"Yes, and the commandant was not happy about it. He does not like change."

"I can imagine. Thank you for sharing this with me."

"You're welcome."

Leaving the acolyte to his chores, Jasper stared up at the meditation wheel a while longer, marveling at its beauty.

"The wagons will be ready in five minutes. Wrap up any sightseeing you want to do," Dragahn announced as he entered the sanctuary. "If we hurry, we'll reach Veliko Tarnovo before nightfall."

Jasper walked to the door and found Lucky waiting for him. "Why did you do that?"

"Do what?" Jasper asked.

"Stand up for Grendel like that. He's just a half-orc."

Jasper looked Lucky directly in the eyes and said, "A man is defined by more than his parents, the money he makes, or the women he beds. There will be times when you — your integrity — will be tested, and that's when you will discover what type of man you really are."

Lucky looked down at his feet.

"Grendel is one of us, and he deserves to be treated that way, even if he looks different. I would have done the same if it had been you or the chief." Jasper relaxed and smiled as he ruffled the young man's hair. "Don't worry. You'll have plenty of opportunities to prove your mettle."

CHAPTER 13
THE SON OF CAYN

October 16, 4235 K.E.

6:25am

"Everyone up!" Dragahn yelled.

Throughout the previous day, the northern road out of Veliko Tarnovo had climbed up into the mountains, paralleling the second escarpment and the Yantra river that ran along its base. Still tired after their flight from Tsarevets, by late afternoon the Percherons plodded along with their heads low. The teamsters stopped early in the first secluded dale that shielded them from the biting wind. Worn out, they had fallen into their bedrolls immediately after supper.

"Come on! We have to make up for the time we lost yesterday," Dragahn called. His breath boiled out in a vaporous cloud.

Grumbling, the teamsters crawled from their one-man tents and struck camp. Though not cold enough for frost, everyone knew it wouldn't be long before the first snow fell. It added a tension to the teamster's conversations since everyone knew that if they didn't complete this trip before the mountain passes closed, they'd be trapped.

The upper rim of the sun peeked over the trees just as they re-hitched the horses and resumed their journey. Mist fell and a thin film of red mud replaced the layer of dust on the road. As the day progressed, the clouds broke but refused to go away. They clung to the horizon, biding their time.

Stiff and sore, Jasper tried to stretch while he sat. To the south and east, the landscape opened with fewer mountains to block the horizon. Over his left shoulder, he lost sight of the second escarpment and the frothy waters of the Yantra River. Colonies of tall aspens lined the road, their thick surface roots spread like tentacles.

"Can I have a try?" Jasper asked.

"Sure," Dragahn replied, handing him the reins.

After they had gone a short distance, Jasper realized the Percherons were capable of leading themselves, so all he had to do was sit and hold on.

"I've been doing some thinking about that ambush," Jasper said as they rode down the backside of a hill.

"Oh?"

"They weren't trying to stop the wagons."

"Looked like it to me."

"Maybe, but don't you think getting past the wheelbarrow was a little too easy?"

"Easy? Could you have done it?"

"No," Jasper admitted. Sneaking a quick glance at the caravan chief, he asked, "Didn't you notice? Those archers were aiming at *you*."

Without answering, Dragahn took back the reins.

6:53pm

By nightfall, the clouds had regrouped, blocking out the starlight. Xandor lay motionless at the base of a small stand of pines, a burbling mountain brook separating him from the teamsters' camp. His perch afforded a good view of the men as they unhitched the horses and pitched their tents.

Jasper stood over a cast-iron pot suspended above the campfire. Beside him, a thin, leather cookbook pulled from his sporran rested on a makeshift stand. Even at Xandor's distance, he could tell the book was well used and had loose pages fitted inside. Jasper flipped it open and traced a passage with his finger.

Using a deep, long-handled spoon, he stirred something inside the pot and occasionally added a pinch of brownish-orange powder from a wooden box with a hinged latch. Each time he did, he dipped the spoon into the concoction and sipped from it. Phrases like "Whew," "Damn, that's hot," or "I'm waiting for the spoon to melt," drifted across the night air. The last phrase was in response to one of the new horsemen, who approached the cook and asked when supper would be ready.

The wind shifted, and Xandor smelled the chili cooking. He frowned, hoping his stomach wouldn't give him away.

When supper was ready, the men formed a line with bowls in hand. Jasper and Lucky helped serve each member, and then they took what remained. It must have been a four-alarm recipe because several of the men pulled out handkerchiefs to mop their sweaty foreheads and runny noses. The ranger grinned and mentally shook his head. He'd tasted some of Jasper's chili before and knew just how spicy the mage liked it.

After supper, conversations turned to non-work-related subjects. Everyone seemed to enjoy the time away from the city; even the chief had settled in by the campfire to relax. Jasper picked up a pot with the dishes stacked inside and carried them to the stream.

He was scrubbing out the last one when something fell with a splash. Looking around, he didn't see anyone and resumed his washing. This time, the pebble fell a little closer. Jasper froze and muttered a few words. He scanned the woods and nearly fell on his bottom when he saw Xandor not five feet away. The cook quickly recovered and continued washing the pot.

The look on Jasper's face was priceless. Xandor savored the moment even though he knew payback would be hell.

The ranger slithered closer and whispered, "How are you holding up?"

"Good, but busy," Jasper whispered back.

"I've brought some news I picked up at Tsarevets. The warehouse burned down the night after we left Pazard'zhik. There are no suspects, but Marcus believes it was arson. Probably the same guy Chert saw outside the advocate's office."

"Any bodies?"

"Three. They were burnt beyond recognition, but the priests were able to divine Advocate Hristova was one of them."

"Sounds like someone's cleaning up."

"I think so, too. Have you had a chance to check out the crates?"

"No, not yet. I'm still biding my time."

"You're enjoying being the cook too much."

"What? Me? No."

"Don't forget we have to find the connection to the Krakov Estate."

"I won't," Jasper replied.

Footsteps crunched through the leaves, and Xandor retreated into the night.

"Jasper, Pyotr's got his cards out. You feel up to a game?" Lucky asked.

Pot in hand, Jasper replied, "Last time we played, I think he cheated."

"He didn't cheat; you were just lousy."

8:48pm

Half in the firelight and half masked by the darkness, Grendel watched Jasper join the evening's entertainment. His mind turned to Tsarevets, but he could only recall what Sachin had said. He shook his head, trying to clear the cobwebs.

As if summoned by Grendel's thoughts, Sachin walked up beside the bodyguard. "Son of Cayn, what are you doing here?" he asked quietly.

"Why do you call me that?"

"It's what you are. You are a son of the sleeping god. The god who created all the humanoid tribes with a single drop of his blood. Though I think you try to deny that side of you."

Grendel did not respond immediately, and Sachin waited silently, giving him some time. "You didn't answer me. Why are you here?"

"What do you mean?"

"I mean you don't belong here. You saw what those soldiers thought of you. They treat you as an enemy here. If you lived amongst the tribes, I have no doubt you would be their chief — their king."

"I am here because you asked for a bodyguard."

"I don't believe that for a second, orcné. You're running from something." After a pause, Sachin continued, "And you're hiding."

Grendel started and turned to face the small man.

Although Sachin's tone was gentle, his words dug into the bodyguard. "You wear that mask, thinking no one will know what you are. How's that worked out for you?"

Grendel continued to stare, but his posture was tense.

"I told you when we first met, I had some experience with your kind. I know more about you and your lineage than you do."

Grendel frowned behind his leather mask. "I am what I am, nothing more."

"That's not true. You are more than you pretend, and you are holding yourself back."

Grendel looked toward the campfire; when he turned back, Sachin was gone. He felt a sense of anxiousness after their short talk, and it weighed on him. Instead of trying to sort out his thoughts, he focused on work. Taking advantage of his night vision, he followed a trail he had marked earlier and did a quick circuit of the campsite.

It was just after midnight when Grendel returned to his post outside Sachin's tent and heard a voice within. Thinking the man was talking in his sleep, Grendel edged closer.

Suddenly, Sachin said, "Yes, D'yakon, everything is going as planned. No, it was only a slight delay. You didn't need to send Marko. I have everything under control. Yes, D'yakon... I know... But... Just make sure Gregori is ready when we get there."

The conversation ended and the tent flap snapped open. Sachin quivered with rage as he stalked out into the cold without a jacket. After a few steps, he ducked back inside his tent.

An hour later, Grendel heard Sachin come up behind him. This time, he held two tin cups filled with what smelled like steaming hot kahve. The small man had apparently recovered from his earlier ire.

Sachin held out the larger of the two, motioning for Grendel to take it. Accepting the cup, Grendel stared down into the dark mixture.

"It's just kahve," Sachin said, taking a quick sip.

Grendel brought the cup to his mouth. The brew was bitter at first but had a surprisingly fiery aftertaste that warmed his stomach.

The two drank in silence and stared at the teamster's campfire in the distance. Grendel drained his cup and felt his muscles relax. The knot of tension in his gut melted away. A hand touched his shoulder, and he turned his head. He tried to focus on who it was, but everything was blurry.

A voice whispered into his ear, "Tell me about your mother."

Grendel's vision cleared, the impairment gone as quickly as it came. He looked around in alarm. The campsite was no longer around him. The smell of unwashed bodies replaced the fresh mountain air and with it came cries of despair.

He knew exactly where he was.

Standing at the side of a dirty bed, a young Grendel looked down at the broken form of his mother. Crying out in horror, he dropped to his knees and pulled her to him. Deep scratches rent her Nubian skin; her legs and arms lay bent at unnatural angles, the joints dislocated. He stared into her almond-shaped eyes, trying to ignore the bruises.

The light was dim, but there was enough for him to see them sparkle when she recognized him. She smiled up at him and raised one hand to touch his cheek.

Something warm and sticky seeped through her ragged clothing where he held her. He didn't know what to do. Tears streamed down his face as he felt her last breath escape her bloodied lips. He crushed her to him, unable to let go.

"Boy, get away from her!" a deep voice yelled from behind him, jerking him out of his sadness.

Laying his dead mother on the bed, Grendel shook with grief as he turned to face his father. He looked into the cold eyes of the murderous creature, and a burning spire of rage coursed through him. With a roar, he charged.

His father deftly stepped sideways and, just as Grendel passed through the doorway, the seasoned fighter slammed the cell's barred door into his son's face. It struck with enough force to break his nose and throw him back onto his mother's bed.

Laughter echoed in the hallway, and Grendel followed the noise to a hulking man with a bull's head standing beside his father. It was Novius, son of Ovius, his owner. "Son of Grendel, save your energy for the arena," he said, still laughing. "You will get your chance soon enough."

Again, Grendel's vision blurred and subsequently cleared. He found himself standing beside Sachin. Everything was as it had been; he still held the empty cup in his hand.

"Are you alright?" Sachin whispered. The concern in his voice matched the look in his eye.

Grendel did not know what to say. The memory had been so vivid, so real. He could still feel his mother's blood on his hands.

He rounded on Sachin and growled, "What was in that drink you gave me?"

"Nothing," Sachin said. "Just some plain black kahve I picked up in Pazard'zhik and a little viski."

Grendel snatched Sachin's cup out of his hand and sniffed it.

"I promise, there was nothing else in it," Sachin said. "Orcné, what is troubling you? You look like you've seen a ghost."

Grendel remained silent for a moment and then handed the cup back to Sachin. "Five years after my mother died, Ovius, my master, allowed me to face my father in the arena. My master made me wear this leather mask; by the time my father figured out it was me, it was too late. When it was over, I took off my mask and held up my sword, still wet with his blood. I placed my foot on his chest and looked down into his dying eyes so there would be no mistaking who had defeated him. I still remember the silence after my father fell. The people at the arena all began to chant *Grendel*. They are the ones who gave me my father's name. Even though I took it, I vowed to never be like him."

"What was your name before Grendel?"

"My mother called me Vanin. She never told me its meaning but said it was from the language of the elves." Looking into the distance, Grendel said, "Right after the fight, my master smuggled me out of the city and gave me my freedom. I have been running ever since."

Sachin stood quietly for a moment, seeming to reflect on Grendel's words. He walked around to face his bodyguard. "Ovius was a minotaur, wasn't he?"

Grendel nodded and answered, "Yes and no. My mother told me the J'Belans had once been human. They were part of a Korellan outpost established in a land far away from the shores of their home continent; it grew into its own country and became J'Bel. During the Great War, J'Bel broke a pact they had made with the Dark One, and he cursed them. Now, every male J'Belan goes through the transformation when he comes of age. I have seen some of them while they go through the bull-rite, even fought a few like Novius. It takes several months, and it is a very painful process."

"Why did Ovius give you a mask?" Sachin asked.

"He did not want my father to know it was me," Grendel replied.

"Are you sure it was only your father he didn't want to recognize you?"

"What do you mean?"

"Well, don't you think it odd Ovius set you free? Why would he do that? Surely, your absence would have been noticed."

Grendel stood motionless, staring down at the small man who struggled with something he wanted to say. Sachin whispered, "Did it ever occur to you he had a reason he didn't want you to stay?"

"What reason?"

"Your mother's death."

"My father raped and murdered my mother," Grendel said a little too quickly.

"Did you see it happen?"

"No," Grendel replied, his eyes wide in shock. "I found her afterwards."

"Then how do you know? Look, if Ovius wanted you and your father out of the way, letting two of his more popular gladiators fight and then releasing the winner..." Sachin left the thought unfinished.

"Why?"

"What if Novius, his son, was the one who attacked your mother? What would have happened if you had found out? Or your father?"

Grendel backed away from the light of the campfire. His eyes shone eerily as he struggled with his emotions.

"Did your mother belong to Ovius?"

Grendel answered, "Yes, she told me her people had been captured — the plunder from one of his many raids."

"And Ovius gave her to your father as a prize?"

"I guess; she never said."

Sachin remained quiet to let Grendel take some time with his thoughts. When the bodyguard reemerged from the shadow, he had taken off his mask. He held it crumpled in his fist. "I do not know what to do," he said quietly. "I kept this mask to honor the man who freed me..."

Sachin stepped forward. "Son of Cayn, you have been hiding behind that mask far too long."

"Stop calling me that," Grendel said.

"You can't hide who you are; what your father was."

Grendel made to deny he was anything like his father, but Sachin stopped him with a raised hand. "Do not lie to yourself," he said. "You are what your father was before they caged him like an animal. Before he became one of Ovius' dogs."

Grendel stared at the mask in his hand. Its empty eyeholes stared back at him as if alive, whispering to him. Was what Sachin said true? Was he hiding from himself? And if he did search for the answers, would he like what he found?

As if in a trance, Grendel walked to the teamster's campfire. Behind him, Sachin followed.

Viktor stood up when the two approached. "Can I get you some —" He started to say but closed his mouth when he saw the look on Grendel's face.

Grendel stopped at the fire, his mask still in his hand, and stared into the light. He dropped the mask into the flames. The crumpled leather curled, blackened, and eventually burned.

CHAPTER 14
DEFEATING THE MOUNTAIN

October 17, 4235 K.E.

6:25am

While the others loaded the wagons, Dragahn kept an eye to the sky. A low-riding bank of dark clouds scudded across the horizon and obscured the tops of the surrounding mountains.

After checking on everyone, Dragahn found the bodyguard collecting Sachin's gear. "Grendel, anything I should know?" he asked, searching the half-orc's maskless face.

"No," Grendel replied succinctly.

Dragahn opened his mouth, and then closed it. Finally, he said, "It's your fault we were delayed in Tsarevets. I just wanted you to hear it from me."

Grendel straightened, his bestial face unreadable. Dragahn wanted to say more. He wanted to tell the half-orc that many Trakyans, especially the soldiers, felt humanoids were nothing more than savage brutes but thought better of it. The half-orc had to know this already. Didn't he?

An hour later, the team rolled out. All the while, Dragahn wore a perpetual frown.

Even with the mountains closing around them, the road ahead remained relatively smooth, and the Percherons made good time. The way dipped down into a mist-filled valley and then climbed higher — the sides of the road bound by jagged cliffs. Long furrows scarred their surface, marking where the Kral's men had carved the pass out of the mountain.

Another dip and the road led into a short, damp tunnel, the arched entrance fashioned with moss-covered stone blocks. Beyond the exit, a wall of rain waited for them. The horses nickered and tugged against their restraints. Dragahn snapped the reins, urging them forward.

Fat drops pelted the horses, moved to the wooden seat and the riders, and then the canvas covered cargo behind them. The water hit the ground so hard it bounced. Noise from the rain assailed their ears but only partially masked Pyotr's stream of curses. The road quickly acquired the texture of an old washboard, and with every bump and jostle, Pyotr's cursing increased.

Jasper was amazed to find the Percherons seemed to have a natural ability to find the best footing, trotting through the mud and heavy rainfall with ease. They hardly ever slipped, and Dragahn was content to let them set their own pace.

Midday, the team pulled into a clearing surrounded by dark trees. Jasper checked with the teamsters, but no one seemed interested in a cold, wet meal. He handed out beef jerky anyway, along with other dry rations from the cache he had prepared earlier for just such a contingency.

"Take the shortcut," Jasper overheard Sachin tell Dragahn.

"We'll see when we get there. It may be impassable."

"Fine, but if there is any chance — any chance at all — we need to take it."

"I'm the one in charge here. I'll make the call."

Sachin didn't respond, he just stared at the chief's back as Dragahn returned to the chuck wagon.

When the horses were ready, Dragahn signaled for everyone to move out. Pulling his cloak tight, Jasper climbed into his seat and hunkered against the wind that blasted down the pass. As they rode, one gust hit the chuck wagon so hard, Jasper felt it drift then suddenly right itself as the horses won their tug-o-war. Along either side of the road, mountain trees shook as more gusts struck them. Their road meandered up toward the mountaintops looming ahead of them and disappeared into the clouds.

They arrived at the fork in the road, and Dragahn called for a halt. With a quick motion, he sent Viktor and his horsemen down the two roads. When they returned, he handed the reins to Jasper and jumped down. Sachin and Pyotr followed suit and rushed to join the chief as he received Viktor's report about what lay ahead.

Jasper sat fidgeting with the reins. The fork to the right stayed relatively flat while the other seemed less traveled and rose steeply. What started as a discussion turned into an argument, with Dragahn pointing farther up the secondary road.   Jasper thought he heard the words "steep," "switchback," and "too dangerous" repeated a few times. The trio argued for a while longer, and then Pyotr, who apparently was losing the argument, gesticulated wildly.   Jasper strained to hear them over the wind and rain.   Suddenly Sachin pointed a finger at Pyotr and then pointed back to the wagons.

It was a seriously pissed off horse doctor who passed. Jasper listened to his muttering and learned a few new Trakyan phrases as Pyotr continued his tirade all the way back to his wagon.

When Dragahn resumed his seat, Jasper looked for some sign of what he was thinking, but the caravan chief wore his poker face and signaled for the team to follow the secondary road.

It wasn't long before Jasper saw for himself the beginning of the series of switchbacks that had been the genesis of the argument. Wind-driven rain and swirling mist obscured the majority of the road, leaving Jasper unsure if this was a blessing or a curse.

The narrow road wound back and forth in tight, hairpin turns, each steeper than the previous. Naked to the elements, only the equally spaced boulders placed along the side of the road offered any modicum of protection. The ride might have been fun on a sunny day, but in the rain, it was just plain stupid.

The Percherons found their footing easily on the slick road. Occasionally, one of the horses' legs would sink to the fetlock when it stepped into a mud-filled hole, and each time, Dragahn held his breath.

The team made it through several hairpin turns without mishap and climbed up the next leg. The mist cleared just enough for Jasper to peer up the slope and see how much higher the switchbacks went. A feeling of dread settled over him as he watched brown rainwater cascade over the edge of the road.

The next rise was even steeper. Although the horses found their footing, the wagons seemed to float whenever the metal-rimmed wheels lost traction. At the top of the fifth hairpin, the horses hesitated, and Dragahn flicked the reins, prompting them to keep moving. The rain slacked off, but water continued pouring down the side of the mountain.

As they reached the sixth and final switchback, the shoulder of the road above them gave way. Water and mud gushed out. It picked up speed as it flowed down the stretch of ground, collecting rocks, dirt, and other debris along the way.

Someone yelled out, and both Dragahn and Jasper looked behind them. Mud flowed around Sachin's wagon, picked it up, and caused it to jackknife. The horses' eyes rolled wildly as they fought the peculiar tugging. Already at an odd angle, the mud relentlessly swept the wagon toward the shoulder and the edge of the road.

The chief hauled back on the reins and handed them to Jasper. He leapt down, ran to the lead Percheron of Sachin's wagon, and pulled on the bridle, urging the horse forward. Sachin yelled at the horses and flicked his whip, but the horses seemed confused by the mixed signals.

"Stop!" Dragahn cried out. "You're making it worse!"

A sharp crack resounded when a rear wagon wheel struck one of the boulders serving as a makeshift guardrail. Spokes buckled and split, causing the rim to warp. With a shudder, the bed shifted and tilted alarmingly.

Grendel jumped down, ran through the mud, and caught the axle. Heaving, he leveled the cart and pushed against the mudflow, trying to realign the wagon. Veins bulged as he strained against the heavy current. With the sudden decrease in the dead weight of the wagon, the lead Percheron took a tentative step forward, followed by another. Dragahn continued pulling the halter, and together they plowed their way through the mud.

Once they reached firmer ground, Grendel held up the wagon a little higher while Viktor grabbed a jack and placed it underneath the axle. He lowered it, slowly letting the weight shift from him to the sawtooth-shaped timber. The strain gone, Grendel arched his back, stretching the sore muscles.

Dragahn spoke softly to the horses while Teodor and Andrei helped Viktor replace the broken wheel. After they finished, he resumed his position on the chuck wagon and surveyed the damage in front of him. The upper leg of the hairpin had lost a sizable portion of the road. Fortunately, the boulders along the edge had simply sunk into the mud; otherwise, they would have rolled down the hill. Unfortunately, deep crevasses had formed around the boulders where the water had eroded channels in the road.

Dragahn waited for the mudslide to subside. When it did, he signaled, and the three wagons hugged the mountain face. Everyone held their breath when their wheels bounced and jostled over the rough ridges and deep trenches. They worked their way past the washout and climbed farther up.

At the top, mists surrounded them as if they were on an island floating in the clouds. Mountain peaks rose to the north and south, a chain of islands in an aethereal archipelago.

Dragahn raised his hand, signaling a stop.

"Good job, Grendel," Dragahn said after everyone had dismounted.

"You saved this one," Viktor said, giving Grendel a congratulatory slap on the back.

Grendel didn't have time to reply as everyone surrounded him, remarking on how strong he was or how lucky they were he was there. Even Pyotr, the smell of alcohol fresh on his breath, thanked him as he checked the half-orc for injuries. Not finding any, the doctor moved on to check the horses.

Uncomfortable with this newfound attention, Grendel stepped to the side and rested. The teamsters congratulated each other, their relief apparent in every gesture, and for the first time in a while, he felt part of something.

3:13am

Surrounded by the collection of one-man tents, Jasper warmed his hands over the campfire. He listened to the snores coming from the teamsters and smiled. Dragahn had finally assigned him a two-hour watch. After making sure the fire had plenty of fuel, Jasper began his patrol.

Hidden in the shadows, Xandor leaned casually against one of the wagons, waiting on Jasper to walk past.

"Rough day?" he whispered.

"Yes," Jasper replied, and he motioned toward Grendel. "Did you see what happened last night?"

Staring past Jasper, Xandor said, "Not really sure. I saw Sachin come out of his tent and talk with Grendel. I couldn't get close enough to hear well, but I thought I heard something about his mother."

Jasper looked back over his shoulder and said, "Let's take a quick look at these crates before someone misses me."

The two found a spot where one of the wagons rested partially outside the perimeter of the firelight. Touching Xandor on the arm, Jasper muttered, "Skoteiní órasi." Both the mage and ranger's eyes began to shine dimly.

"Wow," Xandor said quietly as he scanned the camp with his newly developed night vision. Night had turned into day.

"Be careful. Don't look directly at the fire," Jasper warned a little slower than he should have.

Too late, Xandor jerked his head to the side as the sharp light stabbed his retinas. He stifled a groan and brought his hands up to shield his face. Once his eyes readjusted, he cut a narrow-eyed glare at Jasper. The mage had assumed a pose of pure innocence as he pulled back a corner of the canvas.

Xandor joined him a few moments later and studied the crates.

Similar to what they had found at the warehouse, the crates were nailed shut. But this time, the sigils were unblemished.

"These symbols represent water," Jasper said quietly. "I think they're meant to keep these crates dry. Look, see how the water has beaded up. However, whatever's been done to these nails is so subtle, it doesn't even radiate magic — at least, not arcane magic."

"Are there other types of magic?" Xandor asked in a whisper. Jasper made as if he was going to give a lecture on the topic, but Xandor raised his hands in surrender.

Briefly, the mage appeared disappointed, then continued with his original thought. "I wouldn't have noticed it if I weren't looking for it. Probably why they haven't raised any alarms."

He stepped up to get a closer view as Xandor held the canvas. "I can't tell if there's anything else they do, but I'm certain as long as these symbols are intact, and the nails in place, whatever is inside this box stays dry."

"There are easier and much cheaper ways to waterproof a crate. Why go to all this trouble?" Xandor asked.

"Don't know."

Xandor edged around to look at the ends of the crates. A double-lined circlet entwined by a single rose was branded into the ends, but up close, he noticed each symbol was slightly different. It wasn't simply a case of the rose being in a different position, although, when he looked at the group as a whole, each rose was about forty-five degrees farther around. The vine's leaves and thorns were odd shaped as well, and their pattern changed from crate to crate. It may have made sense if the crates were hand-painted, but each had been marked with a customized brand. He waved Jasper over and pointed it out to him.

"I think it's a message," Jasper murmured. "See how some of the shapes repeat, and these marks here and here repeat over specific ones?" He pointed to several spots where it looked like loose sparks singed the wood. "They remind me of accent marks."

"Have you ever seen writing like this?"

"No. I wish I could send a copy to Guildmaster Velkov in Pazard'zhik or Master Meuricel at the guild library in Tydway," the mage replied.

Xandor pulled out his journal. "Keep an eye out. I'll make sketches and try to find someone who can decipher them." After Xandor finished, the two reattached the wagon canvases exactly as they had found them and headed a distance into the woods.

"What's the plan?" Jasper whispered.

Xandor studied the teamster camp, weighing his options. He could contact Marcus and stop the caravan, or he could let things continue and see where it led. Deep down, he knew his answer.

"Jasper, we need more. Get closer to Dragahn; find out what he knows."

CHAPTER 15
DOBROVNITSA

October 18, 4235 K.E.

6:18am

"Wake up, Cook!"

Jasper looked around blearily and noticed the light of dawn visible through the tent flap. Outside, he heard other voices and hurried to prepare breakfast.

"We should arrive in Dobrovnitsa this afternoon," Dragahn announced while the crew readied the wagons for the day's travels. Everyone cheered. Even the horses seemed eager to get off the mountain as they stamped the ground and jostled in their rigging.

The chief pushed the Percherons to a fast-paced walk. Just after midday, the team climbed the last hill and gave a shout when they caught sight of smoke rising from the scattering of chimneys. Farmland and cottages dotted the valley, each surrounded by low stone walls.

Driving down toward the small town, the wagons splashed through the mud, leaving behind deep ruts, and the horses' hooves made little sucking sounds.

Jasper's stomach lurched when he felt the wagon start to slide. "We're going to crash!" he exclaimed, gripping his seat.

"Calm down. You'll panic the horses," Dragahn replied as he tugged the reins this way and that. The wagon righted itself, and Jasper heard him say, "Never let the horses know you're scared."

Embarrassed, Jasper gave Dragahn a quick nod and turned toward the townsfolk working the fields.

The muddy road led through the middle of Dobrovnitsa, where stables and a krŭchma waited on one side and a two-story inn on the other. Beyond were clapboard buildings, including a blacksmith shop, a farrier, a general store, and a little farther, a church with its tall steeple adorned by a wheel-cross.

4:39pm

The wagons and horses put away, Grendel and Sachin aimed for the warm glow of the inn across the street. Standing to one side, the half-orc pulled open the wood-paneled door for Sachin. Inside, he stopped and let the warmth seep into his bones.

Decorated with animal heads mounted on the wall and animal-skin blankets draped over the furniture, the lobby looked more like a hunting lodge than a wayside hostel. A massive Volhynian cave bear, its face frozen mid-snarl, loomed menacingly in the corner. Against the far wall, a soot-stained stone fireplace crackled with a gentle flame.

Two strangers were talking with the innkeeper. The smaller of the two appeared to be in his early twenties and wore an ermine and gules tunic over a tailored suit of armor fashioned from metal plates that protected his entire body. He had long, jet-black hair and held a visored helmet under one arm as he and the innkeeper discussed room and board for himself and his servant. Against the wooden counter next to him, a round shield lay wrapped in a plain leather cover. An ornate hand-and-a-half sword hung at his waist.

Based on the quantity of pieces and the lavishness of the workmanship, Grendel surmised the armor was probably some type of parade armor rather than munition armor, but when the knight moved, he re-evaluated. It looked heavy, but the weight was evenly distributed. The plates fit together almost perfectly and did not restrict the knight's movement.

Taller than most men, Grendel stood seven-foot, two inches and weighed more than three hundred pounds. The knight's servant was only a couple of inches shorter but looked like he outweighed Grendel by a hundred pounds — all of it muscle. But that wasn't what really pulled the bodyguard's attention away from the knight. The servant was an albino and, from what Grendel could see of his scarred skin, appeared to be completely hairless. He wore a pair of loose-fitting, grey breeches with a tunic, but no boots to hide his clawed feet. Grendel looked up and stared into a human-ish face. Two blood red, reptilian eyes stared back. Strapped on his back was the longest two-handed sword the half-orc had ever seen.

Sachin passed them without a second glance, leaving Grendel to hurry after him.

5:24pm

Over at the krŭchma, the teamsters sat together at a common table and ate their suppers while Andrei went to the bar and ordered more drinks. Everyone was in high spirits, especially after the precipitous climb up the mountain.

Next through the door came Dragahn and the horse doctor. Pyotr was still giving the chief hell about the mudslide and kept telling him how stupid it was for them to have traveled that particular road. They wove their way through the tables and sat with the group.

The barmaid was heading toward them when the knight and his albino companion came through the door. The silence was palpable as all eyes turned to the newcomers. The two approached the bar and pushed into gaps on either side of Andrei. The barkeep set the drink order down while the knight unstrapped his shield from across his back and leaned it against the bar. Next, he took off his helm and placed it on the counter. The albino simply crossed his arms.

"Can I help you, Sir Knight?" the barkeep asked.

"A pint of your best beer," the knight replied.

The barkeep found a clean mug and twisted the tap handle affixed to a wooden keg turned on its side. Meanwhile, the knight placed an arm around Andrei's shoulders.

"Evening," he said. The tone was friendly enough, but the look in the man's eyes was cold and hard, sending an involuntary shiver through the caravan guard.

Surprised, Andrei stared back wide-eyed, and stammered, "Sir?"

"Are you with the caravan that arrived today? I was hoping to find employment for myself and my friend."

Andrei didn't know what to say. He looked back over his shoulder.

Dragahn rose, followed by Viktor and Teodor. "I don't think the boy can help you."

Grinning wolfishly at the caravan chief, the knight released Andrei and said in a smooth voice, "Forgive me, where are my manners? My name is Marko, and this is my manservant, Kourash. We have just arrived from Vratsa, and, as I was just telling your friend, we are hoping you might need two men-at-arms." After he spoke, he offered his hand in greeting.

Dragahn ignored the gesture and replied, "We don't have an opening, but if we run across a team that does, we can point them in your direction."

The knight's face hardened at the insult, becoming almost hostile, and he scrutinized each of the team members carefully. Abruptly, the smile returned. He retracted his hand and waved it airily as he said, "Never mind. I thought you might be able to help us."

Turning back to the bar, the knight focused his attention on the mug of beer the barkeep placed in front of him. Andrei and Teodor edged between the two men, retrieved their drinks, and returned to the table. Lucky leaned over and plied the pair with questions. Jasper, on the other hand, kept his head down and stayed unusually quiet.

When Grendel and Sachin walked through the door, conversations had just restarted in earnest. Before they could cross the room, the albino stepped in front of Grendel while Marko stepped out and approached Sachin. Grendel shifted and stood between them both, effectively stopping their progress.

Sachin stared at the insolent knight. Something must have passed between them because Marko backed down and returned to the bar.

Kourash remained in front of Grendel. The two giants glared at one another, committing each other's faces to memory. After a tense moment, Grendel and Sachin walked around Kourash and sat at the table with everyone else.

"What was that all about?" Lucky asked.

Looking up from his plate, Dragahn said, "They were asking about employment, but I'm not sure who would hire them."

"I thought there was going to be a fight," Lucky said excitedly, then asked, "What is Kourash? I've never seen anyone like him."

"Stay away from him," Jasper said quietly.

"You know what he is, don't you?" Lucky asked conspiratorially.

"No, not really," Jasper said, "but I know trouble when I see it."

Lucky opened his mouth to ask another question but held it.

The team turned its attention back to their meals. All except Lucky, who continued watching the albino. Everyone overheard the barkeep tell Marko that, other than the teamsters, no caravans had arrived that day.

Turning, the knight scanned the crowd. The barkeep refilled his mug. Instead of placating the knight, it seemed to make the warrior more belligerent. Patrons and employees tried to avoid the two men and were, for the most part, successful. Word must have spread outside the krŭchma because, a few minutes later, the captain of the militsiya arrived.

Even though there had been no discussion about it, no one left the table. The teamsters who had finished their meal sat quietly, half-listening to the various conversations. Dragahn kept an eye on the men's progress, and when the last one finished, he stood and laid enough leva on the table to pay for their meals. Following his lead, the team headed toward the door.

It seemed Marko and Kourash were going to ignore the teamsters, at least until Jasper walked past. Kourash quickly moved from his position beside the knight, stepped in front of the portly man, and said with a growl, "You smell funny."

Jasper glanced up, stared Kourash in the eyes, and said, "Yeah? So do you."

Kourash seemed to grow taller and wider as he glared at the fat man. Jasper stood his ground, and the krŭchma grew quiet.

The captain of the militsiya rose to his feet, and his chair scraped noisily on the hardwood floor. "Break it up," he ordered.

Marko laid a hand on Kourash's arm and whispered a few words. The servant abruptly faced the knight, who gave a barely perceptible shake of his head. Kourash turned back and bared a mouthful of sharp, pointed teeth at Jasper in what could have been a snarl or a horrible parody of a smile. "Another time," he said and let the cook pass.

8:16pm

Xandor was in his element — outside with just the stars to guide him. He crept down the narrow alley between the stables and the tavern, making note of the lack of streetlamps. That would make things easier.

He was just in time to see the teamsters emerge from the krŭchma with Dragahn in the lead. Oddly, they huddled together, almost in a defensive posture, and frequently cast anxious looks over their shoulders. Xandor noted Jasper walked near the end of the group without talking to anyone, even though it appeared two or three of the younger men were actively questioning him. Deciding to catch up with Jasper later, he remained in the dark alley and watched the street.

Ten minutes had gone by when Marko and Kourash emerged from the krŭchma. Xandor instinctively backed deeper into the shadows. The two started down the street toward the inn. Some sixth sense caused the hairs on the back of his neck to rise. Not wanting to give his position away, he made no sudden moves. Instead, he slowly retreated, keeping his back to the wall.

Stopping in the street, Kourash suddenly turned toward the alley. Xandor listened and distinctly heard the albino sniffing.

"What's wrong?" Marko asked as he joined his bodyguard.

Kourash did not answer. He kept sniffing the alley. Another minute passed before he growled, "I thought I smelled someone, but I don't see anything."

Marko asked, "Are you sure it isn't two villagers having a tryst?"

"I cannot answer that. I do know that whoever it was, has recently been in the presence of a dwarf, and I haven't seen any dwarves in this town."

"Curious," Marko said. He contemplated the alley with a frown. "Do you think the caravan was followed? This will change things if they were."

Kourash moved into the alley, and a pale green aurora-like glow shimmered in his eyes as they adjusted to the darkness. He knelt and sniffed again, tracing his fingers along a shallow footprint. Marko remained at the entrance and asked, "Anything?"

"Someone was here within the past few minutes. Looks like they stopped here and then walked toward the back of the alley. Do you want me to follow?"

"Do you still smell a dwarf?" Marko asked.

Kourash peered into the darkness, his body tense, and said, "It is not strong, but yes, I still smell it."

Listening intently, Xandor stood just around the corner with his eyes closed, a sword in each hand.

Footsteps scraped on the road.

"Evening, Captain," Xandor heard Marko say.

"Evening. Are you staying at the Yarosten Nosyat?

"Yes. Heading there now."

"Where's your friend?"

"Relieving himself."

There was a pause, then Xandor heard, "I don't want any trouble tonight."

"Captain, I promise my companion and I will be on our best behavior."

"Good. But in case you get any ideas, I want you to know I'll be watching you."

"Not necessary, Captain."

Xandor heard someone walk off. He tightened the grip on his weapons and waited.

After the captain left, Marko turned back to the alley. "Let it go, but tell me if you smell dwarf again."

Kourash exhaled derisively and walked back to the entrance. Together, the two crossed the street and entered the inn.

The ranger didn't breathe until the two men were through the doorway. Once they were gone, two facts registered above all others — they had spoken Rhodinan, not Trakyan, and if the albino could smell Chert, Xandor couldn't approach Jasper, especially if the two strangers suspected the caravan was being followed.

Not good. Not good at all.

CHAPTER 16
JASPER'S TALE

October 19, 4235 K.E.

4:30am

Dragahn paced back and forth in his room. What little sleep he'd managed had been nightmare ridden. Unable to overcome the anxiety of the past few days, he'd finally given up on sleep. His thoughts kept returning to the albino's reaction to his cook. He liked Jasper but needed to know about last night. He shook his head; this was the last thing he needed. Dragahn donned his wools, walked down the corridor past Grendel, and knocked loudly on Jasper's door.

Inside, Dragahn heard a shuffling of blankets and then, "Yes?"

"It's Dragahn."

After a few moments, the bolt slid back, and the door opened. Jasper stood just beyond, wearing his nightgown and cap. In his left hand, he held a lit candle.

"What can I do for you, Chief?"

Jasper stepped back, letting Dragahn enter his room.

Dragahn closed the door behind him and asked, "What happened at the krŭchma last night?"

"What do you mean?"

"The albino; he knew you, didn't he?"

Jasper shrugged, but his expression turned serious.

"Come on, cook. I need to know if you are jeopardizing this trip. I need to know right now."

Jasper took off his nightcap and bunched it up in his hands. He was quiet for a moment while he struggled with what to say. Placing the candle on the nightstand, he sat on the edge of the bed. After reaching his decision, he motioned for the caravan chief to take a seat. Grabbing a wooden chair, Dragahn dragged it in front of the cook and straddled it, propping his forearms across the chairback.

When Jasper spoke, his voice sounded distant. "A few years ago, I worked as the cook for a group of bounty hunters on a mission to the Alashalian Mountains along the western border of Carolingias. It was an area that really wasn't part of any country, but it was near enough to attract some of the bolder Carolingians. They would go into the mountains to hunt or fish. While most returned, some vanished, seemingly without a trace. While not necessarily unusual in the wild country, occurrences grew more frequent. It got the attention of the higher-ups when a nobleman's son went missing on one of these hunting trips. That's how we got involved.

"Long story short, we discovered the missing folks were not dying from accidents or running afoul of a wild, hostile tribe as initially thought. They were being captured and held in a prison of sorts. It looked like an abandoned fort from the outside, but underneath, it actually hid a network of caves and mines. Anyway, we found the missing people, who were working as slaves, and rescued the nobleman's son. That's where we ran into the Seldaehne. There were eight of them, each one just as mean and nasty as the one you saw in the bar. We fought and killed one during our escape.

"Looking back, I'd say we got extremely lucky. Later, the Carolingian and Gallowen governments made a joint effort to dismantle the place and freed a good number of prisoners. I heard they searched that place from top to bottom, but never found the Seldaehne."

Jasper turned his head slightly and looked directly at Dragahn.

"That year, I kept my ear to the ground. One of the more persistent rumors I heard claimed they were half-dragons sired by an evil wizard. If that's true, with all that pale skin, I'd guess they're part frost dragon."

Absorbing what Jasper had just told him, Dragahn sat quietly for a moment. "Is he one of the remaining seven?" he asked.

Jasper shrugged. "He has to be, doesn't he? I've never heard of any others like them."

"I believe he recognized you."

A haunted expression crossed Jasper's face. "Me too."

Dragahn stood and said, "I like you, Jasper. I think you're a good person, but I can't have your past put my team in danger."

Holding up his hand to interrupt the caravan chief, Jasper said, "Wait a second before you complete that thought. I told you what I know not to give you reason to let me go, but to give you information about something that's already taken an interest in you. You know full well those two men are here because of this caravan, not because of me. And what about the ambush?"

The caravan chief stared at the cook, weighing him.

Jasper forged ahead and said, "I may not be good in a fight, but you need me. You need as many friends around you as you can get."

Dragahn sighed. "Everyone is looking forward to your cooking tonight," Dragahn said, more to himself. Coming to a decision, he said, "Fine, but if you endanger this caravan..."

6:25am

Smelling of fresh pine, Xandor leaned against Xerxes with his spyglass propped on the saddle and made occasional notes in his journal. Chert finished packing their gear and walked over to the ranger, grumbling about the man's smell.

"The caravan has fresh Percherons. I bet they cost a pretty lev," Xandor said admiringly to the dwarf.

"You're just jealous," Chert said, then had to dodge as Xerxes tried to step on him.

Xandor ignored the two and readjusted the spyglass' focus. He could clearly see the horsemen and stable hands, all dressed in heavy wools, hitching up the new horses. Jasper was loading supplies onto the chuck wagon. Adjusting again, Xandor panned across the horizon. There was no sign of the knight and his albino.

The ranger watched through his spyglass as the team left Dobrovnitsa. Chert waited beside the ranger, eating jerky.

An hour went by, and the sun rose higher in the sky, warming the air a little. Temporarily putting away his spyglass and journal, Xandor moved them a little farther back into the woods, but otherwise stayed close to the shelter of a grove of maple trees. Another half hour went by before Xandor finally spotted the knight and the albino.

The knight's mount was an elegant, black-coated Frisian stallion. It's thick mane and tail fell in waves that rippled as the horse moved, and the silky feather hair on its lower legs was untrimmed. The Frisian stood about sixteen hands at the withers and walked with a brisk, high-stepping trot. The knight rode with a covered shield strapped to his left forearm, and in his right hand, he held the shaft of a long lance. The weapon's butt rested in a hard leather cup near the stirrup; a dark red pennon flew at its tip. Responding to a nudge from his rider's knee, the horse turned east.

Beside the knight, the albino rode on a tall, grey Shire horse with a lean head, large eyes, and a slightly arched neck that was long in proportion to its body. It was hard to tell through the spyglass, but Xandor guessed the horse was more than nineteen hands and built like an ox. It had to be, considering the size of his rider. They disappeared beyond the far lip of the valley but still Xandor made no move to leave. Ten minutes went by, then twenty, with the ranger's only movement being the almost imperceptible rise and fall of his breathing.

"Xandor, what's going on? The caravan's getting away."

"For a dwarf, you sure can be impatient," Xandor said, not looking up. "While you're waiting, I need you to do something about your armor."

"What's wrong with my armor?"

The ranger glanced over his shoulder at Chert's plate and chain mail and his horned great helm. "It sparkles, and it's loud. I keep thinking I'm being followed by a court jester." The dwarf made an odd choking sound and began to protest, but Xandor talked over him. "There's a spare shirt in my saddlebag. Cut it up and muffle the chain, then dull the shine on the plate and that helm with mud. Please."

Chert hmphed in response but did as the ranger bid.

An hour or so later, Xandor was still hunched over the spyglass, watching where the road disappeared on the other side of the valley. Even he started to have doubts about waiting any longer.

Then he saw it.

At first, he thought it was a trick of light, but then a white, hairless head appeared twenty yards to the right of the road. Although there was no sign of the knight, the albino had doubled back, just as Xandor had expected. The Shire horse trotted along the edge of the valley and stopped at the road, where he met the knight who had approached from the opposite side. The ranger couldn't focus on their faces, but by their relaxed body language, it looked as though they had given up the notion the caravan was being followed.

As soon as they disappeared, Xandor mounted up while Chert stretched and prepared for the long jog. Xerxes needed no urging — the black Andalusian was excited to be moving again — and, without stopping, he trotted through town as Chert hurried to catch up.

When they approached the valley's far end, Xandor stopped and retrieved his spyglass from his saddlebag. He scanned the road and terrain on either side. A mile ahead, the road topped a hill and then disappeared under a canopy of firs and pines. Xandor put away his spyglass and pulled out a map.

Bold letters clearly identified the region as Silva Nigra, or black forest. According to the map, the thickly forested foothills ran eastward from their current position. To the north, it was bordered by the Yantra River and the second escarpment, and to the south loomed a range of tall mountains. After replacing the map, Xandor directed Xerxes to move ahead cautiously. Chert's boots beat a counterpoint to the horse's gait on the hard-packed roadway.

Day turned to dusk when they entered the shadowed line of young conifers. Occasional streams of bright sunlight broke through the trees, revealing a ground covered in reddish-brown pine straw with little underbrush. Clean rows of trees appeared on either side. Their trunks lined up, creating illusions of infinitely long corridors.

Nothing in nature was ever that perfect. Xandor suspected that at some point, the Kral had instituted a reforestation program.

Just beyond the entrance to the forest, Xandor dismounted and knelt to inspect the ground. To anyone else, the road was a series of random ruts, but to Xandor, the road told a detailed story. He confirmed the number of wagons that had recently passed, as well as the number of horsemen, even picking out the Shire's heavy hoofprints from the mix.

Using the Shire's deep impressions in the ground as a simple guide, Xandor could tell the beast had passed twice, the first time at a fairly sedate pace and again, later, at a rapid gait. Following the twin trails, he quickly found where the albino exited the road to double back. Opposite, he found another set of hoofprints leaving the road — those of the knight's horse. Satisfied he'd found the caravan's mysterious shadows, the ranger memorized the tiny features that made each animal's prints unique.

11:36am

Xerxes walked down the East Road slowly enough to let Xandor keep an eye on the hoofprints of the knight and his companion. After a while, the ranger retrieved his map and studied the next few intersections and forks. A thin red line marked the proposed path of the caravan.

They were passing a lone wagon headed west when the knight's trail simply disappeared. Xandor immediately directed Xerxes to one side of the road. The ranger dismounted and guided them farther into the trees.

"Stay here, I'll be right back."

Chert and Xerxes both nodded, then each gave the other a sidelong look.

Xandor crept closer to the crossroads, blending with the trees along the south side of the road. He pulled out his spyglass. Even with the low light under the canopy, the ranger had no problem seeing the intersection, one hundred yards away.

Based upon his notations, the caravan should have traveled straight across. The two riders should have done the same, but he had another one of those nagging sensations that told him to stay hidden. He couldn't explain it, but it had kept him alive on more than one occasion.

Xandor panned his spyglass across the northwest quadrant of the intersection, scrutinizing every deadfall, bush, and tree. Nothing. He took a second to blink the dryness out of his eye, then turned to the next area. As he panned across, a flicker of movement caught his eye. Tightening his focus, he found them.

At first, the ranger couldn't tell if the two men had spotted him, but by the casual way the knight sat his Frisian, it appeared they hadn't. Xandor glanced over to the albino and silently put in a prayer his scent mask would work. He stuck the spyglass through his belt. Xandor thought a moment and then decided on a course of action.

He eased back to Chert and Xerxes and led them through the trees, away from the crossroads. Xandor veered far to the south in hopes of passing the knight and his companion, but when he came within sight of the intersecting road, he stopped.

Once again signaling for Xerxes and Chert to wait, he snuck back toward the intersection, laid down in the pine straw, took out his spyglass, and looked for the two riders. The knight and his bodyguard were still there.

Were they still hoping to catch someone following the caravan? Even to Xandor, who had ridden with some paranoid people, it seemed excessive. Perhaps they were waiting for someone. He decided to wait and watch.

After a few minutes, a bright white light appeared above the northern road and blossomed into a magical portal. Out of it rode two men on short, chestnut-colored horses that bordered on being ponies. Xandor focused his spyglass and studied the newcomers.

Both men had manes of wild, red hair and sported thick mustaches and beards. The two looked enough alike to be related — cousins, maybe even brothers. Swirling tattoos covered every inch of their exposed skin, one a mirror of the other. They each wore a chain vest over sleeveless leather jerkins and carried two broad short swords with slightly curved blades. Sticking out from the saddlebags of each horse was an unstrung longbow and a quiver of sheaf arrows.

When the two Northmen approached the knight and started a conversation, Xandor decided it was time to leave.

A half hour later, Xandor was still riding low in the saddle, dodging low-hanging branches, and navigating Xerxes away from any visible hazards. Chert jogged behind him, easily keeping pace. Finally, the ranger steered his horse toward the East Road, hoping they had gotten ahead of the knight and his men. Once there, he called a halt and checked for signs of passage. Xandor quickly found the trail of the caravan. There were no signs of the albino's horse.

Satisfied, the ranger resumed their journey, with Xerxes moving down the road at a steady trot. All three of them kept their ears alert for sounds both ahead and behind.

They had traveled for half an hour when Xandor and Chert heard the loud jangling of harnesses and hoofbeats moving toward them. Not wanting to take a chance, the ranger guided Xerxes off the road, Chert following.

A patrol of ten regulars mounted on rounceys and holding long spears appeared around a bend in the road. Xandor thought quickly, stepped out, and waved his right hand to get their attention.

The armored soldiers quickly surrounded him. Their commander urged his horse forward. "Identify yourself, stranger."

"Captain, I am a ranger in the service of the Kral, and I need your assistance," Xandor said. He slowly reached into his belt pouch and pulled out the parchment he used for identification.

The commander scanned it. His expression changed instantly, and when finished, he handed it back and snapped a perfect salute.

The ranger returned the salute and said, "Smugglers are using this road. I need a full accounting of everyone who passes this point for the next twelve hours. I am assigning this task to you and your men, Captain. That means anyone traveling this road must be stopped and searched thoroughly, regardless of station. In addition, we suspect foreigners may be involved. If they resist in the slightest, have them arrested immediately. I'll continue ahead and alert the remaining patrols on this road, but I recommend you send a runner to the garrison for backup."

"Yes, Sir." The commander snapped another salute.

Xandor returned the salute and went to retrieve Xerxes. The dwarf was nowhere to be seen, but since the horse wasn't agitated, Xandor let it go. He mounted and rode off, the commander's orders to his men ringing in his ears.

Once he was out of eyesight, he risked a smile.

"That was cute, with all the saluting and stuff. Do you think it will slow down that knight?" Chert said when he appeared beside a moss-covered, rocky outcropping.

Xerxes shied away from the dwarf. Xandor steadied his horse and said, "I don't know if it will slow them down or not, but I hope so." Then he stared down the road and said, "Let's catch that caravan."

5:48pm

The caravan had traveled without mishap and stopped at a campsite along the south end of a small lake. After the horses were unhitched and fed, there was a mad rush as the horsemen ran to the bank with freshly cut cane poles. Jasper's original plan had been to grill pork chops, but after getting a good view of the lake, he opted on panfish for supper. No one argued.

Jasper was alone, busily preparing the fire and the side dishes. Beside him, an open cookbook rested on a makeshift stand.

Sachin had disappeared into his tent, so Grendel left his post and approached the cook.

"How do you like your fish?" Jasper asked as he prepared the salad and grilled some potatoes.

"Do you think those two strangers we ran into yesterday will show up tonight?"

"I don't know," Jasper replied. He stopped what he was doing for a moment, looked around, and said, "Everybody here is wondering the same thing."

"That albino did not like you," Grendel said.

"I get that sometimes," Jasper replied.

Pyotr overheard them talking and approached. "He's right, you know. I wouldn't want to be you the next time he shows up."

Suddenly, Lucky screamed like a little girl, "I caught one! I caught one!" Everyone started laughing. The young man ran up to Jasper, his fish still wiggling on the line.

"That's great, Lucky, but you're supposed to take the fish off the hook first. Now, go clean it."

Lucky's face went from a look of triumph to one of utter defeat. "Ugh, that's gross. Can't you do it?"

Jasper laughed and said, "No way. I'm in charge of cooking them, not cleaning them."

Pyotr grinned and said, "Come on, you big baby." The two walked back toward the lake, where Viktor had set up a small cleaning stand.

Jasper motioned for Grendel to come closer. When he did, the cook whispered, "I have guard duty tonight after midnight. Let's talk then."

Grendel nodded without saying anything and walked back to his post.

Jasper looked up as some of the laughter got louder. He heard Yosif say, "I don't know why they call it cleaning. This is disgusting!"

12:34am

After placing another log on the fire, Jasper patrolled the sleeping camp. Snores and sounds of heavy breathing accompanied the gentle forest noises. He completed his circuit and headed toward the lake, accepting Grendel's nod as he passed the half-orc. Finding a log near shore, he sat and rested his feet.

It was only a couple of days until the new moon. The wind had subsided, so the surface was as smooth as glass. The stars hung low in the sky and silhouetted the mountain peaks. The cook stared at the lake and noted how the surface captured the bright intensity of the stars above. He was not one for staying up late; however, it was pleasantly cool, so he took the opportunity to simply breathe — not worry about the past or the future — just breathe.

Grendel quietly coughed to get the mage's attention. Jasper glanced up and beckoned for the tall half-orc to join him. Grendel cast a last quick glance toward Sachin's tent. Everything was dark, but he suspected his ward was still awake.

The two focused on the surface of the lake and listened to the night's sounds. Without turning his head, Jasper asked, "Everything all right?"

"This trip is not what I expected."

"Me, either. It seems the more you run from your past, the faster it follows you."

Grendel gave the mage a quizzical look when he realized Jasper was not just talking about himself.

Jasper turned, caught Grendel's expression, and asked, "How are things between you and Sachin?"

"Good."

Jasper thought a moment and said quietly, "I can't figure that man out."

With a small warning gesture, Grendel motioned to the tent. Jasper nodded and resumed staring at the lake.

"Why did you provoke that creature at the tavern?" Grendel asked. "He would have crushed you if the knight had not stopped him."

"Don't talk to me about provoking someone. Didn't you put yourself between him and Sachin?" Jasper asked.

"That is my job," Grendel said, his tone serious.

The mage shrugged.

"Jasper, I do not know what history you have with this creature, but do not let it cloud your vision."

"Look, I rolled the dice and won yesterday. Tomorrow, I'll roll those same dice again. Maybe I'll win, maybe I'll lose."

"Those are words of luck, not skill. Luck you did not start a fight in the bar, and luck you did not get attacked last night while you slept."

"You could've taken him."

Grendel shook his head. "The fight would not have been necessary."

"No, maybe not."

Grendel grunted and said, "Do not gamble with other people's lives, especially mine. If yesterday had gone differently, there would have been collateral damage. People might have died."

Jasper's eyebrows shot up, and it took him a second to form words. "You sound very much like an old friend of mine."

"Did he give you the same advice?"

"Pretty much."

They sat in silence for a little while longer. Jasper picked up a small pebble and threw it into the water. It landed with a soft plunk and sent ripples out in all directions.

"I think that creature was a Seldaehne," Jasper said.

When Grendel gave him a questioning look, Jasper recounted what he had told Dragahn.

After he finished, Grendel asked, "Does anybody else know about this?"

"Just Dragahn. *No one* else," Jasper said.

Grendel exhaled loudly and whispered, "We need to tell them."

"I know, but I haven't seen them since before we entered town yesterday," Jasper whispered back.

"Do you think they encountered the knight and the Seldaehne?"

"I hope not."

They both turned when they heard rustling near camp.

Pyotr appeared and asked, "Mind if I join you?"

Looking up at the stars, Jasper gauged their movement and said, "Sure, but you still have a half hour or so before I'm supposed to wake you."

"Couldn't sleep."

Grendel excused himself and resumed his position in front of Sachin's tent.

Pyotr found a spot next to Jasper and sat down. "Chief told me about the history between you and the knight's companion, and I overheard what you told Sachin's bodyguard. Do you think there'll be trouble?"

Jasper didn't say anything, but he couldn't help thinking he should've hired a damned crier and had him announce it from the mountaintops. The thought made him chuff silently, and his mind turned, once again, to old friends. Jasper reached into his pouch, took out a copper lev, and threw it into the water. *That one was for you, Robert.*

Pyotr watched the play of emotions.

Studying the sky, Jasper said, "It's gonna be a nice day tomorrow."

The horse doctor glanced up at the stars and replied, "Looks like it."

After a while, Jasper stood and brushed off his pants. "I'm gonna grab some sleep before Dragahn wakes me for breakfast."

Jasper had just started back when Pyotr said, "Dragahn made the right decision."

The mage stopped, looked down at the horse doctor, and said softly, "Let's hope so."

CHAPTER 17
MARKO ESCAPES

October 20, 4235 K.E.

1:02am

Hunkered down in a small grassy area behind a fallen tree, Xandor watched Jasper and Grendel across the mirror-like surface of the lake. Behind him, an unsaddled Xerxes grazed next to their cold campsite. Taking out his stylus, the ranger wrote several entries in his journal.

"Doesn't that thing ever get full?" Chert asked.

Closing his book, Xandor asked, "How long have you known Grendel?" His eyes still focused on the far side of the lake.

"Seems like forever. Why?"

"Really. How long have you known him?"

"Just over two years now."

"Can we depend on him?"

"What do you mean?"

Xandor turned from the lake and faced Chert. "Before meeting you two, I'd never worked with a half-orc before. Is he really trustworthy?"

"You know, I asked myself that same question when Grendel and I first met. Being a dwarf, you have to know I disliked him from the start," Chert replied.

"What changed?"

"We were both looking for work. Grendel was fresh off a ship from a place called J'Bel, and I had just left my home and my clan."

Chert paused when he heard something plop in the water. When nothing else stirred the night air, he continued, "We were both hired as bodyguards for an elderly druid named Garan. He was traveling to one of their holy sites, where he would compete for the honor of being the Grand Druid. At the time, I thought it strange he hired both of us without asking us any questions about our pasts. Thinking back, I realize now he didn't care. He saw something in us.

A potential, if you will. One that went beyond racial prejudices, and he was right. We became good friends — a dwarf and a half-orc. I learned a lot on that trip about myself and about my faith."

Smiling wistfully, Chert looked at Xandor and said, "Garan had a strange way of connecting everything together. And you know what was funny?"

"No, what?"

"We traveled for a month through forests and hills with Garan teaching us about animals and nature. When we arrived at their holy site, it turned out to be an enormous circle of ancient sarsen megaliths. I almost felt at home. I came to trust Grendel during that trip, and he has never done anything to cause me to question that trust."

"It's still difficult for me. I can only imagine what it must have been like for you," Xandor said.

Reaching over and patting the ranger on the back, Chert said, "Have faith, my friend. If a stubborn dwarf can overcome racial hatreds, then I believe there is hope for you yet."

Chert stepped away from the ranger and retrieved a thick, leather-bound tome from his pack. A silk ribbon looped from the binding marked his place. He found a comfortable spot, sat down, and began reading.

After a minute or two of silence, Xandor asked, "Was it necessary?"

Not looking up, Chert mumbled, "Was what necessary?"

"The druid — did he really need two bodyguards?"

Chert stopped reading and looked up. "No, I don't think he did."

A chill breeze from the lake cut through Xandor's clothes like a knife. "It's starting to get cold. We'll have to wear our furs tomorrow."

Still engrossed in his book, Chert didn't respond. His lips moved as if he were silently reciting a phrase or prayer.

"Chert, I need you to collect some pine straw."

"Why?"

"Camouflage," Xandor said as he rummaged through their baggage.

When the dwarf returned, the ranger crushed the needles in a bowl half-filled with watered-down tree sap until he had a dark-colored plaster. Satisfied with the mixture, he strategically daubed it on his armor and gear, giving it a distinct yuletide smell. Next, he handed the bowl to the dwarf and asked him to do the same.

6:21am

Dawn marked its approach with swaths of pastel colors decorating the rim of the eastern horizon.

A loud grumbling erupted from their tent. "Xandor, what did you do to me?" asked Chert, his voice barely under control.

The ranger lay watching the teamster's camp. Without looking back, he replied, "I didn't do anything to you. Now keep quiet."

Chert poked the ranger in the back with a stick. Xandor glanced over his shoulder and froze.

"You'll pay for this, ranger." Tree sap caked the dwarf's hair, and it stuck out in all directions. Bits of leaves and twigs entangled in his beard made him look like a forest imp.

Xandor's face turned dark red as tears formed in his eyes, and he choked back the urge to laugh. "I'm sorry, Chert. I didn't think about your beard."

Chert stormed off to pack their gear.

Once the wagons were out of sight, Xandor mounted Xerxes and directed his horse to walk slowly back to the road while Chert followed on foot. Before stepping into the open, Xandor gently tugged back on the reins and looked westward again to make sure the road was empty.

Next, he surveyed the ground and looked for anything out of the ordinary. Nothing. He took off his glove, licked his finger, and stuck it up in the air. Xandor said, "The wind's from the west. We should be downwind from that knight and his manservant."

Satisfied, Xandor urged Xerxes across the road and into the forest on the other side.

"You're not staying on the road?" Chert asked.

"No. That patrol would have slowed them down but not stopped them," Xandor replied.

The rows of trees made it easy for Xerxes to maintain a quick walk through the pine straw, and the ranger rode low in the saddle to help his horse avoid the tree roots. They continued north for a hundred yards or so before again turning east.

9:34am

Far to the west, a cloud of dust followed a thunder of hooves. Marko was furious.

Yesterday, after the two Northmen, Mladen and Ognian, joined him at the crossroads, he had set out to catch up with the caravan. They were making excellent time when they came to a long line of travelers stopped on the East Road. He quickly learned the Kral's men had established a cordon and were checking everyone's papers and searching baggage. There was a rumor more troops were on the way to help with the process, but no one knew why the soldiers were stopping people. There was only a vague statement the order had come direct from the Kral's office.

Being a knight usually had its advantages, but this was not one of those times. Marko could have turned around or tried to sneak through the forest and bypass the soldiers; however, it would not bode well for his standing in the family if the Kral's men detained him. Besides, he had nothing to hide.

Marko and his entourage fell in at the back of the line. Two hours later, the cordon where ten regulars were stationed came into view. The soldiers searched each person and their baggage. They were thorough in their efforts and, even though tempers flared, the men handled themselves professionally. Marko judged they probably would not accept a bribe. Before it was his group's turn, he collected everyone's letters of introduction and prepared his story.

The commander motioned him forward, and Marko, with his family crest still concealed behind his leather shield cover, dismounted and introduced himself. The commander took his papers and read each one carefully while his men set about searching the baggage. Everything went smoothly until the commander turned to Marko and said, "Sir, I must ask you to uncover your shield."

Marko stared at the soldier with cold eyes and said, "I have suffered this line of commoners, and I have relented to your search. Your request is most inappropriate, Commander. I respectfully decline."

"You misunderstand, Sir. I made it a request only to be polite. I have my orders, and you *will* remove the cover before I let you pass."

"No."

"Then you, Sir, are under arrest," the commander said, signaling to his men.

Marko responded, "The hell I am!" He punched the commander with his steel gauntlet, bloodying the man's mouth and knocking him backward into the men behind him. Instantly, the sliding of steel resonated through the forest.

The Shire horse charged forward, and Kourash's two-handed sword cleaved through the steel helmet of a young soldier. A sick, crunching sound accompanied the dark, arterial blood that spurted from the collapsing body.

Wielding cutlasses in each hand, the two Northmen easily guided their small horses into the fray. Steel clashed on steel when they crashed into the front rank of soldiers. Four regulars in the second rank thrust long spears repeatedly at Mladen and Ognian. The two Northmen dodged and deflected their attacks but could not stop them all. A spear snuck past their defenses and caught Mladen's horse in the neck. With a scream, the horse went berserk, bucked, and threw his rider. The spear bowed and splintered.

Marko's Frisian reared and kicked with his forelegs, clearing a path for the knight. When the soldiers backed away from the destrier, Marko pressed forward, struck with the edge of his shield, and drew his weapon. Kourash roared defiantly as another soldier went down under his heavy two-handed sword.

The roar echoed and was answered by the clear call of a horn. A score of the Kral's men charged out of the forest from the south. Panicking, the line of people waiting took flight in all directions.

Taking advantage of the brief confusion, Marko yelled at his men, "To me! To me!" as he mounted his horse. Not looking to see if any followed, he raced through a gap in the soldiers' line. The Kral's men renewed their attacks, but their blades failed to dent the knight's heavy armor.

Kourash's Shire crashed through the ranks of regulars and followed the knight. Behind him, Ognian barely fended off the soldiers long enough for the fallen Mladen to hoist himself onto the back of the horse, and then they, too, raced eastward.

Marko looked back over his shoulder. Behind him, six cavalrymen gave chase. They galloped down the road, two to a row, each carrying his long spear high, with the sable and azure pennon fluttering near the tip. Marko spurred his horse to even greater speed as the Kral's men drew closer. However, Ognian's horse, burdened with two men, fell behind. Marko grimaced when he saw the soldiers tighten their ranks and lower their spears.

It appeared they were about to catch their quarry when the front rank of horses screamed and collapsed in a tangled mess of limbs. Several soldiers flew through the air while others disappeared beneath flashing hooves.

Ognian's expression became one of predatory triumph as they raced away.

3:14pm

As the teamsters slowed to camp for the night, another patrol raced past, and Dragahn motioned for Viktor.

"Sir?"

"Did you see those soldiers we just passed?"

"Yes, sir."

"Take one of your horsemen with you and find out what's going on. I want to know if the trouble is ahead of us or behind us."

An hour later, Viktor and Andrei returned and checked in with Dragahn during supper.

"Did you find out anything?" Dragahn asked.

"A patrol was attacked yesterday a few miles outside of Dobrovnitsa. From the description, I think it may have been Jasper's friend and the knight. Soldiers are scouring the countryside for them now."

"What happened?"

"Don't know anything specific, but they killed a whole mess of the Kral's men. One person we spoke with said he heard they had used caltrops." Viktor spit and wiped his mouth with the back of his sleeve.

"I know I don't have to say this, but keep your eyes open."

"Yes, sir," the two men replied.

"Everyone, listen up!" Dragahn called. He waited until he had everyone's attention, including Sachin and Grendel, who walked closer to the group. "Tomorrow evening, we should arrive at Vratsa and the Stena. After that, it will be nine days of hard travel outside the official reach of the Kral. That means tomorrow night will be our last night in civilized country for a while. So, when we get into town, each of you can have the night off to relax and find what entertainment is available."

Everyone started talking at once.

Dragahn held up his hands to quiet them back down. He looked at each of his men and said, "That's not permission to get arrested or get into trouble. Make no mistake, day after next, every one of us will earn our pay. We've been through this territory twice, and each time it was different, so we can't afford to let our guard down. That's how people get hurt. Tomorrow morning, I want to get an early start. The sooner we leave, the sooner we get there. That's all I've got to say."

6:29pm

Sachin stared westward down the road and frowned. A chill had snuck into the air, and he wrapped his cloak tighter around himself.

Next to him, Grendel asked, "Worried about the knight?"

"What? No, just thinking."

After a moment, Grendel said, "Dragahn mentioned we will reach the Stena tomorrow. Do you know what awaits us on the other side?"

Sachin turned and stared up at his bodyguard. "Who can say?" he responded with a shrug. "I expect a few of your brethren."

"They are not my brothers."

"We'll see."

Grendel glared at the small man and fought to control his temper.

"Forgive me. That was uncalled for." Sachin gave him an apologetic smile and continued, "Thirty-five years ago, before the Kral retreated and gave his land to the khumanoid tribes, the area was full of thriving people and their cities."

Grendel looked startled. "The Kral just gave them up? What happened to the people?"

"I can only assume they moved out when the Kral recalled his men."

"He uprooted entire families?"

"I'm sure it was either move out or be captured and forced into some type of slavery — or worse — eaten."

Grendel tried to picture this no-man's land and asked, "What about the Stena? I have heard Dragahn mention the wall several times."

"Full of questions tonight, aren't we?" Sachin asked, then, when Grendel started to back away, he said, "It's alright; these are good questions.

"Others may view it a bit differently, but to me, the Stena is an unprecedented monument to cowardice. It marks the first time the Kral ever conceded territory to his enemies, and by doing so, he left his southern neighbors completely vulnerable to the hordes of khumanoidi. There's even a dark rumor the Kral secretly met with khumanoid chieftains, worked out a bargain to divide the land, and thus saved his sovereignty. In either case, his actions rewrote the world map.

"As for the wall itself, it serves as the eastern border of Trakya. Started in 4201 when khumanoidi first began amassing, it now stretches hundreds of miles, and it's still not finished. Vratsa, the town we arrive in tomorrow, was originally a staging ground for two teams of builders, the north team and the south team, each tasked with constructing the wall and milecastles as fast as they could."

"Milecastles?"

"Gatehouses built into the wall."

"How many men guard it?"

"The numbers vary, but I've heard the Kral has stationed three of his legions, each five thousand strong, to both build and guard it."

"Seems a bit much for a wall."

"Maybe, but it's served its purpose and protected Trakya from the khumanoid tribes."

"I guess so. You seem to know a lot about this wall."

Sachin flashed Grendel a quick smile and said, "No, not really, but I do like to keep up with current events and the geopolitical situation of places we are expected to travel."

"Is that the reason you are not afraid to travel outside the wall?"

"One of them," Sachin replied. After a moment, he said, "Your turn."

Grendel waited, not knowing what to expect.

"From what you've told me, it sounds as if J'Bel is a place far away from here. I want to know what brought you to Trakya."

After taking a moment to think, Grendel said, "I am searching for something I lost."

"What do you mean?"

Looking off into the distance, Grendel answered, "I was given a gift on loan — an ancient labrys with perfect symmetry and balance. It may sound funny, but when I held that axe, it gave me the sense that when I fought, I was not alone. Have you ever felt that way?"

Sachin did not answer.

"It was stolen, and I vowed to the Eternal Father that I would get it back."

"Do you know who stole it?" Sachin asked.

Grendel faced Sachin, a faraway look in his eyes. "No, but I will find it. One day, I must go before the Eternal Father and be judged. With that axe at my side, I can say that, even though I was not worthy, he entrusted me with a great weapon. Then I will return his gift and show I did not disappoint that trust.

"It may be a simple thing, but to me, it represents much more than an axe. It means someone is with me. Someone who cares if I live or die. And it means redemption is still possible. Even after all I have done."

Focusing a fiery, determined gaze on the small man, Grendel said, "Would you not travel to the ends of Gaia to seek out an item like that? To be able to possess something you knew in your heart could mean the difference between Heaven and Hell?"

The question hung in the air.

Breaking the half-orc's gaze, Sachin said quietly, "That's enough for one night." He started back to his tent and, with one final glance down the road toward the west, said, "Sometimes, Grendel, you are destined to travel the road to Hell, no matter how many times you try to turn back."

10:10am

Matching the pace of the caravan the next day, Xandor rode a half mile or so behind the wagons. Rumors abounded about the patrol Marko had attacked, and it disturbed him. He should have warned them, but he had not thought the knight would assault the Kral's men. He had obviously misread him. It also made the ranger wonder what had triggered the encounter. He had spent the bulk of the evening eavesdropping on various camps, but the stories he heard never said.

Chert walked beside Xerxes, enjoying having his feet on the ground. The ranger offered to let him ride, but he turned the man down, muttering, "Horses are unnatural."

"I thought you were a devout priest and loved all of the Eternal Father's creatures."

The dwarf looked up at the ranger and said, "It's not about loving the creatures of the Eternal Father. It's about using what the Eternal Father has given you. Look at you. You ride everywhere you go, letting your legs go to waste."

Xandor choked on his water. "Dwarf, my legs are just fine. I am faster than you, with or without a horse."

"Is everything a race to you, human? You should slow down and smell the dirt."

"Smell the dirt? Are you kidding?"

Chert looked hurt. "No, I'm serious. Have you ever stopped to smell red clay or beach sand? Or have you stood in the middle of a freshly plowed field and smelled that rich, earthy smell?"

"Yes, I have, and it smells horrible."

"You just don't know what you're smelling. Did you know some cultures eat dirt?"

"No. I must have missed that one," the ranger said, shaking his head. "And you said horses were unnatural."

Xerxes whinnied. The ranger patted him on the neck and said, "You're right, boy. Chert, let's talk about something else. You're upsetting Xerxes."

CHAPTER 18
THE EYES AND EARS OF THE KRAL

October 21, 4235 K.E.

6:00pm

Marcus Marchenkov stood in the center of the double-headed eagle seal inlaid in the floor of the Ochi i Ushi chambers, facing four of the most powerful people on the Kral's advisory council. He hurried to finish his report while struggling against the growing tightness in his chest. He croaked out the last bit of information then covered his mouth with his ever-present handkerchief as a coughing fit seized him. Marcus hunched forward, stumbling the few steps needed to grip the edge of a glossy conference table. The wracking, wet sounds echoed from the chamber's dark paneled walls.

When Marcus finally recovered himself, Lord Mitso Tervel, Director of the Eyes and Ears of the Kral, sighed. "Marcus, these fanciful conspiracy theories you have must stop."

"It's no theory that our people are becoming ill. Especially those closest to the Kral. I tell you these people... I was poisoned."

"Poisoned by what?!" Lord Tervel exclaimed, slamming his fist on the table. The dark circles and drooping bags under his eyes made it clear that he, too, was losing sleep over the contagion that had recently struck Pazard'zhik.

"Do you still think Lena Hristova had something to do with this?" asked Asenov, arch-mage and the Acting Guild Master of the White Circle. He sounded tired — or perhaps bored. Of the five people in the room, he looked the healthiest. His bright eyes bored into Marcus, and his long white robes seemed to radiate power. The other two, Lord Bate Marchenkov, Steward of Pazard'zhik, and Lady Maria Sarac, the Kral's Defense Advisor, waited in silence for Marcus' answer to the guild master's question.

"Lena Hristova was burned alive along with Dragahn's compound," Marcus answered. "Her family is missing. What more evidence do you need?"

"Do you question Officer Kostadin's abilities or those of his staff at Tsarevets? Her caravan was searched thoroughly. Dragahn's not hiding anything," Lord Tervel said.

"No, Sir. It's just that..."

"Marcus, let the caravan go. Focus on the events here."

"Besides, the caravan has reached Vratsa. It will be out of our hands by tomorrow," Asenov added. "And I must say, the sickness has not followed it. If this was a caravan of death as you say, wouldn't we hear of it? Wouldn't other towns fall under the same spell?"

"I tell you it's not a disease. It's a poison."

Wracked by another coughing fit, Marcus' whole body shook. He sprawled forward, falling onto the table. The other four leapt from their chairs and backed away. When Marcus didn't rise, Bate Marchenkov cried out, "Quick! Bring us a healer!"

6:05pm

From his office overlooking the dockyards, Georgy Yotsov sipped a steaming cup of tea and watched the last barge of the evening pull away from its dock. Laden with wooden crates, it traveled south on the River Maritsa for the shipyards along the northwestern shores of the Cherno More, the second largest inland sea on the continent of Parlatheas. There, the crates would then be transferred onto two- and three-masted sailing ships that dared the More's sparkling waters.

He could barely make out the first twinkling lights of Burgas, one of several small Trakyan cities dotting the northern shore of the Cherno More, cities the Kral and his ancestors had controlled for the last three millennia. However, his control of the eastern shores was tenuous at best. The Kral would have incorporated those shores into his realm, but with the increasing numbers of humanoids moving into that region, maintaining a presence there for any length of time had proven impossible.

Kingdoms were subject to the same laws as business and trade. More often than not, they were lost, not due to wars and famine, but to the laws of supply and demand. This savvy business sense had enabled Trakya's Krals to rule for as long as they had and still maintain the respect of the people. This also set up pockets of resentment — especially among those wishing to avoid the taxes demanded by such a sprawling country.

In some areas, the Kral built walls to define the boundaries of his realm, but to the south where the inland sea lay, these borders were not and could not be as well defined. Georgy reflected on the petitioners who had arrived just yesterday to request troops. Some of the southern towns had resorted to piracy or smuggling, thinking they could turn a fast golden lev. It wouldn't bode well for them if the Kral caught them. His justice was oftentimes swift and without mercy.

An insistent knock at his door shook him from his thoughts. "Come in," said Georgy.

One of the dockworkers entered. He held his fur kalpak in front of him and said, "Dockmaster, there is something you must see."

Grabbing his coat, he followed the dockworker down to the wharf where a group of men gathered. One held a long gaff hook in his hand. Another wore a thick wool blanket over his shoulders, his pants and boots dripping water. At their feet was a saturated sailcloth tightly wrapped around something the shape of a human body.

"Redjo, what's going on here?" Georgy asked.

"Found it floating in the water, sir," he replied.

Georgy knelt and flipped back a portion of the cloth, revealing the dead man's face. The skin and lips were tinged blue, and the eyes and mouth had been sewn shut.

"He had been weighted down," Redjo said, pointing to a frayed rope tied around the legs.

"Is that Sachin?" a man asked.

"Looks like it," answered Georgy with a frown. The dead man hadn't frequented the docks often, but being from Upper Pazard'zhik, his presence had always attracted attention. "Let's tell the militsiya."

7:00pm

Marcus cracked open his eyes. Light from a single candle by his bedside gave off a comforting glow and the subtle scent of incense. A nun with a kindly face hovered over him, dabbing his shoulders and chest with cool water. In the background, he heard the groans of the sick.

"Where am I?" he croaked as he tried to rise.

"Hush," she replied, pushing him back down with a gentle hand. "You're in the chapel infirmary."

He glanced down toward his feet. He lay naked under a white blanket that had been folded back to expose his chest. Oozing sores and pustules marked his skin. *What was happening to him?* He could literally feel his strength stealing away.

Marcus grabbed her wrist. "I've got to get out of here."

"Father Benesj will be here shortly. Until then try to rest," the nun replied, pushing his hand away.

Lord Bate Marchenkov entered the alcove and asked, "How are you feeling?"

"Uncle, I feel well enough to continue my duties. Tell them to let me leave."

"I'm afraid I can't do that. Stay here and heal."

"You can't expect me to just lie in bed like this. The soap... the poison..."

"Enough, nephew. Master Asenov and his guild are looking into this disease along with the church. Take heart. They will find a cure soon."

"That's right, my son," said a tall man in undyed wool robes from the foot of the bed. He glanced down at his patient. Then turning to the nobleman, he motioned toward the hallway. "Lord Marchenkov, may I have a moment of your time?"

"Of course, Father Benesj."

By the time Bate returned, the nun had left. His face was pale, and he seemed frailer as if the weight of his news were a physical burden.

"What is it uncle?" Marcus asked.

Bate took Marcus' hand and patted it. "You've always been like a son to me."

"What is it?"

"Father Benesj says they're close to a cure. It's just a matter of time."

"You're lying, Uncle."

Lord Marchenkov gave his nephew a sad smile. "You've always had great instincts. You may even be right about the caravan."

"What do you mean?"

"They found Sachin's body at the docks a little while ago. Apparently, he's been dead for some time."

"Oh, no. The caravan. We have to stop it."

"Stay strong. I have already asked the White Circle to send a message to the Vratsa Milecastle. It should arrive tonight."

"Could we also have the church send a message to the Stŭklena Katedrala for me? I have friends there."

"I see no reason why we couldn't. I'll ask Father Benesj."

CHAPTER 19
VALEVATAYA MEHANA

October 21, 4235 K.E.

7:13pm

Bright streetlamps illuminated the faces of off-duty soldiers and their paramours coming and going from inns and taverns. Music flowed from the doors of several establishments, and lively dance tunes beat in counterpoint to softer melodies. Despite the ebb and flow of foot traffic, Sachin had no trouble making headway up the street. One look at the tall, dark figure at his side caused even the bravest of soldiers to give way.

For Xandor, the going was not so easy. Rather than try to mingle, he concentrated on staying at the fringe, moving with the current and bobbing from pool to pool rather than being caught in the main flow.

Farther along, the number of revelers thinned as the neighborhood turned dark, and streetlamps grew less frequent. Sachin moved with confidence through the silent shadows, past weathered houses and crumbling buildings where the poor but proud descendants of the refugees who lost their land so long ago made their homes in shabby tenements.

Taking advantage of the darkened street, Xandor drew closer as Sachin and Grendel entered a narrow, winding lane where the sound of happy laughter vanished. Travelers here did not want to be noticed. A prostitute lingered in a doorway here, a clandestine couple slipped down an alleyway there, and a small-time thug waited for an easy target in the shadows farther on. The occasional sounds of tears or cruel laughter reached the street, traveling the night air like ghosts in a fog, coming at a person from every direction at once and sending a chill down the spine.

Sachin and Grendel came to a stop before a tall, three-story building soaring like the prow of a ship that had run aground upon a weathered, single-story krŭchma with a red tile roof.

A double-sided wooden plaque hanging from the eave by the door read, Валеватая Механа — *Valevataya Mehana* — and bore a rough, carved image of a tankard. Xandor hid himself in a deep recess in the wall of one of the buildings across the street and waited.

The small man descended a shallow set of steps and made to open the door, but something stayed his hand. He scanned the nearby buildings where Xandor stood.

Confident he could not be seen, the ranger remained still. Finally, the small man spoke to his bodyguard and pointed to the steps. Grendel shook his head and said something in a low growl. After a few heated words, Sachin must have won the argument because the half-orc remained outside while Sachin disappeared into the tavern.

After waiting several heartbeats, the ranger crossed the street, stopping beside Grendel.

"Evening."

Grendel arched his eyebrows at Xandor's sudden presence and replied in a deceptively calm voice, "Evening."

"You just supposed to wait here?"

"Yes."

"Doesn't seem like the smartest move he could make in this part of town. I'd better go inside and see what he's up to."

"How is Chert?"

"He's good. I left him at the Glass Cathedral. He's probably asleep on a pew."

Grendel gave the ranger a knowing nod. "Let me know if you need help."

"I will. Thanks."

Xandor walked down several flagstone steps and stopped at a stout oaken door banded with black iron. He paused long enough to adjust the hood of his cloak and take a deep breath before shoving aside the heavy barrier.

Inside, the ranger found himself in a heavily shadowed, four-foot square entry. Beyond lay a dimly lit, cramped main room filled with noise. The smell of sweat, wood smoke, and alcohol assailed him. At his feet, a thick layer of dirt and straw covered the floor. Above him, smoke-stained timbers ran the length of the grimy ceiling.   Patches of white efflorescence stuck to the unpainted stone walls like fungus.

Xandor scanned the room and instantly felt trapped — there were no windows, and the only other exit was a swinging door behind the bar at the right-hand side of the tavern. A small pass-through opening beside the door gave a limited view of the kitchen.

The few tables and benches scattered about the room were full, but there was still plenty of room for the patrons to mill about and circle the roaring fire pit. They carried their mugs as they swapped stories and unwound after a day of hard labor.

Xandor took in all this within a matter of seconds and steeled himself to push through the crowd. No one paid him any attention other than to shift aside enough to let him pass as he wound his way to the bar, but he still felt exposed.

Squeezing into the narrow space between two couples, he gave the bar top a quick double slap to attract the attention of the attractive blonde who stood drying freshly washed mugs, an assortment of casks and kegs with Cyrillic symbols at her back. On the wall in front of Xandor, a variety of odd-shaped bottles stood like dark gypsies along a narrow shelf at the base of a broad mirror covering the unpainted stone. While she poured drinks, the tapster used the mirror to keep an eye on the crowd.

As she walked past, Xandor ordered ale while scanning the crowd in the mirror. His quarry was easy to spot. Sachin stood before the knight and his pale companion. The patrons gave them as wide a berth as they could, amounting to just a few feet, but it was enough for Xandor to also see the two Northmen seated on a bench, their backs to the wall. From Sachin's body language, it was obvious an extremely unhappy superior was dressing down the knight. Interesting.

Both the knight and his companion — Xandor could see now he was not entirely human — listened to Sachin while the two Northmen appeared to sleep. The ranger noted the knight's matted hair and tired eyes were underscored by dark smudges and gave a half-satisfied grunt. *Serves you right, you pompous prick.*

A shapely bosom, enclosed in cream-colored cotton and a leather vest, blocked the view. A mug of ale thudded on the counter and the bartender said, "That's five copper leva."

Xandor produced a silver lev from a pouch on his belt and pushed it across the bar toward her. Without taking his finger from the coin, he looked into her chocolate-colored eyes and asked, "What do you know about those people over there?" He gave a small tilt of his head to the left and saw the woman's dark eyes dart across the crowd and back.

"The knight with the ugly albino?"

"That's them."

She gave a shrug. "Not much. They aren't local and haven't been here before tonight. They came in a couple of hours ago while things were slow. That small man talking to the knight came in just before you did — but you already knew that, didn't you?"

Xandor nodded.

"I don't want any trouble, do you hear? You and your money can leave now if you're thinking about starting something. I don't mind calling for the militsiya."

Xandor pulled out the parchment serving as his identification and handed it to her wordlessly. She scanned it before huffing in exasperation. "Great," she said, a hint of sarcasm in her tone. "You *are* the militsiya."

The ranger smiled in response and said, "I'll do what I can to prevent any unpleasantness or, failing that, take it outside."

She arched an eyebrow at him. "Thanks, I'd appreciate that. We have enough fights in here as it is. Once one person throws a punch, everyone wants to play."

Before he could respond, the young woman moved away to another customer, taking the silver coin with her. He had to give her credit — he hadn't realized he'd taken his finger from it.

Gaze returning to the mirror, he wished he could read lips. The bar seemed more boisterous than when he first came in, and conversations were increasing in volume. A couple of harried young women moved through the crowd, carrying drinks and meals to customers. In the back corner, a minstrel tuned a lute and placed a small bowl on a stand nearby. Once the singing began, it would be impossible to hear anything.

7:45pm

Scowling at the young knight and his bodyguard, Sachin exclaimed, "Of all the idiotic stunts! Have you lost all your senses?" The little man's gaze shifted to the Seldaehne. "And you! A seasoned warrior? How could you let him make such a stupid mistake?"

Kourash glared through narrowed eyes in return, but his hand did not move toward the huge sword propped against the wall at his side.

Marko heaved a sigh and ran one hand through his tangled hair. "I *told* you. We ran into a patrol and had to fight our way out."

"You weren't even supposed to be on this side of the Stena," Sachin said heatedly.

Marko stared at the little man, barely controlling his temper, and said, "D'yakon Krovos said you needed help."

"You call that help?" Sachin demanded. "Your little escapade into Trakya almost ruined everything."

"Maybe, but us getting arrested would certainly have ruined everything," Marko seethed.

"Just be glad you're here. Have you heard from Gregori?"

Marko nodded. "He sends word everything is progressing well, and he is ready to start the next phase of the plan."

"And Chernigov? Have you heard from them?"

"No, not yet."

"I told you, little brother, Bregu Kraagor is not dependable," Sachin said smugly.

"Damn it," Marko said, his fist clenching. "We need him."

"No, we don't," Sachin said. "He can't be controlled."

"I can control him."

Sachin stared at the knight and said, "I doubt that. That's why I have a contingency plan already worked out."

"I'm sure you do."

Kourash lunged to his feet. Sachin took an involuntary step back as the Seldaehne towered over him, but the creature's attention was elsewhere. Marko rose, scanning the crowd.

"The man-dwarf is here," Kourash growled.

"Damn it! How is that possible?" Marko asked as he nudged the two Northmen awake.

"What's this?" Sachin demanded.

"Your caravan is being followed by a man who smells of dwarf," Kourash answered. His tone brooked no argument.

7:50pm

At the bar, Xandor watched the tension build between the knight and Sachin. When the knight's strange companion bolted upright and began scanning the room, the ranger realized he was on the verge of being caught.

Sachin pushed toward the door with Marko close behind. The Northmen made to follow their employer, but he signaled for them to follow Kourash.

Xandor hunched over his ale and tried to keep his face in shadow while still watching the white giant. Perhaps it was fate, perhaps it was chance, but Xandor broke the first rule of surveillance — he made eye contact with his quarry.

There was no hope of remaining anonymous. The Northmen dropped their cloaks at a gesture from a bone-white hand. The two moved in opposite directions through the crowd to flank Xandor while the white warrior headed straight for him, the crowd parting like water. Xandor's options were quickly disappearing. Remembering his earlier promise to the bartender, he leapt onto the bar and rolled into the narrow space behind it.

The young woman working there opened her mouth to protest, but Xandor shouted, "Is there a back way out of here?"

"The kitchen, but —"

Xandor did not hear the rest of her reply. He darted into the kitchen, dodging the cook and several of his helpers. Bombarded by thick smells of grease and cabbage, he spotted another door and ran for it. Angry shouts from the cook were cut off mid-word as one of the Northmen burst into the room with his cutlasses drawn.

Beyond the kitchen's back door, Xandor found himself in a shadowy stairwell leading up into the larger building. High windows let in a minimum of fresh air. There was barely enough light for Xandor to discern a pair of doors at the second-floor landing. He took a chance and ran up the stairs two at a time to put as much distance as he could between himself and his pursuers.

Outside, Grendel waited for Sachin, pondering the wisdom of burning his mask. With the half-orc guarding the door, very few people dared approach his side of the street. He cursed his father's features. Because of them, humans jumped to conclusions and, more often than not, the wrong ones.

The tavern door burst open.

Practically quivering with rage, Sachin stalked out, followed by the knight. Grendel moved to intercept the young man, but Sachin stopped him. When the warrior reached the top of the steps, he said something to Sachin that Grendel did not catch, and the small man whirled, mid-stride, a torrent of words pouring forth. The bodyguard kept his hand near his axe, should things turn ugly, and wondered if Xandor was on the other side of the door, listening.

Sachin's eyes blazed. The caravan being followed was an obvious sign the Kral suspected something. This news made it imperative he get the caravan beyond the Stena and into the wilderness.

Confident in his bodyguard and hirelings' abilities to take care of one nosey man, Marko was much more relaxed about the matter, which only served to infuriate Sachin further.

"What in the name of Sutekh have you been doing these past three days? Why didn't you dispose of this threat before now — or did you think it wasn't important?" Sachin demanded through clenched teeth.

"This is only the second time we've come across him," Marko replied nonchalantly. "There was no reason to suspect him before tonight."

"How many times must I tell you?! We can't afford to be stopped!"

"If I had killed him earlier, you would have screamed about us leaving a trail of bodies. It doesn't matter. My men will take care of him."

"You must leave this town!" Sachin handed Marko what appeared to be a translucent black pearl. "Take your men and we'll meet like we originally planned."

"You have no authority over me. You're out of favor, remember?"

Sachin stepped forward and leaned toward Marko's face. "I am still eldest. You will not fail me again, brother," he hissed, "or I swear to Sutekh I will gut you myself."

"Worry about your own guts," Marko said coldly as he stomped away.

Grendel stood at Sachin's shoulder. He could not understand what they were arguing about. Although some of the words sounded similar to the Trakyan he was still learning, their accents and the speed with which they spoke added levels of difficulty.

Sachin stared after Marko, his eyes burning with hatred. Mumbling under his breath, the small man strode in the opposite direction, retracing their earlier path. Worried about Xandor, Grendel glanced toward the bar, then back at his employer. He dared not linger, and would have to trust the ranger to take care of himself tonight, especially since staying out of trouble seemed nigh unto impossible for Xandor.

CHAPTER 20
AN ENEMY REVEALED

October 21, 4235 K.E.

7:52pm

Xandor grabbed the nearest door handle and pulled, relieved when he found it unlocked. Without entering, he slammed it and crept up the stairs, praying his ruse would buy him time to find his way down to the street.

He was barely halfway to the third floor when the two Northmen entered the stairwell. Xandor froze in place, trusting his cloak to keep him concealed in the shadows along the wall. Peering down, he was rewarded when the two split up to enter the doors on the second floor.

Gliding carefully to the top, Xandor tried the only door; this one was locked. He pulled his graphite rod from his pouch and slid it inside the lock as gently as he could. The tumblers clicked, and the ranger slipped into the room beyond.

Dim light filtered through gauzy curtains, illuminating furnishings with a woman's touch, and the air held the pleasant hint of perfume. Entering the bedroom that overlooked the street, he crept to the edge of the bay window. Below, Marko stood watching the buildings.

With a sudden crash and splintering of wood, the apartment door slammed open and sagged as the hinges cracked. Kourash walked cautiously into the living room, the point of a huge two-handed sword poised in front of him. Behind him came one of the Northmen.

Xandor drew his twin longswords and looked around. Cramped as it was, the bedroom would not give him much room to maneuver, but it also hindered his opponent's ability to swing that big blade of his. Unfortunately, the Northman, with his shorter swords, would have no difficulty at all.

Kourash charged into the bedroom and thrust his two-handed sword at the ranger. Between the Seldaehne's long arms and the fifty-five-inch blade, Xandor was hard pressed in the tight space. He held his blades crossed in an X to deflect each attack.

The bedroom furniture took the brunt of the Seldaehne's fury as each sword stroke tore through fabric and wood alike. It was all Xandor could do to keep from being pinned and still use Kourash's colossal frame to block the Northman. He worked his way toward the window. A thrust by the giant crashed through the glass, shattering the pane.

With a snarl, Kourash shifted his attack. Xandor braced himself for the powerful blow, anticipating the worst, but the swing proved to be a feint that opened the ranger's flank. Xandor realized his error too late as the giant lunged and struck him a hard blow with his fist.

The ranger's head snapped back and slammed against the window frame. Pain instantly blossomed across Xandor's right temple and cheekbone. His vision blurred, and he fought to remain conscious.

Kourash grabbed a fistful of the ranger's shirt and shoved him out the window.

It was a three-story fall to the unyielding surface of the stone-flagged road. The Seldaehne stared out the window with an evil grin, but it turned to a frown when the ranger did not fall as expected — he simply floated down, his cloak billowing around him.

The knight was unimpressed. The man obviously had a magic trinket of some sort. It might save him from the fall but was of no consequence to what waited for him. No longer concerned with maintaining his anonymity, Marko pulled the leather cover from his shield and dropped it. Shield held high and his hand-and-a-half sword at the ready, Marko launched himself at the ranger the moment before Xandor's feet touched the ground.

8:05pm

Cold air helped clear the fog from Xandor's head, even if it did nothing for the ringing in his ears. Twisting like a cat to keep the knight in view, the ranger saw the "sleeve sinister gules on a field ermine" — the heraldic crest of the Madasgorski family, the ruling dynasty of Zhitomir. As the significance of the red sleeve reaching out from the bearer's left, or sinister, side over the black and white field registered, he had to admit that it seemed fitting — sinister indeed. Xandor had a fleeting moment to wonder what interest the knight had in this caravan before he leapt to the attack.

The ranger spun to his left to avoid the knight's initial shield rush and thrust, allowing him a shot at the knight's flank. Marko reversed his thrust into a swiping cut, making Xandor parry rather than attack.

That first strike was all the ranger needed to realize he was facing a master swordsman, making him thankful for the room to maneuver this time.

Circling, the two shifted and feinted as they looked for an opening in their opponent's defenses. An eternity seemed to pass in the few moments it took the two fighters to feel out one another's styles, strengths, and weaknesses.

A crowd of people from the tavern, drawn like scavengers to blood, began to form around the combatants. Talk increased as citizens laid wagers on the outcome. The two seemed evenly matched as stroke after stroke was dodged, blocked, or parried, but the odds were on the knight due to his armor.

"You've been trained by the Iron Tower, but you are no knight."

Xandor was surprised the knight could identify his training. True, the Iron Tower taught a rather distinctive blend of Val Maran Duo Acciaio elegance and Lundellan Två Värja economic brutality, but few swordsmen had the ambidexterity required to master the style with dual longswords. Even fewer warriors could recognize such esoteric styles.

"Who are you?" the knight snarled.

The ranger replied to the knight's question by feinting high with his left and following with a low right. Marko correctly read the move and lowered his shield to block. Instead of striking with his sword, Xandor stepped in, planted his right foot on Marko's shield just above the centerline, and shoved the knight backward. The shield's top edge pivoted back, smacking into the knight's helm with a clang. A line of blood welled across Marko's brow as he stumbled back and dropped to one knee to regain his balance.

Xandor followed up instantly with a double assault, each blade coming in from opposite sides. Marko pulled his shield high and pivoted on his knee, slashing with his bastard sword in a vicious arc at the ranger's ankles. Catching the flash of steel, Xandor leapt over and away from the cut. Both men were back on their feet in an instant, warily circling, looking for an opening in the other's defense.

A flurry of blows passed back and forth, and the sound of crashing metal rang through the dark streets. Cheers and groans erupted from the crowd as the onlookers encouraged their favorite, yet neither man seemed to be able to gain the advantage.

The ranger blocked a heavy blow at hip level with crossed blades, only to find himself buffeted by the shield. The two men were too close for the blow to cause Xandor any real damage, but it threw off the ranger's attack and forced a retreat.

Adrenaline pounded through Xandor's veins, but he knew the fight couldn't go on much longer. Even if the two of them had the stamina, he had little doubt the militsiya would be along soon. He spun both his blades, ostensibly loosening his wrists, as he circled the knight.

The scrape of Xandor's boot on the pavement echoed as he led his attack with his left hand and reverse-gripped the sword in his right for close-in slicing. Anticipating the maneuver, Marko shifted his left foot back, adjusting his stance to give himself extra room to swing the shield like a hammer, forcing Xandor to vent the fury of his attack on the shield face.

Like a hawk, the knight leapt after the ranger, sword high and shield to the fore. Marko's blade descended, and Xandor's blade rose to meet it, beating the sword aside.

Simultaneously, the ranger drove his other blade into the edge of the knight's shield, cutting through the ironbound rim and biting deep into the oak beneath.

Marko twisted the shield to bind the blade and whipped it to the left.

The maneuver almost ripped the sword from Xandor's grip, but the battered edge of the shield broke free, leaving

Marko with an eight-inch chunk of shield missing and Xandor with a sore wrist. The combatants circled each other again, Xandor twirling his swords to work out the soreness.

The ring of spectators shifted as the fighters ranged, each barely avoiding blows from the other, dodging and parrying at the last possible second.

Marko struck with an overhead swing of his sword followed by a low shield bash.

Xandor blocked the blade and braced himself for the shield blow as he brought his other blade around in a powerful arc aimed at Marko's exposed helmet. This time, however, the knight tilted his shield and struck with the edge as he lifted, catching Xandor along the ribs. The ranger's breath whooshed out, stealing enough power from his swing to allow the knight's helm to turn the sword's edge with a ringing clang, leaving a half-inch-deep dent.

Both warriors, mildly stunned, took a moment to reassess and recover. The smell of sweat and blood coated the night air, and the crowd reached a fever pitch. Marko shook his head to clear the stars as Xandor struggled to get his breathing back under control.

A scream from above drew the attention of fighters and spectators alike.

"Back off, or we'll kill the girl!"

Through the broken window, Xandor saw the bartender in the hands of one of the Northmen. He had one hand in her hair, holding her head back to draw her throat taut against his dagger. Unhappy muttering broke out among the spectators. They didn't take kindly to one of their own being threatened.

Finding he had the upper hand, Marko sneered when Xandor stopped circling and shifted back two steps.

"Let her go!" the ranger yelled over his shoulder, still facing the knight in a defensive crouch, both blades at guard positions.

"A truce, warrior?"

"A truce," Xandor replied.

Bringing up his sword, the knight saluted the ranger and signaled for his men to leave. With an evil smile, the knight disappeared into the crowd.

Xandor glanced up at the window to see the bartender standing alone, one hand on her throat, the other on the window frame. He nodded to her as he heard the sound of hoofbeats receding to the north.

With sweat dripping down his face and his swords still in his hands, Xandor stared down the road the knight and his men had taken, wondering if he should try to chase them. All around, the spectators discussed the fight, some drifting back inside the bar, others wandering off down the street. Xandor breathed heavily and knew his energy would soon start to flag. A hand on his arm snapped him out of his reverie.

"Are you alright?" the bartender asked.

"I'm fine."

"Then come inside and have a drink on the house. The militsiya will be here any minute."

He glanced at her, startled to see an angry red mark on her cheek already darkening to a bruise. One by one, he sheathed his swords, wincing as he lifted his right arm.

The bartender's eyes widened. "You're bleeding!" she exclaimed as she saw the dark stain spreading over his armor.

Xandor looked down. "Bloody hell! The bastard got me with his shield."

"Come. The least I can do is bandage that for you."

The two walked back to the tavern, the bartender staying solicitously at Xandor's side. She sent the few patrons who remained out into the street, announcing she was closing for the night. Although there were some grumbles, everyone shuffled out the door. Outside, the militsiya arrived to investigate the disturbance.

"I haven't seen you before," the young woman said. "Are you normally on the wall or the gate?"

Xandor clenched his teeth and shook his head as she helped him remove his damaged leather and the thin shirt beneath. A leather thong supporting a small, bronze Korsun cross contrasted with his pale skin.

"Neither," he replied, then hissed with a sharp intake of breath as the bartender applied a vodka-drenched towel to the wound across his ribs.

"Sorry, but the alcohol will stop any festering. Are you new here, then?"

He nodded. "Just arrived today. My name's Xandor, by the way."

The bartender smiled. "Dana. Press this towel against your side while I get my bag. You need stitches."

His eyebrows rose. "You're going to stitch me?"

"Sure. It's easier than mending a shirt."

"I'm hardly a shirt that needs mending!"

Dana laughed. "Relax. I served my two years of mandatory service in a field hospital. I know what I'm doing. Still, you should probably drink some of this," she said, handing him the vodka bottle.

8:27pm

When the Laytenant of the militsiya entered the tavern, he found Xandor sitting on top of the bar, stripped to his waist. A bottle of vodka sat open beside him, and the barkeep was putting a knot in the last of a line of stitches along his ribcage. She had Xandor hold white gauze over the wound while she wrapped a cream-colored bandage around his torso.

"I'm Laytenant Penko. Can you tell me what happened here?"

Xandor looked around and found his leather tunic. He reached inside and pulled out a folded piece of parchment, which he handed to the officer.

The Laytenant read the document and handed it back with a curt nod. "I thought so. Heard rumors one of the Kral's rangers might be in town."

The barkeep gasped, and the two men stared at her. "Sorry, I... you're a ranger? I thought you were militsiya."

"Who are you?" the officer asked brusquely.

"My name is Dana Valevataya. I own this place."

"Would you mind stepping outside please, ma'am, while I discuss what happened with the ranger? I will have one of the other officers come and take your statement."

"No, you won't," she said, waving her arms. "Have you looked upstairs? It was my home those men tore up. I have every right to know what's going on."

Xandor said, "It's alright, Laytenant. With all those people outside, there's no chance of keeping this story quiet."

Dana gave Xandor a quick nod of thanks.

"So, what happened?" Penko asked.

The ranger explained he was trailing someone of interest and that person led him to the fugitive knight — the same person responsible for attacking the patrol outside Dobrovnitsa. Xandor recounted the evening's events leading up to the fight and provided detailed descriptions of the knight's men, including the heraldic mark on the knight's shield.

"Laytenant, although that man carried a crest of nobility, I expect he is not really a knight, nor does he subscribe to the standard knight's code of honor. When we fought, his tactics were unorthodox. Not only did his men hold this woman hostage, but he used sharpened edges on his shield during the fight — something I have only seen used by Rhodinan mercenaries. The knights I know would view his tactics as dishonorable."

The officer wrote down some notes and asked, "Which way did they leave?"

"The last I saw, they disappeared north into the crowd."

The tavern door burst open, and everybody turned as a young militiaman rushed inside and said excitedly, "Sir, we found them! They're headed for the Stena."

Officer Penko nodded toward the young man. "I'll be right there. Wait outside for me."

As the young man obeyed, Xandor said to Penko, "Be careful. Those men are dangerous."

Looking at the ranger with curiosity, Laytenant Penko asked, "If you don't mind me asking, what's the Kral's interest in all this?"

Xandor jumped down from the counter and said, "Believe it or not, Laytenant, soap."

Shaking his head in disbelief, the officer turned and slowly walked to the exit. He had one hand on the door when Xandor asked, "Can you do me a favor? Please send a runner to the Stŭklena Katedrala. Tell him to find a dwarf named Chert Joalheiro. He needs to know what happened here."

"I'll send someone immediately," replied Laytenant Penko.

"Thanks."

After the officer left, Xandor reached for his blood-soaked shirt, but Dana stopped him, her fingers warm on the back of his hand.

"Where are you going?" she asked. As she said it, she stepped in close to place her other hand on his bare shoulder.

Xandor looked down into her eyes, seeing now that they were flecked with amber. Her tousled hair framed her face in a soft, golden nimbus. She was standing very close, though not quite touching him, and he could feel the magnetic energies between their bodies.

Dana ran her fingers up his arm as she raised herself on the balls of her feet, simultaneously drawing Xandor's head down toward hers. When their lips touched, energy arced between them, and her body seemed to melt against his. The ranger's arms closed around the barkeep, all thoughts of his job forgotten.

CHAPTER 21
EXIT TRAKYA

October 22, 4235 K.E.

6:50am

Up before the sun, Dragahn quickly dressed, packed his gear, and, after one final look to make sure he hadn't left anything behind, exited his room. Nodding to Grendel across the hallway, he aimed for the room a few doors down and knocked loudly.

"Pyotr, it's me. Time to wake up!" he yelled through the door. After a few moments of silence, he knocked louder. He tried the handle but found it locked. "Pyotr! You bastard! Wake up! It's time to go."

A grin appeared on Dragahn's face when he heard cursing from within. He moved to the next door and then the next, banging loudly at each one to wake his team.

Pyotr staggered out of the inn and flinched as the early morning light pierced his bloodshot eyes and throbbing head. Before he reached his wagon, Dragahn caught up to him and handed him a metal flask.

"Here, drink some of my hooch. It'll warm you up."

"Thanks, Chief."

Dragahn laughed. "Are you going to make it?"

"No one likes a wise ass this early in the morning. Of course, I'll make it," Pyotr groused. He held up the flask and said to Dragahn, "To the hair of the dog that bit me." Then he took a deep swallow, feeling the liquor burn its way down.

The last out the door, Sachin glared at the teamsters and the wagons. "Why isn't everyone ready to move?" the small man barked.

Heads turned and Dragahn's jaw tightened as he met Sachin by the bed of the center wagon. "We were awaiting your morning inspection before we mount up," the chief replied. Around them, everyone found something to do to take themselves out of Sachin's immediate reach.

Grendel stood close to his charge. He paid little heed to the tension between Sachin and Dragahn. Instead, he mulled over the conversation he'd had with Jasper earlier that morning.

Before even Dragahn had awoken, Jasper had slipped into the hallway, and they had their first real opportunity to talk. Grendel quickly explained about seeing Xandor, eliciting a sigh of relief from Jasper, and then mentioned Sachin's meeting with Marko, the knight. Jasper's face had clouded with concern, but the cook instructed the bodyguard to stay the course. His final words had been, "We still need to find the connection between this caravan and the Krakov Estate, and we can't do that if we blow our cover now. Besides, if there had been any real trouble, Chert would have found us. I'm sure he knows where we are."

Jasper's words made sense, but Grendel was still worried. He was used to dealing with issues in an open, brutal fashion. All this stealth and clandestine maneuvering was taking its toll on him.

Riding up front with Dragahn, Jasper looked forward to seeing the Stena and Vratsa Milecastle firsthand.

Using the resources of the White Circle, the Mage's guild in Upper Pazard'zhik, Jasper had read everything he could about the Stena and the lands beyond. It had once been prosperous, teeming with trade and civilization, but that was more than thirty-five years ago, before the great sickness befell the land. Before the Plague War.

As he understood it, the Plague War started with strange rumors regarding remote elven villages filled with the dead. Extremely reclusive, the northern elves rarely traded goods or left their lands, so when they fell ill, none but the animals knew it.

Next, it spread to humans. By all accounts, the disease seemed to attack those whose lives were intertwined with magic. Arcane spellcasters were the ones who suffered first and most. The more powerful they were, the faster they succumbed, and during those final stages, their lives ended in horrible, screaming deaths. However, it was not just the mages who contracted the disease. Anyone with the potential for arcane magic was struck with the malady.

As bad as those with an affinity for the arcane had it, the plague still might have gone unnoticed since there were so few of them. Then the normal folk in the towns and cities west of the White River became ill. Priests and lay healers tried every prayer, spell, and potion, but none worked. Their ministrations proved useless against this new evil, and, in the end, they too were susceptible to its deadly touch.

It did not take long for people to blame the spread of the disease on mages and the elves — the very ones who were the most vulnerable. Some of the more outspoken citizens claimed the mages were corrupting the land, and Gaia herself was seeking revenge on those who, as some put it, "raped the land and stole her power."

More and more people turned against the mages as the contagion spread. A few of the fortunate ones who were not sick were driven out, but most fell to the whims of the crowds. Witch hunts sprang up throughout the countryside. They tested everyone, no matter their age or gender, and stoned those who passed. Their bodies were returned to the earth in mass graves to "give back their magic."

Driven to hysteria, the Trakyans and Rhodinans banded together and slaughtered the magical races and the elves still living in the bountiful forests of the region. Even after three decades, some people still hunted the mages, elves, and the faerie folk, blaming them for the plague that killed their brother or sister, or their father or mother.

Into this turmoil erupted the khumanoidi. They varied in all manner of size and shape, from the lowly goblins that scavenged their food from mass graves to the giant nephilim who bathed in the blood of those they killed. Hordes of them came down from the northern tundras and razed whole towns and cities. Eastern Trakya, in its weakened state, provided no resistance to their onslaught.

An army pulled from the people of Pazard'zhik and its neighbors arrived, bringing orders from the Kral — everyone west of the White River must abandon their homes. Wealthy and poor alike packed their belongings — most taking only what they could carry on their backs — and joined the mass exodus. It became a gruesome race against death.

The khumanoidi, driven by some unknown master, ignored those who fled. Instead, they coordinated their movements and struck deeper and deeper south. The White River turned red, and the lands along its banks were no longer safe for the civilized world.

Rhodinan and Detchian countries struck treaties of cooperation and strove to defend their borders, ceding territories along the west bank of the river to the hordes just as Trakya had. Battles raged as the khumanoidi struck time and time again, striving to break the back of the resistance.

Then the plague crossed the White River and moved east. It entered into the northern territories of Detchia, and the hysteria of the masses quickly followed. The Detchian armies were broken.

Free to do as they would, the khumanoidi slaughtered their way east and south — at least until they arrived at the Alashalian Mountains. There the tide of the khumanoidi crashed against the Knights of the Iron Tower. Many a song was written during those months of fighting, but in the end, even the famed Knights were forced to retreat east.

Sutekh, the Dark One as most people referred to him, had returned, but not as an avatar. He traveled through the air and became the invisible death no one could escape. His Sha'iry walked the battlefields, raising armies of undead and using the fallen as fodder. Their black robes and two-handed swords became symbols of fear.

From the ranks of the Sha'iry rose Maa'kheru Bolezni, their high priest. He carried a sickly red orb that oozed black blood. Everywhere he went, disease crept into people's homes and rendered arcane spellcasters useless as they succumbed to its evil. The plague struck down all who stood against the Sha'iry, and there seemed no hope for the common man.

Traveling through the Alashalian Mountains, mercenary barbarians from the north, led by Jongar, bypassed the borders of Gallowen, the home of the Iron Tower, and continued south into Carolingias. With Jongar's army to the north and the Sha'iry Army to the west, York, the capital city of Carolingias, fell to the Dark One and became a spoil of war.

With the Knights of Carolingias in hiding and the queen's own champion disgraced, the Sha'iry and their henchmen dragged the king, queen, and their son onto the steps of the palace, beheaded them in front of the crowd, and drank their blood in celebration.

Bounties were placed on the royal family. Hunted and slaughtered down to the last child, it kept the Carolingian people from organizing any resistance. But the Sha'iry weren't done yet. They filled massive stone furnaces with soaring chimneys with the bodies of the dead, which they burned as sacrifices to their dark lord. Minions of the Dark One constantly threw bodies into the fire, and putrid plumes of smoke rose high in the air, day and night.

To this day, no one knows what caused the disease to stop spreading or stopped the momentum of the Sha'iry and their hordes. Some say it was because the khumanoidi had claimed enough land as their own and were stretched too thin. Others say a deal was struck between the barbarians from the north and the Highlord of the Confederation of Nations. In either case, bards sang of the return of Queen Ambrose Battenberg, the last remaining heir to the Carolingian throne, telling how, with her knights, she struck deep into the heart of the Dark One and united Carolingias.

There were also stories of a humble half-human, half-elf priest whose words shook the foundation of the earth and called down the Wrath of the Eternal Father upon the blasphemous furnaces and the dark cult. Witnesses said holy fire streaked from the heavens and blasted the chimneys along with the clerics who fed them.

In the end, the Sha'iry and their minions were driven back into secrecy and the red orb was shattered; however, the khumanoidi had found purchase in the lands immediately west of the White River and the human armies were powerless to stop them. The khumanoidi took advantage of abandoned cities and towns, and their populations swelled as they became the new masters of the fertile lands between the White River, the Sea of Grass, and the eastern borders of Trakya. The map of the world changed at the conclusion of the Plague War: borders contracted, and entire cultures found themselves on the verge of extinction. These were the lands east of the Stena.

Jasper brought up his hand to cover a low cough and wrapped his coat tighter about him as they passed under the shadow of the Milecastle.

Soldiers in sable and azure rushed forward, led by a tall man with broad shoulders, wearing plate armor.

"Back again, Dragahn?" the Keeper asked.

"This should be our last run for the year," Dragahn replied casually as he climbed down from his seat. "It won't be long until the snow. After that, everything will be covered in mud."

The Keeper laughed quietly, "You got that one right." Skimming the manifest and itinerary, he said, "You know the procedure. Have everyone move inside, and I'll tell you which crates to open."

8:08am

Proceeded by the jangle of harnesses and the rhythmic pattern of hoofbeats muffled by the short grass, the team passed through the earthen ramparts, called the Vallum, and entered the shadow of the Haunted Wood. They resumed their normal positions: the chuck wagon in front, followed by the other two wagons, while Viktor and his horsemen took charge of guarding their flanks. Dragahn kept the horses moving at a slow walk, but he had let everyone know he still wanted to cover at least thirty miles by the end of the day.

Jasper found himself constantly looking from one side to the other. Overhead, barren branches with disjointed sections gripped each other like interlocking skeletal fingers and blocked out the sun. The mage shivered, and not just from the cold air. Screaming faces in the decaying bark leered at him evilly. Always at the edge of his vision, he caught glimpses of pools of blood at the base of the trees and heard an occasional echo of a scream; however, when he glanced at Dragahn, the caravan chief seemed oblivious to the sights and sounds. He cast a quick look over his shoulder and found Grendel asleep.

Viktor rode along the left side of the chuck wagon, keeping a watchful eye on the road ahead. The horseman seemed tense, and he signaled for the others to stay alert. He openly carried a longsword at his left hip, and his yew bow with its quiver of arrows was close at hand. Maybe he felt something, too.

"Is the forest like this the whole way?" Jasper asked.

"No," Dragahn said as he looked around. "This is the worst of it. When Trakya closed the Stena, families of elves were left stranded outside the gates. Rumor is, they were slaughtered by the khumanoidi, and their ghosts still haunt these woods. But don't worry; in a couple of days, it will be more normal, and after that, we'll reach the mudpots."

"Mudpots? What's that?" Jasper asked.

"Just wait. You'll see," the chief said, amused.

"Where do we go after that?"

"We'll stop at a town just on the other side." The amusement in his voice vanished.

"Will we travel all the way to the White River?" Jasper asked.

"No. But we'll be close enough to see it."

"I'm glad I brought enough food," Jasper said, calculating.

"Me, too. Although, if we had to, Viktor's a very good hunter. I bet he could scrounge something."

Viktor smiled broadly and said, "I remember the last time you sent me out hunting. As I recall, I found two squirrels and a rabbit with a bad case of mange."

"We still ate them," Dragahn said.

"*You* ate them," Viktor corrected. "What did you expect? You had Lucky cook them."

"They were good. Even if they were a little scrawny."

"Scrawny wasn't the word for it..." With a gasp, Viktor abruptly stopped talking and hunched over, his face a mask of extreme pain.

Jasper blinked, and everything seemed to slow down. He couldn't believe his eyes as the feathered shaft of a second arrow flew in slow motion toward Viktor's chest. Time suddenly resumed its normal speed, and the arrow slammed into Viktor, knocking him from the saddle.

Dragahn made to snap the reins just as an arrow struck the hand brake at his side, the thin shaft vibrating from the impact. Another struck between him and Jasper. The warning was clear. Dragahn signaled behind him and pulled hard on the reins, halting the Percherons.

Grendel woke at the sound of Viktor hitting the ground. He looked around groggily but couldn't see past the chuck wagon. He growled and started to stand, but Sachin laid a firm hand on his arm and said with a fierce whisper, "Do not interfere, orcné. This is not your fight."

"Yes, it is," the bodyguard said.

Staring into the sleep-filled eyes of the half-orc, Sachin said, "No, it's not. If you go out there, you will only get someone killed. These men are professionals. They won't just aim at you; they will also aim at those you defend."

Grendel's eyes smoldered, burning off his sleepiness, but he remained where he was.

As if by magic, Marko appeared directly in front of the caravan, no more than thirty feet away. Behind him, Mladen and Ognian had their longbows drawn, arrows nocked and aimed at the two men in the front wagon.

Jasper couldn't help but stare at the Northmen. They had removed their shirts and exposed the markings on their upper torsos. As they walked cautiously toward the wagons, their tattoos swirled and blended with the forest, partially camouflaging them. As they passed, Kourash walked out of the woods, holding the reins to their horses. The mage refocused on the two Northmen, calculating the odds. It didn't look good.

"Comrades! It's good to see you again," Marko said with a mock bow. As he straightened, he commanded, "Don't make any sudden moves. I would hate for someone else to get hurt."

After a pause, Marko said loud enough for everyone to hear, "We are taking over this caravan!"

"*Ebi se*! This is my caravan!" Dragahn yelled.

Marko's eyes narrowed and he said, "Driver, do I need to make an example of someone else?"

Dragahn looked down at Viktor, who lay unconscious and bleeding. The Northmen closed, and Jasper judged they had everyone within easy range.

"That goes for all of you!" Marko yelled as he walked closer. "I want these wagons."

Dragahn stared daggers at the knight and said, "You will get no help from us!"

"Driver, I find myself in the fortunate position where I don't need your help," Marko explained. He spread his arms expansively and continued, "But at the same time, I'm not a cold-blooded killer. So, I'm willing to make a deal."

Looking around, Jasper saw everyone watching the chief, waiting on him to give the word.

Dragahn stared at the Northmen and then at the knight. "What kind of deal?"

Jasper heard muttering behind him. He guessed it was either Lucky or one of the younger horsemen, possibly both.

"I want you to drive these wagons down this road, just like you originally intended. Nothing more."

"What do we get?"

"Your lives, of course. In exchange for delivering these wagons, I will let you go free. However, if you resist, I will have my men kill everyone here. Got it?"

Dragahn cast a quick glance at Jasper. Despite his heart pounding in his chest, Jasper tried to appear relaxed and keep his face expressionless. He wasn't scared but the odds of surviving this trip kept dwindling. In the back of his mind, he listened for Xerxes, hoping Xandor would show up at the last second to save the day.

"Seems we have no choice," Dragahn said slowly.

"No. You don't."

Marko motioned for Kourash to come forward with their horses. He took the Frisian and mounted. The two Northmen quickly jumped into their saddles and rode to the back of the line, using their legs to guide their horses while keeping their bows ready; however, Kourash didn't follow everyone else's lead. Instead, he tied the reins of Viktor's rouncey to Dragahn's wagon. When he was done, he approached Jasper. Standing beside the wagon, he was tall enough to glare directly into the mage's face.

"We have unfinished business," he said in a deep, menacing tone.

"Knight!" Dragahn yelled before Jasper could do something stupid.

"Yes, driver?" Marko steered his horse closer to the chuck wagon.

"Keep a leash on your man here. Otherwise, we may lose the best cook this side of the White River."

Marko stared at Jasper a moment. "A cook?"

The knight looked at Kourash, questioning. The Seldaehne inhaled deeply, and a somewhat confused look came and went. "I smell spices," he said simply.

Dragahn kept an eye on his cook and said quickly, "I don't know exactly what business your friend here has in mind, but if it's what I think it is, you will miss out on some of the best-tasting food you've ever eaten. Look in the back if you don't believe me. That's all his stuff."

Marko glanced at the chuck box and said, "You'd better be right, Driver. Cook, what's your name?"

"Jasper, Sir."

"Are you as good a cook as this man says?"

"Better."

Marko gave him one of his wolfish grins and said, "We'll see." The knight motioned for Kourash to back off. "Let's go. We're burning daylight."

"What about Viktor?" Pyotr yelled out.

Marko pulled on the reins. The Frisian turned, letting the knight get a good look at the speaker. "What about him?"

"We can't just leave him here. He'll die. Dragahn, let me help him."

Marko stared hard at the horse doctor and said, "Stay where you are unless you care to join him. Driver, let's go. We need to make some time."

Dragahn turned to look at Pyotr, who was fuming. He gave him a helpless look, turned back around, and flicked the reins. As the team moved down the road, everyone gave Viktor a parting glance, hoping against hope they wouldn't be next.

CHAPTER 22
MILECASTLES AND MILESTONES

October 22, 4235 K.E.

8:37am

Chert paused in the hallway outside the third-floor apartment. Part of the door sagged on its damaged hinges, while the rest lay on the floor in splinters. In the living room, weapons, armor, and clothes lay where they fell. The dwarf followed the trail of castoffs to a darkened room where Xandor and someone else lay sleeping in the bed under a thick pile of fur blankets. The furniture looked like it had been used for sparring practice, and a heavy blanket hung on the wall. Chert walked over and peered behind the fabric to find the remains of a window where something, or someone, had been thrown out.

"Ahem."

Nothing. Just the gentle rise and fall of the blankets.

"Ahem!"

Still nothing.

He reached over and snatched the blankets off the bed. Frozen air washed over two naked bodies. The shock brought both of them wide awake, and angry protests filled the room.

"It's time we were leaving, Xandor."

The ranger opened his mouth to argue, but when Chert held aside the makeshift curtain to reveal the growing daylight, he closed it. Xandor turned his gaze to the blushing woman at his side. She had managed to retrieve a portion of her blankets, but his mind's eye saw the curves of her body. He shook his head to clear it.

"The caravan left over an hour ago," Chert said.

"What?! It can't be that late!"

"Well, I would have been here sooner, but I received a message from Marcus."

Xandor rolled out of bed and collected his discarded clothing and weapons.

"What did he have to say?"

"The note was brief. Apparently, a plague has struck Upper Pazard'zhik. They aren't sure what's causing it, and the healers are at a loss as to how to cure it. Several members of the royal family are deathly ill. Whatever it is, Marcus has it too."

"Marcus? Are you sure?"

"Aye. The message said he's been coughing a lot, and he's developed sores on his skin that won't heal. He's even spit up some blood. It's like whatever's ailing him is eating him from the inside out."

Xandor made a face. "Ugh. Did he say how this might be related to our mission?"

"Not really, other than to say they were investigating common denominators and our soap was on the list. One of many."

"That narrows it down," Xandor said sarcastically.

"There's something else. They found Sachin's body."

"What?! Where's Grendel?"

Chert held his hands up to calm Xandor and said, "You don't understand. Dockworkers fished Sachin's body from the River Maritsa."

"Then who was I following last night?"

"I don't know."

10:18am

Sable and azure flags fluttered in the frigid breeze, marking the border to the land ruled by the Kral. Xandor and Chert stood twenty-five feet in the air atop a stone tower. Below them was the famous milecastle of Vratsa.

At first glance, Xandor had to admit he was not impressed. The milecastle consisted of a simple, gated courtyard surrounded by crenelated walls of stone. Its footprint measured roughly fifty feet by sixty feet and housed several support buildings for the garrison manning the Stena. However, when he turned and looked to the north and south, he quickly revised his opinion. The line of the Stena traveled endlessly over hills and into valleys.

The curtain wall stood twelve to fifteen feet high, and men armed with long halberds patrolled the battlements. A third of a mile away in each direction, a single turret defended its portion of the wall.

Xandor reflected on the morning's events. Dana had sent him on his way with an ardent kiss and an admonition to catch the bastards who wrecked her home. Although she hadn't blamed him, Xandor felt responsible and arranged to have the apartment repaired.

Through the militsiya, he commandeered a small, light reddish-brown pony for Chert. The dwarf had protested heavily when he saw the beast but seemed to concede when Xandor reminded him of the lengthening gap between them and the caravan. They needed to move faster to have any hope of stopping the wagons. Xandor suspected their conversation was not over yet, because the normally stubborn dwarf had given in far too easily.

In the distance, four lopsided peaks pierced the eastern sky. Xandor studied the dark trees beyond the Vallum. These weren't young trees like those in the Silva Nigra. These were old, gnarled hardwoods with branches that overhung the road. The harder he stared, the more he thought he saw faces in the bark — inhuman faces that screamed in agony. He had heard rumors in Pazard'zhik about the Haunted Wood, but until he saw it with his own eyes, he had taken them as just that — rumors.

"I don't like those trees, Xandor," Chert said, his breath forming a white cloud. The dwarf had cleaned and polished his chain and plate armor. Under his arm, his horned great helm shimmered. Neither man nor dwarf were concerned with stealth anymore.

"You haven't liked any of the trees we've come across."

"Aye, but I really don't like *those* trees."

"Maybe it's just your imagination," Xandor said hopefully.

"Now, that's a load of scrap metal. Dwarves don't *have* imaginations, and even I can see those faces."

Xandor looked down at the dwarf and said dourly, "We still have to go down there."

"I know."

Taking a deep breath, Xandor inhaled the crisp morning air. He knew he needed to stop the caravan. The knowledge someone was impersonating Sachin troubled him deeply.

Grendel and Jasper could be in grave danger, and he didn't know what Sachin and Marko were planning. The report he had left behind for Marcus said as much.

"Let's go," Xandor said finally.

Their horses were saddled and waiting for them down in the courtyard. At the sight of Xandor coming out of the tower, Xerxes pawed the ground, obviously anxious to be on the road again. *'Of course, he hasn't seen the trees yet,'* Xandor thought to himself. The pony, on the other hand, cast dubious looks at her rider.

Chert and the pony faced each other. Immediately, everyone in the courtyard felt the tension in the air. The soldiers stationed at the milecastle stifled laughs. No one could tell if the two were simply sizing each other up, or if there was going to be a fight.

For his part, the dwarf looked ready for battle. The long horns affixed to his great helm added a foot to his short stature, and the ancient chain armor that peeked out from his heavy cloak whispered with his every move. In his left hand, he held at the ready a small, round steel shield emblazoned with the silhouette of a mountain. His right was empty, but it itched for the ornately inscribed hammer that hung through a belt loop.

The bay Connemara stood only thirteen-and-a-half hands at the withers, but her head still towered over the dwarf. Xandor had chosen the Connemara because they were a strong and sturdy breed, considered agile and with good jumping ability. They were also known to be excellent mounts for children, but watching the two, the ranger began to have misgivings.

"There's no way you are getting me on that beast," Chert said through gritted teeth.

"Chert, we talked about this, remember?" Xandor said patiently.

The Connemara's powerful hindquarters tensed as the pony assumed an aggressive stance. She stomped the ground nervously and gave a loud snort. Xandor stepped between the two before they escalated into all-out warfare. He put a hand on the pony's muzzle and said calmly, "Sky

Una." The pony looked at the ranger, and her muscles relaxed slightly.

"Sky, you must carry this dwarf. We have friends in danger, and we cannot get there without your help."

Chert started to say something to the contrary, but Xandor silenced him with a quick motion of his hand. The pony stared past the ranger at the dwarf, and she reluctantly nodded her head, giving a small nickering noise. Keeping his voice neutral, the ranger said, "Alright, Chert, it's up to you. This girl knows what to do. All you have to do is hold on, keep your balance, and stay in the saddle."

The dwarf stepped closer to the ranger and whispered, "Xandor, I don't know if I can do this."

"You must.

"You don't understand. I'm a creature of the earth. My feet *always* touch the ground."

"Do it for Grendel."

Chert nodded curtly. He knelt down and picked up a small handful of dirt. Rubbing his hands together, he approached the pony and gingerly stepped into the stirrup, hoisting himself into the saddle. It wasn't pretty, and Chert nearly fell twice, but with Xandor's help, he managed to stay seated. With the dwarf's inexperience and heavy armor in mind, Xandor hoped to get a knight's saddle with a high pommel and cantle, but there wasn't one small enough for the pony. Instead, he acquired a saddle based on the Korellan four-horn design.

"Just remember, Chert, this pony knows what she's doing. Give her the benefit of the doubt, and she'll not fail you."

Xandor could not see the dwarf's expression through the slits of the great helm, but he knew fear when he smelled it, and so did the pony. Chert white-knuckled the saddle horns and breathed deeply through his nose. Xandor wondered if he should tie the dwarf in place.

Meanwhile, if Xerxes had been less of a horse, he would have been rolling on the ground laughing. Justice had finally come to the small, irritating man.

The soldiers struggled, and those who could not keep a straight face made themselves scarce. All except for the milecastle commander, who approached Xandor before he could mount up.

"Ranger, are you chasing the Zhitomiran knight?"

"Yes and no," Xandor replied, his mind still focused on watching the dwarf handle riding the pony.

"Well, there's something you need to know."

Xandor turned to look at the commander.

"I don't know if you knew Laytenant Penko or not, but he was with the militsiya patrol chasing the fugitive knight through the city last night." He gestured south. "I was on the ramparts when they reached the base of the Stena. Instead of being trapped, the knight threw something at the wall, and a bright, yellow light erupted, forming a large hole. The knight and his men raced through the opening and out the other side.

"Laytenant Penko and two of his men were right behind them. They followed them into the light, but they never made it out the other side."

Xandor eyes went wide at the news. "What happened to Laytenant Penko and his men?"

The commander's face darkened as he said, "The opening was temporary. After the knight and his men passed through, it closed. When the stone blocks filled back in, those three men and their horses became trapped inside.

"Ranger, the knight and his men could have escaped through the wall at any time, but they intentionally waited for someone to follow them through. I heard the men and horses screaming as the milestones fused with their arms and legs." Rage filled the commander's words. "I believe there is a special circle of hell set aside for evil like theirs. If you find them, remember what they've done."

"I will, Commander," Xandor said as he mounted Xerxes.

CHAPTER 23
THE HAUNTED WOOD

October 22, 4235 K.E.

10:43am

Xandor led Sky through the passage within the main tower, under murder holes and the viciously spiked bars of the heavy portcullis suspended above them. Once past the Stena, they followed the causeway across the Vallum.

Thirty feet from the wall, they passed the first bulwark, a six-foot high embankment that immediately dropped off into a twenty-foot-wide by ten-foot-deep ditch filled with sharpened wooden stakes. Hooves slowly pounding across wooden planks, the two continued to the other side, where the causeway sliced through a four-foot-high mound embedded with crisscrossed stakes along the top. On the other side, the land sloped steeply, adding to the defenses of the Stena against any invaders from the forest.

At the edge of the Haunted Wood, they stopped. All the trees were dead. Everywhere they looked, decaying bark clung like a disease to the hardwoods. Cracked boughs supported barren branches that splayed out in odd directions, like disjointed fingers. From within their shadow came an undercurrent of something watching and waiting. There was anger here, and a looming threat of death.

Xandor generally found himself refreshed when entering a forest, but not this time. Even the sunlight dimmed along the road as though it did not feel safe within the trees. Here and there, bottomless pools of shadow obscured the forest floor as effectively as the blackest night. The ranger caught himself rubbing his Korsun cross between his thumb and forefinger. These trees looked like they all died at the same time. Only the Plague Wastes along the southern border of his homeland in the Alashalian Mountains came close to the same level of eeriness, although the Wastes lacked the air of impending doom present here.

Chert looked around, not saying anything. His initial impressions of the trees did not improve; if anything, they grew worse. His forte was metal and stone; the trees and their maladies were a mystery to him.

Both Xerxes and Sky cast dubious looks at the forest. Sky snorted and shook her mane as her pace slowed, and Xerxes looked back at his rider as if questioning the man's sanity. Xandor made reassuring sounds and gave both animals pats on their necks.

Feeling the need to be moving before fear infected the horses, the ranger handed Sky's reins to Chert. "Remember, trust your pony."

"Easy for you to say."

The ranger directed Xerxes into the Haunted Wood. As they traveled deeper into the dark forest, noises from above assailed the two riders. Boughs creaked and groaned though there was no hint of wind.

Brown grass covered the roadway. Along the edges, piles of brambles and sticks lay heaped haphazardly, leaving Xandor to wonder who had taken the time to clear away the debris.

The two continued slowly for the first mile while Xandor leaned forward in the saddle, studying tracks and signs. He estimated the wagons were only a few hours ahead. Unfortunately, the knight and his men were ahead of the caravan.

Xandor straightened in the saddle and made a loud clicking sound as he touched his heels to Xerxes' sides. His mount leapt forward to chase down the caravan, with Sky a pace behind. A loud crash brought the three to a halt. The ranger looked back and saw Chert sprawled in the middle of the road like a turtle flipped on its back.

Amidst the grumbling and Chert's cursing of all four-legged creatures, Xandor said, "You have to hold on."

"The blasted creature dropped me!"

Sky looked as if she might trample the hapless dwarf, so Xandor jumped down to interpose himself between them.

"Sky!" Xandor said sternly and pointed next to Xerxes. "Stay!"

"Chert, get up and get back on that pony. We aren't going to catch the caravan if you can't hold on."

"I know. I'm sorry, Xandor," Chert said as he picked himself up.

"Don't tell me, tell Sky."

Chert glared at the pony suspiciously.

"No way am I going to apologize to that beast."

Xandor looked at them both. "Sky didn't drop you; you fell. Get over there and apologize, or we might as well pack up and go back to Vratsa."

Grumbling, Chert walked up to Sky and said something incoherent. Sky looked to Xandor for a translation.

"I think that was his apology," Xandor said with a shrug.

The bay pony gave the dwarf a skeptical look, but she nodded and stepped closer to him. Grabbing the saddle horns, Chert hauled himself up.

"Are we ready this time?" Xandor asked as he mounted his saddle.

"Aye, I'm ready," the dwarf grumbled.

Xandor made a clicking noise with his mouth, and the horse and pony both cantered into the forest. Chert held on this time, both hands tight on the saddle.

Without warning, Xandor raised his fist and signaled for Sky to halt. Up ahead through the dim light, the ranger spied several turkey vultures waiting in the trees. Their brownish-black wings blended with their surroundings, but their bald, red heads made them stand out. Signaling the horses to proceed cautiously, Xandor rode several more steps before spotting something on the road.

The ranger and the dwarf dismounted and approached a body adorned with a pair of feathered arrows. Senses alert and weapons ready, Xandor scanned the forest, anticipating an ambush, but nothing was there.

Chert took off his gloves, leaned down, and checked the horseman's vitals. He was still alive, but barely.

One arrow protruded from just below his collarbone. The other had driven completely through his kneecap and poked out the back side of his leg. From the feel of him, the horseman's internal body temperature was lower than normal. He had lost a lot of blood from his wounds, and his colder inner core was not letting the blood clot.

"He's too cold," the dwarf muttered. Chert closed his eyes, laid his hands near the uppermost wound, and prayed. A bright blue light spread from his touch and enveloped the man's entire body. The light faded. Chert opened his eyes and laid a hand on the horseman's brow. As he waited, Xandor paced back and forth, watching over Chert's shoulder, anxious to get back on the road.

"You're hovering," Chert said to the ranger. "Go check for tracks or something."

"What are you waiting for? Shouldn't you pull those arrows out?"

"If I take them out now, I'll kill him."

"Whatever you're doing, hurry it up. They're getting away."

"Can't do that, either. Even with the Eternal Father's help, his body temperature has to rise slowly."

Xandor stalked away, staring intently down the East Road.

A few minutes later, blue light pooled around the two wounds. Still with one hand on the man's brow, Chert reached up and grasped the arrow. The dwarf's muscles bulged as he yanked it out, revealing a wickedly barbed steel arrowhead. Blood gushed. Dropping the shaft, Chert placed both his hands over the wound and prayed. Blue light spread throughout the man's body. The wound closed, but the horseman did not regain consciousness.

Chert opened his eyes and focused his attention on the knee. It wasn't bleeding as badly, but the joint was obviously shattered. "Xandor, I can take out the arrow and fix the entry and exit wounds, but he'll probably remain unconscious for some time."

"Do what you can," Xandor said. Out of the corner of Chert's eye he saw the ranger investigating the tracks on the ground. As he read the signs, the ranger said aloud, "He was shot off his horse and landed where we found him." Kneeling to get a better look at the road, the ranger studied a disturbed area. He pushed aside a patch of brown grass and fingered the bent blades. "That knight and his manservant were here."

Blocking out Xandor's voice, Chert forced the arrow farther through the knee before using his knife to cut the thin shaft directly above the arrowhead. Next, he placed one hand on the shaft just under the feathers and the other on the leg. As gently as he could, he slid out the remaining piece of wood in one smooth motion. He laid the shaft beside his knife, placed both hands on the knee, and prayed. Blue light spread and grew stronger, enveloping the entirety of his knee.

"I've done all I can. The rest is up to him and the Eternal Father," Chert said, rising. "He really needs to go back to Vratsa."

Xandor stopped looking at the ground and stared at the dwarf.

"You can take him. Just let Sky do all the work."

"Not with me trying to hold him," the dwarf said quietly. "Xandor, I'm worried about Grendel and Jasper, too, but I can't leave this man here, and I can't save him alone."

The ranger's eyes closed briefly as he fought an internal battle against frustration and anger.

"Fine," he said. His voice held a hardness that wasn't there before. "We'll head back."

2:52pm

It took the better part of three hours to return Viktor to the garrison at Vratsa and deliver him to the nearest kŭshta na iztselenie. Xandor paced the hall outside the wardroom where Chert and a group of healers examined the horseman. Finally, the dwarf emerged with an elderly man in clerical robes and the deep blue stole of a senior healer.

"Monsen'or Bansko, may I introduce Xandor ap Kynan, a ranger serving the Kral," Chert said.

"Thank you," the priest said. "Viktor would have perished without your help."

"May I see him? Is he able to answer questions?" the ranger asked.

Monsen'or Bansko held up a placating hand. "Patience is paramount, especially with cases like this, since even a partial recovery can take quite some time. After all, Viktor has survived a near-death experience."

"Isn't there anything you can do, Monsen'or? He could have information vital to my mission for the Kral."

"I'm sorry, but it could be several days before he regains consciousness. The best thing for him is rest. To force him awake at this point would be detrimental to his recovery."

Xandor's fist clenched at his side, but he said nothing. Instead, he gave the healer a curt nod and strode from the House of Healing. Behind him, he heard Chert murmur a goodbye and hurry after him. On the stoop, the ranger spun on his heel and slammed the side of his fist against the wall.

"I'm sorry, Xandor."

He exhaled noisily, forcing out his frustration. "There's nothing left to do but hurry and catch that caravan."

"Then let's get to it."

The two hoisted themselves back into their saddles and raced across the Vallum into the Haunted Wood. It didn't take long for them to reach the point where they had originally found Viktor. Xandor slowed and hung low in the saddle as they rode past.

"They've increased their speed."

"What does that mean?"

Xandor quickly calculated when they could intercept the wagons. All total, he figured they were at least six hours behind. By himself, he could have easily made up most of the lost time, but with the dwarf, he hoped to simply keep pace and catch up to them after dark. The ranger straightened in the saddle, held Sky's reins tightly, and said, "Chert, hold on. We need to make tracks."

The dwarf wasn't quite sure what the ranger meant, but he had a sinking feeling he was about to find out. Chert gripped his saddle and held on tightly. "I'm ready, Xandor."

Xerxes bounded forward, followed closely by Sky. Chert tried to mimic the ranger's profile and lean into the wind, but after ten minutes of racing down the roadway, his posture and profile resembled a sack of potatoes.

CHAPTER 24
THE KISS OF DEATH

October 22, 4235 K.E.

3:04pm

The Percherons had no trouble keeping up with the fast pace Marko set. The dead trees passed in a blur, and Jasper couldn't help but feel the knight wasn't just in a hurry. He was running from something — or someone.

The teamsters did not fare any better than Chert. The increased speed caused every bump and rut to resonate, and Dragahn swore under his breath each time the wagon jostled or groaned.

Their afternoon break was a quick affair that only served to increase the tension between the two groups. Jasper distributed dry rations and tins filled with water while Teodor and Branimir fed the horses. Marko informed everyone they didn't have time to unhitch the horses, so Pyotr and Andrei spent their time rubbing them down and applying poultices to spots rubbed raw by the harnesses.

During the stop, Marko and Kourash constantly kept an eye on the road, checking to see if anyone followed. The knight seemed extremely agitated about the delay, and within the half-hour, they were back on the road racing east.

4:26pm

To the north, four crooked peaks topped a thirty-mile-long mountain range. Lacking any foothills, they rose sharply above the dead trees. Dragahn and his team of wagons passed three of the four, and still Marko looked harried. It wasn't until they passed the fourth mountain an hour later that the knight seemed to calm. He finally called a halt with the sun dipping precariously in the western sky.

The Percherons' coats were glossy from sweat. Pyotr and the horsemen quickly unhitched them and gave each animal a rubdown while the others unloaded their gear.

Jasper retrieved several pounds of pork tenderloin from one of the covered pans. He had planned to save it, but if this was going to be his last meal, he wanted it to be a good one. He scrounged around the wagon and found a dozen small red potatoes along with some carrots and a medium-sized sweet onion. The cook smiled when he looked around and saw Lucky already setting up the grill, but his smile quickly disappeared when Kourash appeared at the end of the chuck wagon. The Seldaehne made it obvious he was watching every move the cook made. *'Fine,'* Jasper thought. *'Let him look.'*

The cook walked to the fire and handed the items to Lucky. "Here, cut this meat into inch-thick strips, then wash these vegetables and cut them up for me. I'll be right back."

Not giving the young man time to protest, Jasper walked toward Kourash. The Seldaehne looked amused but let the portly cook pass without a word. Jasper filled a large bowl with zucchini, speckled butter beans, and several dark red tomatoes. Retrieving a Detchian campfire oven from the chuck box, he carried everything to the fire. Kourash followed close behind, observing everything the cook did.

"Go find someone else to watch," Jasper finally said to the Seldaehne.

Kourash pointed and said, "What do you wear?"

Jasper patted his tunic. "Clothes," he responded.

"No. I mean your purse."

Jasper looked down at his sporran and held it up. "You mean this?"

Kourash nodded.

"It's not a purse; it's called a sporran."

"I do not care what it's called. What is in it?"

Jasper opened the pouch to reveal two books and a jumble of small, oval and rectangular snuff boxes. "Cookbooks and spices," he said.

"Cookbooks? Let me see," Kourash said reaching out. Jasper handed him one. The Seldaehne skimmed the pages, but his expression made it clear that he didn't really know what he was looking at.

With a final humpf, Kourash held out the cookbook to Jasper. Before Jasper could touch it, Kourash let the book fall to the ground. A harsh grating sound leaked from the

Seldaehne's throat as he walked away. It took Jasper a moment to realize the humanoid creature was laughing. Trying to ignore Kourash, he knelt and picked up his book. Brushing the dirt off the cover with his sleeve, he slid it back into his sporran.

After washing his hands, Jasper placed the cast iron oven on the grill, drizzled olive oil inside, then added the chopped onion and two cloves of minced garlic. He stirred them around in the sizzling oil until the onions were clear, then added a handful of flour, along with a measure of both salt and white pepper.

Lucky eyed the pot uncertainly.

"It's called roux," Jasper explained. "A little technique for starting gravy that I picked up in Francesca. Watch and learn."

Jasper added water to the pot a little at a time, stirring constantly. The browned flour drank the liquid and fluffed up like a cake at first, then slowly transformed into a thick sauce as Jasper continued to add water. Once satisfied, Jasper allowed Lucky to add the potatoes and carrots. Next, he placed the strips of tenderloin inside, chopped the remaining vegetables atop the meat, and covered the pot with a heavy lid. "We'll let that simmer a bit," he said. "Why don't you go set up your tent and bedroll."

Approaching the campfire, Marko inhaled deeply and said, "That smells good."

"It'll be ready in about an hour," Jasper said to everyone.

It seemed the normalcy of the evening meal relaxed the teamsters a little, but Jasper could tell everyone was scared — everyone except Sachin and Grendel. The two remained aloof, and for some reason, Marko did not seem to care or be concerned.

When supper was ready, Jasper pulled out a stack of bowls and several loaves of bread before tapping his ladle against the oven's iron lid as a dinner bell. The teamsters lined up. Jasper began filling bowls while Lucky passed out tin cups of water.

Noticing the activity, the knight cut in line and said to Jasper, "This better be good."

Jasper handed him a plate, but Marko shook his head and said, "You first."

The cook dipped a small chunk of bread in the bowl, scooping up a bit of potato and pork. Popping them in his mouth, he chewed slowly, and exaggerated the motion as he swallowed. "There. Satisfied?"

His eyes never leaving those of the cook, Marko grabbed the bowl from Jasper and tried it. Arms crossed, Kourash stood behind the cook, waiting for Marko's decision.

"Not bad," the knight grudgingly admitted. "Let's see what he cooks tomorrow."

Jasper let out a sigh of relief.

Kourash stepped closer to the cook and whispered low enough so no one else could hear, "You're mine, Cook. It's only a matter of time."

Jasper watched the Seldaehne walk away before handing a dish to the next teamster in line. He tried to make small talk as they waited their turn, but the conversations dried up after the first few words. After he served the last teamster, Jasper portioned out some food into two bowls and headed toward Sachin's tent.

Grendel was leaning against a wagon when Jasper approached. The giant's hands never strayed far from his axe handle and his eyes constantly followed Marko and his bodyguard. Jasper handed him the food. When Grendel didn't say anything, Jasper turned to leave. Before he had taken his first step, he heard Grendel whisper harshly, "You should have done something when you had the chance. This charade of yours is going to get these people killed."

5:30pm

With the level terrain, Xandor and Chert made excellent time down the roadway. They had just passed the second mountain when the sun dropped below the horizon, and the temperature dropped with it. The trees gave off an ominous feeling as the shadows deepened, something that only worsened the farther they went. They had seen no animals and heard no calls, which set them both on edge.

The colors of the western sky began a rapid transition from the red orange of sunset to the dark blue of night.

"Chert, how good is your eyesight?" Xandor asked, noticing the golden color of the dwarf's eyes when they occasionally shined in the evening light.

"Getting better," he replied.

"Is it good enough to keep us on the road?"

"You won't be able to go as fast, but aye, its good enough to keep going."

Stars dotted the evening sky, making it look like the forest was staring down at them with cold white eyes. Behind the trees loomed the third mountain.

Without warning, splintering wood and snapping branches shattered the eerie quiet. A tree crashed across the road, causing Xerxes and Sky to rear and shy away.

Chert shouted in surprise as he tumbled backward and landed with a loud clatter.

Not able to see, Xandor hugged his horse and murmured unintelligible words, the sound keeping both animals from panicking.

Xerxes gave a warning snort just before sounds of movement reached the ranger from both sides of the road. Giving Xerxes a quick pat on the neck, Xandor slid out of the saddle and drew his swords.

"Forest trolls," Chert spat.

"Trolls? How many?"

"Three."

"Where did they come from?"

"Is that a religious question?"

Xandor didn't respond. Instead, he shouted, "Aduro!" Instantly, golden flames engulfed the blades of his swords, illuminating the road and woods around him. An inhuman scream echoed off the trees as the firelight silhouetted two trolls standing at the edge.

Large, clawed hands shielded their faces. Each stood more than eight feet tall. Their ruddy skin sagged in fatty rolls from their jowls and down the length of their torsos to drip over animal-hide breeches. Dull, black eyes glared at the ranger, darting to and fro in time with the dance of the fiery swords.

"Come on!" Xandor yelled as he swung his longswords back and forth, his Alashalian accent becoming thicker. The flames whipped as the blades cut through the air, causing shadows to jump from tree to tree. Behind him, Xandor heard the quick rush of wind, followed by a dull thud and thunderous crack. Loud, guttural yowls erupted from the other side of the road.

"Stick your nose out again!" Chert challenged.

Small boulders, each about a foot in diameter, flew out of the woods toward the ranger.

Xandor ducked his head and rolled his shoulders to avoid the projectiles. As he started to straighten, a massive foot kicked out toward his face. Passing his right leg behind his left, the ranger let the foot slip past and stomp the grassy road beside him. Xandor twisted at the hip, plunging his burning blade into the troll. The creature's flaccid skin blistered and oozed viscous, pale liquid.

The troll shrieked and reached for the ranger, its wide-open mouth revealing teeth filed to jagged points.

Instead of staying in front of the creature, Xandor spun sideways on his heel and let it rush by, yanking out his sword in the process. Turning, he followed up with a left-handed slash, cutting deeply into the troll's side.

The creature howled in pain as the skin melted away and fat boiled from the wound.

Without warning, the other troll grabbed Xandor from behind, sending one of his blades spinning away. Its flame winked out the moment it left his hand.

The ranger staggered under the troll's weight and almost retched as its foul stench engulfed him. Strong arms squeezed the air from his lungs. In front of him, the injured troll stopped thrashing and turned around.

Black spots formed in Xandor's vision as the troll lifted him off the ground. Struggling to not lose his other blade, he jabbed it toward the troll's head. Then, reversing the grip on his weapon, Xandor dug the tip of his sword into the troll's thigh.

Letting go with a screech, the troll reeled backward. Before Xandor escaped the reach of its gangly arms, it threw a wild swipe and caught the ranger on the side of the head, its claws leaving three bloodied scratches.

Swinging his sword back and forth, Xandor tried to distract the two creatures and keep them at bay long enough to catch his breath.

Both trolls respected the fiery blade enough to keep their distance, but the ranger knew it was temporary. He cast a quick glance around and saw Chert faring a little better. His shorter stature made it hard for the third troll to pin him down, and every time it tried, his hammer lashed out.

With a savage yell, Xandor leapt toward the troll on his right, and, with a perfectly timed two-handed slash, completely severed its leg at the knee. The troll lost its balance and fell over with a gurgled scream.

On his left, the other troll charged.

Hard pressed to avoid the flailing claws, Xandor ducked under one, but the other caught him with a glancing blow, knocking him off his feet and throwing him into the woods.

Xandor heard the slapping of naked feet as the troll raced toward him. Taking a quick look around, he got his bearings and managed to pick himself up in time to avoid being trampled. The ranger grinned viciously, tucked and rolled back onto the road, and came up with his lost sword. The blade ignited.

"Troll, your death awaits!" Xandor taunted in Alashalian.

In response, the troll at the edge of the trees picked up another boulder and threw it.

Xandor dodged right, feeling the stone pluck at his cloak as it hurtled past. Anticipating another incoming stone, the ranger spun back to face the thrower; as he did so, motion in the corner of his eye caught his attention. Glancing down, he saw the grasping hand of the one-legged troll reaching for his left ankle. With a cry of surprise, the ranger leapt away before the fell beast snagged him.

Between the crash of his hammer and the smack of his shield against troll-flesh, Chert shouted, "Would you quit playing?"

"Who's playing?" Xandor growled.

Another boulder flew toward Xandor, and the ranger danced out of the way. The rock sailed past, shattering the trunk of one of the barren trees. The ranger backed into the woods opposite the troll and let out a sharp whistle.

Clutching a length of splintered wood as thick as Xandor's upper arm, the troll stalked onto the road but kept just outside the firelight. Malevolent eyes glared at the man and dwarf.

Xandor circled the closest tree, entering the road between Chert and the troll. Step by step, he pushed forward, forcing the troll down the road.

With all the strength he could muster, Xerxes struck out with his rear hooves, planting them squarely in the troll's back. Arms whirling, the creature flew toward the ranger. Xandor stood ready. Twin arcs of flame swept forward. The ranger pivoted on the ball of his left foot as the troll plunged into his trap and past. Xandor's swords crossed paths and reversed directions without stopping. He finished his turn with each blade in a guard position, one high and one low, ready for another attack. The troll landed in three distinct pieces.

Everything grew still, punctuated by the sizzle of the troll's skin.

A slow scraping sound echoed from the trees. Xandor turned and found the one-legged troll crawling toward him. The creature snarled and rolled to a sitting position, lobbing a stone at the ranger's head, but the throw was clumsy, and the stone flew wide. The troll's dark eyes simmered with hate as it watched the grim ranger approach. Before the creature could stand, Xandor formed an X with his swords and beheaded it. The head rolled to the roadside, its eyes still glaring. The rest of the body spasmed and jerked as it fell away.

Chert watched the life fade from the scowling troll head, then turned to Xandor. "Do you think someone sent them?"

In response, an aethereal wind howled through the trees. They swayed back and forth, their boughs creaking as their branches knocked against one another. The air turned icy, and the rage of the Haunted Wood pressed against the two warriors and their horses from all sides. Dark, malevolent faces with red eyes loomed eerily in the firelight of Xandor's blades.

Chert hurried over, his hammer and shield covered in bloody pulp. Behind him, the pulverized remains of his troll lay scattered about. He looked around uncertainly and said, "I don't like this."

Black spectral shapes closed about them. Their bodies absorbed the warmth from Xandor's blades, extinguishing them.

With frozen hilts burning his hands through his gloves, Xandor slashed at one of the dark forms. His blade passed right through without stopping. Cold breath kissed his face, and the cloying scent of death filled his nostrils, overwhelming his senses. His lungs fought for air as fiery pain blossomed in his throat and chest.

Then, it was gone.

Falling to his knees, Xandor gasped in a lungful of cold, fresh air, and relief flooded the ranger. His entire body ached, and all he wanted to do was curl up and rest. Instead, he forced his head to turn. Beside him, Chert was on his hands and knees, his lips moving in a silent prayer. A soft azure glow enveloped him.

Xerxes and Sky stood nearby, the wild look in their eyes speaking volumes.

Out of the trees, slim, pale figures surrounded the dark specters, and the two aethereal forces clashed. Black voids and brilliant white lights filled the forest.

Xandor and Chert huddled in the middle of the road with the horses, not daring to move.

The feeling of rage grew, along with an undercurrent of sadness. Silent flashes illuminated the swaying of the trees and the twisting of the limbs. Faster and faster, the lights flashed until Xandor and Chert had to cover their eyes.

As quickly as it arrived, the rage fled, leaving only profound sadness. With it, an eerie calmness reigned, and the two warriors slowly peeked to see who had won.

It was hard to make out individual features, but the ranger had the distinct impression the ghostly figures surrounding them were elves. Their mouths formed words, but neither the dwarf nor the ranger could make out what they said.

The ghosts drew closer, their cold, inner light consuming the bodies of the trolls, turning them to dust. Xandor and Chert grabbed both Xerxes and Sky's reins and backed away, careful not to touch the light. Behind them, more ghosts appeared from the Haunted Wood. Just before the four ran out of room, the ghosts stopped and formed a circle around them.

"What are we supposed to do?" Chert asked quietly, hefting his hammer in anticipation of another fight.

"You're the priest. Don't you know how to deal with ghosts?" Xandor whispered back.

"Sure, if you want me to give them their last rites."

"Do you think that's what they want?"

"How should I know?"

Looking around, it was difficult for Xandor to tell. The ghosts seemed to be staring at the two warriors, weighing them — wanting something. Hate filled their eyes, but it was tempered by tremendous sadness.

Chert switched to the musical language of the elves and said, "Friður sé með þér," in a halting voice. *Peace be with you.*

The simple elven phrase sent a ripple of motion through the ghostly figures. In the blink of an eye, the elves disappeared, and the four were left alone in the dark.

Xandor's swords reignited, the golden firelight driving off the frigid cold.

"What was that all about?" Xandor asked when he finally found his voice.

The dwarf shrugged.

Xandor extinguished his blades, and Xerxes and Sky whinnied nervously in the darkness. The ranger took out his stylus, shook it to light it, and checked the horses for injuries.

Beside him, Chert fished around in his pouch and pulled out several small jars of ointment and some bandages. "Xandor, let's take a look at those scratches on your face." The ranger knelt beside Chert and waited patiently while the dwarf cleaned and doctored his wounds.

"I hate the way this stuff smells," Xandor said while Chert rubbed a healing salve into the scratches.

"Just count yourself lucky the troll didn't rip your ear off."

Chert made Xandor stand and turn around. "Do you hurt anywhere else?"

"Just my shoulder."

"I don't see any blood, but better safe than sorry."

After handing the dwarf his stylus, Xandor removed his leather jerkin and wool undershirt. Chert made him kneel again while he inspected his shoulder. "You're going to have some serious bruises by morning, but you'll live."

"I guess we're done for the night," Xandor said as he redressed.

After a few hours of twisting and turning, Xandor gave up on sleep. The feeling of being watched kept him awake. He looked around for the hundredth time, but there was nothing there — only the pitch black of the forest. Even the stars seemed farther away. Slipping out of his bedroll and pulling out his journal and stylus, Xandor started writing.

Chert groaned as he awoke and stretched. "I'm getting too old for this."

Xandor stopped and quirked an eyebrow at the dwarf. "How old are you?"

Holding up his hand to count his fingers, Chert answered, "Sixty-two."

"Wow, you are old."

Chert laughed. "Not really. Some dwarves live over four hundred years. My great-grandfather's four-hundred-fortieth birthday is next month. I'm sure everyone will be there."

"You miss your family, don't you?"

Chert said sadly, "I'm one of the last Joalheiro." He reached into his pouch and pulled out an ugly-looking red rock with jagged edges. Rubbing it with his fingers, the dwarf said, "Stonework is a gift given to my clan by the Eternal Father." Small bits of red dust sprinkled the ground as he continued working the stone. Finally, he stopped and handed it to the ranger. "Here, take it."

Xandor held it up — a ruby. One half sparkled brilliantly in the light of the glowing stylus, while the other half remained rough and dull. Admiring the stone, Xandor asked, "Why did you leave?"

A faraway look overtook the dwarf. "I've been looking for more of my kin, but all I've found are old, forgotten cities they abandoned long ago."

"Like Pazard'zhik?"

"Yes, like Pazard'zhik. I keep looking for some hint of where they went, but there's not much out there. Even at Pazard'zhik, the Trakyans destroyed or built on top of most of what my kin created."

"I hope you find them, but I expect they are well hidden."

Chert looked at the ranger and asked, "What makes you say that?"

"I'm not as old as you," Xandor said good-naturedly, "but I've noticed how we humans seem to take everything for granted. We tend to be opportunistic when it comes to expansion." He gestured toward the trees. "Eventually, the Kral will have to take this area back. His people will continue to multiply, and he will run out of land. One day, the countries of Rhodina will cross the White River to reclaim their lands. Battles will be fought, and new borders will be drawn. I'm afraid there won't be much room left for the races of elves and dwarves."

"Guess that's why my people retreated into the earth," replied Chert.

"Sorry, I didn't mean to dampen your spirits. I didn't sleep well, and it's put me in a foul humor."

Chert patted Xandor on his good shoulder and said, "You must have faith, my friend. I will find my people one day, and you will find peace."

"Maybe, but not today," Xandor said, standing.

"No, not today."

CHAPTER 25
BISON BLOCK THE WAY

October 23, 4235 K.E.

6:15am

Wearing a heavy wool jacket, Jasper stoked the campfire, watching the sparks drift skyward. It was an hour until sunrise, and a pale layer of white frost covered the ground.

The teamsters were asleep in their tents. It felt odd not having one of them on watch duty, but Marko's men were now handling that responsibility. Then it struck him: he didn't see any signs of Marko or his men.

Walking to his wagon, Jasper opened the chuck box and rummaged around, looking for the ingredients for breakfast.

Jasper peeked around the edge of the cabinet. Still no sign of the Northmen; however, he did see a faint light shining in the woods. Curiosity got the better of him, and he decided to investigate.

Concentrating, he channeled a little magical energy into the air around him. It rippled slightly and to anyone watching, Jasper simply vanished as he stepped behind a tree.

Using the dead trees for additional cover, the cook followed the light and found Marko and Kourash talking with a spectral figure. Ignoring the fear churning in the pit of his stomach, Jasper stepped close enough to overhear their conversation.

"The trolls failed," the figure said in a hollow voice.

Marko's face darkened in the light of his small hand-held lamp and he said, "D'yakon Krovos, who is this ranger? The trolls should have succeeded. And what of the lemures? Surely, he didn't have the power to turn them."

"They were stopped by the elves."

"The elves? What elves? They're all dead," Marko said a little too loudly.

"Like the lemures, they, too, are doomed to walk these woods for eternity."

"Why were they there?"

"I don't know why they took an interest in this matter. Sutekh has not revealed this information to me."

"This complicates things," the knight mused to himself. He waved a hand toward the tents and wagons. "D'yakon Krovos, I have my hands full with this caravan. It's up to you to stop them."

"Sir Marko," the spectral figure said, his voice calm and measured, "you can't expect me to drop everything to cover for your incompetence. The khumanoidi rooted out a band of Rhodinan scavengers yesterday afternoon and have them on the run, even as we speak. If I do as you ask, we will lose them."

"Can you spare any of them?"

After a moment, the figure replied, "I suggest we work together. Send one of your men west. Have him meet me."

"It will be done, D'yakon," Marko said with a bow. The figure returned the gesture and disappeared.

Jasper followed Marko and Kourash back to camp, giving them a safe lead. Occasionally, Kourash turned back as if he sensed something, his reptilian eyes scanning the pre-dawn forest. Each time, Jasper held his breath lest the Seldaehne catch him. Once they passed the chuck wagon, Jasper dropped his glamour and busied himself with breakfast.

The knight and his companion continued on to Sachin's tent. Grendel stepped out of the shadows and placed himself between them and the opening. Behind him, Sachin gave the knight permission to enter the tent, leaving Kourash and Grendel outside to face each other. The quiet tension between them was palpable. Fortunately, neither seemed ready to provoke the other — at least, not yet.

A few minutes later, Marko emerged from the tent, his face a mask of neutrality. He approached a secluded part of camp where one of the Northmen lay hidden.

Not wanting to arouse suspicion, Jasper pulled out strips of bacon and a dozen eggs from the rear of the chuck wagon. He glanced back in time to see the Northman disappear behind one of the tents and then reappear mounted on his horse. With a snap of the reins, the horse leapt forward and galloped back down the road they had just traveled.

The smell of kahve, bacon, and eggs filled the small campsite, waking the teamsters. Dragahn and Lucky were the first, followed quickly by Pyotr and the rest of the horsemen. Soon, a crowd formed around the campfire.

Marko motioned to Kourash, and the two converged on the teamsters. Jasper noted the brisk, angry pace that replaced Marko's normally cocky stride.

Breaking in at the front of the line, Marko took the plate and cup of kahve intended for Dragahn. Next to him, Kourash turned his nose up at the cooked food, and Jasper could only imagine what the Seldaehne considered a normal meal. Apparently attracted by the smells of breakfast, Sachin and Grendel walked over and joined the back of the line.

Marko scowled at the teamsters, spoiling for a fight. Everyone, including Sachin, gave him plenty of room and let him eat. This change in attitude did not go unnoticed. It seemed even the normally haughty man was cowed in the presence of the knight.

After everyone was seated, the second Northman stepped forward and grabbed the last plate. He sat down a short distance away, his bow in easy reach.

Head down, Jasper watched the teamsters' reactions when they realized one of the Northmen was missing. Their expressions ran the gamut from curiosity to speculation to nervous tension.

Dragahn brought his empty plate to the cook and held out his tin cup for a refill. "I notice you don't have any extra food. Camp's one man short this morning," he murmured.

"I saw him leave while I was getting things together. He headed back the way we came. I'll say one thing. The look on his face would have curdled fresh milk."

"Wonder what that means," the chief mused.

"Can't say," Jasper said.

As soon as the kahve pot was empty, everyone busied themselves with striking camp while Jasper and Lucky loaded the chuck wagon.

Marko mounted his Frisian, watching Jasper close the chuck box. The cook remained a mystery. During his conversation earlier, the Northman told him the cook had walked into the woods. Marko could only presume he had overheard his conversation with D'yakon Krovos, but that's not what bothered him. What bothered him was the cook had managed to get past both himself and Kourash undetected.

Dragahn gave Marko the signal, and the knight smiled knowingly. The caravan chief knew the chain of command.

7:48am

Dragahn cursed silently when he realized the knight was setting another fast pace, one that would eventually cause an accident. Although the land they traveled had flattened, grass covered roads could easily hide holes or ruts.

For their part, the Percherons were ready. Yesterday's ride had allowed them to stretch out their stride a little, and they seemed eager for more.

The morning flew by, and the day warmed as the sun reached its zenith. To either side, live mountain firs, crowded amongst older, dead trees, fought for sunlight. Random patches of black shadow marked the treed landscape where vine covered ruins of abandoned buildings seemed destined to never see the light of day again.

Just as they passed a small lake on the right, Marko raised a clenched fist and gave the signal for everyone to stop. Ahead, the trees gave way to open grassland. As far as the eye could see, a herd of light-brown bison grazed peacefully on the grass. They appeared unconcerned with the sudden presence of the caravan and had no intention of moving out of the way.

Dragahn turned to their fearless leader and waited for his instructions. After a few minutes, when Marko still looked unsure of what to do, he climbed down and approached the knight. "Sir, if I may?"

Marko sat his horse calmly, but inside he was furious, cursing the god who created such foul beasts. He glared down at Dragahn and asked, "Do you know how to clear the road, driver?"

"We can't clear the road, but I think I can get us past the bison."

At first, the knight was suspicious of the driver's intentions, but not finding any obvious subterfuge, he tipped his head slightly and said, "Very well.   I temporarily relinquish command of the caravan to you, driver."

Dragahn patted the lead Percheron on the neck as he walked back to the wagons. He stopped next to Sachin and said calmly, "Everyone listen up. We are going to take this slow and easy."

"You're not thinking about going into that herd, are you?" Pyotr interrupted. "That's crazy!"

Dragahn looked directly at the horse doctor and replied, "Yes, I'm planning on taking this caravan through the herd, and no, it's not crazy as long as you do exactly what I say." After giving everyone a few seconds to let his words sink in, he continued, "I will take the chuck wagon and hug the right-hand side of the road where there aren't as many bison."

Everyone turned to look at the road.

"I want all the horsemen riding between us and the woods. Whatever you do, do not stop. I repeat, do not stop. If you keep the horses moving, everything will go just fine."

Walking back to the end of the line, Dragahn made sure everyone had heard him and understood what they needed to do. He made a point of giving each of the lead Percherons some attention before he resumed his seat.

Except for Pyotr, the teamsters seemed in good spirits. Jasper, for his part, could hardly contain his excitement. He had no clue what was about to happen, but he was thankful Dragahn knew what he was doing. Or, at least, he was really good at faking it.

The caravan chief looked behind him. He received nods from each of the teamsters and from the knight. With a flick of the reins, the chuck wagon moved forward slowly. Dragahn steered the wagon closer to the edge of the road and aimed straight for the herd.

At first, it didn't look like the bison were paying any attention, but at the last second, the few in front stepped aside. Jasper twisted in his seat and looked back over his shoulder as the last wagon entered the herd. Behind them, the bison closed their ranks.

Jasper gave the caravan chief credit. Even though some of the larger beasts seemed annoyed with the presence of the caravan, they continued to open a path with little more than a snort.

Everyone remained quiet, and Jasper caught himself holding his breath when they passed within touching distance of one of them. It stood six feet at the shoulder, and Jasper estimated it must have weighed over a thousand pounds. Its head and forequarters were massive, and it was easy to imagine the short, curved horns goring a person.

They traveled several miles before Jasper saw the edge of the herd. The slow, tedious pace wore on everyone's nerves, but Dragahn seemed unaffected. He held the reins tightly and didn't relax or increase the tension the entire time they were within the herd.

When they came out the other side, everyone sighed in relief. Marko motioned to the horsemen, and they resumed their positions along each side of the wagons. As the knight passed Dragahn to take back the command, he bowed his head slightly toward the driver, much to Jasper's surprise, and said, "Let's find a place to circle the wagons and regroup."

CHAPTER 26
THE BUNKER

October 23, 4235 K.E.

6:57am

Holding her reins, Chert led Sky through the boughed tunnel. Beside them, Xandor and Xerxes listened for signs of ambush, but there did not seem to be anything living in these woods. It unnerved the ranger not to hear any of the animal movement typical of a healthy forest.

The rim of the sun limned the dead trees with a fiery glow. Shielding his eyes, Xandor called for a stop. He jumped down and scanned the grassy road, hoping to find signs the caravan had slowed. Instead, it seemed that they, too, had traveled late into the evening. When he pushed aside some crushed underbrush, he found the day-old spoor of a big cat. From the size, it looked to be a Parlathean lion — one of those rare, solitary maneaters that hunt the hunters. *'At least there's one animal in this godforsaken forest,'* Xandor thought with a wry grin.

"You ready?" asked Xandor.

"Whenever you are," Chert replied, stepping into the stirrup, and gripping the saddle pommel.

"Good. Maybe we can catch them today," said Xandor. He climbed onto Xerxes, letting the horse take the lead, while he searched the ground.

As they rode, the sun climbed higher, and the light drove out some of the shadows lingering in the Haunted Wood.

"Smoke," Chert said, pointing south of the roadway. Xandor looked up from his inspection of the road and saw the dark plume through the line of trees.

"Should we investigate?" Chert asked.

Pulling back on the reins, Xandor stooped low in the saddle as he studied the roadway. The tracks indicated the caravan had slowed, which probably meant they had camped nearby. Judging distances, the ranger suspected the smoke was too far off the road to be from their campsite, but he needed to be sure.

The smell of smoke grew stronger, even as the cloud above the trees thinned. Xandor frowned. Whatever had fed the fire must have burned itself out. With all the deadwood lying around, it was fortunate the fire hadn't spread. It probably meant the fire had been contained, which also meant it had been set intentionally.

"What do you think?" Chert whispered.

Shaking his head, Xandor signaled for the dwarf to stay quiet.

They topped a tree-covered knoll and dismounted. A smokey haze blanketed the area, but none of the surrounding boughs appeared to have suffered fire damage. On the other side, down in a hollow, were the charred remains of an underground bunker.

After motioning for Chert to remain with Xerxes and Sky, Xandor crept toward the bottom.

Stacked one on top of another, blackened logs, sealed with mud, held back the earth and made up the rectangular sides of the bunker. Once forming a series of interconnected rooms and hallways, interior partitions poked through the collapsed remnants of the roof. Xandor heard the crackle of smoldering wood and spotted an orange flame dancing inside one of the hollowed-out timbers.

Creeping closer, the ranger used all his training to remain hidden. A portion of an interior wall fell under its own weight, and fresh smoke billowed up. The wind shifted, and the ranger caught the pungent odor of burnt corpses. Expecting the worst, he raced toward the bunker and looked down. Charred roof rafters covered the bottom, burying anyone who might be below.

"Chert! Get down here!"

With the heat of the scorched earth seeping into their boots, the two raced toward one end of the bunker, where a portion of the roof clung tenaciously to the timber retaining wall and formed a steep ramp to the bunker floor. Xandor slid down it and quickly cleared a path through the debris as best he could. Behind him, Chert did the same as they searched for survivors.

"I hope we don't find the teamsters," Chert said.

"Me, too."

Their first body was an adult male, burnt beyond recognition, lying next to what appeared to have once been a desk. Sweat beading on his forehead, Xandor searched nearby and found blackened bits of charts and maps that were brittle to the touch. Opening and closing the drawers, he discovered the burnt remains of a journal. The cover and outermost pages disintegrated when touched. A few yellowed pages near the middle were legible enough to see the passages were written in Rhodinan.

"These weren't the teamsters," Xandor concluded.

Responding from another room, Chert replied, "Aye, I think you're right. I found three more bodies. Looks like they were caught sleeping. Whoever did this, stripped them of their gear."

Following the sound of Chert's voice, Xandor walked into the other room. He found the dwarf kneeling beside a body, administering last rites. When Chert finished his prayer, he rose and moved to the next one. The ranger watched briefly, then decided to continue searching the bunker. Like Chert, he did not expect to find anyone alive, but he couldn't give up without checking.

Xandor entered a short hallway, stepping carefully over the splintered wood. He continued toward the next room, but before he cleared the threshold, something slammed into him from behind and knocked him into the wall.

Chert looked up and saw Xandor staggering toward him with a thick-shafted arrow sticking out of his back. Hand on his hammer, Chert peeked through a small opening in the debris and spotted two muscular humanoids at the upper edge of the bunker.

'*Eotenas*,' Chert thought grimly.

Humans near his homeland on the island of Hy Breasal called the beasts ogres. More than nine feet tall, they were larger, more primitive versions of Grendel. They had long, greasy hair that only partially hid their cruel features. It didn't take much imagination to know what would happen if they caught Chert or Xandor. Ogres typically brutalized and devoured their victims.

The two ogres followed Xandor and Chert's trail toward the ramp-like end of the bunker. They carried oversized axes, the likes of which Chert had never seen. The weapons bore a steel labrys, or double-headed axe, at each end, connected by a long oaken shaft wrapped in leather strips.

Thinking quickly, Chert crawled under a pile of charred debris that lay against one side of the bunker. He took out his dagger and dug into the brittle retaining wall, pulling chunks of black wood loose. He worked quietly and eventually exposed raw earth. Pressing his hands against the surface, he pushed them into the soil. Instead of creating an opening, he simply forced his body inside.

The feathered shaft of another arrow streaked toward Xandor from somewhere above. Knowing he could not avoid it, he twisted aside and succeeded in turning enough that the arrow missed his heart. Even so, it was a grievous wound, and he tasted blood in the back of his mouth. The barbed head had punctured his lung. With a sharp swipe of his hand, he broke the shaft and dove for cover in the nearest room.

Xandor knew he was dying. He felt the arrow in his back but couldn't reach it to break the shaft. He tried using the wall, but the round logs and mud-filled joints caught the shaft at an odd angle and only drove it deeper. Blood soaked his leather shirt. He tried not to think about it as he worked to control his breathing and listen.

Leaning heavily against the wall beside the doorway, Xandor coughed blood. Fighting to stay conscious, he scanned the trees at the edge of the valley but still didn't see the archer. He peeked around the doorjamb and saw two ogres climbing down the charred framing, oblivious to the heat. Then he saw their weapons. His lips compressed to a bloodless slash, and his eyes narrowed.

He ducked back around the jamb and struggled to get his feet under him. It was slow, painful work, but he managed to stand and draw both swords.

"Aduro." Golden flames coursed along the edges of the blades. If today was his day to die, then he would be taking company.

The ogres advanced cautiously through the bunker. Shoulder to shoulder, they walked past the desk and headed into the former sleeping quarters. The one on the left split off and approached the portion of collapsed ceiling where Chert had disappeared. He struck the debris hard with his axe, crushing the brittle wood framing, but no one was there — only raw earth.

"The dwarf's in the walls," the ogre said, speaking Rhodinan in a guttural voice.

They both glanced around, quickly checking the other openings in the hallway. With a grunt, the one on the right pointed toward the doorway ahead. The one on the left stepped forward and spun his labrys, and the blades cut the air with a soft whirring sound.

When the ogre stepped across the threshold, Xandor staggered out and struck with both blades. The monster deflected one with his axe, but the other sank deep into its stomach. The ranger twisted his wrist as he wrenched it out, causing the steaming wound to widen.

The ogre snarled viciously, reverse spun his axe ninety degrees, and caught Xandor across the right leg with the flat of his blade. The close-quarter maneuver caught the ranger by surprise as he stumbled to one side. When he did, he caught a glimpse of the other ogre behind the first.

'*This just keeps getting better.*'

Retreating, Xandor swung his swords back and forth, hoping to gain breathing room. The ogre in front of him pressed forward, reversed his spin again, and aimed for the ranger's head. The axe blade missed, but it took everything Xandor had to dodge it.

Chert exploded out of the earth above the rim of the bunker and landed on the ogre in front of Xandor. The dwarf's weight rocked the ogre sideways, and Chert rode him all the way down to the ground.

Not wasting time, the second ogre charged Xandor, his blades spinning faster and faster. The ranger ducked around them, thrust his left blade into the ogre's thigh, and dove into a room on the right. Again, the reverse spin caught Xandor, this time with a shallow cut across the back, breaking the arrow shaft there.

With a roll, Chert put distance between himself and his opponent, and hurled his hammer. It flew past the axe blades, struck the ogre a crushing blow on the shoulder, bounced, and flew back into Chert's waiting hand.

"Liked that, didn't you?" Chert taunted.

With a low snarl, the ogre advanced. Again, the hammer flew from Chert's hand and struck the monster, this time in the rib cage, bounced, and returned.

Letting loose a berserker cry, the ogre charged. He swung his axe in a ferocious arc that struck Chert's shield. He reversed the spin, and the dwarf nearly lost his arm when his shield went flying across the bunker. Not missing a step, Chert gestured with his now-free hand, pointed at the ogre's head, and yelled, "heofonléoht!"

The ogre staggered back, blinded by white fire erupting from his eye sockets. He blinked, trying to escape it, but the fire originated within his own head. He dropped the double labrys and pressed his palms to his eyes as the flame seared into his brain, driving him mad with pain.

Using his hammer, the dwarf followed up with a swift strike to the ogre's leg, crushing the knee joint. The ogre landed hard, holding his head, and howling.

The world spun as Xandor dodged to one side to avoid another swing of the double-bitted axe. Blood seeped from several small wounds on the ogre, but none were near the humanoid's vital areas.

By contrast, the ranger remained standing for one reason — he would not go down alone.

Xandor struck at the ogre again, feinting with his left blade. The ogre brought his weapon around to block it, but this time, Xandor didn't follow up. Instead, he waited.

The ogre reversed his weapon's spin, expecting to catch the ranger, and it left him wide open. Gathering his strength, Xandor put all his weight into one last desperate thrust. He plunged his flaming blade deep into the ogre's chest, piercing his heart.

Chert raced over in time to see the ranger perform his coup de grâce. Both ogre and ranger fell together in a pool of mingled blood.

Before the dwarf could reach Xandor, a shadow crossed overhead. Chert dove for cover too late. A thick arrow cut through the links of his chain armor, impaling his chest. The arrow hit with such strength it knocked him to the ground and pinned him to the charred floor.

His last vision before blacking out was that of the tattooed Northman and the spectral shape of a tall, bald man in dark robes beside him.

CHAPTER 27
THE VOW

October 23, 4235 K.E.

12:12pm

*D*ragahn found a sparkling pond surrounded by thick grass for the caravan's midday break. Old moss-covered foundation stones dotted the ground.

The horsemen jumped down from their saddles and unhitched the Percherons to let them graze near the water. Everyone seemed happy to be walking around again and less nervous around the knight and his companions.

Jasper eavesdropped on small conversations about the day's events while he and Lucky prepared lunch. Even Marko and Sachin seemed more at ease now that they were clear of the bison. They stood together, conversing in low tones.

Without warning, Grendel threw a small work hammer, striking the Northman in the head with a high-pitched metallic tone. The man collapsed instantly.

In the moment of stunned silence that followed, Grendel undid the leather loop and bone toggle supporting his battle-axe, slipped behind Marko, and held the blade against the knight's neck. A rivulet of blood ran down and disappeared beneath Marko's plate armor.

"No one move!" Grendel growled.

Kourash drew his two-handed sword. "You won't make it out of here alive."

Looking for backup, Grendel gave Jasper a hard stare, but the mage hadn't moved. He simply watched from the chuck wagon, his face unreadable, and a feeling of dread came over the half-orc.

Marko inhaled sharply as Grendel pressed harder. Glancing at the teamsters, then back at the chuck wagon, he silently urged Jasper to do something, but the cook only frowned and shook his head slightly.

Kourash took a tentative step, and Grendel glared at him, daring him to try it.

Suddenly, Grendel's muscles tensed and froze.

Sachin stood behind Grendel, wielding an ornate, silver dagger covered in arcane runes. The tip rested against the side of the half-orc's neck just under his right ear.

Marko grabbed the handle of the battle-axe and pushed as hard as he could. It didn't budge. With Kourash's help, the knight managed to slip out from Grendel's grasp. After freeing Marko, the Seldaehne gripped his sword tight with both hands, opened his stance, and reared back.

Sachin stepped between Grendel and the huge blade.

"What are you doing? He's too dangerous." Marko's voice sounded ragged, and his lungs heaved. A crimson stain bloomed on the cloth he held to his throat.

"That's exactly why I chose him as my bodyguard, you idiot," Sachin replied, his haughtiness back in full force.

Dragahn caught the exchange and asked, "Who are you? You're not the Sachin I know."

Sachin removed the thin, gold chain from around his neck, and morphed into a tall, long-legged woman in her early thirties. Her medium-length, raven hair hung loose above her shoulders and framed a pale, square face with a slightly upturned nose and elegant neck. The riding clothes she wore no longer fit properly, nor could they hide her near-perfect proportions. Her dark eyes captivated the teamsters as if with magic and held them prisoner.

"You should let me kill him, sister," said Marko.

"Why? Because you were careless?" She laughed. "Oh no, I'm keeping this one. If I had not stopped him, he would have killed you while your Seldaehne stood helpless. You owe me your life."

The woman looked away from Marko and caught Dragahn staring at her, his mouth open. She walked over to the chief and closed it for him.

Amused, she said, "No, Dragahn, I am not Sachin. My real name is Aleksandra Madasgorski, cousin to the throne of Zhitomir and widow of Baron Gavriil Krakov, former advisor to the Kral. This knight is my younger brother, Sir Marko Madasgorski."

Every man in camp remained riveted to her every move.

"Oh, this is priceless," she said with a smile, basking in the attention.

Dragahn coughed to clear his throat and asked, "What happened to the real Sachin?"

A shadow briefly crossed Aleksandra's features, and she said, "He's dead."

Jasper watched Dragahn struggling to think clearly. In fact, all the teamsters seemed to be reacting toward her the same way, and it did not take long for them to become completely enamored of her. All except Jasper. He couldn't explain it. Maybe it was his training, or maybe it was something else. Regardless, he seemed immune to Aleksandra's charms. One thing was certain. They had finally found the connection to the Krakov Estate. Stepping away from the chuck wagon, he asked, "What are you going to do with us?"

She focused on Jasper, curious, and said, "Nothing. You made a deal with my brother. There's no reason for me to break that deal. Now, please excuse me while I change into something more appropriate."

Aleksandra retrieved the luggage stowed under the seat of her wagon and changed on the far side, teasing everyone with glimpses of soft, fair skin. When she returned, she still wore the same style of riding clothes, but these were tailored to her figure and complemented her natural beauty. Her dark hair was parted down the center and fell in layers, with a light twist through the tresses giving her a roguish look.

"Jasper, please make sure everyone is fed; Pyotr, please check on Ognian and see how badly he's hurt. I would hate to waste this break."

"Of course, milady," Jasper said before he realized it.

Paralyzed by the touch of Aleksandra's dagger, Grendel stared straight ahead, his arms and weapon still poised to hold Marko trapped. Kourash filled his field of vision, his sword propped on his shoulder, awaiting the signal to dispatch the half-orc. Adrenaline pulsed through Grendel's veins as he struggled against the unseen bonds seizing his muscles. His mind replayed the scene, and each time, he felt more betrayed by Jasper. Grendel knew they could have saved the teamsters, but because of the mage's cowardice, they were still prisoners.

The first sign his paralysis was wearing off was when he could move his eyes, followed closely by his first blink. Words could not describe the relief that coursed through his body.

Aleksandra approached Grendel, and his battle of emotions reached new levels. Her dark eyes peered into his, and it seemed she felt what he was feeling. Maybe she even knew what he was thinking. She traced her finger along his jaw and down his arm. Her touch sent electricity through his body, and he found it difficult to think about anything else.

"My orcné, what am I going to do with you?" she whispered softly, an affectionate hand on his cheek. "I certainly didn't expect you to try to rescue everyone."

Still unable to speak, Grendel blinked and felt the muscles in his face relax.

"I'm sorry I had to do that. I couldn't have you kill Marko. He is family, after all." She edged closer, and her voice dropped to a soft murmur. "Did you attack Marko to rescue me? Or did you have some other motive?"

After a brief pause, she said, "You will soon regain your ability to move. Before that happens, I want you to think long and hard about your next course of action. I didn't save your life only to have it taken away from you. You have passed the final test, and I want to keep you as my bodyguard. Can you live with that, son of Cayn?"

Looking deep into those mesmerizing eyes, Grendel saw something there, something different. It was hard to fathom at first, but he swore he saw hope.

"Do you promise not to harm these people?" he finally asked in a voice dry from lack of moisture.

"Of course," Aleksandra replied.

"It seems I have little choice."

"The decision is ultimately yours."

Grendel cast a quick glance at Jasper, watching as he served dry rations to the horsemen, and temporarily put aside his angry feelings.

"I..." he began, but Aleksandra stopped him with a finger across his lips.

"No, you have to start with my name."

The words formed in his mind, and before he could stop himself, he said, "Lady Aleksandra Madasgorski, your life is my life. Your honor is my honor. I vow to safeguard them both."

A self-satisfied smile spread across Aleksandra's perfect face. "Ya prinimayu. Ya soglasen." *I accept. I agree.*

CHAPTER 28
ON THREE

October 23, 4235 K.E.

1:38pm

"Get up, mountain boy!" Not satisfied, the sergeant-at-arms leaned over and yelled again, "Get up, Alashalian! Move your ass!"

The brown sludge rippled slightly when Xandor raised his head. With one torturous move after another, he crawled through the slurry with three heavy, painted rocks tied to his back.

The sergeant stood over him, wearing a black and silver surcoat over a suit of shiny chain mail. Ahead, Xandor saw the yellow rope marking the finish line.

As part of the last test to be a ranger, the Knight Commander selected ten of his best students to participate in the three-day event. It started at the gates of Tydway, the capital of Gallowen. Each candidate was required to follow a specific trail and find three rocks marked with the symbol of the Iron Tower.

The test wasn't just pass/fail. The person who ran the course the fastest typically got their choice of assignments, and there were only six assignments. They weren't allowed food, water, or lights. Just the clothes on their back, their boots, and whatever they found along the way.

Horses were not allowed, either, so all ten ran, searching for their prizes. Each had a different course to navigate, and as soon as the trial started, the ten students quickly separated and disappeared into the forest west of the city. Some had to climb trees while others dove into clear pools of water.

It took over twenty miles of navigation for Xandor to find his first rock, and it was at least another twenty before he found the second. By the last day, he had lost count of the miles, and all he knew was he was exhausted and tired of carrying his three rocks.

"You are a Ranger, and this is the Iron Tower!" the sergeant shouted, leaning over and staying with him. Xandor snapped out of his reverie and inched forward through the slurry. He wouldn't be the first to cross the line, nor the second, but he was going to cross that line.

"Ooh-rah!" Xandor yelled, spitting out a mouthful of mud.

"You are a Ranger, and this is the Iron Tower!" the sergeant repeated.

"Ooh-rah!" Xandor responded again, this time louder, and deep, deep down, he found a small reserve of energy. He clawed through the brown goo and reached toward the yellow rope until finally he grabbed it and pulled himself out.

Somewhere inside his head, Xandor heard that sergeant still yelling at him, "You are a Ranger... Get up, mountain boy... This is the Iron Tower!"

He mouthed the words, "Ooh-rah!"

Pain coursed through his body as his chest muscles contracted around the arrow wounds and protested at the movement. He was so thirsty.

Xandor opened his eyes. Staring back at him were the vacant eyes of an ogre.

Looking past the body of the dead ogre, he saw Chert lying face down, the feathered shaft of an arrow sticking out of his back. He wasn't moving.

"Get up!" he heard the sergeant yell.

Xandor spit the blood out of his mouth, grabbed a handful of the ogre's tunic, and pulled. Inch by inch, he crawled closer to Chert. After an eternity, Xandor drew close enough to the dwarf and checked his pulse. He was still alive.

"Chert, wake up," Xandor whispered hoarsely, shaking him.

Nothing.

Nearly losing consciousness, he pulled out a small brass vial of Spirit of Hartshorn from his pouch. Opening it, he waved it under the dwarf's nose. Instantly, Chert twitched and wrinkled his nose.

"That's vile. Where did you get that stuff?"

Xandor mustered a weak smile and said, "Welcome back."

"Where are we?" Chert said as he slowly pushed his helmet off his head and looked around, his movement causing an involuntary groan.

"Please tell me you're still on good terms with the Eternal Father," Xandor said.

Chert looked at him askance and said, "And you're not?"

"That's not what I meant."

Chert smiled back and said, "I know."

Still pinned to the floorboards, the dwarf fished out his knife, pushed up slightly with one arm, and notched the shaft just above the arrowhead. With a heave and loud grunt of pain, he broke the shaft and pushed himself the rest of the way off the floor.

Turning his attention to Xandor, he laid a hand on the ranger's shoulder and prayed. Blue light flashed and disappeared beneath the ranger's armor.

Xandor sat up. Another blue light flared, and Chert managed to stand. He still had a broken arrow shaft sticking out of his back, so he turned around and asked Xandor to take it out.

"On three?"

Chert nodded curtly and listened for the count.

"One."

Xandor yanked out the shaft and threw it to the side. The dwarf never had time to tense up.

Chert looked over his shoulder with a shocked expression but held his tongue. His gaze dropped to the dark patches of blood covering the ranger's armor — most of it his own. "Your turn," he said calmly. "Shall I count, or just rip them out?"

Xandor looked down, and his complexion paled.

Chert cut out the arrowheads while simultaneously praying for healing. Even with thaumaturgy, it took more than an hour to complete the procedure, and when the dwarf finished, he and Xandor both fell into an exhausted sleep.

5:29pm

When the caravan passed a solitary mountain rising from the treetops in a jagged spire, Marko called for their evening halt. Dark clouds obscured the setting sun, throwing a pall over the landscape.

At the back of the chuck wagon, Jasper reached up and lowered the odd-looking panel, turning the lid into a worktable. He placed beef, onions, and potatoes on the surface and chopped them into bite-sized pieces. Grabbing a cast-iron pot, he dumped the food inside and walked to the campfire where Lucky had his cooking gear ready.

Out of the corner of his eye, Jasper spied Ognian sitting with his head in his hands. From time to time, the Northman would slowly peer out into the camp between his fingers, shudder, and cover his eyes again. Apparently, the world still spun a little too fast for him.

The cook could feel eyes boring into him while he worked. He wiped his brow on his shirtsleeve and caught Marko staring at him with open suspicion.

Near the edge of camp, the Seldaehne had positioned himself to watch everyone, weapon in hand. At the sound of hoofbeats, he growled, "Mladen's returned!"

Marko ran to the road, and Mladen jumped from his saddle to greet him.

Jasper turned back to the pot, added chunks of flour dredged beef to the caramelizing onions and potatoes, then sent Lucky for more water. When Marko strutted back into camp, a sinking feeling crept into Jasper's gut. If it was good for the knight, it had to be bad for the rest of them.

All eyes went to Aleksandra when she emerged from her tent. With a broad smile, Marko offered her his arm. Together, they crossed the camp, discussing whatever news the Northman had brought.

Reaching the campfire, Marko asked, "What's for supper tonight, cook?"

Jasper looked up from stirring the pot and replied, "Beef stew and flatbread."

"It smells delicious. What's in it?"

"A little of this and a little of that," Jasper said casually as he brought up his spoon to taste the broth, not looking at the knight.

Marko slapped the spoon away and said, "I asked you a question. I expect an answer."

Glaring at the knight, Jasper said curtly, "I gave you an answer."

"Jasper," Dragahn warned, "just tell him what's in the stew."

"He saw me cook it. He should know what's in it," Jasper replied.

"You have a smart mouth on you, cook," Marko said. "Be glad I like your food."

Jasper wanted to reply, but Dragahn grabbed his arm tightly and shook his head.

"You'd better listen to the driver, if you know what's good for you," Marko said, daring the cook to say something else.

Jasper yanked his arm out of Dragahn's grasp, grabbed another spoon, and dipped it into the stew. "Try a taste first before you get mad at me for wanting to keep the recipe to myself."

Marko noticed the teamsters watching him. The men liked and respected Jasper, but the cook seemed to have the natural ability to get under his skin. Marko felt the fat man had somehow trapped him. He could push the cook further, but looking around, he concluded he had already lost this round. He took the spoon from Jasper, sipped it, and a smile spread across his face.

"I'm glad you like it. Lucky, grab the knight here a plate and fill it for him."

The young man instantly produced a plate, laid a thick piece of fresh flatbread on its surface, and ladled a mound of beef and vegetables atop. Passing it to Marko, he prepared a second plate for Aleksandra. The two departed with their stews in hand, the small confrontation forgotten for the time being.

Everyone else formed a line with dishes in hand while Lucky dipped the stew. It was a quiet crowd, and when Mladen helped Ognian join the line, everyone stepped aside so they could go right to the front.

"Here ya go. Fresh from the pot," Jasper said, offering Grendel a plate.

Grendel took it without saying anything, but the cook felt the hostility rising from the half-orc.

"There was nothing I could do, Grendel," he whispered.

"I have heard about what you can do, so do not expect me to believe you were helpless. We could have ended this."

Jasper met Grendel's narrow-eyed glare and said quietly, "Taking out Marko would not have ended this. There's more going on here than just him and the baroness."

"How many of these people have to die or get hurt before you are willing to step in and do something?" Grendel whispered harshly.

The cook opened his mouth and, catching himself, shut it. He thought for a moment and said, "We cannot give up now." He held up his thumb and index finger a scant half-inch apart. "We are this close."

"Close? We know the connection to the Krakov Estate — the baroness is that connection. What else is there to do?" Grendel said a little too loudly, and some of the teamsters looked their way. "At this rate, none of us will make it out of these woods alive."

Jasper glanced around and whispered, "Let's wait on Chert and Xandor."

5:59pm

Xandor woke as twilight fell and found Chert snoring loudly next to him. Although the forest was dark, the bunker remained lit by the dim light radiating from the ogre's head, like a gruesome jack o' lantern. He gave the dwarf a sharp poke to the ribs.

Chert startled awake, hands scrabbling for a weapon to fend off another attack.

"Wake up, sleepyhead. It's past dark."

Glancing about in confusion, the dwarf sought his bearings.

"You going to make it?" Xandor asked. He rolled his shoulders and stretched out the kinks in his muscles. Considering the day they'd had, he felt good.

"Getting there." Chert rolled to a sitting position and, with a prayer of thanks, took some jerky from his pouch. He offered some to the ranger, who declined.

Xandor examined one of the arrows. "Did you get a good look at who shot us?"

"One of the Northmen."

"Damn," Xandor swore. "Did you see the other one?"

Chert shook his head.

"I didn't expect them to work with ogres."

Chert climbed to his feet and said, "It gets worse."

The ranger studied the dwarf. "How so?"

"The Northman wasn't alone. He had a Sha'iry with him."

"Are you sure?"

"I'm sure."

Touching the Korsun cross at his neck, Xandor said, "If Sha'iry are involved, Jasper and Grendel are in more danger than we thought."

At the edge of the bunker, Xerxes stared down at them and neighed. The ranger relaxed and asked, "Have you been there the whole time?"

The Andalusian bobbed his head up and down and pawed the ground.

"You're right. We need to catch that caravan. Chert?"

The dwarf finished swallowing his bite and replied, "Ready whenever you are."

After a quick search of the bunker, Chert found his shield and reworked the strap so he could hold it correctly.

As he passed the glowing head of the ogre, Xandor said, "That's disturbing."

"Aye, he'll be like that for at least a couple of days," Chert replied, placing his helmet on his head.

"Maybe we should take it with us?"

Chert glanced obliquely at the ranger and replied, "No thanks."

CHAPTER 29
ALEKSANDRA'S TOUCH

October 23, 4235 K.E.

11:53pm

The clouds had cleared, and the stars shone down through the branches, crisp and cold.   Outside her tent, Aleksandra stood beside Grendel, staring up at the night sky. Wrapped in a wool blanket, she leaned into her bodyguard and let the heat radiating from him seep through her.

"Orcné, come inside my tent," she said.

Grendel glanced down at her before quickly scanning the camp, then replied, "I should stay out here and keep watch."

She grabbed his hand and said with a laugh, "Don't be scared. I'm not going to bite..." *Much,* she added silently.

With some gentle urging, Aleksandra led Grendel through the tent flap. Once inside, he stretched to his full height and stared at the amount of space she had — a foldout cot, a chest of drawers, and a desk with a lit oil lamp lined three walls, and there was enough room left in the center for a thick rug.

Despite the cold outside, the air inside the tent was comfortably warm. Aleksandra let the tent flap fall into place and released the blanket. The wool slithered down her body to pool on the floor.

Grendel turned, and his jaw dropped.

Aleksandra stood naked, her eyes filled with lust. She approached him and said in a husky whisper, "I've never tasted a J'Belan."

His mouth closed with a snap. Gripping her shoulders, Grendel stopped her from getting any closer. "Milady, you cannot have me," he growled.

She reached down toward his waist while staring into his eyes, willing him to give in to her. He pushed her roughly away and said, "I am only a half-human, not some handsome prince. Go find someone else to play with."

"What does it matter if you're part human or part orc? Your father was part ogre, and your mother was human. You must have wondered what it felt like — to feel the soft skin of a human woman."

Aleksandra licked her lips in anticipation as he struggled against himself. Abruptly he tore his eyes away, found her desk, and stared at it.

She slid between him and the desk and recaptured his eyes. "You can say I bewitched you, if you're worried what the others might say."

"I am not my father."

"Then be Vanin and take me."

"No."

She laughed and asked, "Are you worried you might hurt me?"

Pain filled his eyes, and he bowed his head. She knew she had guessed right and changed tactics. "Look at me."

Before he could turn away, she stepped forward and cupped his cheeks in her palms. "Look at me," she repeated, softer this time. "You are not going to hurt me."

He stared down at her and asked, "How do you know?"

For an answer, she took a couple of steps back and rotated her leg. Deep white scars scored her upper thigh. "When I was twelve years old, a demon raped me, Grendel. Compared to it, you are a handsome prince."

Horror flooded his expression only to be swept away by a look she had never seen before. "Your family did not protect you?"

"Protect me?" she asked incredulously. "They were the ones who gave me to it. I guess you could call it a rite of passage. Every girl born into the Madasgorski family is given over when they come of age."

"Why?" he asked.

"It doesn't matter," Aleksandra answered. Her voice quivered, and she inhaled sharply as she turned away from her bodyguard. She heard him move and was surprised when he draped the blanket around her.

Aleksandra turned swiftly before Grendel could see her face and buried her head against his chest. He felt her shaking and wrapped his arms around her.

It could have been minutes, or it could have been hours. Grendel held her, one hand around her back, the other softly stroking her hair. His tenderness was alien to Aleksandra, and she had no idea how he expected her to react. Her mind raced, and she thought of all she had lost in the last few months. She let the hot tears of rage flow, certain this man was unlikely to use them against her. Eventually, she began to breathe softly.

Grendel gently picked her up and placed her on the cot. He stepped over to the desk and dimmed the lamp to a bare flicker before pushing out of the tent into the cold night air.

In the wake of his passage, a smile of satisfaction curled Aleksandra's lips.

CHAPTER 30
PYOTR, THE MAGE?

October 24, 4235 K.E.

7:08am

"The horses can't keep this pace," Dragahn said.

"They can, and they will," Marko said, pointing his finger at Dragahn's chest.

"Are you trying to run them into the ground?"

Marko made like he was going to turn away, then spun and punched Dragahn's jaw with a solid right cross. The caravan chief fell, sprawling in the dirt.

Instantly, everyone was wide awake. Kourash stepped into the firelight, his mere presence quelling any resistance from the teamsters.

"Don't ever question me again!"

Dragahn wiped the blood from his mouth with the back of his hand and said, "Yes, Sir."

Pyotr rushed over and knelt beside the caravan chief. Dragahn brushed him aside.

"You can punch me all you want, but it doesn't change the fact you're killing these horses."

A woman's voice echoed across the camp. "He's right, brother." Dressed in heavy riding clothes, Aleksandra approached Dragahn, whose lip was already starting to swell. She looked at Pyotr and then back at the caravan chief. "Can we get one more good day out of the horses?"

The two looked at each other. Reluctantly, Dragahn nodded affirmatively and said, "Perhaps, Milady. I think so."

Muttering, Pyotr stomped off toward the wagons.

"Good, then let's get everyone up and the wagons ready to go."

1:13pm

When the wagons stopped for the midday break, Jasper and Lucky jumped down from their seats and immediately built a small fire to prepare the trail rations. While they worked, Jasper overheard Pyotr and Dragahn discussing the condition of the horses. They talked a lot about horseshoes and whether some of the horses were favoring one leg over another. The cook couldn't keep up with what was said, but he knew it didn't sound good.

Aleksandra had said one more day. Looking around, Jasper found her in good spirits and unconcerned about the condition of the horses. Whatever was going to happen, it would be soon.

A loud crashing echoed through the woods, and everyone turned. Marko emerged, cursing in Rhodinan. He kicked and stomped and occasionally struck trees with his sword. The noise he created was loud enough to spook the Percherons, and the drivers rushed to calm them with soothing words and gestures. Aleksandra took her brother aside, and the two talked briefly. As they did, her good mood noticeably darkened.

Marko motioned curtly for Mladen. The Northman flinched and approached the siblings like a man summoned to his execution. When the Northman blanched beneath his tattoos and ran for his horse, Jasper said a silent prayer to the Eternal Father to keep Xandor and Chert safe.

2:33pm

After a few miles, the knight picked up speed and moved faster, pushing his Frisian, but Dragahn made no effort to keep up. He held his Percherons back, allowing the gap between them to grow larger and larger without the knight knowing.

"You're going to get yourself killed," Jasper whispered out of the side of his mouth.

"That *kuchi sin* is going to kill these horses if he keeps this up, and I've got way too much invested in them to just let them die like this."

Eventually, Marko turned and saw the gap. Furious, he trotted back toward Dragahn. Matching the chuck wagon's pace, he yelled harshly, "You'd better push those horses, driver, or I'll have my men kill someone right now!"

Keeping his head forward, Dragahn ignored the knight and kept the horses moving at a steady pace.

"Driver, this is your last warning. Do not test me on this. You will lose," the knight said. When Dragahn still did not respond, Marko gestured to Ognian, who rode beside the second wagon. The Northman turned and fired directly at Lucky with his longbow.

The teenager stared wide-eyed as the arrow sped toward his chest. He didn't have time to react, throw his hands up, or try anything to block it. Just before the arrow hit, the air in front of Lucky coalesced and the shaft veered downward, striking the bed of the wagon.

Marko immediately screamed for a halt, and, with one fluid motion, put the edge of his blade to Dragahn's throat. "What was that?" he yelled. When no one responded, he yelled again, this time louder, "What was that?"

The knight removed his sword and directed his Frisian down the line toward Lucky's side of the wagon. "Comrades, we have a magic user amongst us," Marko said angrily. "One of you is not what he seems."

Kourash nodded toward Jasper and said with a growl, "There's your spellcaster."

Looking where the Seldaehne indicated, Marko asked the cook, "Did you save this boy?"

Avoiding eye contact, Jasper said, "I'm just a cook."

"We'll see about that," Marko said as he stood in his stirrups. His sword arm drew back across his chest. The knight swung his sword, but before it struck home, a voice cried out, "It's me!"

The blade stopped mid-swing. Everyone turned, and cries of disbelief went up amongst the teamsters. Pyotr shook with fear, but he looked at the knight and stated, "I'm the mage you're looking for."

Marko gestured toward Ognian, who aimed his next arrow at Pyotr's chest. The knight guided his horse around the wagon to within reach of the self-proclaimed mage. "You may be a horse doctor, but you're no mage," Marko said confidently, "but I bet you know who is."

"I swear it's me. There's no one else," Pyotr said, his voice quivering. Beside him sat a small tin of hooch.

"Fine, it's you. Do something else."

"I can't. I didn't even know I could do that until just now," Pyotr said quickly. Marko eyed him suspiciously. "You know that by claiming to be a mage, you have condemned yourself to death."

"Then get on with it."

Marko laughed and said, "I want these horses moving, doctor, with no more excuses. If I kill you, will that get me what I want?"

Turning away from the doctor, the knight shouted, "Dragahn!" As he spoke, he reached back and stabbed his sword into Lucky's side, cutting him deeply but not fatally. Pulling out his sword, he wiped the blood from the blade using a red kerchief.

Pyotr stood and yelled, "You were supposed to hurt me, not him!"

"Sit down, doctor! You try my patience," Marko replied. "Dragahn, get these wagons moving. This man doesn't have all day, and if you stop, slow down, or even scratch an itch, I'll stab another of your men. You understand me?"

Dragahn's brow drew down as he stared hard at the knight. "Yes, Sir."

"Finally, some progress. I promise when we stop for the evening, your precious doctor can spend all night saving the boy."

Grabbing a cloth from beneath the seat, Pyotr handed it to Lucky and whispered for him to press it against the wound. The doctor hoped it would be enough to stop the bleeding, but he doubted it. At a minimum, the boy needed stitches.

With a snap of the reins, Dragahn's Percherons continued down the road and, this time, he matched Marko's pace.

CHAPTER 31
GREGORI

October 24, 4235 K.E.

2:36pm

Cursing his lot in life, Mladen galloped west along an old woodsman's trail. The four-beat gait rapidly put distance between him and the caravan. After about ten miles, the Northman slowed. The dead woods had not changed, but something felt different.

He passed several large rocks piled on the side of the trail, forming a small cairn. The topmost boulder had been marked with a blackish-red handprint. He pulled sharply on the reins, bringing his horse to a halt, and dismounted. Taking a gold disc embossed with a claymore from his pouch, he placed it on the ground.

D'yakon Krovos' spectral shape rose and scanned the area. Nodding his head, he said, "Very good, Northman. The Anak'im is here."

"Can he defeat this ranger?"

"It is the will of Sutekh. The ranger must die."

The D'yakon raised something to his lips and let out a shrill whistle. It felt intrusive in the deathly quiet wood. They listened, and after a few minutes, the sound of something crashing through the woods reached them.

One of the dreaded Anak'im, a descendant of the feared Nephilim, approached. The giant stood more than fifteen feet tall and reeked of death. Greasy black hair fell about his twisted face, and deep scars covered every exposed inch of his bone white skin. He wore the thick brown pelt of a Volhynian cave bear over his heavily muscled torso, leaving his legs bare, and wielded a thick wooden club embedded with long iron spikes.

Mladen's horse reared and screamed. The Northman gripped the reins and managed to control the beast, but the horse trembled beneath him, blowing and snorting as its eyes rolled.

The giant's eyes gleamed wickedly in the filtered light beneath the trees as he peered down at the humans and said in a ground-rumbling voice, "Why do you summon me?"

"Sutekh requires your help," D'yakon Krovos said. "You must kill a ranger and his dwarf companion."

The Anak'im looked west and said, "The wind speaks of this ranger and dwarf. They bested the trolls of Tartarus Peak and killed both Gath and Calliades. The spirit of this wood will not touch them."

"Mighty One, we offer you gold and silver," Mladen said. He opened one of his saddle bags and revealed heavy ingots.

Baring his stained, pointed teeth, the Anak'im said, "What need have I for gold or silver? You have nothing I want."

D'yakon Krovos replied, "This ranger is but a harbinger — a messenger from the Kral. It is his intent to take back this land. You will be driven out."

The Anak'im's evil eyes narrowed dangerously. Mladen added hastily, "Help me kill him, and we will stop the Kral's plan before it starts."

Gripping his club so tightly it creaked, the Anak'im growled ominously, "The Kral owes me a debt of blood. I will aid you, but the body of the ranger is mine. I wish to send the Kral my own message."

4:39pm

A few paces ahead of the caravan, Marko gestured for Dragahn to slow. The knight swept his head from one side of the road to the next as if to find a place to camp.

The mood of the teamsters had not improved during the afternoon; if anything, it had worsened. Each of them cast worried glances toward Lucky, hoping he would make it until they stopped, but the cloth pressed against his wound had turned a deep crimson, in stark contrast to the youth's extremely pale skin.

Preceded by rustling in the overhanging boughs, clouds of yellowish-white smoke erupted around the wagons.

Shouting out in warning, Dragahn snapped the reins. Fumes clouded his vision, and his movements became sluggish as the world spun. His head lolling as he lost muscle control, Dragahn caught sight of the group's outriders falling from their horses. Next to him, Jasper lurched forward. Unconscious or dead, he didn't know.

The caravan had stopped. Dragahn fought against the lethargy and gripped the reins with both hands. He had to get everyone moving. Suddenly, his muscles relaxed, and he slumped in his seat.

Four orc warriors, wearing black masks and black leather armor, dropped from the tree branches above and searched the wagons to make sure everyone was asleep. Staying clear of the smoke, Marko turned his horse around and waited while, at the other end of the caravan, Kourash and Ognian did the same.

In the middle, Aleksandra, her face covered by her scarf, checked to make sure Grendel was unconscious. Once confirmed, she climbed down from her seat and studied the other teamsters.

"I think they're out," Kourash growled.

Moving like a shadow amongst the wagons, a man wearing a dark cloak with the hood pulled up, gently touched each of the bodies, exposing a cadaverous hand with blackened fingertips.

"Gregori," Aleksandra said, "I wasn't expecting you here."

A hairless face that wept with open sores turned toward her. His feverish eyes bored into hers as he leaned heavily on his staff. "I wanted to see for myself what gifts you brought."

She shuddered involuntarily and said, "You look horrible."

"A side effect. Nothing more." His eyes roamed over the sleeping forms as he added, "Yes, these will do just fine."

"What are you going to do to them?"

Gregori stiffened. "Corrupt them like everyone else... like the guild... like Pazard'zhik. Do you really care what I do to them?"

"No, of course not. Just curious about your work" she replied quickly.

"My sister's grown soft," Marko said with a sneer. They both turned at the knight's approach. "We are wasting time," he added before Aleksandra could respond. "Where's your camp?"

Waving his hand, Gregori pointed toward a now-visible side trail.

CHAPTER 32
HUNTING THE HUNTER

October 24, 4235 K.E.

5:20pm

"What's going on here?" Xandor said to himself as he stared down at the trampled grass. This was different than the bison tracks from earlier. These tracks had a purpose. Dismounting, Xandor scratched his head.

"Xandor?" Chert asked, fidgeting with the reins.

"A troop of humanoids, probably orcs, came through last night," Xandor replied. "They're chasing a band of humans."

"Are you sure?"

Xandor gave Chert a slant-eyed look.

"Sorry, oh master of reading tracks," Chert snarked.

Turning back toward the road, Xandor knelt. "The Parlathean lion has returned, too. It came through a couple of hours ago."

"Should we worry?"

Xandor thought about his last encounter with a lion and gave the dwarf a cheeky grin. "We, no. You, maybe."

"That's not funny, ranger. I don't like cats."

"I'm sure they don't like you either," Xandor said and remounted Xerxes.

The sun dropped below the horizon, and the two continued traveling. With Chert using his night vision to help them avoid low-hanging branches and trusting the instincts of their horses to keep them on the road, they moved as quickly as they could through the looming darkness. After several miles of riding this way, Chert and Xandor spotted a faint glow just off the roadway. Pulling back on the reins, Xandor directed Xerxes toward the pale light.

Beside the road, an elf raised his hand in greeting or maybe in warning. A white nimbus surrounded the figure, causing the two travelers to squint against the glare.

Speaking the language of the elves, Xandor asked, "Kuinka voin auttaa sinua, väkiljós meistari?" *How can I help you, master elf?*

The elf looked at the ranger and pointed west, back the way they had just come.

Xandor replied, "We can't do that."

The mouth of the elf did not move, but a hollow voice echoed all around them and said, "The sleeping god grows restless. In his dream, he has sent one of the Anak'im to hunt you. You must flee now, or he will kill you."

Xandor and Chert exchanged a puzzled glance. Neither had seen an Anak'im. Xandor had read a little about them during his ranger studies, but even those references were vague and often contradictory.

"We cannot leave. Our friends are in danger to the east. Perhaps you can show us a safe route around this Anak'im?"

The elf stared at them, the expression on his face unreadable.

"Elf, help us or get out of our way," Xandor said, angry at being threatened.

The elf's eyes glazed slightly, giving the impression he was listening to something only he could hear. When his eyes came back into focus, he stared at the ranger. After a slight bow, the elf vanished, and with him went every creak and groan of the forest.

"Great, you chased him off," Chert muttered.

"He wasn't going to help us."

"At least he warned us."

Xandor searched around for the elf, trying to see if he had reappeared elsewhere, but darkness reigned. Giving up, he applied a little pressure to Xerxes' sides, and the horses started forward at a slow walk. "He warned us about some mythical beast that crushes men's bone for bread and bathes in their blood. That's not a warning. It's a bedtime story."

No sooner than the words left his mouth, the stench of death and decay enveloped them.

"You were saying," Chert whispered.

"Shut up."

Xerxes pawed the road and tossed his head, but the stallion made no other sound to give away their position.

Xandor rubbed the horse's neck, peering vainly into the darkness for signs of this new threat.

Dismounting, Chert and Xandor silently led their horses behind a massive granite boulder standing sentinel near the roadside. The ranger whispered to each animal while he removed their bridles and stowed them in the saddlebags. When he was done, he crouched beside a jumble of smaller rocks while Chert stood by the boulder, checking his armor.

The dwarf could not believe his eyes. Walking down the road was a massive giant with a spiked club braced against one shoulder. Chert's eyebrows climbed higher when he spotted the redhaired man riding slowly beside the giant. It was the same Northman who had shot them at the bunker.

The dwarf glanced over and saw Xandor give the signal. Whispering a silent prayer, Chert gestured sharply. Silvery-white light erupted in front of Mladen's horse, causing it to rear and throw its rider.

The Anak'im stopped and raised one of his massive hands to block the glare.

Taking advantage of the confusion, the dwarf shouted another prayer and hurled his hammer. It whooshed through the air and struck the giant in the lower chest. A loud crack echoed off the trees. With a sharp intake of air, the Anak'im stumbled back as the hammer bounced off the flattened bear hide and returned to Chert's waiting hand. Meanwhile, Xandor ghosted away into the woods.

Emitting a thunderous bellow, the Anak'im swung his club in a circle, striking several dead trees. They crashed and fell toward the dwarf.

Chert ducked behind the boulder to avoid flying branches. He closed his eyes to keep out the dust and, when he reopened them, found himself surrounded by a sea of splintered wood. Feeling trapped, he watched the giant wade through the destruction toward him.

With another shouted prayer, Chert side-armed the hammer. White flames enveloped the head. It struck the giant in the shoulder with an explosive boom, leaving his left arm hanging limp.

The Anak'im's twisted face snarled in anger, and slimy spittle escaped from the corner of his mouth, splattering on

Chert's shield. Roaring as he raised his spiked club high in the air, the giant struck the boulder, shattering it into a thousand tiny pieces. Shrapnel flew, and Chert found himself deafened by the rain of stones pelting his helmet.

Using the havoc caused by the Anak'im, the ranger circled the light radiating from the road and slowly closed the distance between himself and the Northman.

The boulder exploded, and Mladen raised his bow. Arrow already nocked, he drew back the string.

Out of the corner of his eye, Xandor saw Chert standing dazed amid the boulder's pulverized remains. In one fluid motion, he stepped and threw one of his blades overhanded. Spinning through the air, the sword hilt struck the Northman's extended left arm.

With a cry, Mladen dropped his bow and spun in place, simultaneously drawing his cutlasses.

Xandor charged across the short, well-lit distance, his remaining longsword raised for a mighty, downward, two-handed cleave. At the last second, he dipped his shoulder under the rising block and slammed into his opponent's solar plexus. He straightened explosively, hurling the Northman back.

Trailing arrows in his wake, Mladen crashed to the ground in a sliding roll. He came up in a low crouch and brought one of his cutlasses into a high block and attacked with the other in a low slice.

The Northman glanced about, surprised. Instead of attacking, the ranger had retrieved his fallen weapon and waited in silence.

Fighting the dull pain in his chest, Mladen sent his tattoos swirling. He knew the psychological impact the display had on his opponents and searched the ranger's face for the fear his tattoos normally inspired.

Instead, what he found was a cold, pitiless gaze.

Mladen shook himself and fought against the worm of fear in his mind. Errant thoughts jumped into his head. *'I killed this man. I saw the arrows go in. I saw him fall. He was dead.'* The words kept repeating in his mind, feeding his fear. Words he had used with Marko.

"Are you a ghost?" he finally screamed.

Xandor answered the tattooed warrior's query by advancing.

Mladen rushed forward. He feinted with his left blade while slashing up from a low guard position with his right blade.

Xandor blocked and dodged the first, but was a second too slow with the other, earning a bloody gash along his left calf, just above his boot.

Mladen's expression turned predatory when he saw his opponent wasn't a ghost. Looking into his foe's eyes, he searched again for an emotion, any emotion. The ranger's expression remained impassive, his bicolored gaze cold. What kind of man was the Kral's ranger? Did he have no fear of death? Mladen yelled, "I killed you once. I'll do it again!"

Growling loudly, the Anak'im swung his club at the dwarf.

Partially trapped by the fallen branches and deafened by the noise, Chert could only stand his ground and watch through the eye slit of his helmet as the club began its downward arc. Bracing himself, he yanked his shield up over his head in a vain attempt to stop the crushing blow.

The club landed with a deafening crunch, and several of its spikes punched through the steel shield, driving Chert to his knees.

With an alarming metallic scrape, the spikes grated against the side of Chert's helmet as the Anak'im raised his club. Wrenching the torn piece of metal back and forth, Chert couldn't pull his shield free of the club. His forearm began to throb. He glanced up and saw the bloodied tip of a spike protruding through the steel vambrace he wore over his chain sleeve. The dwarf hung on like a gristly piece of meat and rode the club into the air as the giant slowly raised it over his head.

Pivoting, the Anak'im found a fractured tree trunk. He inhaled deeply and drew back his club in a long arc, preparing to drive the impaled dwarf into the knifelike projections.

Ignoring the spasms of icy pain that shot through his arm, Chert desperately struck at the spikes trapping his shield with his hammer, hitting them with everything he had. Frantic, he worked his shield back and forth, and the spike trapping his arm became more and more brittle with each pass, but it also rent his flesh. Gritting his teeth, he pushed against the almost-vertical club with his feet, finally snapping the spike between his arm and the shield.

Pain consumed his world, but through divine grace, he clung to consciousness. When the club stopped for a brief moment at its apogee, Chert was free. He twisted and held on as best he could with blood dripping steadily down his mangled arm.

The Anak'im brought his club around swiftly, but the dwarf didn't slam into the broken tree. Instead, he let go of his shield and dropped the few feet to land on the giant's head. Chert grabbed a handful of the greasy hair, and with all the strength his short frame could muster, he smashed the thick skull of the Anak'im repeatedly with his hammer.

Enraged, the giant reached up, grabbed the dwarf by the leg, and flung him.

Focused on his opponent, Xandor saw he needed to move faster. The play of emotions on the red-haired man's face was clear: the Northman was afraid. The two circled for a moment more before Xandor launched his attack. Swinging his swords in opposite arcs, he forced Mladen to split his attention. The Northman succeeded in blocking both blades but could not avoid the ranger's head butt.

Blood running down his chin, Mladen staggered back. Xandor kicked him in the groin. The wounded man's tattoos ceased swirling, and his eyes lost focus as he sank to the ground.

Gasping in pain, the Northman instinctively rolled, putting distance between himself and the ranger.

Xandor closed and was ready when the Northman came up with his high block and a low slice. This time, the low slice skimmed the surface of the roadway, throwing a spray of dirt and gravel into Xandor's face. Stumbling back, the ranger held his swords defensively as he blinked the grit from his eyes.

Taking advantage of the distraction, the Northman dodged sideways and hurtled into the darkness, crashing through the underbrush.

Through watery eyes, Xandor watched the distorted form of the Northman vanish into the darkness.

A sudden clamor of metal on metal drew his attention, and Xandor glanced in Chert's direction in time to see the dwarf's meteoric arc and inevitable crash landing.

Ignoring the Northman, the ranger's eyes darted to the discarded bow. He scooped it up and let an arrow fly toward the giant's backside. Before the arrow hit its intended target, Xandor melted into the edge of the forest and readied another.

Breathing loudly through its nose, the Anak'im searched for his new tormentor. A few heartbeats later, a second arrow flew out of the trees and struck the giant in the chest.

The giant saw only the empty road and the devastation he had caused. Chert's light disoriented the Anak'im, making the darkness under the trees impenetrable. Squinting to see better, the creature rubbed his head with a beefy hand and found several sticky lumps where the dwarf had struck. Blood trickled from the arrow wounds and soaked into his bearskin.

Another stinging pain penetrated his thick hide, and he turned, searching for the archer. The arrows were coming too fast. A fourth flew, striking the giant's chest once again, and then a fifth. Finding the point where the arrows originated, he hurled his club.

Xandor looked on with grim satisfaction as the club flew past him and crashed into the trees. Across the way, the horns of Chert's great helm moved steadily through the woods toward the giant.

Whispering the arcane command word, Xandor sent golden fire licking up his blades as he stepped into the light and shouted, "Missed me!"

The Anak'im swung around and glared at the impudent human. "Die, little man!" He snatched up a nearby boulder and strode forward, winding up to hurl the stone. He took two steps and met Chert's hammer. It smashed against the side of the giant's skull with a loud thunderclap.

Tree branches crashed down behind Xandor, shorn off twenty feet above the ground by the giant's errant boulder. The ranger charged forward, both blades swinging. Chert's blow had turned the Anak'im toward the dwarf, so Xandor passed behind, hamstringing the giant with both burning blades.

Falling to his knees, the giant screamed in rage and grabbed wildly for the fleeting shadows that darted in and out of his darkening vision. His horrific cries merged with another thunderclap and turned into a weak mewling.

Xandor passed the dwarf, saying only, "Finish it." He extinguished his blades and disappeared into the darkness. A few feet into the trees, he paused to give his eyes time to adjust after the brightness engendered by Chert's prayer and to listen. The Northman crashed through the dry underbrush a hundred yards away.

'*As long as he keeps that up, catching him won't be a problem,*' he thought. Using his ears more than his eyes, he headed in the direction of the noise, his motions in harmony with the woods around him.

Seconds later, the noise ceased, replaced by an eerie quiet. Xandor heaved a resigned sigh. '*I knew it was too good to last,*' he thought as he cut through the woods to catch up.

Cautiously putting distance between himself and the leather-clad warrior, Mladen eased through the dark underbrush. Just as he thought he had lost the ranger for good, the darkness was rent asunder by a leonine roar.

Mladen froze. The great cats of Parlatheas — both the lions who hunted the Sea of Grass and the Wasteland tigers of the far north — feared nothing, but one who dared brave these ghostly woods would be especially dangerous. Only the Anak'im and their kin walked here without concern.

With a fresh dose of adrenaline singing in his veins, Mladen struggled to control his breathing and remain still. Keeping his sweaty palms close to the hilts of his cutlasses, he strained his ears for the slightest of sounds.

Dry underbrush crackled and rustled in the darkness, but it was too far away to be the cat. It must have been the Kral's ranger.

The cat roared again, giving Mladen a direction and rough distance. A sinister gleam in his eyes, he turned and headed away from the approaching ranger, stomping and breaking branches along the way. Mladen wanted the ranger to hear him as he placed the cat directly between them.

With no moon in the sky, there little in the way of light. Xandor pressed forward through the darkness, trying to close the distance before the Northman went silent again. He froze when he heard the low warning growl of the great cat less than a dozen yards away.

"Keep your distance, San Sebek-wy."

Not moving a muscle, Xandor struggled to find the talking cat.

"The man-thing you follow is my kill," the sleek female said with a low growl. Seven feet from nose to base of the tail, the Parlathean lioness crept forward, keeping its head close to the ground.

Without conscious thought, Xandor responded, "No, little sister. He is mine."

The cat flicked her tail.

Xandor tensed, expecting the lioness to challenge him. Instead, she said, "I am Sahmaht. We hunt together, friend of the Akshan."

The Akshan. Hearing the strange title the felines bestowed upon the one who was both their alpha and protector sent a flood of relief through the ranger. Akshan was also the name of a sentient artifact that had gifted the ranger with the ability to speak with felines.

The great cat waited, her tail flicking with impatience.

"We hunt together," Xandor agreed, taking a respectful step back. He let the lioness guide him, and the two moved carefully along the path taken by the Northman, low growls and hisses passing between them.

Disappointed the ranger hadn't screamed yet, Mladen stopped briefly and looked behind him, listening. What was the ranger doing?

Uncertainty gnawed at him and, with it, an idea of what he could do to tip the odds in his favor. It did not take long to find what he needed, despite the weak light from above.

He felt a surge of self-satisfaction as he covered the ground with a scattering of leaves. Afterward, he doubled back and left a trail, something he was sure the ranger could follow.

Thankful the cat found hunting one human with another to be fun, Xandor followed her lead. Without her eyesight and keen nose, he would never have been able to follow his quarry. Unfortunately, she did not know how to identify traps. Xandor bit back a curse when the vine grabbed his ankle and whipped forward, yanking his leg with it.

Breaking partway through the arc, the field expedient trap turned Xandor from a captive into a projectile. He hurtled into a tangle of brittle tree branches, which burst in an explosion of splinters.

The ranger came to rest at the base of the tree, stunned and in pain. Before he could shake it off, the lioness bounded up and nosed his side. "Do you live, San Sebek-wy?"

A wicked grin split Mladen's face when he heard the tree whip upright. He froze and strained his hearing, certain he heard a muffled curse followed by sharp cracks and a dull thud. Feeling much better about things now, he listened for a moment more before he hurried onward, his own path laid out in his mind.

Sitting with his back to a tree, Chert heard the great cat's roar. "Hope that beasty finds its dinner elsewhere."

He plucked at his ruined vambrace with a pair of pliers and pried the jagged pieces of metal out of his arm. Blood dripped freely, warm and sticky inside his armor. Beside him lay the discarded tip of the Anak'im's spike.

When he pulled out the last piece, he rotated his arm and worked the buckles loose, letting the vambrace fall to the ground.

Pulling up his chain sleeve, he examined several deep, jagged wounds in his forearm. He dug his fingers into the soil beside him and pulled up a fistful. Rubbing the earth into his wounds, he mixed it with his blood and whispered a healing prayer. Blue light illuminated his arm and slowly the wounds closed, leaving thin, white scars.

Chert spent the next few minutes healing his other wounds. Once finished, he stretched his arm and tested the muscles. Feeling sore but otherwise unhurt, he stood and checked on the horses.

Xerxes was missing.

He had no idea where the stallion would have gone, but he was betting it involved trouble — like rider, like horse. Thankfully, Sky remained where they had left her. Chert patted the pony on the nose, surreptitiously glancing around to see if anyone noticed.

Searching the battleground for anything useful, Chert found his mangled shield still impaled on the Anak'im's spiked club and took a few minutes to dislodge it. Next, he crossed the road and retrieved the Northman's bow and several of his arrows. After a moment's thought, he set his load down and pulled out his knife to make a few modifications to the bow. With a grin hidden beneath his beard, he left the bow and a few arrows randomly scattered where Xandor and the Northman had fought earlier.

Chert went back to Sky and was startled to find not only her, but also Xerxes and another horse. He blinked in surprise, and his mouth worked silently for a minute. Finally, he spluttered at the two larger animals, "Where did you go... and where did you come from?"

Six big liquid eyes stared back at him.

"Be that way," Chert grumbled. Then it came to him. He wagged a finger at the charger. "You're a smart one, aren't you? You brought back the Northman's horse."

Xandor hated their slow pace, but he had to keep a wary eye out for more traps. Of course, the Northman had to slow to set them, so it was a trade-off of sorts. The gamble, naturally, was whether he had set any others.

Fifteen minutes of slow movement grew tiring. Xandor gently stepped down on the ball of his foot, carefully putting weight on it to avoid breaking anything underfoot.

"We hunt a hunter, San Sebek-wy," the Parlathean lioness growled.

"He's dangerous prey, but fighting is not his preferred way. He likes to ambush or set traps." Xandor closed his eyes as a thought occurred to him. He oriented himself to the path he and the cat were following — the Northman was circling!

"He's going back to the road! Come, let's surprise him."

CHAPTER 33
SAN SEBEK-WY

October 24, 4235 K.E.

7:12pm

Hidden behind a thick tree trunk, Mladen eyed the dwarf rummaging through one of his saddlebags. Nearby, he saw his bow and arrows at the edge of the lit zone. Easing down onto all fours, he carefully crept through the woods, staying low and moving as quietly as possible. Reaching past a jumble of debris, he lifted his bow and two arrows into the safety of the darkness.

Her eyes fixed on the Northman, Sahmaht brought her legs in underneath her, preparing to jump, but Xandor put a restraining hand on her shoulder. "Wait," he hissed. "My friend is not that careless. Let's see what happens."

Flicking her tail in irritation, the cat focused on the crawling Northman.

Seemingly oblivious to the attention he was getting, Chert opened the Northman's saddlebag and slid out a silver ingot. He let out a low whistle and put it back.

Behind the dwarf, the Northman slowly raised himself to a kneeling position.

Mladen nocked an arrow and pulled his bowstring back, sighting on the dwarf. When the string became taut, his humor turned to horror as it snapped with a loud twang. The dwarf whipped around.

Chert tossed the glow stone hidden in his left hand toward the noise, took a single step, and hurled the hammer in his right.

The Northman threw himself to the side, barely avoiding what could have been a fatal strike. Still, the hammer landed a glancing blow to his shoulder and spun him to the ground. He was on his feet in an instant. Drawing his cutlasses,

Mladen snarled, only to find the dwarf waiting for him, the hammer already back in his hands.

Erupting from the edge of the underbrush only yards away, the buzzsaw roar of a feline challenge mingled with a barbaric war cry split the night as both Parlathean lioness and leather-clad ranger charged toward the surprised Northman.

Chert and Mladen gaped at the sight. Mladen recovered first and fled into the darkness, but his flight was cut short as the snarling cat swatted his feet out from under him. The Northman hit the ground hard.

Rolling to the side, he came to his feet as quickly as he could, one leg burning as though on fire. He whipped both cutlasses up in a desperate attempt to parry the ranger's incoming attacks. The intricate web of blades mostly succeeded, but one of the ranger's blades snuck through, leaving a small current of blood running down the Northman's left arm.

Even as he fought the ranger, Mladen's mind gibbered frantically as he tried to come to terms with what had just happened. The cat and the ranger hunted together, and they hunted him!

He swept his blades in short, sharp arcs, trying to put distance between himself and his attackers while panic reigned in his mind. Who was this ranger?

Igniting his blades, Xandor blocked the short swipes and stabbed low with his left blade, slicing the Northman's right thigh open with an audible hiss. However, he caught a short score on his own left bicep in return.

The ranger danced back and settled for blocking any swipes that came close enough to threaten him. He made a few probing attacks but mostly waited for the Northman's energy to bleed off.

Circling behind the Northman, the cat contented herself with keeping her new brother's prey from fleeing into the night and watched them battle with their steel fangs.

Feeling the weight of the cat's stare behind him, Mladen's eyes widened with the realization the ranger must be one of the Neuri — a werebeast. It was the only explanation that made sense. It explained how he survived the bunker and now, how he hunted with a Parlathean lioness. Rather than comfort him, the explanation only fed the knot of fear inside him. He had never seen a Neuri before, but he had heard tales of the shapeshifters. They were rumored to be amongst the most cruel and vicious hunters known.

Outnumbered and out of his league, Mladen sought an escape route. Any path out of this nightmare would do. His frenetic attacks clashed again and again against the ranger's defenses, his fear feeding every strike.

Xandor and Mladen traded more blows and with each riposte, the Northman's swings became wilder.

Taking advantage, Xandor swept both blades around in a low-to-high arc from the left. He beat aside the Northman's blades with his right blade and opened a deep gash in his ribs with his left. Blood steamed as it poured from the wound.

Before the ranger could bring his fast-moving blades back to a guard position, the berserk Northman charged. Screaming, Mladen plowed a shoulder into the ranger's chest, driving him to the ground.

Not looking back, Mladen sprang for the darkness of the woods. Xandor shot back to his feet and raced after him, his passage marked by the glowing trail of his burning blades. Behind him sped the lioness.

Chert's eyes grew wide at the hungry look the cat bestowed on him before chasing after the two men. He continued to stare in their direction for several moments. Then he shook himself, closed his mouth, and turned back to find Xerxes watching him.

"That is the strangest human I have ever met," Chert said to the horse.

Mladen crashed to a stop at the edge of a thicket and turned, vainly searching for salvation. His eyes fell on the ranger charging after him, swords aglow with a hellish light, and he let out a frightful shriek.

Xandor saw the glint of the Northman's blades as they rose to intercept his charge. The ranger pulled back, but his feet slid on the layer of twigs and broken branches carpeting the forest. He dropped to his back, barely holding onto his blades, and kicked out with both feet. His boots impacted his opponent's stomach.

With a grunt, Mladen doubled over. "No!" the Northman gasped. Eyes wide with panic, he stumbled off amid a spray of bone-white needles.

Dodging between the close-growing trees, Xandor followed close on the Northman's heels. '*This has gone on too long,*' he thought. Sahmaht growled as she raced by him.

A moment later, a bloodcurdling roar erupted near Mladen. The Northman spun away from it and raced down a steep slope, his chest heaving.

"San Sebek-wy, you will find him in the ravine," Xandor heard as he passed the cat's position.

Hooking an arm around a slender tree, Mladen caught himself at the edge of the rocky cliff. There was a sickening moment when his lower body flew out over the edge. His stomach fell back into place when his feet touched the ground again.

A wide chasm spread out before the Northman. Knowing there was no other choice, he hastily picked his way down the face, ignoring the trail of blood he left.

Xandor stopped at the edge of the ravine. A bloody handprint marked where Mladen had started his descent.

Extinguishing his blades, he leaned over and used the thin trickle of starlight to watch his foe. After several steps back and a deep breath to center his mind for more combat, Xandor sprinted for the edge and leapt.

Mladen looked up from the base of the cliff, expecting to see the ranger clambering down behind him, or at least the glow of his burning blades. The starlight teased him with glimpses of trees, roots, and brush.

A soft swish overhead and the sound of something heavy striking the ground set his pulse pounding louder than khumanoidi war drums. Nothing moved at the rim of the hollow. He swallowed against the lump in his throat and turned to make his way along the ravine.

The darkness exploded with flaming light. Mladen cursed when he realized he had trapped himself with the Neuri. He snarled and slashed the air in front of him with his cutlasses. Desperation ruled — if he could just escape! Deep down, some part of him knew the ranger would not allow that.

Cornered, the Northman was far more dangerous. But even backed by fear and panic, Xandor noticed the Northman's injuries were taking their toll, robbing him of the energy needed to maintain the fury of his attacks. His breathing came in labored gasps, and blood ran freely from his growing number of wounds, darkening his clothes.

"Yield," Xandor demanded amid strikes.

The golden flames from the ranger's blades reflected off Mladen's wide eyes. "Never! You'll have to kill me!" As he spoke, the Northman's cutlasses crashed against Xandor's defenses.

"I don't have to kill you. All I need to do is wait," Xandor replied. The ranger shoved Mladen back using both his blades. Above their heads, the roar of the lioness echoed off the walls of the ravine.

Again, Mladen charged. He led with both blades extended, each aimed at Xandor's head, but at the last second, he dropped his guard. Xandor's block turned into a thrust and cleanly slipped between the Northman's ribs, piercing his heart.

Mladen stared up at the ranger as he fell to his knees, his eyes open but unseeing.

Taking a step back, Xandor felt a freezing cold shadow pass over himself and the Northman. Yellow eyes glared out of the darkness with such malevolence it almost became a physical barrier. Sheathing one of his blades, Xandor reached for the cross around his neck.

The shadowy form dug both its hands into Mladen's body, wrenching out his heart as if flesh and bone were mere paper. Anchored to the heart was the frail image of the Northman. It screamed and writhed, trying to escape the shadow's grip, and all Xandor could do was watch. Even shutting his eyes, the image stayed with him.

Then, all was quiet, the feeling of malevolence gone.

Xandor opened his eyes and prayed.

The lioness waited for Xandor at the top of the ravine. "You fight well, San Sebek-wy. Why do you not eat your prey?"

"He's only fit for the vultures, Sahmaht."

She thought for a moment, then said, "That was an impressive leap. You would make a good cat."

"Thank you," Xandor said. Turning his face skyward, he told the Akshan, "But I would prefer to stay human!"

The lioness stared at him curiously, letting the comment pass. With a sigh of relief, Xandor retraced his steps.

Light from a glow stone illuminated the rim of Chert's shield. The dwarf grabbed it firmly with both hands, placed one foot on the opposite edge, and pulled, slowly bending the warped metal back into a round shape. Raising the shield, he eyed it critically, then shook his head in dissatisfaction. It would never truly be round again, and he needed a proper forge to repair the holes caused by the Anak'im's spiked club. Still, it was all he had for the time being. He would have to make do.

The dwarf was busy hammering the bent and split edges around the holes back together when the ranger materialized out of the darkness.

With a start, Chert yelled, "I hate it when you do that!"

"Sorry. Habit."

The dwarf asked, "Did you get him?"

When Xandor didn't answer, Chert stood and said, "Let me see those wounds."

They were both silent while the dwarf bandaged and dressed the ranger's injuries, healing the more grievous ones. While he worked, Chert studied the ranger, noting the distant look in his eyes. Finally, he asked, "You alright? You look like you have something on your mind."

If he weren't watching so closely, Chert would have missed the slight shake of Xandor's head. Frowning, he took the glow stone and directed the light into the man's eyes for a moment before pulling it away again, watching the pupils respond.

"What are you doing," Xandor asked as he jerked his head back, "trying to blind me?"

"No. Just checking for a concussion."

"What?"

Chert eyed his companion warily. "Were you hit on the head? Come on, let me check you for lumps on that thick skull."

Pushing the dwarf away gently, Xandor murmured, "No, I wasn't hit on the head. It's just..." He paused, seeming to gather his thoughts, before he said, "Something's out there. Something evil. It took Mladen. I can still see its face." Xandor heaved a loud sigh and added, "I've fought and killed before, but this — this was different..." He drifted back into silence. The tiny muscles around his eyes twitched, as if he fought some as-yet unidentified pain. "Do you ever forget the people you kill?"

Chert shook his head sadly and replied, "No, I remember every single face. Every last breath, it seems. Each one of them was trying to kill me, but their deaths still haunt me. Probably always will." He eyed the ranger gravely. "What do you think is out there?"

"A demon maybe. I don't know." Shrugging off the phantoms, he stood, looked at the saddlebags, and asked, "What have you been doing?"

"Well, while you were traipsing through the forest, I took care of our giant friend there, gathered the dropped weapons, and perused the contents of the Northman's saddlebags."

"Not bad. I'm glad you thought to retrieve his horse." At the dwarf's shamefaced expression, Xandor asked, "That wasn't you, was it?"

"No, blast it — Xerxes did! But I did go through the saddlebags."

Xandor chuckled as they gathered everything together. Once done, he introduced himself to the rouncey. "You can go with us or go your own way. There is danger in both choices, but know that where we go, the danger will only be worse."

The horse sidled closer and lightly butted the ranger in the chest.

"Alright, you can come with us," Xandor responded with a sad smile as he rubbed the horse's head.

They saddled up, and headed down the road at a comfortable pace, the way ahead lit by the dwarf's light.

"You still look like you were poleaxed," Chert said, hiding a smile.

"Do not."

"Do, too."

CHAPTER 34
CAPTURED

October 25, 4235 K.E.

8:18am

Jasper didn't know how long he had slept. He woke with a throbbing headache and a mouth full of cotton. Opening his eyes was a mistake. Bright sunlight flared all about him, causing tears to stream down his cheeks.

Squeezing his eyes shut, he felt his surroundings and discovered he was in a rectangular cage with cold metal bars and grated floor. Focusing, he used his other senses. He smelled the fresh air of the outdoors, heard heavy breathing — probably from the others sleeping — and movement nearby. The tiny hairs on his neck rose. Something made a wet, slurping noise, like jelly sliding out of a glass jar.

He peeked through teary eyes and instantly wished he hadn't. In the cage next to him, a purplish-grey mass of pulpy flesh writhed and pulsed. Jasper couldn't tell for sure, but it looked like a human elbow stuck out through its folds. The thing shifted slightly, exposing blood-covered tentacles. Underneath were half-eaten remains.

As his vision grew accustomed to the daylight, other cages came into focus, each with a person inside, scattered about a grassy clearing. He searched the faces of those near him and found all the teamsters asleep in similar metal cages — all except Grendel, Branimir, and Teodor. Looking further, he counted six more humans he didn't recognize — two adults and four children. Rivulets of blood trickled from their noses and mouths.

On the far side of the clearing, three cages stood clustered by themselves. Two held prisoners with long, lean bodies and hair the color of corn silk. Despite the distance and their emaciated condition, the style of their clothes and pale facial features made them unmistakable: they were Väkiljós — the People of Light — elves of the northern

Alashalian Mountains. The ruined remains of the third cage stood empty.

The two elves did not have the same symptoms as the humans, but they, too, seemed to be suffering from some type of illness. Their skin had an unhealthy grey pallor, and their bodies seemed soft, almost mushy. At least, that was the only way Jasper could describe it.

He turned and looked a little harder at the mess in the cage next to him. The more he stared, the more the pieces fit together. Bile rose in the back of his mouth when he realized he had found one of the missing horsemen.

Beyond the cages, the barren trees of the Haunted Wood bordered the clearing like silent sentinels. There were no signs of their captors or guards, nor were there any signs of the wagons, the soap, or the road. They'd been abandoned.

On the ground beside his cage, he spotted a metal bowl filled with water and was struck by a terrible thirst. He reached for it and was about to take a sip when he heard a hoarse elven voice call, "Ära drekka!"

Bowl still in his hand, Jasper lifted his gaze to the two cages across the way. One of the elves motioned weakly with his hand and repeated, this time in Trakyan, "Don't drink it. It will put you back to sleep."

Jasper studied the water and noticed the oily residue at the bottom. When it suddenly moved, he jerked and dropped the bowl, spilling the water. The bowl rang like a dinner bell.

The creature in the adjacent cage ceased pulsating. It didn't have a head or anything that resembled ears, but it remained poised as if listening.

Clearing his mind, Jasper reached deep inside and found his magic. He focused his energy on the locking mechanism of his door, working it through the keyhole and around the tumblers until the lock clicked.

The creature slunk out of its cage and shambled toward him. Still groggy, Jasper stumbled out of his cage only to come face to face with the horror. There was no head or eyes or any other sensory organs, just a writhing mass of flesh. It reared up and two of the tentacles lashed out, striking the mage hard in the chest. Like a ragdoll, Jasper crashed against a nearby cage and bounced off the bars.

The creature followed up with another crushing blow from one of its tentacles. This time, however, Jasper was ready and shaped the air in front of him into a shield. The tentacle smacked sickeningly against it, leaving traces of bloody mucus.

Grimacing, Jasper held his ground, using his low center of gravity to help keep his balance. He concentrated on one of the rings on his right hand and yelled, "Pyros!" A lance of yellow fire leapt out and struck the creature.

Tiny mouths opened along the underside of the tentacles, and a thousand screams echoed in the clearing as the creature flipped backward into the air. It landed several yards away with a squelching noise that made Jasper cringe.

Flailing its tentacles, the thing struggled to right itself. Mouths opened and closed, spitting black mucus. Steam hissed from the gaping hole near where two of its tentacles connected to the main body, but the wound quickly filled with black slime. It sealed without leaving a scar.

Preparing another spell from a ring on his left hand, Jasper advanced cautiously.

The creature struck again, this time lashing out with three of its rubbery tentacles. Jasper deflected the first two with his shield of air, but the third snuck under his defenses and wrapped around his knee. Agony coursed through the mage's nervous system.

Compartmentalizing the pain, he made a fist with his left hand, focused on a different ring, and rasped, "Īlios!" Bright white light speared downward into the tentacle, and the purplish-grey flesh peeled away as it melted, revealing a black mass of quivering muscle.

Jasper wrapped his left hand around his right wrist and intensified the light, moving it farther up the tentacle and cutting deeper into the body. Sparks sprayed from the wound. The creature screamed in agony and released its hold to retreat, leaving a black trail of slime and mucus.

Jasper's leg throbbed. Acidic spittle had eaten through his pants and left tiny red circles the size and shape of the creature's multitudinous orifices.

With a juicy slosh, the hungry monster launched itself into the air. Flailing tentacles spread wide, its body blocked out the sun, and the mouths opened wide.

"Jasper!"

The mage's eyes darted to the right, and he caught sight of a long staff, charred at one end, hurtling toward him. Reaching out, he concentrated and called the staff's name.

The creature smacked against Jasper as his fingers closed around the wooden shaft. Tentacles wrapped him in an enormous hug, and the folds of its purplish-grey flesh bulged and throbbed, hiding any view of the mage.

A thunderclap shook the clearing, and the thing attempting to devour Jasper exploded. Black and grey flesh fountained into the air.

Surrounded by a smoky haze, Jasper sat up, dripping black mucus. What remained of the creature's body collapsed around him and dissolved into the earth.

"Take that, you bastard!" Jasper yelled in defiance.

Xandor and Chert ran to the mage, armed and ready for action.

"What was that?" Xandor demanded.

On shaky legs, Jasper bent over with his hands on his knees, gasping deep breaths. He held up a finger. "Give me a moment."

"Where's Grendel?" Chert asked, looking among the cages.

Jasper remained quiet, not sure what to say. The dwarf stood before the mage, giving him a dark look.

"I don't know. Grendel isn't here."

Chert turned and grasped Xandor's wrist, fear and anxiety written clearly in his eyes. "We have to rescue him."

"We will," Xandor assured him.

"But first, I need you to see about saving these people. Especially the boy," Jasper said, pointing to Lucky's cage.

While Xandor and Jasper caught each other up on recent events, Chert wrenched open the cage door with a word of prayer. Removing his helm, he knelt beside Lucky and unwrapped his bandage. Fresh blood seeped out and pooled on the ground. He pressed his hands against the boy's side, closed his eyes, and prayed to the Eternal Father to heal him. In response, the teenager's skin glowed with a bright blue light, and the wound closed, leaving an angry red line. Afterwards, Chert rewrapped the wound and continued praying. "Sleep. Heal," he whispered to the youth when he was done.

Chert moved from cage to cage, but when he came to the children, he stopped. "I think the two of you should take a look at this."

Xandor and Jasper hurried across the clearing. On the way, Jasper whispered, "Katharízo," and the black mucus covering him disappeared, leaving him looking cleaner and fresher.

As they approached the unconscious child, they noticed clumps of his hair had fallen out. Oozing blisters and ulcers covered most of his body, and odd symbols, written in what looked like black ink, scored his cheeks and brow.

Xandor asked Chert and Jasper, "Do either of you recognize those symbols?" They both shook their heads.

"It doesn't appear to be arcane in nature," Jasper said as he studied the markings, still a little out of breath.

"It's not arcane."

All three turned simultaneously and saw a semi-transparent figure standing beside the caged elves. It was the same ghost who had warned Xandor and Chert about the Anak'im.

"What is it, then?" Jasper asked.

"It's the language of Ka'Sehkuur, the sleeping god — or Cayn, as humans call him."

The three of them stared blankly at the ghost. Beside him, one of the elves in the cage coughed and raised his arm to wipe his mouth. A black smear glistened on the back of his grey-skinned hand — the same as the creature's trail of slime.

They approached the ghost cautiously, but it never moved from the sickly elf's side. Looking closer, Jasper could see a resemblance between the two.

Xandor said, "Chert, please see what you can do for him."

While Chert worked the lock to the elf's cage, Jasper quickly inspected the unconscious elf in the other cage and saw he, too, drooled a small trail of black mucus from the corner of his mouth. The third cage sat empty. Several of its bars ended in jagged nubs three feet above the ground, as if the iron had been melted.

Xandor examined the ground in front of the cage. A trail of black slime led toward the teamsters.

The conscious elf tugged up his tunic hem, revealing black symbols painted on his torso.

"Is he turning into whatever that was I just fought?" Jasper asked the ghostly elf.

He nodded, and his luminous eyes filled with hatred.

Chert stared at the elf, a concerned look on his face. "Any idea how to stop it?"

"None," Jasper said simply.

"That thing, does it have a name?" Chert asked.

"A dwolma," the ghost answered.

"I've never seen or heard of anything like it. Is it some type of demon or extraplanar creature?" Jasper asked.

"It is one of the beasts of Ka'Sehkuur."

Xandor returned and motioned for Chert to continue opening the cage. The dwarf gave him a questioning look but bent to finish. With a loud metallic screech, the door swung open.

Stooping down, Xandor gently helped the tortured elf out of his cage. The elf's body sagged, as if his bones had lost their hardness and become spongy. Holding the elf's head so he could drink, the ranger dribbled water from his canteen into his mouth. The elf tried to gulp down the water, but Xandor held him to just a few sips. When the elf finished, Xandor laid him on the ground so Chert could begin his examination.

Chert closed his eyes in prayer. The moment his hand touched the elf's grey-skinned arm, the elf screamed. Chert drew back his hand as if stung, leaving behind an ugly red handprint. "I don't think there's anything I can do for you," the dwarf said quietly.

Standing, Xandor asked the elven ghost, "What can you tell us about this Ka'Sehkuur?"

"The sleeping god is one of the original brothers."

Xandor, Chert, and Jasper stared at each other.

"Brothers?" Chert asked. "As in the brothers, Cayn and Havel?"

"Yes."

Seized by a fit of choking, the elf vomited the water. Chert sat him up so he wouldn't drown. He looked at Xandor and said, "He doesn't have much time."

"You must listen and understand," the ghost pleaded. "There is an ancient story we tell our children about our creation. A tale of two titan brothers: one elven, — Dioth Cyela, or Havel, as you call him — and the other, human — Ka'Sehkuur, or Cayn. They fought a terrible battle in a faraway land; no one remembers the truth of why. Some believe it was jealousy, but other storytellers say that Ka'Sehkuur touched the face of Chaos and went mad." As the ghost spoke, images formed in his audience's minds. Behind him, other ghosts arrived, filling the clearing with pale, cold light that competed with the sun.

"Brother struck brother using swords fashioned from the very stars, and where their blood touched the earth, it brought forth life. It is said Dioth Cyela cried with sadness at every swing of his sword. His tears streamed down his face, falling as rain. When they fell on a tree or flower or blade of grass, an elf was born.

"Ka'Sehkuur screamed with an insane rage when he saw the goodness his brother created. He cursed and spat fire. His blood turned black as pitch, and every time it landed on a newly formed elf, they became corrupted. Thus were the eotenas and orcnéas born. It must have been a horrible sight to see... the creation of both abominations and the beautiful.

"Toward the end of the battle, Dioth Cyela struck Ka'Sehkuur a mighty blow, sending him crashing to the ground. He pushed up tall mountains and formed deep valleys. Cut by one of the jagged peaks, black blood pooled around Ka'Sehkuur's head. The pain brought clarity to his thoughts, and his eyes gained a sense of lucidity.

"Temporarily freed from his madness, he begged his brother to slay him before chaos and evil consumed him once again.

"Dioth Cyela looked down at his newly-created elves and could not bring himself to taint their birth with further violence. He threw down his sword, creating a rift between the lands, which quickly filled with his tears.

"Ka'Sehkuur slowly brought himself to a kneeling position. His elven brother turned his back on him and walked away, with all his children racing after him. The battle between madness and lucidity raged inside the human brother. Madness won, and Ka'Sehkuur hurled his sword at the departing form of his brother, felling him.

"Before he claimed the body, he glared up into the sky and shook his fist at the Eternal Father in defiance. Unbeknownst to him, their younger brother, Sutekh, shrouded by his shadows, had reached into the steaming waters and picked up Dioth Cyela's discarded sword. He snuck around the newformed mountains and stabbed Ka'Sehkuur in the back.

"Many of our stories conflict after that, but all say Ka'Sehkuur did not die. I believe the Eternal Father exacted a price for the killing of Havel — he made Ka'Sehkuur anathema and cursed him with sleep. Now, he bides his time, awaiting the day he will be reawakened." The images faded, and the three men found themselves once again in the clearing.

"It is because of this fight there is a lake of darkness in Altaira," the ghost said. "It is a lake of such depth of color it gives off no reflection of the sky above. The lake lies in a valley the shape of a man's head, but it's not filled with water. It is filled with the Blood of Ka'Sehkuur."

"My people tell a similar story," Chert said, "but Cayn and Havel did not carry the power of creation in their blood or tears. Neither had wives, and Havel died childless." He leveled a narrow-eyed glare at the ghost. "The Eternal Father forged the races with the fires of creation using rocks and minerals. Its why humans have iron in their blood and elves have palladium."

Xandor made a cutting motion with his hand and said, "Chert, not now."

Arms crossed, Chert asked, "How does this relate to the soap or that creature Jasper killed?"

Jasper thought for a moment and said, "The Blood of Cayn. Is that what created the creature? Is that what affects these people?"

"Yes," the dying elf rasped. "It hides in the bowls of water."

Xandor's brow furrowed as he asked, "Where did they get it? From the lake?"

Wracked by another fit of coughing, the dying elf spat black mucus, trying to clear his throat. "I don't know how to reach the lake, but there is an old, Väkileyna village far to the northeast, beyond the Valge Jõgi," the elf said, "the White River in Michurinsk." As the memory overwhelmed him, black tears streaked his face.

"Väkileyna?" Xandor asked.

"The Hidden People," the ghost replied. "We were separated from our cousins, the Väkiljós — the People of Light — in your Alashalian Mountains. These two are far from home." The ghost knelt beside his distant kinsmen and said, "There were never many of us, only a scattering of small, beautiful villages deep in the forests of Michurinsk and eastern Trakya where humans feared to tread... before the Plague War."

Bitterness filled the ghost's words. "The humans loved our wine. Each fall, we sent a wagon full of small casks to Pazard'zhik. During that last trip to Trakya's capital, we traded our wine for barrels of corn meal, fruit, and other items we could only get from the west. The wagon returned to our village like normal; however, during the unloading, one of the barrels broke open and spilled black blood all over those nearby.

"The transformation took less than a minute. The driver and workers holding the barrel instantly turned into the cursed dwolmas and attacked our people. Several quickly succumbed to the dwolma and they, too, were transformed.

"Sacrificing themselves, the Elders remained behind and bought time for our mages to create a containment circle around the entire village."

The ghost laid a pale hand on his kinsman. Touching, yet not touching. "Their sacrifice allowed a small group to escape. They fled to a monastery south of Chernigov, taking the Tear of Havel with them. War tore through the countryside, and my kindred were massacred. The Tear of Havel has been lost to us ever since."

The ghost clenched his fist, and his body shook with emotion. "The Kral forbade us from entering the Stena. His soldiers watched from their battlements while we were slaughtered. None raised a hand to help us in our time of need, and now none may pass the Haunted Wood without feeling our wrath."

"What of the barrel?" Xandor asked.

"The barrel? We never found out where it came from. Somewhere along the way, maybe even in Pazard'zhik, someone must have placed it there to destroy our village and start the Plague War."

Jasper scratched his chin as he thought back to the sliver of soap he examined in Pazard'zhik, and the strange black speck he glimpsed in the melted residue. Looking at his hand, he said, "I bet the soap is tainted with this same stuff. Somehow, the Zhitomirans must have gotten their hands on the blood that sabotaged your village."

Xandor looked up, surprised. "You mean the Madasgorski knight?"

"Yes, Marko and his sister, Aleksandra Madasgorski-Krakova."

"What! You saw her?"

"She was impersonating Sachin."

Xandor stared at the teamsters in the cages.

"Did Grendel know?" Chert asked.

"Yes."

The dark expression on Jasper's face made Chert ask, "What happened?"

"He fell under Aleksandra's spell. He even slept with her a couple of nights ago."

"No! I don't believe it."

"Chert, I didn't see it personally, but some of the other guys said they saw him enter her tent."

Before Chert could respond, Xandor said, "Enough. We'll ask Grendel when we find him. Let's focus on the task at hand. Elf, who captured you?"

"A human mage, but I never saw his face. He always wore a heavy cowl." Spasms wracked the weakening elf. His body contorted in pain as he fought the thing growing inside him. "You must kill me before I change." Another convulsion shook the elf.

Xandor looked at Jasper, but the mage simply shrugged. The sad look in his eyes said it all.

Gently brushing his fingers down the elf's face, Chert closed his eyes and whispered a silent prayer for the elf's soul.

Pulling out his sword, Xandor raised it and saluted him. The ghosts pressed closer, but none made a move to stop him.

"What is your name, Elf?"

"Alvar."

"I wish there was something else we could do for you."

"Thank you." The elf stared into Xandor's eyes and said, "Do not worry. I've led a good, long life."

Black mucus seeped out of the elf's pores. Xandor ignited his blade and stabbed, piercing the elf's heart. The ranger expected at least some resistance when his sword struck bone, but the elf's skeletal structure had softened from the transformation process. Passing through his body, the sword bit deep into the dirt below.

The golden flame ignited the black mucus, and everyone stepped back from the sudden heat. Flames rose from the elf's body and smoke trailed into the sky. The ghosts slowly disappeared back into the woods until only one remained.

"You must stop this. You must stop the past before it repeats itself." The ghost's demand echoed off the Haunted Wood, then he, too, began to fade, leaving only his words behind.

Stunned to silence, the three men stared into the dying flames.

Shaking himself, Chert turned to the other elf. He knelt beside him and quickly confirmed his fears. The elf was changing too, but there was no way to know how long he had or if the transformation could be reversed. Frustration and sadness settled on his face. "Without knowing more, I can't help this elf."

"Let's talk to the teamsters," Xandor said. "Maybe they can tell us something."

CHAPTER 35
A MAGICIAN'S LAB

October 25, 4235 K.E.

9:32am

Xandor gripped Dragahn's shirt, pulling the collar tight against the man's throat, and he slammed the caravan chief against a cage. Pyotr and Andrei stood nearby, held back by Jasper and Chert.

"Where are the wagons going?"

Dragahn clutched the ranger's wrists in a vain attempt to loosen the pressure on his windpipe. "King Kraagor."

"Who's that?"

"A nasty orc chieftain in Chernigov," Pyotr supplied.

Relaxing his grip, Xandor asked, "Why?"

Dragahn tugged at his shirt and rubbed his throat. "He controls the White River."

"What do you mean controls?"

"Well, his orc patrols pretty much stop anything moving up or down the river."

"Why hasn't Michurinsk rooted him out?"

Dragahn shrugged. "They probably tried."

"How did you get into Chernigov?"

"We didn't. We met with his orcs at an old, abandoned town and unloaded there. We never had to go into the city."

"Dragahn! What the hell were you thinking, trading with orcs?!" Jasper demanded.

The teamster shrugged again. "The money was good, and I thought it was pretty damned ironic to sell soap to humanoids."

"Who arranged for the pickup?" asked Xandor.

"Sachin made all the arrangements. It was always touch and go, but they mostly left us alone."

"What about the marks on the crates? What do they mean?"

"I assumed it was Advocate Hristova's branding. The crates came in a day or two ahead of each soap delivery."

"They looked similar, but each one was custom," Jasper informed Dragahn. "I believe they contained cleverly concealed messages. Most likely, their final destinations."

"Do you think the crates from the previous trips are still there?" Xandor asked.

"I doubt it."

"Any idea where they went?"

"Down river."

"Do you *want* me to hit you?" Xandor seethed.

"Listen, I'm sorry. I didn't know what they were doing with the soap. I mean, what we carried seemed innocent enough. How could I know it was tainted?"

Pointing at the blackened smear on the ground where he had killed the elf, Xandor glared at Dragahn and said, "You see that? If what they said is true, you supplied orcs with a weapon no one will recognized until it's too late."

Jasper laid a hand on Xandor's shoulder. The ranger fixed a fierce gaze on the mage before stomping off with clenched fists, putting distance between himself and the caravan chief.

As he walked away, Xandor heard Pyotr tell Dragahn, "I told you so."

Jasper pondered the elder elf's story as he sat with his staff across his lap and watched the teamsters dump the bowls of water from the cages, careful not to spill any of it on themselves.

The elf's words repeated in his head, and he wondered if he, too, had been poisoned with the Blood of Cayn. He didn't feel any different. He just had a mild cough from time to time. He looked at the teamsters. Were they befouled as well?

Dragahn, Pyotr, and Andrei didn't seem sick. Under Chert's care, Lucky's color was closer to normal, but the other people in the cages were still unconscious.

Xandor had the prisoners brought out carefully and laid side by side. While he took the time to go through the tattered remains of their clothes, Chert and Pyotr examined them for physical ailments. Placing a hand on the last child's forehead, Pyotr commented, "They all have high fevers."

Looking up, Chert replied, "Aye, I noticed. They're trying to fight it off, but I think they're losing the battle." The dwarf knelt and tugged gently on a small tuft of the boy's hair. It came out easily at the root. He shook his head as he examined all the little ulcers and blisters. "He's bleeding real blood, not black slime. Whatever's in their system is killing them from the inside out, similar to the elf, but it's affecting them differently," Chert observed. "It's definitely a poison, not some disease."

"So, it's not contagious?"

"No. At least not in the traditional sense."

"Can you do anything for him?" Pyotr asked.

In answer, Chert closed his eyes and placed his hand on the boy's arm; pale blue light appeared and seeped into his skin. The youth's face creased in pain and a groan escaped his cracked lips. When Chert looked up, he wore a grim expression.

"No."

"Looks like someone's trying to start another Plague War," Xandor said as he sat next to Jasper. "Everyone here is sick with the same ailment described in our last message from Marcus at Vratsa."

Jasper stared at the staff balanced across his knees. "How bad is it?"

"I don't know. Members of the nobility and merchant class have become extremely ill. He described a few of the symptoms, similar to what we're seeing here, but they couldn't trace the cause to anything specific. He did mention their healers were helpless against it."

Chert ambled over in time to hear the tail-end of the conversation. "I'm afraid I'm not much help either."

"It's not a disease," Jasper said. "It's the soap or whatever's inside it."

"Do you think the elves knew what they were talking about?" Chert asked. "That it's the Blood of Cayn?"

"Yes," Xandor said, "I do."

Jasper tilted his head toward the sick prisoners, his face clouded with concern. "Where do you think those people came from?"

"My guess, they're cottars from Trakya," Xandor answered.

"Let me take a look at them," Jasper said, using his staff to help him to his feet. Chert and Jasper went from person to person, double-checking them for anything out of the ordinary.

Xandor rose and studied the clearing. Although he told Chert and Jasper that he believed the elves' story, and someone was inciting another Plague War, uncertainty gnawed at him. This disease, this poison, was different from anything he'd heard from his parents or Iron Tower instructors about the war and disease thirty years ago. If it had been the same, they'd all be sick — or dead. This seemed to target specific groups of people. He studied the teamsters. Having thrice traveled with the soap, they remained immune to its effects.

Across the clearing, Xerxes and Sky grazed with the Northman's horse between them. As Xandor turned away, he spotted a shimmering in the air. "Jasper, what do you make of this?"

Looking up from examining one of the children's wounds, the mage found Xandor staring into the woods. "Looks like a bunch of dead trees to me," he replied.

Xandor kept staring at the woods.

Jasper gave up and joined the ranger. Mimicking his stance, the mage tried to see what Xandor was seeing. At last, he saw a slight distortion in the air in front of them. Whispering a few words in the arcane tongue, he put out his hand and felt a solid structure.

"It's hidden," Jasper said, ignoring the disparaging look his friend gave him.

The portly mage felt along the surface, trying to get a feel for the dimensions, and discovered a recessed entry near a corner. Running his hands down the door, he found the latch and grasped it. Concentrating on the door, the mage closed his eyes and whispered, "Orámata ephanerōthē."

At first, nothing happened, then alien images filled his head with vivid clarity: towering trees harboring derelict homes, a greenish dome of energy that blotted out the sky, a blood-covered temple in a swamp, and crazed figures performing a cacophonous ritual around a sleeping giant. Bringing his hands to his ears, he tried to block out the noise. It was all so incredible — so real — he had trouble controlling the visions.

His knees buckled and sweat streamed down his forehead before he finally sorted through the images and found the clearing. In his vision, he saw a man wearing dark red robes walk to the magical construct, grasp the doorknob, and murmur, "Patefaciam." The door opened, and the man walked inside.

As Jasper released the spell, he shared a final vision: amid his frenzied worshipers, the giant stirred, and with his waking came the presence of raw madness. The feeling of madness grew, and Jasper knew he had to break free. Dimly, he heard a sleepy voice ask inside his head, "Who are you?"

It shook him to the core, and panic almost overwhelmed him. Focusing his will, he pictured the grassy clearing, the trees of the haunted wood, and the cages. He made everything feel as real as he could, anchoring himself, but without giving away his friends.

"Snap out of it!" Xandor yelled, shaking the mage and slapping him across the cheek.

Jasper lay on the ground, staring blindly at the sky. The ranger kept shaking him, with no response. Pyotr joined them and offered his flask, but the ranger refused in favor of his vial of Spirit of Hartshorn. Despite the foulness of the compound, Jasper did not rouse.

A minute passed, then two. Finally, Jasper blinked and took a deep ragged breath.

"What happened?" Xandor asked.

Wide-eyed and obviously frightened by something, the mage gibbered, "We've got to get out of here. It knows where we are!"

The ranger grabbed the mage by the shoulders and gave him another sharp shake. "Jasper! You're not making sense."

Jasper blinked again, and his wide brown eyes met the ranger's heterochromatic gaze. He swallowed the lump of fear in his throat and said in a shaky voice, "There's something out there — something powerful — and it knows we're here."

"What knows we're here?"

Jasper's voice dropped to a whisper. "Cayn."

Xandor leaned in close and said, "Jasper, focus. Tell me what that thing is."

Jasper pressed the heel of his hand to his forehead and grimaced. He drew in a deep breath, squared his shoulders, and answered, "An invisible portal. I think."

"To where?"

"How should I know?"

"You're the mage."

Sorting the wild images floating in his head, Jasper said, "I don't know where it goes, but the man who poisoned these people went inside."

"Can we follow him?"

"I think so. Help me up."

Xandor reached down and gave the mage a hand. "You alright?"

"Just rattled." Composing himself, Jasper faced the door. "Get ready."

Xandor positioned himself between Jasper and Pyotr, drew his blades and ignited them.

Giving the two a quick nod, Jasper said, "Patefaciam."

The outlines of a door appeared in front of them. It opened slowly, revealing a cool, dark interior with a low ceiling. A faint odor of death wafted out as Xandor crossed the threshold, blades first.

Not seeing anyone, Xandor sheathed his weapons in favor of the light from his stylus. Shattered glass and other debris covering the floor glittered in the red light and crunched under the ranger's boots.

Directly in front of them, wooden frames with slate boards filled with magical and astrological symbols and alchemical formulas lay in jumbled pieces against the righthand wall. In the middle of the room, a stout oaken table held the shattered remains of an alchemical array. On the opposite side from the door, just within the limits of the light, sat an ornate writing desk and wooden stool. Viscous liquids pooled on the floor, some still dripping.

Instantly engrossed, Jasper sorted through the various sized slate tiles as he tried to piece them together like a puzzle.

'*Repsaj.*'

Jasper turned his head and asked, "Xandor, did you say something?"

"No," Xandor replied as he went by to search the desk.

At the door, Pyotr said, "What a mess." He walked to the table and picked up a wooden rack, the only thing still upright. A trail of slime spread from the base. In the rack were three cold-wrought iron vials stoppered with wax. Next to it was a small brush made from animal parts, its bristles stained black.

Xandor rubbed his chin as he studied the desk and the glistening gore down its front. He knelt and pried open a large drawer using the tip of his knife. Inside, he found a half-dozen rubies, sapphires, and diamonds, each about the size of a grape, identically cut with thirteen facets. As he stooped to pick one up, he saw a shape flicker inside. His fingertips stopped a hair's breadth away, caution staying his hand.

"Back here. There's someone in the bed," Pyotr called from the far corner of the room.

Jasper and Xandor looked around and found the doctor in the mouth of a shadowy alcove. Expecting the worst, the ranger unsheathed his swords while Jasper prepared a spell.

With a single motion, Pyotr yanked the sheet back and the stench of decay flooded the room. Under it lay the remains of a man in dark red robes. A deep cowl obscured his face.

Jasper poked the body with the tip of his staff, but the figure remained unmoving. Xandor pointed with a sword. The corpse's fingers were all stained black.

Easing up to the bed, Jasper studied the robes. He cautiously reached down and pulled back the hood, exposing the corpse's face. The dead man's head was completely hairless and covered in the same ulcers and blisters as the humans outside. Dried blood caked his nose and mouth.

As though it had merely awaited an audience, the corpse's skin rotted away, and his soft tissue began to putrefy at an alarming rate.

Jasper closed his eyes again and used his magic to enhance his senses. Maggot-like tendrils consumed the man's flesh. Jasper's eyes shot open, and he backed away. He thumped against the table, taking in ragged lungsful of air. "Something's eating the body," he gasped.

"What?" Xandor and Pyotr blurted as they both took an involuntary step back.

Jasper stared at the dead man's face, and his eyes grew round. "I know this man."

"I can't take you anywhere," Xandor said incredulously.

"Several years ago, in Tydway, I attended a lecture on spirit possession at the Academia. The core lesson centered on the dangers of depression and sickness, and how it can leave you vulnerable to the various entities that travel astrally. The lecturer was a necromancer called Gregori Saso. He was a highly acclaimed expert on the subject."

Disbelief and revulsion warred on Xandor's face.

"What? Look, there aren't that many of us around, and you don't often get a chance to learn from experts in a specific field of knowledge. Most of us dabble, but there are some real artists out there."

"You sound like you admire this guy."

"I respected his work. Xandor, not all necromancers are evil. They study the living as much as the dead. Some have been known to restore lost limbs, graft flesh, and develop new medicines to combat diseases. Gregori —"

'*Su nioj.*'

Jasper looked around, his brow creased in concern as he sought the origin of the strange voice. He spotted the open drawer with its contents sparkling merrily in the light streaming through the open door.

"I doubt Saso was in that body when it died."

"Explain — and pretend I don't know anything about magic, because I don't."

"His spirit was elsewhere when his body died."

"How?" asked Xandor.

"It's complicated to explain, but, basically, he'd need a specially prepared gem." Jasper pointed to the open drawer and said, "He's probably in there."

Pyotr asked, "Why would someone do that?"

"Some mages use it to transfer their consciousness to someone else. Swap places, so to speak. At the Academia, there were rumors Saso was a practitioner. If so, he could escape his body and take someone else's."

"Magic can do that?" Pyotr asked, still not believing.

"Oh, yeah," Jasper whispered with a fervent gleam in his eyes that made the horse doctor turn pale.

"Stop that," Xandor said. "You're scaring him."

"He's already scared."

"Pyotr, Jasper and I can handle this. Go find Chert and tell him what we've found."

When the horse doctor was out of earshot, Xandor asked, "Are you saying he's in one of those gems?"

"Maybe, maybe not."

"Great," Xandor replied. His tone implied otherwise. "We'll add his name to the report for Marcus. For now, is there anything you learned in your lecture that can help us?"

A distant look appeared in Jasper's eyes as he sorted through the lecture's salient points. "Not much, but there are two things we know for sure — that's Gregori lying there, and there's a bunch of gemstones in that drawer."

"Do you think he found someone else to possess?" Xandor asked tentatively.

"Considering we don't know how many prisoners he had, and at least one of the horsemen is unaccounted for, I'd count on it." Looking around, Jasper said, "I can't believe Gregori would have just left this place where we could find it."

"Maybe the sickness affected more than just his body; maybe it affected his mind, too. What about the writing on the slate? Did you notice this?"

Looking where Xandor pointed, Jasper saw where someone had erased portions of the various formulae and replaced them with nonsensical scribbling.

"I'm not a mage, but even I can tell whoever wrote that wasn't in their right mind."

'Rood eht esolc.'

Jasper swatted at the air as if trying to bat away the voice in his head. When it quieted, he bent down to get a closer look at the writing on the piece of slate. He stopped when he noticed Xandor staring at him. "What?"

"Are you alright?"

"Yes. Why do you ask?"

"You're acting funny...er."

"Long day, I guess."

The ranger backed away and panned his light about the laboratory. "What do you make of all this?" the ranger finally asked.

Straightening, Jasper replied, "It's hard to say. Maybe one of those dwolma ransacked the place. Jasper looked around. "Have you seen a spell book?"

"No," Xandor replied.

"Must have taken it with him."

"Can you decipher those formulae and come up with a cure?"

Scratching his chin, Jasper didn't answer immediately. "I don't think it's something that can be cured."

'*Won, rood eht esolc, Repsaj! Regnar eht part*!'

Worry crept up Jasper's spine. He cast about the room, checking every corner. With a look of alarm, he realized what the voice was saying and yelled to Xandor, "Get out! Get out now!"

Xandor did not hesitate. He bolted toward the door, which was shrinking.

Jasper pushed the ranger out even as the walls around them shimmered. With a frantic jump, he landed on Xandor. He turned in time to see the portal suddenly become visible, rise in the air, and disappear with a loud *pop*.

"What just happened?" Xandor asked in a muffled voice.

Jasper rolled off him and said, "Gregori was watching us. He tried to trap us inside, and it almost worked, too." It wasn't a complete lie. Jasper had felt Gregori watching them, but it was the voice that had the mage's hands shaking. He wanted to tell Xandor about it but decided to wait until he knew more. At least, that's what he told himself.

"Did you get a chance to look at those formulae?"

Thankful for something to focus on other than the voice, Jasper replied, "I'll need to write them down before I forget, but I think I got a good look at most of them."

"Do you think you and Chert can use it to find an antidote?" asked Xandor, rising to his feet.

"Maybe, but it'll take us some time, especially with those portions rewritten like they are. And while we're here trying to figure it out, Grendel's out there with the caravan, heading to Chernigov. We can't just sit here."

"I know." Xandor looked around at the men in the clearing and said, "But we can't just abandon Dragahn and his men. It would be a death sentence for sure. These woods are dangerous, and every minute we stay, we run the risk of attack. Especially after the noise and smoke from earlier."

"What do you recommend?" asked Jasper.

"Go get help."

Jasper pursed his lips in thought. "I can talk with the White Circle in Pazard'zhik, take them what we have, and bring them back here."

Pyotr and Chert ran toward the two men with Dragahn two steps behind. Xandor took them aside and described what they had found inside Gregori's laboratory.

While the ranger talked, Jasper sat cross-legged on the ground. He dug into his sporran, pulled out some paper and wrote down the formulas from memory, including the symbols that, as Xandor said, didn't make any sense.

When Xandor finished explaining their options, Dragahn said, "No matter what happens to us, you've got to stop that caravan. You don't have a choice."

"We know," Xandor replied, his face grim.

The scratching of a quill on paper filled the silence that followed. Chert left with Dragahn and Pyotr to find water and set up camp.

Xandor sighed and pulled out his journal. As soon as the mage put down his quill, he asked, "Can you make another copy for me, and also write down what the elves told us?"

Surprised by the request, Jasper looked up but opted not to ask. Instead, he said, "Sure. You want me to put it in that journal of yours?"

With a nod, Xandor handed him the thin book and stylus. The mage took it and flipped it open. All the pages were blank.

Jasper gave Xandor a questioning look.

"Don't ask."

The mage studied the journal intently but did not find anything unusual. He could have used his magic on it, but he respected Xandor enough to let it go for the time being. Instead, he flipped to the first page and started copying his notes.

Once finished, he handed it back to Xandor, who quickly glanced through the pages before putting it away.

"Not bad. You do all that from memory?"

"Yes." Jasper stood and stretched. "Have you decided yet?"

With a curt nod, Xandor said, "Go. Get help. But be quick about it. Chert and I will rescue Grendel and stop those wagons."

Jasper reached into his sporran and handed a small item to the ranger. "Keep this with you. It will help me find you, no matter where you are."

Xandor looked down and saw the mage had given him a metal canister with one word scratched on the outside — *spice*.

Jasper gripped the ranger's arm and said, "Good hunting."

"You, too," replied Xandor.

Taking a few steps back, Jasper drew a circle with the end of his staff and stepped inside. In each of the four cardinal directions, he drew an elaborate symbol. Next, he closed his eyes in concentration and tapped the dirt thrice while whispering in the arcane tongue.

A few seconds later, Xandor could have sworn he heard the faint whisper of a response. He blinked, and Jasper was gone.

CHAPTER 36
ACCEPTANCE

October 25, 4235 K.E.

9:47am

Grendel awoke on the seat of the wagon. Beside him, Aleksandra looked straight ahead, holding the reins to her four Percherons. They followed the chuck wagon, and he briefly wondered whether he had dreamed the attack or if it had been real.

Up front and a little to the left of the chuck wagon, Marko rode his Frisian, but he couldn't quite make out who drove the wagon. Behind him, Teodor rode on the seat of the last wagon instead of Lucky, and Ognian held the reins. Riding beside them on horseback were two soldiers wearing black leather armor with the red sleeve sinister emblem of the Madasgorski family fixed above their hearts.

Grendel did not ponder any further; the attack had been real.

Running parallel to the caravan were a dozen or so olive-skinned orcs who easily kept pace with the Percherons. Grendel could see he shared some of their facial features; however, they ran hunched over, making them more apelike than human, and their true height hard to guess. Heavily muscled, they looked to be stronger than most humans. Each wore a blood-colored mail shirt, hard and hand-linked, and a wickedly curved scimitar tucked under a small, wooden shield strapped to their backs. As they ran beside the caravan, they carried themselves proudly — the elite of a warrior race.

Grendel's exposure to orcs was limited. He had fought and killed a few of their kind in his youth as a harēna tironis, but they were weak, pathetic creatures by comparison. Watching these orcs lope through the woods, he realized he really didn't know anything about them. They were much like his father, and yet, so different.

"Good morning," Aleksandra said.

Snapping back to the moment, Grendel asked, "What is going on? Where are the teamsters?"

"I'm afraid we had to swap personnel during the night. We should be able to make better time now."

Feeling like his head was stuffed with cobwebs, Grendel tried to recall what had happened, but could not remember much after Lucky was struck by Marko. He double-checked his gear and found everything to be in place, untouched.

Not knowing what else to do, he grabbed Aleksandra roughly by the hair with his left hand, pulling her head back. With his right, he drew his dagger and placed it against the exposed skin of her neck.

"Stop the wagon. Now."

Without showing any signs of resistance, she tugged on the reins and slowed the Percherons to a halt. Behind them, Ognian stopped his wagon and retrieved his longbow from under the seat. He nocked an arrow and aimed at the half-orc.

The orc leader sent two of his orcs ahead to signal for Marko and the chuck wagon while the rest held their positions at the tree line.

"You have everyone's attention, Grendel. What do you plan to do now?"

"Where are my friends?"

"We are your friends," she replied.

He tightened his grip on her hair and pressed the dagger harder against her neck, stopping just short of breaking her soft skin. His grip should have hurt, but she seemed to be unaffected... at least, in the way he expected. He was taken aback when her breathing came faster, her skin grew flushed, and excitement shimmered in her eyes.

"You are not my friends," Grendel said slowly. "I want you to tell me where they are. Now."

"You mean the teamsters? They weren't your friends. They were never your friends. But, if you must know, we left them in a small glade last night. They're alive, or at least they were when we departed."

"Do not lie to me. Did you kill them?" Grendel asked.

"I'm not lying to you. Every one of them was alive when we left."

The orcs moved from the trees as the knight arrived on his Frisian.

"Let her go, half-orc," Marko commanded. "Your life will be forfeit if you hurt her."

"He's right, you know. Look around you," she said.

With a quick glance, he realized his options were extremely limited.

"I am going back, and I am taking you with me," Grendel said as he stood. Aleksandra remained submissive and let him drag her off the wagon. As he lifted her to the ground, he caught a new scent in the air, at once strange, yet familiar. It held a hint of musk. Adrenaline coursed through his body despite his best efforts to control the surge in his blood. He pulled her back against him and started walking toward the rear of the caravan.

Marko and the orcs formed a ring around Grendel, preventing him from moving any farther.

"Back off, or I kill her."

Marko didn't move, and he signaled for the orcs to stand fast.

Grendel hesitated. He could not hold Aleksandra and fight. He knew he'd be a fool to try. Still, there had to be a way out.

For her part, Aleksandra could feel the tension quivering in every muscle pressed against her. When Grendel hesitated, she knew she had him. She ran her hand up between his legs, causing his inner thigh muscle to jump and spasm. Grendel unconsciously flinched, and his grip on her hair loosened. With a quick spin, she turned and pressed her breasts against him. In her hand, she held the tip of her own dagger against his groin.

"What do we do now?" she asked in a husky voice.

He made the mistake of looking down into her eyes. He saw an emotion there he could not identify, and it gave him pause.

"My brother isn't going to let you drag me into the wilderness to do who knows what." She paused and licked her lips hungrily. "I'd much rather you didn't get yourself killed over a bunch of men who don't give a damn about you anyway. Think, Son of Cayn. I'm the one who has stood by you at every turn."

"It does not change the fact you promised me no one would get hurt, and your brother stabbed that boy. With a wound like that, he is not likely to survive."

"The boy's wound was superficial. Marko is an excellent swordsman. Besides, we left him with the horse doctor."

His resolve wavered. "Do you swear?"

She smiled up at him. "I swear to you, Son of Cayn, no one was in danger of dying when we left."

The dagger at Grendel's groin disappeared into the folds of Aleksandra's clothes despite the fact he had yet to loosen his grip on her hair.

"You might not have found your axe, but you have found acceptance — a purpose," Aleksandra said. "What say you? Shall we climb back on the wagons and discuss matters of friendship in a more civilized manner?"

Grendel looked around at the men and creatures surrounding him and realized there was only one way to get out of the situation alive. With a parting glance back down the road, he flipped the dagger around in his hand and slipped it back into its sheath. His other hand released Aleksandra's hair, and he gently rubbed the back of her head before dropping it to his side.

"You are right, of course, Baroness, the teamsters were never my friends."

His tone and sudden change in attitude made her stop. She studied his stoic face with curiosity. He was not defeated, and whatever he was planning intrigued her.

Armed with her best smile, she gave him her hand and said, "Call me Sacha." They mounted the wagon and readied themselves to go.

The others remained in position, staring at them.

"Let's go, Marko. We don't have all day," Aleksandra said.

End of Book I

The adventure continues in <u>City of Cayn</u>!

THANK YOU FOR READING!

We hope you've enjoyed <u>Son of Cayn</u> as much as we enjoyed bringing it to you! No author would be where they are without readers, so please accept a HUGE thank you for taking a chance on our endeavor. Whether you loved it, hated it, or landed somewhere in between, it would be of immense help to us, as well as other readers, if you would take a moment to leave a review on Amazon and/or Goodreads. Even a single sentence will mean a lot.

We love to hear from readers! Feel free to drop us a line at mcdonald.isom@gmail.com Let us know what you loved (or what you hated). If you have questions about the story, we'll do our best to answer them. For more information about cultures, countries, creatures, and races of Gaia, visit the glossary on our website, www.mcdonald-isom.com. You can also find us on Facebook, @McDonald.Isom.author.

There are more adventures yet to come!

Turn the page for a sneak peek at <u>City of Cayn</u>!

CHAPTER 1
THE BYAL KRŬG

October 25, 4235 K.E.

11:08am

Standing in a clearing surrounded by teamsters, five days from the nearest town, Jasper knew of only one place to find help: Trakya's Byal Krŭg, or White Circle. According to their historian, the White Circle was the oldest Mages' Guild on the continent of Parlatheas, having received its original charter more than three thousand years ago, during the height of the Korellan Empire. Despite a long and sordid history, including multiple wars and a fire which gutted the building and destroyed many of its original tomes, the White Circle remained one of the three largest repositories of learning in the civilized world, alongside the *Academia des Artes Magicae* in Gallowen, and Vologda's *Taynaya Biblioteka.*

He concentrated on his teleportation spell, driven by hope the White Circle could find a remedy for the Blood of Cayn.

The moment he spoke the last incantation, Jasper felt something *other* slither through his magic. He recoiled at the alien presence, but it was already too late. It altered his spell ever so slightly. With some arcane magic it might not have mattered, but accuracy was paramount with a teleport spell. A wave of nausea seized him, and, for an instant, he felt his feet materialize inside stone before the failsafe triggered. Wrenched from death, he found himself guided like a novice.

Helpless and more than a little embarrassed, Jasper arrived safely inside a dark, round chamber. Breathing a sigh of relief, he waited for his eyes to adjust to the low lighting. Set in the stone floor immediately surrounding him was a narrow band of burnished gold, intricately engraved with arcane runes of both protection and guidance.

Outside the circle stood two men dressed in dark robes. Each carried a tall, wooden staff of darkest oak. Their hoods were up, hiding their faces. Raising their staves in unison, they chanted and pointed with their free hands. Jasper felt the air around him constrict. Tucking his chin, he inhaled sharply, filling his lungs, and poked out his stomach without being too obvious. When they finished, Jasper relaxed, creating a small gap between him and the wall of air. It wasn't much. He still couldn't move, let alone cast an immediate counter spell, but it was something.

One of the mages patted him down and removed his belt and sporran. The dark mage rifled his belongings and fished out the small sliver of soap. Evidently satisfied, he dropped it back in the leather pouch and carried the pilfered items from the room while the other mage stood guard.

This was not the reception Jasper had anticipated. The only thing he could figure was the guild knew about the soap and had set up some sort of detection spell. Either they had discovered it was the cause of the sickness — or they had known all along. The more he thought about it, the more concerned he became.

Beyond the guard, he noticed fresh scorch marks on the wall.

Jasper didn't have time to waste; he needed to find Marcus Marchenkov, second-in-command of the Eyes and Ears of the Kral. Barely able to move his lips, he called upon his own magic and used it to probe the binding spell. He searched for any weakness that might help him.

The two mages had cooperatively cast the spell. Although the binding was exceptionally strong, he found the wood of his own staff had interfered with their spell by absorbing some of its energies. Thankfully, they hadn't thought to utilize the magic circle at his feet.

Sweat beaded on his forehead as he layered magic upon magic into the staff, using it as a conduit. The staff, in turn, focused and amplified his power until the binding spell developed tiny cracks. He would have to be quick. Both casters would know the instant their spell failed. He pushed more magic into his staff.

With a flash of light and a haze of ozone, the binding collapsed.

The guard reacted a half-second too slow. Jasper swung his staff with all his might and struck the guard hard on the side of the head, knocking him to the floor. He knelt beside the fallen mage and placed his staff across the man's throat. Using his bulk to maintain leverage, he applied pressure, little by little, with his knee until the mage stopped struggling.

Reaching down, he threw back the other mage's hood to reveal his face. It was Ivo Indzhev, one of Jasper's old instructors from Tydway. He had seen him a few times in the halls, but the two rarely traveled in the same social circles.

The mage glared at Jasper with cold, dead eyes. Something alien had replaced the man's humanity, and it saw Jasper not as a person but as an object — a mere bug. If positions had been reversed there was no doubt Ivo would have taken his life. It sent an icy chill down the portly mage's spine.

Jasper grabbed the dark mage's hand. The fingers and fingernails were pitch black, and the hand felt warm to the touch. Worried furrows creasing his brow, Jasper pressed his hand flat against the other's forehead: a high-grade fever. Shifting his weight slightly, Jasper pressed even harder with his staff and cut the mage's airflow.

After making sure the mage was unconscious, Jasper crossed the room and listened at the door. Not hearing any traffic on the other side, he peeked out. A massive, barrel-vaulted corridor trimmed with a dark wainscot along each side stretched into darkness. Sticking his head out farther, he looked up and down the hallway. Concern etched his features as he felt how quiet this once-busy thoroughfare had become. He stepped cautiously out of the chamber and closed the door behind him. With a quick weave of magic, he locked it.

At the far end of the hallway was the central stair that led down to the ground floor. Trying to remember the shortest route out of the maze-like guild, he moved in that direction, the sound of his boots echoing eerily in the deserted hall.

A tingling sensation coursed through his hands, followed by another wave of nausea that caused his steps to falter.

'Kcab eomc, Repsaj.'

He leaned against the cool stone wall, clutching his stomach until the spasm subsided. Taking a deep shuddering breath, he brought up a hand to swipe at his suddenly damp brow. The tips of his fingers and his fingernails had turned grey. Images of Gregori's corpse swam before him.

The thudding echo of Ivo banging on the door jarred him from his thoughts. It wouldn't be long before someone heard him and raised the alarm. Putting aside his symptoms for the moment, Jasper fled, not caring how much noise he made. At the head of the stairs, he heard the echo of voices below, followed by the opening and closing of a door as someone released Ivo.

His thoughts racing, Jasper retraced his steps. Going out the front was no longer an option, and if he didn't come up with a real plan, he would be trapped.

At a side passage, inspiration struck. Tilting his staff so the charred tip angled back toward the central stairs, he summoned a thin sheet of ice. Once the floor was covered, he tossed out a bit of fleece and whispered, "Psévdo íchnos."

A solid-seeming image of himself raced across the ice and down the hallway toward Ivo and the arrival room. Jasper snuck down the narrower side passage. Maintaining his concentration on the image, he let it get close enough for the men to see it before he made the phantasm turn and flee to the central stairs.

Jasper rounded a corner and stopped. He glanced back toward the main corridor just in time to see two armed soldiers flash by with Ivo right behind them. All three were hot on the trail of his simulacrum. Back pressed to the wall, he listened to the curses of the men as they slipped on the ice and fell down the stairs, bringing a satisfied smile to his face. From the sound of it, they were broken but not dead.

He continued down the new hallway until he came to an intersection. An elaborate arch adorned each side passage. Jasper turned left and found himself at the entrance to the private chambers set aside for visiting mages.

A dark-robed mage patrolled the hall. He walked with an odd shuffle, as if he couldn't bend his knees properly and leaned against his staff with every other step. Luckily, the mage had his back to Jasper, allowing him to retreat and prepare.

Taking the chance he could talk his way through, Jasper strode confidently down the hall. As he approached the dark-robed mage, the pungent stench of decay and excrement assailed his nostrils. On either side, doors stood wide open. He caught glimpses of groaning men and women on straw pallets, their bodies consumed by the contagion.

He wondered how the sickness spread so fast. Then it dawned on him: a communal bath. If the guild had bought a block of that soap, it would only have been a matter of time before everyone became sick.

"Stop! This area is off limits," the dark-robed mage commanded when he saw Jasper. "What are you doing here?"

"I'm on my way to the kitchen," Jasper answered. He patted his stomach and gestured toward the door at the far end of the hall.

"The kitchen's closed," the other mage said automatically. "Return to your quarters." He cocked his head as though listening to another voice.

'*Damn it,*' Jasper thought. '*What is going on here?*'

Not taking any more chances, he threw a fistful of iron filings at the other mage, intending to bind him with a similar spell to what the dark mages had used against him earlier. The other mage countered it with a simple wave of his staff.

'*How did he do that?*'

The dark-robed mage flicked his left hand, sending three streaks of searing red energy down the hall. Jasper concentrated, and the air in front of him shimmered. The lights struck the barrier, causing it to buckle and ripple, but it held. They ricocheted off the magic shield, blasting the corridor wall.

Jasper didn't understand what was happening, but he knew it wouldn't be long before others showed up. He tightened his grip on his staff and struck the floor with its tip. Magic flowed through the wood shaft and out. A shuddering boom of thunder blasted the dark-robed mage off his feet and slammed him against the far wall. Jasper ran past the dazed man without looking back.

At the end of the hall, he threw open a narrow wooden door. With shouts and the sound of footsteps close on his heels, he dared not look back as he ducked inside the antechamber. The landing led to a tight-radiused spiral stone stair intended for servants, not portly mages. Sucking in his gut as best he could, he wound around and around, passing several doors, all marked with white, stylistic numerals.

The walls around him stretched and distorted as if alive — someone was trying to trap him, using the building itself. He raced on, fighting the vertigo blurring his vision, until he reached the bottom. There, a utilitarian hallway stretched into the distance, each side lined with doors labeled with simple block letters.

Ducking into a soot-stained corridor, he felt the weight of the centuries embedded in the old and immovable walls here. It never ceased to amaze him how old the guild was. By comparison, the Academia de Artes Magicae at Tydway, where he had originally learned his trade, was still in its infancy — not even two hundred years old.

Jasper came to a door with *КУХНЯ* written above and threw it open. Silence and the smell of rot greeted him. Shutting the door behind him, he surveyed the kitchen.

Dust motes danced in the thin streams of light filtering through tiny windows set in the ancient block walls. He had made it to one of the original perimeter rooms.

Pots and pans cluttered long rows of countertops and cabinets. Along the far wall sat several wood-burning stoves, now cold and dark. Cutlery and cooking utensils hung from racks built under tall, overhead cabinets. From the looks of it, the staff were hustled out in the midst of their work, and no one had been down here for at least a week. Jasper worked his way around the counters toward the iron-bound door at the other end.

The door from the main dining hall burst open, and a pair of guards armed with short swords rushed him. With a wave of Jasper's hand, sharp knives leapt out of their blocks and flew toward the men.

Although they tried, there were too many blades to fend off. The men fell to the ground screaming as various sized knives and long-pronged forks buried themselves in their forearms, stomachs, and chests.

Jasper exited through the back door and found himself in a tight alley. He breathed a sigh of relief when he found the way clear. After closing the door behind him, he frowned in concentration as he wove magic through the lock and fused the bolt in place.

Abrupt banging and yelling from the other side rattled the door. The men had already thrown off the effects of his illusion. Jasper ran toward the street in front of the guild, the noise fading with each step. As he approached the main thoroughfare, a black wrought iron gate with sharp spikes barred his way. Jasper used his staff to push open the gate.

Locked.

Three stories above, a man exited the conical turret and leaned over the crenelated edge of the roof, peering down into the alleyway. With one eye on him and another on the gate, Jasper threaded his magic into the locking mechanism and rolled the tumblers. When the lock gave, he whispered, "Metaschimatízetai," and then boldly stepped out of the alley into the daylight. Dressed in the dark robes of a mage, he tugged at the edges of his illusory hood, making sure his face was completely concealed.

The area around the mages' guild was prosperous, lacking the accumulation of filth found elsewhere in the city, especially Lower Pazard'zhik. Along each side of the Bulevard na Kralete stood two- and three-story live-work affairs, housing the merchant class. Board and batten upper floors overhung walls of mortared stone and provided sheltered porches where people could avoid the traffic and harsh weather. In a few more weeks, their steeply pitched roofs would shed the weight of heavy snow into narrow alleys between buildings.

With a purpose in his stride, Jasper walked up the hill toward the Kral's estates. Using the porches for cover, he ducked inside a nearby store and cancelled his disguise spell.

He turned to leave, and found himself facing the sharp end of a crossbow aimed at his chest. Holding the crossbow was a buxom woman with shoulder-length, curly, dark-brown hair who stood a few inches shorter than the mage.

"Who are you and what are you doing in my shop?"

Glancing around, he noticed he was in a women's dress shop. There wasn't anyone else in the store except himself and the proprietor. Anger and fear warred for dominance in her expression, and she struggled to control the trembling in her hands.

"What's going on around here?" he asked, keeping half an eye toward the door.

"You answer my questions first."

"My name is Jasper Thredd. I'm a mage from Tydway," he said truthfully. "I'm here to help the Kral."

"You're not sick?"

"Do I look sick?"

"I heard all the mages were ill. Some say the Plague has returned, and war is coming."

"I know. I'm searching for the cure."

"In my dress shop?" she asked, still pointing the crossbow at him.

Shaking his head, Jasper said, "Actually, I was hiding."

"In my dress shop?" she repeated.

"I promise, I intended no harm. I only needed to get off the street."

Looking out the window, he noticed several dark-robed mages questioning passersby.

"I don't have much time," Jasper pleaded. "I really am trying to help the Kral, and I have friends who will die if I don't help them soon."

Her face softened, and the tip of her bolt dipped slightly. Apparently reaching a decision, she nodded toward the window.

"You may need a better disguise," she said.

The dark-robed mages were approaching her door.

"Can you hide me?" Jasper asked quickly.

"Sure, there's a dressing room in the back." She pointed with her crossbow toward a small work room.

Jasper shut the curtain behind him just as the two dark-robed mages walked inside. Listening, he heard them ask the proprietor if they had seen a fat man enter her store. Everything grew quiet.

His hands shook and he tried to steady them. The expenditure of magic was taking its toll. Finding his center, he called up what magic he had left.

The curtain slid open. "They're gone," she said.

Jasper slowly peeked out from behind an elevated cutting board. He let out a deep sigh of relief. The proprietor still held her crossbow, but, thankfully, there was no sign of the dark mages.

Eying the wares in the back room, he thumbed through several dresses hanging on the racks and said, "You make your own dresses." After a moment Jasper asked, "Do you have one my size?"

Several long minutes later, a rotund woman appeared at the door to the dress shop wearing a plain blue dress that just brushed the ground. She wore a matching hat and gloves and carried a tall walking stick wrapped in strips of dyed leather.

"You'll need this."

Jasper looked around and saw the proprietor holding up a brightly colored scarf. He stepped closer to let her tie it around his face.

"Sorry. I forget I've let my beard grow out."

"Don't get yourself killed. I would hate for you to ruin my dress."

Jasper's face was unreadable behind the scarf. He took her hand and said, "Thank you. I'll let the Kral know what you have done."

"Just come back and see me when this is all over."

Letting her hand go, Jasper stepped outside and made to head toward the Kral's estates again. Before he took a step, he stopped and looked back at the proprietor. "I never got your name."

"Violeta Galabova," she answered and pointed. "It's on the sign."

"Oh, yeah," Jasper said, flummoxed. "Thanks."

Walking in a dress proved more challenging than Jasper had anticipated. The skirt billowed this way and that with any errant breeze, and he found himself afraid the unruly thing would blow up and reveal his pants underneath or get snagged on something and rip off. At least he was wearing comfortable shoes.

Jasper strode past the dark-robed mages, giving them the same wide berth everyone else did. He continued up the hill toward an imposing stone wall and gatehouse. Behind him, the Bulevard na Kralete aimed straight toward the Majna I Vira and the stone buildings atop the edge of the Escarpment, the three-hundred-foot cliff that separated Upper from Lower Pazard'zhik and the Maritsa River.

Along the way, Jasper noticed several shops with doors marked with freshly painted crimson crosses, their windows dark and wares abandoned. The merchant traffic was steady, but most of the conversations he overheard dealt with this person or that person being sick. He hoped Chert was right and the Blood of Cayn wasn't contagious, but he had a sinking feeling in his gut.

The men at the mages' guild had taken his pouches, which also meant they had taken his identification. He wasn't sure how he was going to get past the guards at the gatehouse. As he approached the stone wall, he came up with and discarded more than a half-dozen ideas. On the other side resided the royalty of Trakya and their various estates, most related to the Kral in one way or the other. Most, but not all. High-ranking dignitaries were also allowed to lease property from the Crown and build their mansions.

It was on that side of the wall where the Krakov estate once stood — before the Kral discovered the Baron and Baroness were in league with the Dark One. Security increased at the gate after that incident, but only the royal family and the Kral's Eyes and Ears knew the real reason for it. It had stung the Kral deeply to learn the Dark One's cult was not just at his front door but inside his proverbial house. Jasper had never met the Kral, but he respected Marcus Marchenkov, who had hired him for this mission. Jasper just wished he could get a message to him.

In mid-stride, an epiphany struck. At the next intersection, Jasper turned left and walked parallel to the wall. He continued, passing block after block. It was well past noon by the time he left the merchant district and entered the section of town that catered to the military.

Walking around in his blue dress, he felt conspicuous, but he didn't have the time to change or magic to waste.

Stopping in front of a thick door with a stylized chevron painted in bright red, Jasper thought, *I guess this is what's meant by girding up your loins.*

Taking a deep breath, he opened the door and walked inside. Dim light filtered through high windows, illuminating a rustic tavern full of soldiers, most of them female, eating a late lunch. All were of similar appearance, with shoulder-length hair and petite, athletic builds. Each wore a tight-fitting uniform consisting of sky-blue leather tunics and breeches with a different-colored chevron emblazoned on their right shoulders and, on their left, embroidered patches of various types: eagles, gryphons, dragons, and hippoæti. Next to them on tables or empty chairs sat blue, fur-lined leather kalpaks with a sable-colored Parlathean lion, the symbol of Trakya, stitched onto the front.

All conversation stopped when Jasper stepped inside. Even the bartender stopped polishing her glass.

Jasper scanned the bar and noticed various military awards and plaques hung on the wall. Quickly finding who he was looking for, he walked confidently through the crowd to the back of the common room, ignoring the open stares. He waited in silence.

In front of him were four fit-looking women dressed in the same type of uniform. They stood in a line, side by side, and as the one on the left counted, they drew and threw daggers in smooth, fluid motions, aiming at a row of small targets on the wall. Even to the casual observer, the contest wasn't just one of skill and accuracy, but also of patience. Each person had to hit their target dead center or run the risk of obstructing the target of their teammate next to them. These four soldiers competed against other squads, and watching them practice, Jasper understood how they had won three of their last four annual competitions.

After the round, the one on the left stepped up to the target board and calculated their score. She turned, about to congratulate her team, and stopped. Her mouth remained partly open; the words that had rested there forgotten.

He simply waited and watched the play of emotions unfold, unable to avoid the inevitable chain reaction he knew was coming. Surprise quickly turned to raw bewilderment, followed by denial and, finally, dawning recognition.

She burst out laughing. Her teammates turned and discovered a plump woman standing behind them dressed in a frilly blue dress, wearing a dainty scarf over her face. They didn't know what to do, causing their team leader to laugh harder.

Jasper yanked off his scarf and complained, "Yana, you could've done the decent thing and waited until I had my back turned before you laughed at me."

It took several minutes for Yana to collect herself, but she eventually managed and motioned for the bartender to bring her team a round of drinks.

"And bring one for my mom, will you?"

"Funny. Very funny," Jasper said, finding himself thinking he should have kept the scarf on.

Once their drinks arrived, Jasper and Yana found a quiet table away from the front door.

"You look silly in a dress," she said, wiping a tear.

"I need your help."

"Sorry, I'm not that kind of girl."

"Would you stop? I'm serious."

"I know, sorry. Go ahead."

"I need to see your brother."

All merriment disappeared. She turned up her glass and finished it in one swallow, slamming it back down on the table. "You can't. They have him at the chapel with the others. They say he's dying," she said sadly. "Our aunt's with him now."

Jasper reached over and placed his hand over hers. "Yana, that's why I'm here. I'm trying to find the cure. Have you heard if anyone has made any progress?"

"The mages' guild is supposed to have one ready any day now but, no offense, I think they're just sitting on their collective arse."

"I just came from there," Jasper whispered. "They tried to hold me prisoner."

"What! That's insane. They wouldn't dare do that."

"They would if they didn't want me to tell the Kral what they're doing."

"What *are* they doing?"

"I have my theories, but no evidence — at least not yet — so let's pass on that question."

"You just said they tried to hold you prisoner. Isn't that evidence enough?"

"It's my word against theirs, and I don't think that would hold up if I took it to the local constable."

"Why didn't you go straight to the Kral instead of coming to me?"

"The mages took my papers and my pouch when I arrived. I wouldn't be able to get past the gate."

A knowing look came over Yana and she said excitedly, "Put your scarf back on, Mom. You and I are going for a ride." She left the table to collect her team. While she was away, Jasper reached for his drink, downed it, and asked the bartender for another.

ABOUT THE AUTHORS

Jason McDonald

An engineer by day and a world builder by night, Jason is an advocate for using both sides of the brain. Unfortunately, it seems his best (and worst) ideas come to him while driving — much to the chagrin of his family and coworkers.

With his stepfather as a guide, Jason traveled the worlds of Edgar Rice Burroughs, Robert E Howard, and JRR Tolkien at an early age. As he grew older, he discovered Dungeons and Dragons and the joys of creating his own campaigns. Combined with the creative genius of his co-writers, whom he met in college, these adventures grew more complex, and an entire world sprang to life.

During all this, Jason graduated from Clemson University, embarked on a career in engineering, and became a partner in a successful engineering firm. Still a practicing engineer, he continues to design a wide range of projects. His attention to detail and vivid imagination helps shape the various scenes and adventures that challenge his characters.

Alan Isom

Alan began his adventure with science fiction and fantasy literature as it should begin: with JRR Tolkien's The Hobbit, read to him as a child by his father. Since that auspicious beginning, he has fostered a love of reading a variety of fantasy and science fiction types and that led him to RPGs, most notably Dungeons & Dragons, where world building became a fascination.

Growing up in northeast Alabama, Alan moved north to South Carolina for college. He fell in love with the Upstate of South Carolina and forgot to go home afterwards. While initially majoring in Physics at Furman University (Go

Paladins!) and then moving on to Clemson University for additional studies in Civil Engineering (after deciding that his options for a Physics career were decidedly thin), he became a licensed engineer and now works for an international Engineering-Procurement-Construction company. During all of this he served a number of years as a soldier with the Army National Guard. Each of these careers, as well as a multitude of hobbies, helps bring depth and creativity to the characters and worlds he brings to life.

Stormy McDonald

Born in the midst of a thunderstorm in the darkest hours of a solstice morning, Stormy has been told she has a personality to match: full of sound and fury, and highly unpredictable. She comes from a family of traditional, oral storytellers, so it's little wonder that she's driven to weave words as well. She can't remember a time when she didn't love books — from the feel and smell of the pages, to the information they hold, to the tales that they tell. However, storytelling is a labor of love, which doesn't always pay the bills. Over the years, she's worked a ridiculous variety of side jobs to support her writing habit, including waitress, security guard, library minion, engineering drafter, and small business owner.

www.ingramcontent.com/pod-product-compliance
Lightning Source LLC
Chambersburg PA
CBHW060248100726